Mother Material

Doretta Warnock

Brookside Avenue, Irvington, NJ
Late Summer, 1908

"Can I help you there, little lady?"

Emily took her eyes off the growler in her hand to stare at the thin man towering over her. Despite the thick hair covering his head and face, Emily could still see his glazed eyes. He wobbled on his feet as he yanked the tin pail from her hands. If a strong gust of wind blew through the unopened tavern door, she thought he might fall down, or worse, knock into her brother's baby carriage, resting by her side. She pushed the pram with her foot, rolling it safely out of his way. The man made his way behind the bar, filling the container himself, as if he owned the place.

"What do you think you're doing, Charlie? That's my job," said Patrick Sullivan, the bar's owner.

"I don't want you cheating a little girl. Just keeping you honest."

Emily looked at Mr. Sullivan. He was a short man with a red complexion and a bushy white beard. His suspenders were working hard to hold his pants up over his immense belly. With his long-sleeved red shirt, he reminded her of Santa Claus. He filled the growler, watching the foam rise and stop just before it reached the top. Then he placed the tin lid on top, locking it on.

"Don't just stand there, Emily. Pay Mr. Sullivan the dime," said Mama. Even standing on the foot rail, she had to reach across the bar to drop the dime into Mr. Sullivan's hand. "You can expect my Emily in here a lot. She's starting school next week, and if she is old enough to start school, she's old enough to take on more chores, like taking her papa's beer to work on her school lunch break."

Ignoring her mother, Emily studied her surroundings. The tavern was long and narrow, like a railroad car. A single electric light bulb hung from the dingy metal ceiling, covered in years of cigarette smoke. The patrons wore mostly white shirts and narrow black ties. Some gathered at small tables against the wall, while others played darts in the back. But most of the men stood at the mahogany bar, immersed in a heated discussion while drinking shots of whiskey. She heard words she didn't understand like socialist, government, and taxes. The raised voices frightened Emily.

Looking away from the men, she saw a mountain of dirty glasses sitting in the sink behind the bar, within easy reach of the patrons. Emily hoped they wouldn't throw them. She tried to move, but the dirty floor, caked with dried whiskey and beer, made her shoes stick.

She wished she were back in the comfort of her own home. Mama was an immaculate house cleaner. Her floor was spotless. There were never dirty dishes in the sink or dust under the bed, nor a speck of dirt on the furniture.

"Gentlemen, tone it down. We have women and children in here." The men all stopped to stare at Emily. Mr. Sullivan's broad smile and warm pat on the arm were reassuring to her.

After they left the bar, it was time to make the short walk to the firehouse where Papa eagerly awaited his brew and lunch. Emily carried the food and growler, while Mama pushed John down the dirt path.

"Mama, what's a socialist?"

"Where did you hear that word?" replied Mama.

2

"I heard the men in the bar say it," said Emily.

"Nothing to worry your pretty little head about."

"I don't like that place."

"And you should keep your opinions to yourself. Children should be seen and not heard. And don't worry, you won't be spending much time in there. Just get the beer and be on your way."

Emily looked at her mother. The corners of her lips drooped ever so slightly, leaving her mouth in a perpetual frown. Happy or sad, it always looked the same to Emily. And Mama didn't talk much either, never showing her emotions. She thought people would think less of her if they heard her German accent.

Two blocks later, they came to a pond. Emily said, "I'm sorry, Mama, but Papa's beer is heavy. Can't we stop for a while and maybe feed the ducks?"

"I think you know the answer to that question. With Papa's salary, we barely have enough money to put dinner on the table. I'm not wasting any food on ducks. But I'm glad that you brought it up, because that pond is your first landmark. When you reach this park bench, you turn right and head down Springfield Avenue."

Emily and her mother pivoted the corner. A young boy whizzed by on an oversized bicycle, clipping Mama. She went down with a thud, tearing the rickrack trim from her yellow house dress. "*Verdammt noch mal!*"

"Mama, Shush! English only." Mama had broken her own rule, to speak only English in public and German at home. But when Emily saw the cut on Mama's calf, she understood why she had cursed.

Her brother, John, began wailing in his carriage. Why was he crying? He's not the one who got hurt.

Mama was tough. She bounced back up, removing a hanky from her knitted purse. She grabbed the growler from Emily, pried off the lid with her fingernail, and soaked the handkerchief into the beer. Emily watched Mama dab it onto her calf. She

3

applied pressure until the bleeding stopped and the hanky turned pink. "Don't just stand there, Emily. Settle down your brother."

Emily couldn't understand why her mother still made her do this. John was way past his teething years. Dipping her fingers into the beer, Emily plunged them into her brother's wide-open mouth. He suckled them and the crying stopped immediately. Mama rose to her feet, tucking the bloodstained cloth back into her purse. She put the lid on the container and handed it back to Emily.

Brookside Avenue was lovely with the ducks, but Springfield Avenue? When Emily turned the corner, she stepped into a new world. The buildings grew another three floors. She could no longer see the sun. Horse-drawn carriages packed the street, moving every which way around the electric bus, clanging its bell trying to get the horses to move over. Throngs of pedestrians held their hats as they huddled under the awning of the tobacco store, shielding them from the wind. The smell of the beer mixed with the horse manure in the street made Emily nauseous. She held her breath until she maneuvered her way to the bakery on the corner. The smell of freshly baked bread wafted into Emily's nose. "I wish Papa worked there. It smells so good! Can't we go in just for a minute so I can rest my feet?"

"No, but you have an uncanny way of pointing out the landmarks. At the bakery, you turn left onto Park Place and follow it all the way to the firehouse on Glorieux Street," Mama said.

"What does uncanny mean?"

"A strange way of knowing something. You have the gift, and you'll have no trouble remembering this route," Mama said.

"I guess my brain works well, but not my feet. They hurt." Emily stopped to remove her buttoned black shoes, which were a little too small, and massaged her feet.

"Alright. We'll switch jobs. You can push your brother and I'll carry the food."

She had to push the carriage uphill and stop every so often

to kick the wobbly wheel back on the axle or tilt the umbrella to keep the sun off her brother's face. John was almost four years old and weighed almost as much as Emily. He had to bend his knees to fit properly in the carriage. Emily thought if she was old enough for school, then her brother was old enough to walk. But then again, he didn't own a pair of shoes yet.

She was out of breath when they finally reached the firehouse driveway. Several firemen were bathing the horses in front of the bay doors. They stopped to look at Emily and her mother. One of them said, "I can tell you two are related. Those big brown eyes are a dead giveaway."

Emily looked at her mother. She hoped she didn't have her mother's dreary mouth, but she had her mother's beautiful eyes. "Where is Papa?"

"In the back feeding coal into the furnace," said one man.

Emily took the sandwich sack and beer from her mother and headed toward the boiler room. She felt water on her head and looked up. One of the firemen had squeezed soapy water from a sponge onto her head.

"Hey!"

He only laughed at her. "Don't fret, little one."

Emily stomped loudly to the back of the building. She didn't want to startle her father working so diligently shoveling coal into the furnace. He was sweating profusely, and his hand shook ever so slightly as he dumped the heavy load of coal into the monster's mouth. He stood up to greet her. She noticed he had trouble standing up straight. He had developed a small hump in his back. Boy, did Papa work hard!

"Papa, take a break. I helped Mama make your lunch. It's your favorite: cucumber and tomatoes on rye bread." Papa's smile was bigger than ever. His white teeth looked enormous with his soot-colored face.

"Thank you, Princess," said Papa. Emily loved that nickname. It made her feel special. "Come sit with me while I eat."

Papa unwrapped the paper, hardly making a sound, but

Patches, the resident Dalmatian, heard it. The dog put his head in Papa's lap. Emily laughed, "I guess next time I'll have to make an extra sandwich for Patches. Papa, do you have to go right back to work?"

"No, I still have some time left."

"Can we play a game of hearts? Mama come join us. John is busy playing with his paper airplane."

"Sure. I know how you like card games."

Papa whipped a deck of cards out of his pocket, just like a magician. His skillful card mixing mesmerized Emily. She did love playing cards, a love she inherited from her father.

He dealt the cards, and they played a hand. When Papa won the round, Emily threw down the cards.

"What's the matter, Princess?"

"You always win. How come I never win?"

"It's because you recognize all the picture cards but don't know all the numbers yet. Once you start school, and learn your numbers, you will play much better. And you will be able to keep score too."

"I'm looking forward to it. Do we have time for another round?"

Papa glanced at his pocket watch. "Afraid not. Maybe next time. I'll see you at dinner tonight."

But Papa came home late. Mama and her children ate dinner without him. "Get started on those dishes, Emily," said Mama. She hated washing dishes, but ever since Emily was tall enough to reach the sink without standing on a chair, it became her permanent job. But she still had to drag the chair across the room to put the dishes in the cabinet. Couldn't Mama at least do that? She was just putting the last bowl in the cupboard when Papa came home carrying another full pail of beer. He hung his hat on the hook by the door and pulled the bow open on Mama's apron. "Stop that, Henry. You only do that when you're drunk," she said, retying her apron.

"You have no sense of humor."

6

Papa raised his hand to his mouth, but it wasn't in time to stop the vomit from exploding on the floor. Emily jumped out of the way, but Mama was a bit too late. Some of the projectile landed on her shoe. Papa staggered to his over-stuffed easy chair and collapsed, snoring loudly.

"Quick, Emily. Get the rags, dustpan, and bucket so we can clean this up." Emily didn't like the sound of "we." She sure hoped Mama was going to clean it up herself. He was her husband. This wasn't a job for an almost six-year-old girl. She watched Mama scoop the vomit into the bucket and dilute it with water, then mop the floor. "Here, Emily. Dump this down the outhouse."

It was times like these that Emily hated living on the second floor. She ran down the stairs at lighting speed, not spilling a drop. When she got to the first stall, she found it occupied. The second one was available, and she quickly disposed of the waste.

Emily walked by the Taylor apartment on the way back to her own. Despite the evening hour, Mrs. Taylor's laundry still hung on the clothesline. Emily noticed the generous supply of clothespins that Mrs. Taylor used. There were four clothespins holding the sheet in place. Emily repositioned it with three pins and put the fourth pin in her pocket. There it would stay as an insurance policy. She feared this could become another regular chore. At least next time, she could put the clothespin on her nose to block the awful stench.

Back in her own apartment, Emily's emotions rushed in like an out-of-control freight train. Would this happen again? Was Papa going to be alright? How could she talk to her mother about it when children should be seen and not heard? And Mama, in her usual way, said nothing about it. Not that evening, nor the next morning. It was like it had never happened.

Emily felt delighted to see her parents at the kitchen table eating *brotchen* and marmalade for breakfast. Papa seemed fine but complained about a headache. "Perk up, Henry. You have work again today."

"And I'm bringing your lunch again. This time I get to go alone, but Mama will be following close behind to make sure I don't get lost."

"Can't wait, Princess."

Emily couldn't wait either, and lunchtime came fast enough. Remembering all the steps, she filled the growler and gave Mr. Sullivan his dime. When she exited the tavern, she looked at her mother a block back. Mama waved, and Emily waved back. With confidence, she continued, remembering to turn right at the pond, and left at the bakery, and walked straight to the firehouse all by herself. She turned around to look for Mama, who was now only ten steps behind her. Mama gave another wave, but this time Emily didn't wave back.

"Mama, you can go home. I can find my way back."

"Alright, but if you aren't home in an hour, I'll come looking for you."

"Don't worry. I will be."

Emily heard a bird squawk and looked up at the watchtower. That place was eerie; she was glad Papa didn't work up there. She walked past the horses sheltered in their pens. In the kitchen area, ten men, all with identical uniforms and mustaches, sat crowded around a round table designed for six people, playing poker. Eight men puffed on cigarettes. At least someone had the wherewithal to open a window and let the smoke out before the neighbors thought the firehouse was on fire.

Coughing, Emily walked to the boiler room, looking for her father. Instead, she found Patches nestled in the corner next to the furnace. She patted him on the head. "Hey, boy. Have you seen Papa?" Patches wagged his tail. "Papa, I've got lunch."

"Boo!" Emily jumped as Papa came up behind her. "I've been waiting for you. What fine lunch did you bring me today? I'm starving."

"It's just baked beans on rye, and of course, your beer."

8

"Let's go over to the table. We can eat it while we play Chinese checkers. It's all set up. You can be red, I'll be blue."

Papa and Emily sat with Patches trailing behind. Papa opened the wrapper and took a big bite. A few beans fell onto the table. Emily picked them up and gave them to Patches. He swallowed without tasting them. "Boy, that dog sure does like you."

"And I like him. Oh Papa. My birthday is next week. Do you think I could have a dog for my birthday?"

"I don't know, Princess. We'll see. Your mother isn't much of a dog person." Papa usually let Emily win Chinese checkers, but today she was so distracted thinking about dogs she couldn't win.

"What's on your mind? You made many careless mistakes in the game."

"I keep thinking about having a dog."

"Well, get it out of your head. Concentrate on the way home so you don't get lost."

"I won't."

"I knew you could do it. I'm so proud of you," Mama said when Emily got home. The three of them ate their own baked bean sandwiches. Emily laughed when John spilled the beans on his shirt. He wiped them off his shirt and flicked them onto the floor.

"Mama, do you think we could ever have a dog?"

"They're too much work. I clean enough after your brother, never mind a dog. Now come on, get started on the dishes."

Emily's sixth birthday fell on Labor Day. Papa said, "I'm sorry Princess, I have to work. You'll have to wait until dinnertime to get your present. But trust me, you're gonna love it. Don't pout, your Aunt Annie and Cousin Blanche will stop by later to share your special day with you."

Aunt Annie and Cousin Blanche could keep Emily entertained for hours. How they came up with the fun ways to spend the hours, Emily never knew, but she couldn't think of a better way to spend her day. She waited patiently by the door, flinging it open as soon as they arrived.

Mother and daughter wore matching cotton dresses of diagonal navy blue and white stripes. Aunt Annie looked so much like her younger brother. They had the same prominent forehead, narrow nose, and ears that stuck out a little too far. Aunt Annie came bearing gifts and dinner. Emily took the presents from her aunt's hands. "Oh Mama, can I open them now?"

"Let's wait until your Papa gets home for dinner."

Blanche and Emily spent the afternoon putting on plays for their mothers, portraying animals in the zoo, an unruly student and teacher, and an absent-minded chef and her assistant. Before Emily knew it, it was time for dinner.

Mama was the most regimented person who Emily knew. Breakfast at seven, lunch at twelve, and dinner at six. Not a minute later. And Papa knew it. Where was he? "Henry is late again," said Mama.

"That sounds like my brother. That man will be late for his own funeral. I can't tell you how many times we ate dinner without him growing up. Let's just eat without him."

Putting Henry out of their minds, the four of them dined on bratwurst and sauerkraut. For dessert, Aunt Annie placed six candles and one for good measure on top of her famous Black Forest cake with coconut icing. They sang "Happy Birthday" to Emily before she blew out the candles. "Can I open my presents now, Mama?"

"After you finish the dishes."

"Oh, Margaret. You're in America now. You don't have to be so anchored to the rules. It's the child's birthday. Can't she have the night off?"

"No, she has to learn responsibility."

"Alright. I'll help her do the dishes, but let her open her present first."

Emily ripped off the wrapping paper, revealing a set of rosary beads and a German primer reader book. "I know you speak German at home, but I thought the primer would help you learn how to read and write German, since they'll only be teaching you English in school. As for the rosary beads, well, I don't want you to forget your Catholic upbringing."

"Oh, Aunt Annie. *Danke*, you're the best," said Emily.

"You're welcome. Now let's tackle those dishes. Together, we can do them in no time."

Emily watched her aunt fill the sink with the dishes, adding the water and an extra large portion of Borax soap. The bubbles were overflowing.

"Your Mama tells me you can sing the alphabet, so now we're going to learn how to say and write each letter. Hop up on the chair."

Aunt Annie drew a large letter "B" in the suds.

"Now you try it. That is the letter "B." It makes the sound like you hear in b-all or b-us."

Emily traced the letter "B" as she said it. Boy, this was fun. They tried the letters "G" and "F." When they got to "D" for dog, Papa came home. His timing was perfect.

"Are you ready, Princess? I have a big surprise for you. Close your big brown eyes."

Emily closed them so tightly they hurt. She heard scraping across the floor, and then she felt a big slobbering lick on her face. She opened her eyes and there stood the mangiest dog she had ever seen. The dog weighed 50 pounds, give or take a pound. Its tan and black hair was so matted, Emily figured it might take weeks to cut them all out. And it had a beard. Could dogs even have beards? But this one did, and Emily loved it. This was her dog.

"This is Queenie," Papa said.

"Henry, take that mutt back. Dogs are too much trouble to take care of."

"Oh, Mama, I promise I'll do it."

"They also take money to feed them," Mama added.

"Not this dog. She'll eat table scraps. I'll even give her some of my dinner."

But Mama put her foot down. "She goes back to the pound tomorrow. In the meantime, I don't even want her in this house. We might catch fleas. She can sleep on the porch tonight."

Aunt Annie watched the rush of excitement on Emily's face drain to sadness in just a matter of minutes. Why was Margaret so cruel? What did her brother see in her? Did she forget what it was like to be a child? Would her brother stand up to Margaret and let Emily keep the dog? Not able to watch the outcome that she already knew was coming, she politely excused herself.

Without asking Mama to heat his dinner, Henry ate his bratwurst cold. He took a generous helping of cake for dessert, washing it down with the last of his beer. "Happy Birthday, Princess."

"Thanks, Papa." Emily couldn't watch him eat. Why didn't he stand up to Mama? Why didn't he let her keep the dog?

"Margaret, I need more beer. Why don't you run down to Sullivan's pub and get another round for me?"

"Haven't you had enough today?" Two beer runs a day was a bit much. Henry's drinking was getting out of hand. At least Margaret got Emily to make the runs at lunchtime, but Margaret didn't feel like getting beer in the evening on nights like these when Henry demanded more beer.

"Mama, I'll get the beer. I'll take Queenie with me. It'll give me a chance to spend more time with her before you send her back to the pound tomorrow." Emily hoped her good deed would change her mother's mind.

"Thank you, dear."

Emily picked up the growler before heading out to the back porch. The mutt wagged her tail like a whip, hitting the railing.

She lurched toward Emily, yelping when she reached the end of her leash. Emily unhooked her from the railing and headed to Sullivan's pub.

It was a slow night in the tavern; Mr. Sullivan was regretting his decision to open up on Labor Day, but when Emily walked through the door with her dog, it was like a breath of fresh air. "Who do we have here?" he said, petting the mutt on the head.

"This is Queenie. Papa gave her to me for my birthday present, but Mama says I can't keep her."

"Why not?"

"She says it costs too much to feed and take care of her."

"Food shouldn't be an issue. Just give her table scraps."

"That's what I told her."

"What if we give her a reason to keep her? What is a job that your mother hates doing?'

"Fetching Papa's beer. I'm doing it at lunchtime now, but she still does it at night sometimes."

"This dog is an Airedale terrier. A very smart breed of dog. What if we train her to fetch your father's beer?"

"Do you think we could? I bet Mama would let me keep her for sure."

Patrick Sullivan saw dollar signs in the back of his mind. He thought about the business he would receive when patrons came to the bar to see this beer fetching dog. He put the growler around her neck. She shook her head until it fell off. "We have a lot of work to do," he said, laughing.

"Dogs learn by repetition. Starting tomorrow, I want you to walk your dog down to the bar every night at the same time." Patrick looked at his watch. "Say 7:30. That way, I will know when to expect you. You put the dime in the growler, and the growler around her neck, and this is important. You say, Queenie, fetch beer." He took the dime from her and filled the growler with beer. Then he placed the growler around her neck, gradually releasing his grasp until the Airedale bore the entire weight of the beer-filled growler. "Queenie, go home.

13

Emily, you take her home and see if your mama will let you keep her."

"Thanks, Santa. I mean Mr. Sullivan. You're the best."

Emily walked her dog home. Mr. Sullivan said Airedale terriers were smart, but they must be strong too because this one made it down the block and up the stairs carrying the heavy load. Inside the apartment, Emily gently removed the growler from her neck. "Emily, what on earth are you doing?" asked Mama.

"Mama, I know how you hate those beer runs. What if I train this dog to do it for you?"

"Emily, I don't know if that is even possible, but if you can do it, and it saves me time, this dog will have a home for life."

"Good. Then it's settled," said Papa, winking at Emily.

At 7:30 the next day, Emily followed her instructions from Mr. Sullivan. She put the dime in the growler, placed the growler around the dog's neck, and said, "Queenie, fetch beer." Then she put on the dog's leash and walked to Sullivan's pub. Mr. Sullivan took the dime, filled the pail with beer, and said, "Queenie, go home." They walked home without spilling a drop of beer.

After a month, Emily was ready to give up. "I don't think this is working. I'm the one getting the beer. She wouldn't be getting it if I wasn't here to pull her along," Emily said to Mr. Sullivan.

"Remember, I told you that dogs learn by repetition? She is learning the route. Do you want to try the next step?" Emily nodded. "Tomorrow night, we are going to help her along with a treat. Put the growler on, but not the leash. Let her smell the table scraps in your hand. If you don't have any, then try soaking a small piece of bread in milk. That should work too. When you say, 'Queenie, fetch beer,' make her follow you, but don't give her the treat until you're at the door. Then put the leash on and come here to the pub as usual. Eventually, when you say, 'Queenie, get beer,' she'll go right to the door where you give her the treat."

Emily followed Mr. Sullivan's instructions again. Emily didn't know if her dog was smart or just knew where to go to get a treat. It only took her three days to go to the door. Emily didn't even have to say, "Queenie, get beer" anymore. Just putting the pail around her neck made her go to the door.

When Emily told this to Mr. Sullivan, he was quite pleased. "It's working. She is learning by little steps. "Tomorrow, we're going to get her to go down the stairs by herself. When she comes to the door, don't give her the treat. Let her smell it in your hand, then have her follow you all the way down the stairs, before you give her the snack."

Mr. Sullivan's instructions were right again. In about a month's time, the dog walked down the stairs and waited for Emily to give her the treat. Then Emily extended the distance halfway down the block to the mailbox before giving her the reward. And finally, Queenie made it all the way to the bar where Mr. Sullivan gave her the treat.

It took another month to teach the dog the route back home, stopping again at the mailbox, the porch steps, and finally the kitchen door. At last, Emily was ready to show off her dog training to her skeptical parents.

"Mama, Papa, come watch."

Papa put his newspaper down, stood up from his overstuffed chair, and pulled his suspenders back up. Mama wiped her hands on her apron and walked toward the kitchen door.

Emily opened the door and put the growler around her dog's neck. "Queenie, fetch beer," she ordered. The Airedale scooted out the door with Emily peering out the door behind her. She watched her run all the way to the pub. A hand reached out to open the tavern door. Emily couldn't see the body attached to it, but Queenie bounded in.

When her dog didn't reappear again in ten minutes, Emily said, "Something is wrong. I'm going to see what the problem is." Emily ran all the way to the bar. Mr. Sullivan stood like a statue with his arm extended, pointing toward her house.

He said, "Queenie, go home." Then louder again, "Queenie, go home." She wasn't moving.

Emily barged in. She said, "Queenie, go home," in the most authoritative voice she could muster. She still won't move.

"I was afraid that this might happen. It might be confusing for her to take commands from two people." Mr. Sullivan pulled a dog whistle from his pocket. "Here, this might help. Blow it," he said as he handed it to Emily.

She puckered her cheeks and blew as hard as she could, but nothing happened.

"I don't think it's working. I don't hear it," Emily said.

"Give it a minute. It works on a different frequency. People can't hear it, but dogs can." Emily's dog howled like a wolf.

"Take Queenie and the whistle home, and let's try this again. You wait at home. After I put the beer in the growler, I'll put her outside. When you see her, you can see her from your house, right?"

"With the mounds of snow, I'll have to stand on the second-floor porch and lean over the railing to see you."

"Good. So as I was saying, when you see her, give a long tout on the whistle. If it works correctly, Queenie should come running home."

Emily ran home with her dog right behind. She couldn't wait to try again. First, she emptied the beer into a pitcher and placed it in the icebox. She put another dime in the growler. "Queenie, fetch beer."

Off the dog bounded. She ran right to the bar. Emily waited for Mr. Sullivan to do his thing, and then, on cue, he pushed Queenie out the door with his foot and gave Emily an enormous wave. She puckered her lips and touted loudly on the dog whistle. She blew so hard her ears hurt. Emily could hear the dog's howl, and that mutt was almost a block away!

Queenie ran right up to Emily, but so did two other dogs. She recognized Nellie, Mrs. Taylor's poodle, but the other dog must have been a stray. She laughed. Papa pulled the family's dog into the house, slamming the door on the other two dogs. Emily cleaned up the snowy footprints before Mama could complain.

From that moment on, Emily knew her dog could stay. She put the dog whistle on a string, and the string around her neck where it would remain, close to her heart.

But with Queenie came darker days. Mama and Papa fought more and more, always about Papa's drinking. One day, Papa repeatedly pulled the bow open on Mama's apron. Papa was drunk again. Emily reached into her pocket to make sure the clothespin was still there. It was; she clenched it tightly. If she is forced to take Papa's vomit to the outhouse again, at least her nose will be ready this time. She wondered how much longer Mama would put up with it. After the twenty-fifth pull and retie of the apron, Mama yelled, "Get out and don't come back until you sober up."

Papa tried to leave, he really did, but he fell asleep right in the doorway. She let go of the clothespin. Mama said, "I'm going to teach your father a lesson." She grabbed Papa's razor and shaved off his entire mustache. Emily laughed. Her younger brother, John, didn't recognize his father. He ran around the neighborhood in his bare feet yelling, "I have a new Papa. I have a new Papa." Worried that John might get frostbite on his toes, Mama ran right after him.

Papa never complained. He must have thought he deserved it. He never had time to grow back another mustache because the last fight happened about a week later when Papa reached for the old coffee can in the cupboard over the stove. "What do you think you're doing?" Mama said.

"I need the money to pay our bar bill. Patrick says we can't buy more beer until we pay it off. Queenie, come here."

"No Henry. We're behind on the rent. That's more impor-tant," Mama said with her pleading eyes.

"Stop looking at me. I can't resist those eyes. I promise this will be the last time," Papa said. He shoved a five-dollar bill in the growler while Mama quickly did the math in her head. Mama and Emily always paid for the beer they bought, but somehow Papa had another 50 beers that he didn't pay for. "How are they not paid for?" Mama asked. But she already knew the answer. Henry was drinking another pint of beer on his way home from work.

Without answering Mama's question, Papa opened the door and sent Queenie on her way. Mama was nervous. This was the most money her dog ever carried. She watched out the window.

"No, no, no!" Mama snatched the red umbrella from its stand and disappeared down the block. Emily ran outside to find out what was going on. Mama was pummeling the dogcatcher over the head with her umbrella. He was a thin man but managed to feign off Mama and keep a firm grip on the stick holding the stray in place. "Give me back my dog," Mama screamed.

"Sorry, lady. This dog has no license. She is now the property of the city."

"At least give me back the dog's harness and pouch," Mama pleaded.

"No."

Mama surrendered. She sat on the front step of her house in tears as Queenie was driven away in a cart pulled by the dogcatcher and his two horses. Emily tried to give her a hug, but Mama brushed her away like she was shooing away a fly.

"Get out," she yelled at Papa. This is all your fault. I never want to see you again."

Emily felt like a freight train ran her over. Everything was coming at her so fast. First, someone took her dog, then Mama snubbed her, and now Papa was leaving. This was all too much to bear. Emily began shaking and crying uncontrollably as she watched her father pack his shoes in the old valise. He packed a bottle of gin and wrapped his clothes around it, adding it to the contents. She hugged her father and said, "Papa, please don't go."

"Emily, be brave. I'm counting on you to take care of your mother. I'll be back when things get better."

"Don't forget your hat," Mama said. She threw it so hard at Papa she could have made the Olympic discus throwing team. Papa merely picked it up, plopped it on his head, and went on his way.

Without Papa, things didn't get better, they got worse. Yes, the house was quiet. There was no more fighting, but now there was unimaginable hunger. The cupboards were empty. Most nights, dinner was a piece of bread soaked with water and sugar. One day, when Emily came home from school, Mama stood in the street with her hands on her hips. Someone had strewn everything they owned- clothes, furniture, pots, pans, and dishes- in the street, and there was a big padlock on the apartment door.

Twenty-First Street
1909

E mily gasped. She wiped the tears from her eyes and said, "Mama, what happened?"

"Calm down, Emily. Here, I made you a doll." Mama handed her the toy with a reassuring smile on her face. It wasn't much of a doll, just an old stuffed sock with button eyes, yarn hair, and a painted mouth and nose. It had arms and legs, a piece of red yarn pulled tightly, creating the hands and feet, but it had no distinctive fingers or toes. Emily hugged the doll so tightly, that if it had been a real person, the eyes would have popped out of their sockets.

"Emily, I'm so sorry. Please stop crying. I need you to be a big girl. Help me move the furniture out of the street before it gets run over or stolen." Emily felt as strong as Hercules as she helped her mother drag the couch, Papa's chair, the kitchen table, and all the beds and bureaus to the alley next to their former home. She didn't even feel the pain when she dropped the couch onto her foot.

"That was a lot of work. I'm hungry. How are you gonna cook dinner, Mama?" Emily asked. But she already knew the answer. Without pots and pans, or a kitchen to cook in, there would be no dinner.

"I'm sorry, baby. We'll have to skip dinner and sleep in the alley tonight. But it is only temporary. One night. I'll pick you up from school tomorrow and walk you to our new home. I promise. Look on the bright side; at least it's not raining." That was it, no emotion, no explanation, and certainly no admission of guilt.

To say sleeping was rough would be an understatement. Emily kept her shoes on all night, but even that didn't keep her toes from getting numb in the bone-chilling winds of the early spring air. She slept huddled next to her brother for warmth, using clothes for pillows and blankets, their heads separated by the doll. The clomping of an occasional horse woke her up every few minutes. With the wind came the stench of the community latrines. When it reached her nostrils, she gagged. Where was her clothespin? She had lost it weeks ago.

In the morning, Mama bought four apples from the street vendor on the corner for breakfast. They each ate an apple. Emily savored hers, eating every piece, sucking out all the juice. She tried to imagine that she was eating apple strudel, but nothing helped to relieve her hunger pains. The last apple Mama gave to Emily for her school lunch. "Remember, I'll meet you after school and show you our new home. I can walk you to school this morning too if you want me to."

Emily felt delighted that her mother still wanted her to go to school on this traumatic day. Most mothers would make their children stay home to help move, but not Mama. She valued education in her own way. Every day she asked Emily to tell her one thing she learned in school. But Emily's mind wasn't on school. She worried if this would be her last day in this school. Would she have to say goodbye to her friends when they moved? If her mother asked what she learned, what would she say? Would she have the nerve to say: I learned that my teacher isn't very observant. She didn't notice I had the same clothes on two days in a row. "That's alright, Mama. I can walk by myself."

When school was dismissed, Mama went to the girls'

entrance to meet Emily. They walked to their home on Twenty-First Street. Emily didn't bother learning landmarks to get from school to home. She knew she would be enrolled in a new school because the walk was too long.

"Emily, this is your new home. We're on the third floor." Emily followed Mama up the rickety staircase that creaked with every step they took. The first thing she noticed was the bathroom out on the back porch. "No more trips down to the alley at night in the cold and rain. We only have to share it with people on our floor."

Mama opened the door and ushered Emily into the parlor. She felt at home immediately when she spotted her couch, Papa's chair, and the gold-framed mirror hanging on the wall. She smiled until her roaming eyes found the strange man sitting at the kitchen table next to her brother.

"Mama, how did our furniture get here? And who is that man?"

"This is Bill, our boarder. He helped me move all the furniture here while you were at school. He'll be living with us now, paying rent and helping with the bills," Mama said. Bill waved at Emily. "Come Emily. Let me show you your room. You and John will share a bedroom."

There were only two bedrooms off the kitchen. Emily could see her bed and John's bed in the small bedroom. The space between the beds was so narrow, Emily would have to sashay sideways just to pass through. They moved on to the other bedroom. Mama had already set up her double bed with the pink bedspread. Emily wondered if Bill would be sleeping on the couch until she saw a man's watch on the dresser and a pair of men's pajamas under the pillow on the bed.

From the very first night in her new home, things got better. Bill was a butcher by trade, so there was always meat on the table at dinner. Tonight's dinner was *sauerbraten*. Emily couldn't help but stare at the "boarder." He was an ugly man. His thin nose pointed down while his rounded chin pointed up. She watched him chew and thought that the chin and nose might meet. It was pretty darn close. Emily tried not to laugh.

After a hearty pancake breakfast, Mama walked Emily to her new school. There were no landmarks to remember; it was a straight walk down 21st Street. She waited patiently in the office, twirling the bow on her dress while Mama filled out the paperwork. The secretary walked Emily to her new classroom. She wondered what lay ahead as she looked back over her shoulder to watch Mama exit the front door.

Her new teacher, Miss Carter, had full command of the classroom. "Welcome, Emily. Isabel, slide over and let Emily sit next to the pot-bellied stove."

Emily felt honored. The warmest seats next to the stove were for the best-behaved children. Now that she had that seat, she intended to keep it.

The day flew by, and Mama met her at the door to walk home again. About two blocks away, Emily noticed Isabel following them. Emily slowed down so she could catch up. "Where do you live?" Emily asked.

"179 21st Street Apt. 4D."

"That's where I live, but we are right below you in Apt. 3D. This is great. Maybe we can play together sometime."

"Yes, but not today. Emily still has some unpacking to do," Mama said.

Emily frowned as she waved goodbye to her new friend. She watched Isabel climb the steps until she rounded the corner. What was Mama thinking? It would not take very long to unpack her four dresses and two pairs of shoes, and there would still be time to play. But the damp weather in the alley last night was not kind to their clothes. Mama had to rewash and iron all of Emily's and John's clothes, as well as her own, and unpack the remaining kitchen dishes and pots. As the daylight hours faded into dusk and Emily's stomach growled for supper, she realized she would not be playing with Isabel today.

The next morning, Emily awoke to a strange sound. Was

that Mama's alarm clock? It couldn't be; it was Saturday. John was still sleeping with his mouth wide-open and one leg dangling over the side of the bed. It took a minute to realize that this was her new home, and the tapping was coming from the window. A bucket hung from a string banging on the window. Emily opened the window, looked up, and saw Isabel's head leaning out.

"Wake up, sleepy head. I left you a message in the bucket."

Emily grabbed the bucket and removed the note inside. It read, "Let's play today."

"I'll have to ask Mama. How did you know this was my bedroom?"

"I figured your apartment was just like mine and this was my room, so yours would be just below mine, and I guessed right. We'll play in my apartment. Come up after lunch and bring your dolls."

"I will see you then."

During lunch, Emily thought about what Isabel had said. She said bring your dolls, but Emily only had one doll. Did Isabel have more than one? She must be rich. Emily scrutinized her doll, wiping a stain of apple juice from its arm. Why hadn't she asked Mama to wash it with the clothes last night or sew the holes that John put in them? Oh well, it would have to do.

Ten minutes later, Emily stood aghast in Isabel's room. The room had lacy white curtains and a child-size table with four chairs set for a tea party. A porcelain doll sat in one chair, a teddy bear in another, and the other two were left vacant for Isabel and Emily. Another five dolls dressed in plaid dresses sat on top of a hope chest observing the tea party. Emily hid her doll behind her back.

"Let me see your doll."

"I didn't bring mine. I forgot it."

"Yes, you did. I saw you hide it behind your back."

Emily slowly revealed her doll.

"I like it. She is so soft. I bet you sleep with her every night. I'm afraid my dolls might break, and they're too hard to cuddle with. What's her name?"

"She doesn't have one. It's just a doll."

"I think you should call her Dolly."

Emily's inhibitions slowly faded away as she attended the first tea party of her life.

The next day, it was Isabel's turn to play in Emily's apartment. Emily felt worried again. What would she think of her room? How could they play with John hanging around? What would they play? So they sat in the parlor and Emily showed Isabel how to play Chinese checkers. Isabel loved it, and she was a quick learner. Emily's fears melted away.

They became inseparable after that. Spring became summer, and Emily spent hours with Isabel jumping rope in the alley and swinging in the park. On hot days, the firemen would open the hydrants so the neighborhood children could have their day at the beach. Isabel and Emily fought the other children to get up close. They loved the way the rushing water carried them away. When the cooler days of autumn arrived, it was back to playing dolls, Chinese checkers, cards, and styling each other's hair. No one could tie braids as tight as Isabel.

Winter came with a vengeance, blanketing the streets with layer upon layer of snow. Emily didn't mind. Thanks to Bill, the boarder, the Miller family was going to have their first Christmas tree. It was a little thing, with sparse branches already shedding needles onto the floor. And today Isabel was coming over to help make a gingerbread house and string popcorn for the tree.

"Emily, what are you going to ask Santa Claus for this year?" asked Isabel.

She thought about it. There were so many choices. She longed for a doll like Isabel had, or a teddy bear, or a collection of beautiful hair ribbons. She didn't know what to say without appearing greedy. Mama stood close in the kitchen listening to every word. She was making cookies. The smell was wafting into the parlor.

"I'm asking for a pair of ice skates. Why don't you ask for the same thing, and we can skate together in the park?" Isabel said.

"Skating is bad for your ankles. First they hurt, and then arthritis sets in," Mama said, coming out of the kitchen.

"Don't believe it, Emily. That is an old wives' tale."

Emily didn't want to hurt her mother's feelings. "I'll be happy with anything." Deep inside, she wanted everything on her list, and she hoped with Bill living with them, Christmas would be magical. And it was a Christmas that Emily would never forget. Mama made hot chocolate to enjoy by the crackling fire. There were so many candles! From her seat on the floor, Emily couldn't see the candles on the mantel, but their reflection made the star on top of the tree shine brightly, like a light from heaven. Under the tree were four presents for Emily and John, each wrapped in silver paper with an enormous bow on top. John snatched his first gift, shredding the wrapping paper. Emily reached for hers.

"Wait a minute, Emily. One at a time. Let John open one first and then you. I want to see everything you got."

Emily waited patiently while John opened up his gift. It was a new pair of britches, and his first pair of shoes. An uninterested John threw them aside like trash.

"My turn." Emily ripped her wrapping paper off in a slow, lady-like motion. It was a beautiful blue pleated dress with puffy sleeves and a high collar lined with lace. Emily held it up in front of the mirror to admire it. It was the perfect length just above her ankle. "Oh, Mama, can I try it on?"

"Of course."

"I might need help. There are so many buttons on the back."

Mama buttoned the dress, and Emily modeled it for Bill. "You look like a princess."

He may not call me princess, she thought. That was Papa's

name for her, and Bill was not her papa. "Can I open the rest of my presents now?"

John had already opened a wind-up train that was chugging along the floor, a yo-yo, and a collection of jigsaw puzzles. Next, Emily opened up a porcelain doll wearing an identical blue dress to the one she was wearing.

"The next two presents you and John can open together."

"Are you ready, John? One, two, three." In unison, they tore off the wrapping paper. Each held a teddy bear, Emily's with a pink ribbon around its neck, John's with blue. "I'm going to name him Henry after Papa."

"I saved the best for last. This is from Bill and me," Mama said as she handed Emily and John their last present. Each unwrapped a pair of black ice skates with shiny silver blades.

"Oh, Mama. Thank you so much. Can you come skating with me?"

"I don't think so; it's not very ladylike. Besides, I have too much to do. Maybe you can skate with Isabel tomorrow."

"Sure, if she gets a pair of skates too."

"Oh, I know she will."

"Wait, you're not done yet. Look in your stocking."

Emily ran to the mantel, hopping over John's train. She stood on her tiptoes, reaching deep into the red wool stocking. She pulled out an apple, an orange, and a Hershey's chocolate bar. But deep down at the bottom was a collection of bows for her hair. There was a blue one, a red one, a white one, and a black one, one that could match any dress she wore.

But the day was not over. The family celebrated Christmas American style, eating a delicious turkey dinner with corn, green beans, potatoes, and gravy. Watching Bill eat was revolting. He had to wipe the gravy gathering in the reservoir south of his mouth and north of his chin after every bite. Emily smacked herself on the leg. How could she think of anything so mean on a wonderful day like this? She went to bed snuggling her bear,

Henry. She wished it was the real Henry, her papa. His absence weighted on her heart.

The next day, wearing her maroon coat and gray woolen skirt, Emily pounded on Isabel's door. When Isabel answered the door, Emily proudly held up her prized ice skates. "Look what I got for Christmas."

"Me too." Isabel momentarily disappeared, then reappeared holding up her skates. "I just have to put on my long johns and grab my coat and we can go skating. Sometimes I hate being a girl. How come our legs get to freeze under our skirts, but boys get to stay warm in pants? I hope someday girls can wear pants too. I'll be right back."

"Isabel, I don't own any long johns. Do you think I could borrow a pair?"

"Sure. I don't think my mother will miss them."

The girls slid their flannelette long johns on under their skirts and headed for the pond. Emily's skates were a little too big for her. Mama had shoved a sock into each skate, telling Emily it was only temporary until her feet grew into them. She didn't complain; she thought it might keep her toes warm. They sat on a big rock to lace their skates. Even with the extra layer of clothes, the coldness permeated through to their rear ends. The skates had high ankles, and there were at least twenty eyelets to master as they laced up.

"Have you ever skated before?" Emily shook her head. "Tie the laces tight. That way, your ankles won't hurt. Here, let me show you." Isabel laced them so tightly Emily wasn't sure she could stand up. But she worried about nothing. Isabel pulled her until she was steady on her feet. "Let's go."

Emily put one foot forward. Her second foot didn't want to budge, and down she went. Her hands broke her fall, but her mittens got wet. She wasn't sure how long it would be before she gave up. "Let me help you up. I'll hold your hand until you get the hang of it."

Isabel was an outstanding teacher, and before long Emily was skating. Her strides were short, and she wasn't graceful, but she was skating. She let go of Isabel's hand, glided another twenty feet, and tripped over a tree root semi-frozen in the ice.

"I forgot to tell you. Rule number one, watch where you're going," said Isabel, giggling.

Emily pulled herself up. Her skirt and long johns were soaked. The wet mittens were frozen, and so were her fingers and toes. "I think I've had enough for today."

"Me too."

But Emily could tell by the disappointment on Isabel's face that she was just getting started. She didn't fall a single time, and her clothes were still dry. The girls sat on the rock to put their shoes back on. "I'm sorry, Isabel. I'm just so cold. Maybe after I practice more, we can stay longer."

"Don't worry about it. Look over there, by the swings. I see smoke. Maybe someone built a bonfire and we can warm up."

They crept closer to investigate. Three older boys had built a bonfire. One was warming his hands in the radiating heat while the other two roasted marshmallows on thin sticks.

"Can we come join you?" Isabel said.

All three heads turned around, but only one boy spoke. "Aren't you the butcher's kid?"

"You mean Bill? He's not my father. He's our boarder."

"My mother says he overcharges."

"I wouldn't know anything about that."

"Sure you don't."

The boys didn't exactly say the girls could stay, but they didn't say no either. Something in the boys' demeanor concerned Emily. Her immediate reaction was to leave, but her hands were numb. She took off her gloves, laying them on a rock to dry. First, Emily rubbed her fingers together for circulation, then placed her hands, palms up, toward the fire. The heat was a godsend.

The boys stared and snickered, licking their lips as they ate their marshmallows. She couldn't stand it another minute. Her stomach was growling, and dinner was still three hours away. Emily pleaded, "Oh, please, could we have a marshmallow?"

"Well, that all depends. Prove yourself worthy first. What do you think, Ed? What should we have them do?"

"How about jumping over the fire?"

Emily hesitated. "If you show us how, we'll do it." She thought that would be the end. They wouldn't jump, would they? But each of the boys took a running start and leaped over the fire.

"Your turn," one of them said to Emily. Although she was afraid, she didn't want the boys to know. She paused for a few seconds, raised her skirt, and took off, pushing off harder than she needed to. Emily easily cleared the burning logs and fell forward, skinning her knee. The boys laughed. "Your turn," they said to Isabel.

"Isabel, you don't have to," Emily said. Isabel was shorter than her, and she might have trouble with this, but before Emily could say anything else, Isabel was off and running. She jumped too early, landing on the edge of the fire. As she stood up, her skirt was ablaze. In a matter of seconds, flames totally engulfed her. Isabel screamed and kept on running with a tail of flames behind her. "Isabel, stop running."

Emily seized her arm, knocking her to the ground. Covering her with mounds of snow, she looked for the boys for help, but they were long gone. Finally, Emily could see nothing but charred cloth and smelled something like burnt meat. Isabel laid on the cold ground. Emily lifted Isabel's skirt and found her legs severely burned. The sateen lining of her coat had melted into her skin. Pieces of flesh hung from her face. Both of them were in shock.

Emily flagged down a young man who miraculously had gone out for a run in the park. He ran for help while she ran back to wait with her trusted friend. The smell of burning flesh coupled with Isabel's painful moaning brought tears to Emily's eyes. She used her arm to cradle Isabel's head while she waited for the ambulance. She hoped it was a motorized one like the ones she heard about in Philadelphia. It would be way quicker than a horse-drawn ambulance. But the longer she waited, the more she feared it would be the horse-drawn type.

The ambulance and police arrived simultaneously in identical black motorized vans, one marked ambulance and the other police department. They had white tires with spoked wheels that looked too small to hold up their weight. The police officers dispatched to the scene wore dark blue uniforms with a double row of eight gold buttons. Two gold badges mounted on their chests and hats looked official. The men quickly loaded Isabel onto a stretcher and whisked her away, leaving a shaken Emily behind.

Emily told the police all she could remember, including a description of the boys who had run off. The policemen vowed to find the boys and took Emily home, where facing her mother would be the tough part.

To Emily's surprise and relief, her mother did not raise her voice. She simply gave her a few sips of beer and told her to go to bed. Emily fell asleep clutching Henry, wishing it was Papa.

Morning came, but Emily felt sicker than the night before. She sauntered into the kitchen and collapsed into a chair. Bill was nowhere in sight. Mama stood at the griddle, a stack of steaming French toast on the plate beside her. It was Emily's favorite, but the butterflies in her stomach wouldn't allow her to eat them. "Emily, what were you thinking?"

"Mama, I feel bad enough. No lectures, please. Did you hear from Mrs. Danover? How is Isabel?"

The doorbell rang. "Maybe that's her now. Let's go see."

Mama opened the door to a distraught Mrs. Danover. Her hair was disheveled and her eyes puffy and red. "Isabel's condition is quite serious. The doctor is not sure if she is going to make it." Mrs. Danover could hardly speak.

Mama hugged her and rubbed her back. How could Mama

show such compassion to neighbors? When Emily needed a hug last night, it never came.

Mrs. Danover glanced at Emily. "And you, this is all your fault. If it weren't for you, my Isabel would be fine. I forbid you to see her ever again."

Emily darted to her bedroom, slamming the door behind her. "Please, Mrs. Danover, keep us posted on Isabel's condition. We'll pray for her. Now, if you'll excuse me, I need to attend to my Emily."

Mama knocked on Emily's door, then entered without waiting for an answer. "Mama, how could you let her speak to me like that? It's not my fault; it was just a terrible accident."

"There is no need to punish you further. I think your guilt is punishment enough." She kissed Emily on the forehead and left the room.

By dinnertime, Emily's stomach was rumbling. She ventured out to the kitchen. Mama fixed her a cup of tea and some dry pumpernickel toast that Emily ate willingly. The doorbell rang again. "Let me get it, Mama. Maybe it's news about Isabel." Mama nodded.

She walked into the parlor. Bill sat in the easy chair, smoking his pipe. Emily stepped over his feet to answer the door. "You're not Mrs. Danover."

"No, it's just me." It was Mama's friend, Mrs. Baker. Emily thought her name was perfect because she owned a bakery. Mrs. Baker always smelled different depending on what she was baking. Today it was cinnamon. She held the Newark Evening News in her hands. "Are you alright?" She gave Emily a big hug.

"I'm fine. But how did you know?" asked Emily.

"There is a story on the front page of the paper. See. Fire Injures Local Girl. It says Isabel was wearing flannelette long johns that acted like a fuse igniting her clothes quickly. She is in critical condition at the hospital with burns over 35% of her body."

"Let me see that," said Mama, seizing the paper from Mrs.

Baker's hands. "Oh, my God! It mentions Emily by name. Now the entire world knows our business. They'll think I'm a terrible mother letting you play with fire." Emily couldn't believe it. Here her friend could die and her mother was worried about her reputation as a mother. It was always about her.

Mrs. Baker said, "I'm so glad you're not hurt, Emily. Poor Isabel. Is there any word on her?" Emily shook her head. "Well, I'll pray for her. I'll stop by in a week. You can keep me posted."

Emily retreated to her room and played marbles with her brother. She thought about how wonderful Christmas was; the joy in her brother's eyes when he unwrapped his toys. Nothing would ever be the same.

Mama knocked on her door. "Here, have some more beer, drink the whole mug. You need it to help you sleep." She didn't argue and finished every drop.

The next morning, somehow Emily just knew that something was wrong. The sun peeked through the curtains just like it did every morning, but there was no clattering of dishes in the kitchen and no Bill reading the paper or smoking his pipe. She ran to Mama's bedroom. There were no sheets on the bed, no comb and brush on the dresser, no clothes in the closet or bureaus, no valise, and, most importantly, no Mama. Where did she go? Would she be alone to care for her brother? Emily thought about the beer Mama gave her last night. Was that to make her sleep so she wouldn't hear Mama and Bill slip away into the night? How long would they be away?

She had no choice but to accept the job of caregiver for John. The first order of business- the waning heat. Emily shoveled more coal into the stove. Fortunately, there was an abundance of coal in the box. Emily estimated it would last them at least three days.

When her belly could take it no longer, she rummaged through the kitchen for food. She looked in the icebox and found some leftover *wiener schnitzel,* unwrapping it before she remembered Mama didn't want her to use the stove. She put it back in the icebox. Instead, she poured two glasses of milk; one for her and one for her brother. They dined on some celery and cheese, washing it down with the milk. In the next few days, Emily and John polished off all the crackers, jelly, bread, jarred fruit, and vegetables from the pantry.

The coal and the food ran out on the same day. They couldn't do much about the heat, except to wrap themselves in blankets. But the food? Emily remembered how Mama used to store their extra money in a coffee can above the stove. Was it still there? She dragged a kitchen chair across the floor to reach the cabinet. Her eyes lit up like a Christmas tree, finding the can in its usual place. She took it down, looking inside. Empty. Darn you, Mama. Emily threw the can across the kitchen. It ricocheted off the icebox and rolled under the stove. Reaching deep under the stove, she fished out the can with some dust bunnies, and a nickel.

That nickel was a gift from God. Following her mother's example, she left John alone to go to the corner market and buy a loaf of bread. Using another trick of her mother's, she dipped the bread in water and sugar. It was their only source of food for three days.

But when the bread was gone, she didn't know what else she could do. Maybe she could knock on Mrs. Danover's door and ask for help, but her pride won't let her. If Mrs. Danover never wanted to see her again, then so be it. Emily realized that she hadn't talked to an adult in over a week. Her mind imagined the worst. Boy, would her mother be in trouble when she came home and found her children dead from starvation. That would surely get Mama's name in the paper. Imagine the embarrassment.

She tried praying. Her Guardian Angel came with a ring of the doorbell. She rushed to open the door. There stood Mrs. Baker, smelling like lemon.

"I came by to check on Isabel. How's she doing?" Emily hugged her around the waist and burst into tears.

"Emily, what's wrong? Where is your Mama?"

"I don't know. She and Bill packed all their clothes and left us."

"Left you alone?" Mrs. Baker opened every drawer in the kitchen. She saw no food in the house. "How long ago did they leave?"

"About a week ago," Emily said.

"A week? Well, pack up your things. You're coming with me."

11th Avenue
1910

E mily couldn't stop shaking as she took Little John's hand, pulling his thumb out of his mouth for the tenth time that day. Her mother once told her that on days that bad things happen, you would remember exactly what you were doing at the moment in excruciating detail. She looked at the armchair with the sagging springs, the water-stained ceiling, and the flow-ered wallpaper, peeling at the seams. "What happens if Mama comes home? How will she know where we are?" Emily wasn't sure if Mrs. Baker heard her words. She was already in the bedroom, rummaging through the dresser.

A few seconds later, Mrs. Baker's head stretched out into the hall. "Don't worry, dear. It's only temporary until we find your papa. I can't find a valise. Don't you have one to put your clothes in?"

"We only had two. Papa took one when he moved out, and Mama took the other one."

"This will work." Emily watched Mrs. Baker yank the table-cloth off the table. It reminded her of the magic show that Mama had taken her to where the magician pulled off the table-cloth and left every dish on it, but Mrs. Baker was no magician.

The saltshaker teetered, then fell, raining salt all the way to the floor.

Emily collected all John's and her clothes and tossed them into the middle of the tablecloth while Mrs. Baker gathered up the sides and heaved it over her shoulder. She looked like Santa carrying his sack. "You can bring one toy each. I don't have that much room in my apartment."

Emily's eyes stared at the Christmas tree innocently standing in the corner. She wasn't bringing her ice skates, that was for sure. Quickly, she grabbed their teddy bears from under the tree, brushing off an avalanche of pine needles. Mama was right, those Christmas needles stick around until spring. Emily felt the corner of her lips turn upward, realizing the joy these toys brought to her and her brother.

Emily's little legs were bare, and she could feel the rush of the frigid air in every bone in her body as they walked to Mrs. Baker's house. She was proud of John, walking in his new shoes without the aid of his stroller. As Emily wrapped the scarf tighter around her neck, she wondered, how long would she have to stay at the bakery? Could Mrs. Baker find Papa? When was Mama coming back?

The wind slammed the door shut, pushing the trio into the Apples Galore Bakery. Three bells above the door jangled violently, rescuing Emily from her thoughts. She rubbed her legs to warm up and noticed how different the bakery looked in the dark. The flame of the gas streetlight cast eerie shadows on the empty glass counters.

"Bert, Bert, where are you?" Mrs. Baker bellowed. Footsteps echoed on the wooden stairs and Mr. Baker stood in the doorway, like an emperor. "What is the matter my dear? Whose children are these?"

Emily covered her mouth to keep from laughing. She had never seen Mr. Baker before. He was so fat; the buttons on his shirt looked ready to pop. Emily wondered if Mrs. Baker made him taste all of the food before she sold it, eating his way through the profits.

"These are Margaret's children, John and Emily. Margaret disappeared and left the dear ones behind. They'll be staying with us for a while. Now go and fetch the cots from the basement, and also bring up the orange crates."

Mr. Baker did as he was told.

Mrs. Baker took the children through a swinging door which led to their home at the back of the bakery. "This is the parlor. You will sleep in here once Mr. Baker sets up the cots. I know it is small, but we only have one bedroom. I'll leave you to get settled in for the night. You'll get the tour of the kitchen in the morning. In the meantime, you stay out of there. There are too many ways for children to get hurt in there."

Mr. Baker set up the cots and the children untied the tablecloth, placing their meager belongings into the orange crates. Since times were hard, Mrs. Baker only provided thread bare blankets and two skimpy pillows with the feathers spilling out. They both huddled under the covers, Emily hugging Henry, and John holding the only toy he had in the world.

Emily didn't fall asleep until the wee hours of the morning. The bar in the middle of the cot hurt her back, so she slept on her side, but all she could see were the slats in the back of a chair, making her feel like she was in a crib. And that cuckoo clock sang every hour. How long would it be until Mrs. Baker found Papa?

"Rise and shine. Time to get up." Emily thought she must have been dreaming. She heard Mrs. Baker's voice, but the cuckoo clock said it was only 4:00.

"It's not morning yet. It's still dark out."

"In a bakery, we rise early. There are lots of chores. Now, get up." When Emily didn't budge, Mrs. Baker pulled her blanket off. She looked over at John, who was already sitting up rubbing his eyes.

Emily put on her blue dress, laced up her shoes, and reached for her blue bow. "You can't wear that. Customers don't want hair in their food." Mrs. Baker handed her a baker's hat and helped Emily tuck in all the hair. Emily looked in the mirror. It looked like a giant mushroom on the top of her head.

Mrs. Baker took Emily by the hand into the kitchen. A huge white icebox with claw legs and the biggest black stove that Emily had ever seen took up one entire wall of the kitchen. Another wall had a shelf lined with pots and pans, dishes, and every baking tool you could imagine. Under it was a baker's rack that could hold 50 loaves of bread. The third wall housed the sink with white tieback curtains. Fresh daisies rested on the window ledge. On the last wall was a vat for mixing bread dough big enough to take a bath in. A warm bowl of oatmeal waited for Emily on the table next to it. As she ate, she counted eight barrels scattered around the room used as cooling racks for the plethora of bread they would be baking.

"Hurry and eat, Emily," Mr. Baker said. "We have deliveries awaiting us." It was bad enough getting up early, but today was Sunday. Wasn't Sunday supposed to be a day of rest?

Emily finished her breakfast and joined John and Mr. and Mrs. Baker, already waiting in the alley behind the bakery. "We are expecting five deliveries today- apples, flour, milk, ice, and coal. Emily will help with the apples, and John will help with the rest."

A scrawny horse pulling an apple cart stopped at the door. Emily thought the horse needed something to eat, so she reached for an apple and tried to feed it to the horse. Mrs. Baker slapped her hand. A shocked Emily dropped the apple onto the ground. "Pick it up. It's not bruised, is it?" Emily picked it up and examined it thoroughly. She shook her head. "Good. We are making 20 pies today. We need ten apples for each pie. There are 50 apples in a bag, so grab four bags."

"How do you know there are 50 apples in each bag?"

"Because I have never been short-changed yet. You can count them."

"No, I believe you."

"But we would have been short if you fed that apple to the horse."

"But he is so skinny."

"That's not our horse. It's up to the owner how he wants to treat him. Here, I'll help you carry these bags into the kitchen so you can start peeling." Surely Emily would not have the task of peeling 200 apples by herself, would she?

Mrs. Baker covered Emily with a full-size apron, tying it tightly, over and under her arms. It was so long, it dragged on the floor. Emily feared it would cut off her circulation.

"Have you ever peeled apples before?" Emily shook her head. "It's easy. Watch me. Now you try."

It looked easy, but with the first pull of the paring knife, she nicked her finger, dripping blood into the bowl. She hoped Mrs. Baker didn't notice. Soon, she got the hang of it and Mrs. Baker was pleased with her new helper.

"See, I knew you could do it. We only have 199 more to go. With my help, we'll finish in no time. And each day you'll get faster and faster."

Each day? How long did Mrs. Baker think she would be here? "Did you find my papa yet?"

"Not yet."

As the girls peeled, they watched Mr. Baker and John unload the rest of the wagons. First came the bottles of milk. John did a good job putting them in the icebox spilling no milk and breaking no bottles. Next came the flour. John squeezed a bag too tightly, shooting the flour into his face and setting off a sneezing fit.

"You look like a ghost." Emily said, trying not to laugh.

"I'd like to see you try it."

"No, that's alright. I got my hands full peeling apples." Emily continued to peel as she watched John and Mr. Baker shovel the coal into the stove and lug the heavy block of ice across the floor, depositing it into the icebox. John tripped in a puddle of water. The water turned the flour into dough; he was going to need a bath.

"Emily, why don't you help your brother clean up? I'll finish the apples. When you come back, you can watch me make the pies and bread for the day."

"Can't I help bake? That looks like the fun part."

"No, you're too young. I don't want to see you burn yourself on the stove. Remember, never touch it without an adult present." Emily would have no trouble remembering that rule, after watching Isabel get burned, she didn't want to be anywhere near a fire.

So a cleaned-up Emily and John watched diligently as the Bakers made ten loaves of bread at a time. They poured the dough into the big mixer and stirred with what looked like an oar. Emily and John helped shape the bread and put it in the oven. When it was done, Emily got to take the bread out of the oven and put it onto the cooling racks. The Bakers cleaned the mixer and made the dough for the apple pies, repeating the process. At last, the pies and bread were ready for customers, but the work wasn't done. Emily helped Mrs. Baker carry all the baked goods to the front counter of the bakery and greet the customers. John helped Mr. Baker sweep the floor and wash the fingerprints off the glass counter with a mixture of water and vinegar and an old rag.

Emily had no idea how much hard work went into running a bakery. Even with the 17 nicks on her hands, the hard bed, and the cuckoo clock, she had no trouble falling asleep the second night. Tomorrow was Monday and she would be glad to go to school. Suddenly, school seemed easier than running a bakery.

But at 4:00, Mrs. Baker woke her up again. "Rise and shine, little lady."

"Why are you waking me up so early? School doesn't start until 9:00."

"You're not going to school. It will only be a few days until we find your papa. I'm sure school won't mind, and I really could use your help."

Everything became clear to Emily. Mrs. Baker wasn't looking for Papa, and she wanted Emily to be her employee, or more like her slave. On Thursday, Mrs. Baker came to her with terrible news. Emily's friend Isabel had passed away from her injuries. Deep sadness set in, and Emily performed her chores like a robot, without emotion. Days turned into weeks, weeks turned into months. Emily asked every day where Papa was, and the answer was, "I'm still looking." She worried that she would forget her German. Mrs. Baker didn't speak a word of it.

One day, Emily noticed an advertisement attached to the side of a bag of flour. She couldn't read all the words, but she could tell it was some type of bread-making contest for children. She showed it to Mrs. Baker. "Do you think I could enter?"

"How can you? You don't even know how to use the stove."

"I'm a quick learner. If I can win, it'll bring you a lot of business."

"How on earth would you know that?"

"It worked for Mr. Sullivan. Customers came from near and far to see my dog fetch beer for Papa."

"Let me see the notice. We only have a week to practice. We better get started." Mrs. Baker was already gathering baking tools onto the table. She opened her cookbook. "I think we'll use this recipe. It is the simplest one to learn." She measured the milk and water and called Emily to the table to join her.

"I'm going to show you how to light the stove, but remember what I told you: only do this when a grown-up is present. Do you understand me?" Emily nodded. "Open up the flue so the smoke goes up the chimney. Then crumble some paper and stand up pieces of wood like a teepee. Use the lighter to light the wood. When it catches, shovel in some coal. Let me see you do it." Mrs. Baker stopped talking to watch Emily's every move. "Good job. Now pour the milk and water into the pot until it boils."

Mrs. Baker left Emily alone to stir while she got the smaller bread mixer off the shelf. "When we're only making one or two loaves, we use this mixer." Emily felt delighted. She didn't think she was tall enough or strong enough to stir the big mixer. "The milk is boiling. Pour it into the mixer to cool. Now we're going to make a yeast sponge. Mix the yeast into warm water and add a few teaspoons of flour. Let's cover it and wait for the milk to cool down. Do you want an apple while we wait?"

Emily felt surprised that Mrs. Baker had any extra apples to eat, but she took her up on her offer. By the time Emily finished her apple, the milk had cooled. Mrs. Baker took the lid off the yeast sponge. "Come and look."

"Wow, how did that happen? Was it magic? How did it grow like that?"

"Yeast is the secret ingredient. We're going to add the sponge to the milk with some salt and flour. You can start mixing now. Look at the clock. When the big hand hits the three, it should be ready."

"Mrs. Baker, why didn't you use all the flour?"

"That is the tricky part. After 15 minutes, the dough might be too sticky and then we'll add more flour, but it might be fine. We can always add more flour; we can't take it out."

"What happens if we add too much flour?"

"It will make the bread too dry."

"It sounds hard."

"It'll take practice to get it right. We'll practice every day until the contest."

After 15 minutes, Emily was glad to stop. Her hands cramped up. She wiggled her fingers to get back the circulation.

"Now we have to knead. Watch. Fold the dough to the center and flatten it out over and over again."

"That looks like fun. Let me try." Emily loved kneading the dough, but she didn't enjoy having to do it for so long. Her hands ached again. "Is that the last step? I hope we're done."

"Almost. I'm going to cover the dough and let it sit for two hours at room temperature. Where do you think I should put it?"

"How about on this barrel?"

"No, it is too close to the stove, but this one will do. It's in the middle of the room, not too cold and not too hot."

"I feel like Goldilocks. It's just right."

Mrs. Baker laughed. "Let's go for a walk. We can come back in two hours."

Two hours later, the dough had doubled in size. It was ready for the oven. Mrs. Baker helped Emily form two loaves and place them in greased pans. "Can we put them in the oven yet?"

"It has to be high heat. We need to add more coal first. Shovel in two scoops of coal and move the damper. That will allow the oven to heat up quicker. Now put in the loaves for 15 minutes. They will be done when the big hand hits the 5 this time."

Emily watched the clock intently. Exactly 15 minutes later, she opened the oven door. "That doesn't look done to me."

"That's because it's not. Move the damper again to lower the heat and cook it for 45 more minutes."

"Can we play gin rummy while we wait?" asked Emily.

"Sure. I'd love to. I love to play cards, but Bert only plays poker." Emily appreciated that Mrs. Baker would take time off from her busy work schedule to have some fun with her.

Emily had her own bread with butter for breakfast the next morning. It tasted great. The next few days, she made the bread completely by herself under the watchful eyes of Mrs. Baker. One day it was too dry, another day too moist, and one day it tasted fine, but lacked the proper shape. But by the fourth day, she had perfected it. I'm ready for the competition, she thought.

The day of the contest finally arrived. Emily wore her white dress with the red satin sash and her white bow. She carefully wrapped her bread in a clean cloth, and she and Mrs. Baker set off on the 20-block walk down to Main Street Park. The sun glowed brightly. Emily hoped it was a good omen.

The closer they got, the bigger the crowds got, until they were just pushed along with the crowd. "There is the registration table. Let's wiggle our way through this crowd. Hold on to my hand so we don't get separated." Emily tightly gripped Mrs. Baker's hand. She saw a man bump into a girl about her age, knocking a loaf of bread out of her hand. Emily clutched her loaf tighter. She wasn't about to be eliminated before she even got started. Mrs. Baker shoved her way through the crowd to reach the table. "This is Emily Miller. She wants to register for the contest."

The woman behind the table was small. At first Emily thought she was a contestant herself, but upon closer examination, she realized this was an older woman who wore a blue velvet hat with a light green feather. Her meticulous eye make-up accented her green eyes, and her cherry red lipstick emphasized her perfectly straight teeth.

They approached the table where all the contestants stood in line. "You are entry number 35. Here, Emily, is it? Pin the number on your dress." Mrs. Baker filled in Emily's name and address and certified by signing that she had not helped Emily. "Emily, you can have a seat over there with the other contestants, and Mrs. Baker, you can have a seat with the spectators in the bleachers."

"Emily, see the open area three rows up? I will be seated there so you can find me after the contest. Good luck."

Emily took her seat in the second row next to a girl about her age. "Hello. My name is Ruth. Nice to meet you." She put out her hand and Emily shook it. Ruth wore a blue dress with a baker's cap on her head. Emily worried she was supposed to wear that hat, but when she looked around, only two other girls wore them.

"Pleased to meet you. I'm Emily Miller."

"You look like the only friendly face in this crowd. All the other entrants wouldn't even say hello. They are so snooty."

Did Ruth say snooty? She wasn't sure. It was hard to hear

over the band playing "God Bless America" right behind them. But when she surveyed the other girls sitting up perfectly straight with their hands folded in their laps, she knew exactly what Ruth meant.

An older girl wearing a blue dress with a sailor's collar and number 18 on her dress strutted by with her chin up in the air, rolling her shoulders from side to side as she walked. "Who is that?" Emily asked.

"That is Mary Rickers. She won the last three years in a row. The way she is walking, I think she thinks she is going to win again. That's probably because her mother helps her bake the bread." Emily thought that was cheating, but she would never say that out loud. "Oh, no. Look at the judges' table. Her mother is a judge this year. We're doomed."

Emily spotted Mrs. Rickers easily; she had the same prominent forehead and ski-jump nose as her daughter. She wore her black hair in a bun, and she was the only woman mingled with four male judges. They all sat beneath a banner reading "1910 Children's Bread Making Contest." Ruth didn't think she'd have a chance to win, but Emily was an optimist. Mrs. Rickers held only one vote of the five; she was convinced the men would be fair.

At last, the winner was to be announced. A man stood behind the podium with a microphone. Emily crossed her fingers. "This year's winner is Emily Miller." She jumped up and ran for the lectern. When Emily passed Mary Rickers, Mary extended her foot. Emily jumped over it. *Was she trying to trip me, or merely cross her legs?* Emily, being so good-hearted, thought it must be the latter.

Emily received a loving cup and a certificate that read "Home of the 1910 Children's Bread Making Contest Winner." The crowd cheered wildly, except for Mary Rickers, who sat emotionless. Mrs. Baker stormed the stage and gave Emily a big bear hug. Mayor Brown shook her hand. The three posed for a picture that made the front page of the local newspaper. Emily floated home; it was the happiest day of her life. And if she was lucky, Papa would see the picture and rescue her from Mrs. Baker.

Mrs. Baker allowed Emily to keep the trophy, but she insisted on posting the certificate in the front window of the bakery "It's good for business," she said. And so it was. Every pie, cake, cookie, and loaf of bread sold. Emily had never seen an empty counter before.

One day, when Emily was alone at the counter, an odd woman entered the bakery. It was hard to see her face. She had a knitted shawl pulled up to her neck and a cream-colored hat pulled low over her face. Who was she? She looked familiar, but Emily couldn't place her.

With that, the woman looked at her with daggers in her eyes. "Aren't you supposed to be in school?"

"I don't go to school. I work here."

"Well, can I see your mother? I would really like the recipe for your bread."

"Mrs. Baker, can you please come out here? There is a customer that would like to speak with you."

Mrs. Baker pushed open the swinging door. "Yes, can I help…" She froze in the middle of her sentence. "What do you want?"

"I was wondering if you could share the recipe for your bread; it is most delicious."

"Why dear Mrs. Rickers, why don't you use your own recipe? Mine is an old family recipe that I am not willing to share."

Mrs. Rickers stormed out while Mrs. Baker and Emily laughed behind her. But the next day she was back with a police officer whose badge read "Truant Officer."

"Mrs. Baker, is Emily your daughter?"

"No. She is Henry and Margaret Miller's daughter."

"Why is she here, and why is she not in school?"

There was a pause in the conversation as Emily waited for

Mrs. Baker to respond. But since Mrs. Baker had no answer, she remained speechless.

"Well, little lady. We're here to take you and your brother back to your papa. Go pack your things and come back out here. We'll wait."

Although Emily had sympathy for Mrs. Baker, she felt delighted to go back to Papa. She packed up John's and her clothes in the tablecloth that they had come with and took John by the hand. When she walked through the bakery, she couldn't look Mrs. Baker in the eye. The last thing she remembered was Mrs. Rickers ripping the certificate off the glass window.

Belmont Avenue
1911

Even by car, it was a long way to Papa's house. Wooden houses gave way to identical brick apartment buildings as they traveled deeper into the heart of the city. The car slowed down to a crawl, passing through throngs of people. "Hop out kids; this is it."

Alighting from the car, the stench of the community latrines filled Emily's nostrils and made her gag. The wind wrapped an old newspaper around Emily's leg like a snake. Shaking it off she said, "How do I know which building I will live in? They all look alike."

"Look for the number 76 on the front. It should be easy to remember; it's the same year we became a country." Emily and John followed the truant officer, who never told them his name, into the building. He pushed the button and the elevator door opened, sending the scent of urine into the hallway. "We'll take the stairs," he said.

"What floor are we on?"

"The sixth."

As they trekked up the stairs, the nameless truant officer carried their belongings, making Emily smile. He knocked on Apartment 6A. A large bearded man answered the door. He was missing his front teeth and had a gun holstered on his right hip. Emily clenched her fist as John hid behind her. "Are you Henry Miller?"

"Wrong apartment. He's next door in 6B."

"Pardon the interruption."

Emily ran down the hall and barged into the next unit. Apartment 6B was a one-room apartment with flowered wallpaper. A braided rug covered the wooden floor. A huge white fireplace stood directly in front of her, a picture of Emily and John displayed on its mantel. The fireplace split the room in two. Two wrought-iron beds, two closets, and a chamber pot filled one side, while a kitchen area with a sink, icebox, stove, and washing machine, and a living area with a blue couch filled the other. Henry Miller and his mother Adele sat at a small table in the corner.

"Papa, you grew your mustache back." Emily gave her father a big bear hug.

"*Ich habe dich vermisst.*"

"I missed you too, Papa."

"I can see that the children are in good hands. I'll be on my way." The truant officer handed Papa a paper to sign. He signed it, shook the truant officer's hand, and showed him out the door.

Adele Miller stood up, towering over her son. She had a long, thin neck with an unfortunate mole that even her long ringlet curls could not hide. Adele wore a blue dress with long sleeves lined with white cuffs and a white apron, signaling to Emily that Grandma was living here.

"Papa, why didn't you come rescue us from Mrs. Baker's house? Every day I thought you would come, and you never did," Emily said.

"Believe me, we tried. We've been looking for you ever since that no-good Bill ran off with your mother, but nobody saw you. It wasn't until Mrs. Rickers contacted the truant officer that we got a lead. We're so glad you're here now."

"I bet you can't wait to start school tomorrow. Unfortunately, we don't have a bed for you yet. It's being delivered tomorrow. Just tonight, you and John will have to sleep on the couch," Adele said all in one breath.

After a supper of chicken soup with bread and butter, Emily played three games of Chinese checkers with Papa, just like old times. Then Papa played regular checkers with John, while Grandma helped Emily fix the sheets on the couch. It was good to be home!

About 2:30 in the morning, loud voices from apartment 6A woke the household. Papa put on the light. "What is that?" asked John.

"That is Vinnie Romano, our neighbor."

"Is he the man with the gun?" asked John.

"Yes. It's 2:30 in the morning. The bars just closed. Vinnie probably had too much to drink again, and now he's getting into a fight with his wife, Pinky," said Papa.

"What kind of name is Pinky?" asked John.

"I'm sure it's just a nickname."

"Did you ever ask him what it stands for?"

"No, he's not the friendly type. And I would suggest you kids stay away from him."

Emily would heed his advice. An angry drunken man with a gun was a dangerous thing. She worried about Pinky's safety. "Now what?" Emily could hear the whistle of a train as it approached growing louder and louder, then softer and softer as it passed through town. At least it drowned out the Romanos. She looked at John; he was shaking. "How is anyone supposed to get any sleep around here?"

"I promise you'll get used to it. But until you do, I'll get you a pair of earplugs."

"That will be great, Papa." Taking on the role of the big sister, Emily picked up John's teddy bear that had fallen to the floor during the night and handed it back to him. She put her arm around him until the shaking stopped and they both fell asleep.

Emily woke up with her teeth chattering, a chill throughout her body. She could smell urine; John had wet the bed. She cleaned herself up and got ready for school. Then she stripped the sheets.

"Don't worry about it. I'll wash them and have them all ready for you on your new bed when you get home from school." Emily hugged her grandmother, grabbed a cinnamon bun, and headed off to school with John.

When Emily and John walked in the apartment at 3:30, their new bed had arrived, already made with the rewashed sheets. Grandma sewed the last piece of lace onto their new brown bed cover and threw it on the bed. Two sets of wax earplugs rested on the dresser.. Emily wasn't sure if she would use them; she thought the wax would itch her ears.

Papa came home for dinner carrying four wagon wheels and some strips of wood. "Not only does the elevator stink, now it doesn't work at all," Papa said, trying to catch his breath from hiking up the six flights of stairs.

"What's that for?" John and Emily asked together.

He kicked the crate in which the bed had been delivered. "See, nice and sturdy. I'm using this to make a wagon. Sorry Princess, no games tonight. I'm going to be busy."

John spent the evening helping Papa with the wagon, while Emily studied her primer. She got used to the train whistle, and Vinnie and Pinky Romano only had two more fights. Emily felt brave enough to throw out her wax earplugs.

One day, two burly men burst into the apartment, plopping a moaning Papa onto the couch. "Adele, Adele, come quickly. Henry got hurt." Adele dropped her sewing and approached the men. Emily and John watched from their bed.

"What happened?"

"The coal wagon ran over his foot, and it was a full load."

"Please tell me he wasn't drinking."

"He was, but this wasn't his fault. There are more and more

automobiles on the roads these days. A car backfired. It spooked the horse, and it took off."

"Let me see it." The man gently lifted off his shoe and sock, and Grandma raised his trouser leg to the knee. His foot suffered a crushing injury. It was three shades of purple with dried blood caked on it, extending all the way to his big toe.

"Thank you, gentlemen. I've got it from here," Adele said, waving the men out the door.

Papa's head rolled back and he moaned profusely. "Grandma, how can I help?" Emily was trying to be brave, while John started shaking uncontrollably.

"Get me some whiskey and bandages." Emily removed the whiskey from the icebox and some cloth rags from under the sink. Grandma poured the whiskey on Papa's foot and wrapped it in a bandage. Then she poured more whisky down his throat.

"Your father is in terrible pain. This is one time I don't mind him being drunk. It will numb his pain. Anytime during the night if you hear him moaning, give him some more whiskey or beer. Hopefully, the pain will stop by morning. And Emily, this will take a long time to heal, if at all. You're going to have to be the lady of the house now and cook and clean. I'm going to find a job cleaning houses so we can pay the rent and eat."

Clean the house and cook? Yes, she could bake, but baking and cooking were two different things. Who would teach her how? What about school? She didn't have the nerve to speak out loud. What was it that Mama said, children should be seen and not heard? These words still resonated in her head. At night, she lay awake in bed, giving her father beer twice and rubbing John's back to ease his shaking.

Emily woke up cold and wet. "Grandma, John wet the bed again."

"I'm not washing the sheets this time. That is your first job as the lady of the house."

"I don't know how."

"Come, I'll show you how. First, you fill the tub with water.

I know you know how to light the stove from working in the bakery. This works the same way. When the water is hot, add the sheets and clothes. Then add some soda crystals and Lux soap flakes. Use the dolly stick to agitate. If the stains don't come out, then use the washboard to scrub them out with peroxide. Push the sheets through the wringer to get out the excess water. Then hang them on the line to dry."

"Is that my only chore for the day?" Emily was afraid to ask.

"No, while the clothes are drying, take John to the street vendors and buy some chicken and green beans. Come back, cook dinner, iron the clothes, and remake your bed. I should be home by then."

"That's going to take all day." Emily thought about her schoolwork. She thought that would have to wait until after dinner.

"Probably, but tomorrow should be easier. You won't have to do the laundry."

"Good luck with the job-hunting." Emily kissed her grandmother goodbye. She took on her chores with authority, quickly discovering that the laundry was a job she hated. The hot water burned her fingertips, but holding the growler of cold beer quickly relieved her pain. She held it so long that she was afraid Papa would complain the beer was too warm, but he didn't notice. To make cooking dinner go faster, she had John snap the beans. Grandma came home bearing flowers for the centerpiece.

"Emily, dinner was delicious. And since you did such a good job, I'm going to do the dishes."

"Thank you, Grandma. Then I can have time to work in my primer." But the drudgery of the day and the rules for adding 'ing' to words put Emily into a deep stupor. Grandma gently removed the book from Emily's lap and carried her granddaughter to bed.

During the night, a cat howled on the fire escape, waking up Emily. She looked at her brother who was still fast asleep. Where were those earplugs? She put the pillow over her head. "Get out of here, you stupid cat. Some of us need to sleep."

Suddenly, three loud pops made her jump. Emily didn't know if it was her jumping out of bed or the gunshots that woke John, but he was wide awake. "Was that a gun?"

"Yes, it was Mr. Romano shooting at a stray cat."

"He won't shoot us, will he?" asked John.

"Of course not. Now go back to sleep."

In the morning, Emily realized that the easy workday she was expecting was not to be. John had wet the bed again. Darn Mr. Romano and his gun. It was going to be another long laundry day without a chance to do some schoolwork.

Within a week, Papa started feeling better. He still couldn't walk, but he was well enough to stay sober and play some Chinese checkers and hearts. Emily fit in the games between her chores.

Papa taught her how to play poker using peanuts for poker chips. It wasn't a simple game to learn; Emily could never remember which hand was higher. In one round, Emily had a full house. She wasn't confident it was a good hand, but she bid five more peanuts anyway. Papa had a pretty good hand himself- three of a kind- so he tossed in his five peanuts, matching her raise.

"Wow, you have a great poker face."

"What's a poker face?"

"It means you show no emotion, so I can't figure out if you have a good hand or a bad one. I thought you were bluffing, trying to trick me into thinking you had a good hand, so I called your bluff. It turns out you weren't bluffing. You had a great hand."

"I didn't do it on purpose. I just got confused which hand is the highest."

"Let me write you out a list so you can keep it straight."

As Papa was writing the list, the doorbell rang. Emily

answered it. Two strange men wearing overalls stood before her. "Can I help you?"

"Is this the Miller apartment?"

"Yes."

"We are here to repossess your furniture."

"Papa, what does that mean?"

"It means someone purchased this furniture on time, but they haven't made any payments in three months. We are taking it back to the store," said a man as he handed Emily a paper. She didn't know enough words to read it, but she knew it was bad. Why was she wasting time playing games with Papa when she should use her free time to learn to read? She watched each man pick up an end of the couch. She quickly jumped on the sofa, hoping her added weight would be too much for the men, but it didn't deter them at all.

"Emily, get off the couch." She saw the pain in her father's eyes, and she obeyed. Without adding another word, she watched the men take all the furniture- the couch, Grandma's bed, Papa's bed, Emily's and John's bed, and the table and chair set. Only the mattresses were left behind. Emily started crying.

"Don't cry, Princess. As soon as my foot gets better, I can go back to work and we can buy the furniture back." But wasn't Grandma working? Wasn't her salary enough to pay the bills? Why were they buying beer and cigarettes instead of paying for the furniture? She opened the kitchen cabinets; a sparse food supply greeted her. There wasn't much money for food either.

Emily knew things were bad. She thought about her mother. Where was she? Didn't she love her anymore? Mama had been gone two years now; surely no one remembered that article about Isabel Danover. It was time she came back. Just thinking about Isabel and Mama brought a fresh round of tears to her eyes.

When Grandma came home, the pain only intensified. "It looks like you had a bad day around here. I have to say I'm not surprised. I knew this would happen. Emily and John come sit by me. We need to talk." They gathered on Grandma's mattress, and she continued. "My salary barely covers the rent. I'm going to need more help from the two of you."

"Yes, Grandma. What can we do?"

"We're going to cut back on food."

"What do you mean?" Emily couldn't imagine how they could possibly eat less.

Grandma walked over to the coal bin and lifted the lid. "Since we have no coal to run the stove, we will be skipping breakfast tomorrow. I need you two to go to the coal yard tomorrow. Wait until the men finish bagging the coal, and you can take some from the scrap pile. Get enough for lunch and dinner." But what about the day after that? Would this become a new chore?

Emily deliberately slept in the next morning since there was no breakfast to be had. She waited until Grandma left for work to drag herself out of bed. John followed. "I'm hungry," he said.

"Try not to think about it." Her stomach was growling too. "Get yourself dressed. We'll figure something out along the way."

John rummaged through the closet, pulling out his white shirt. "Not that one. Wear your black shirt."

"I can't; it's dirty."

"Wear it anyway. It's only going to get dirtier today." Emily put on her navy blue dress. She thought about washing these clothes and shuddered.

Emily and John took a burlap bag from the shed behind their apartment building, put it in their wagon, and started down Belmont Avenue. Two blocks into the walk, they came upon the 11th Street Bakery. The smell of cinnamon teased their noses and stomachs.

"I have an idea to get us some breakfast. You stay right here around the corner. Don't let the baker see you, but listen to what I do because tomorrow, you can do the same thing."

Emily waited patiently while the man in front of her ordered a cruller. She stepped up to the counter with her poker face on. "Please, ma'am, do you have any day-old bread to spare?"

"Do you have any money? You'll have to pay for that."

"No ma'am. I'm an orphan and I'm starving. I didn't eat all day yesterday."

"Oh, you poor child." She reached into the counter, pulling out a loaf of French bread. "I can spare it. Enjoy."

"Thank you, ma'am."

Emily ran out the door as fast as she could, giving the woman no time to change her mind. She broke the bread in half and gave one half to her brother. He took a big bite, tearing it off with his teeth. "You know what would top this off? Some milk. Look ahead, what do you see?"

"The milk wagon," John said. Emily watched the milkman place four quarts of milk on someone's front porch. She waited for him to leave and helped herself to a quart.

"That's stealing."

Emily didn't know how to respond to that. She tried to convince herself that it wasn't.

The Lehigh Valley Coal and Charcoal Yards sat on the corner of Clinton Avenue and 19th Street. The establishment included a factory with an attached office building. Four stacks expelled plumes of black smoke into the air. Emily and John counted 31 cars of coal waiting on the tracks to be unloaded. They finished their bread and milk as the men completed their work. Some men dumped the coal from the train onto the ground while another group of workers shoveled it into bags and buckets. A third group of men loaded the coal wagons. The dust the men created grew in size until it met the smoke from the chimneys, forming one homogenous cloud. Black soot covered the men from head to toe.

When the dust settled and the men left their positions, Emily and John pulled their wagon closer to the tracks. They sifted through the remnants, finding pieces big enough to drop into their burlap bag. Soon, another dust cloud formed. Emily quickly learned not to breathe in the fumes, holding her breath, and turning her head to steal an occasional gulp of air. But John coughed his way through this task. Finally, after raking through nine piles with their hands and looking like black bears, their bags were full.

Lugging the wagon home was challenging. Coal was heavy, and it took all the strength they could muster to pull the wagon uphill. Several times, Emily lost her footing. On the fourth fall, Emily landed on her face, splitting her lip and spewing a collection of soot, blood, and tears onto the sidewalk.

When they got home, Emily left John to guard their treasure while she ran up to her apartment to clean up. But Grandma wasn't home, and Papa was in a drunken stupor on his mattress. Badly in need of help, she didn't know where to turn until she thought of Mrs. Romano. She pounded on her door, hoping Mr. Romano wouldn't be home in the middle of the day.

"My goodness. What happened?" Pinky said as she coaxed Emily into her home.

"I was gathering coal and fell on the way home." This was the first time Emily had ever set foot in this apartment. She immediately understood why Mrs. Romano was called Pinky. Everything was pink- the couch, the curtains, the bedspread, her dress. She even had a pair of pink pumps with a black bow on each shoe.

"Let me clean you up." Pinky washed the soot off Emily's face and applied some salve on her cut lip. The ointment worked its magic, and the stinging diminished.

"Thank you so much, Mrs. Romano," Emily said as she headed for the door.

"Can't you stay and visit for a while? It gets pretty lonely here by myself all day, and I have some oatmeal cookies fresh out of the oven."

"Maybe another time. I have to look in on my brother."

"Take a cookie for yourself and one for John. He is such a sweet boy."

"Thank you again." Emily would have to tell Grandma about her visit; Pinky was a very kind lady.

The next day, one of the charcoal workers returned unexpectedly and discovered John and Emily sifting through the coal. "What are you doing?" he asked them.

"We're trying to find coal to bring home to our family," Emily said feeling embarrassed and worried that this man might report them to the authorities. "Is it alright to be here?"

"You're not the only ones. Children come in here all the time. But you're looking in the wrong place. You see, when the workers start loading the bags of coal, they start at the front of the train, but as the day goes on, they get tired and leave bigger piles toward the last few train cars. If you go there, you will find bigger chunks and will finish your work quicker."

"Thanks, mister."

They walked down to the 27th car. Emily was mad at herself for not thinking of this sooner, but the trains were so long she couldn't see all the cars around the bend. There were other children bagging nuggets here, and they joined in without incident.

Gathering coal became the morning ritual for months. Emily and John took turns getting day-old bread from the kind baker; she never turned them down. They kept to the back streets and took a bottle of milk each day, always from a different house, and never getting caught. But with the rigorous work, Emily developed calluses on her fingers and John's cough became chronic.

One day Grandma said, "It's a beautiful day today. Let's play hooky."

"You mean we don't have to go to the coal yards?"

"That's right. We're going to have a picnic right here on the fire escape. Put the blanket down so we can have a place to sit." Emily did as she was told. Grandma and Emily each grabbed Papa's arms and helped him hobble over to the blanket. "John, Emily, have a seat and close your eyes." Emily sat with her legs crossed beneath her, shifting her weight. It was hard to get comfortable with the cold metal bars rubbing her bottom. "Alright, you can open them now."

In front of her, a feast made for a king was laid out. Emily and her family munched on fried chicken, potato salad, and watermelon. It was the best meal they had in a long time. Grandma always had a way of making things special. Emily thought about her mama. She couldn't think of one special thing they had done together. She wondered what her mother was doing right now. Did she ever think about Emily and John?

Distant music interrupted her thoughts. "Do I hear a marching band?" Grandma said.

Emily turned her head to see a 13-piece brass band rapidly approaching playing "Alexander's Ragtime Band." Emily counted one tuba, one trombone, two French horns, two saxophones, six trumpets, a big bass drum, and the marchers all clad in navy blue uniforms with high collars. They stopped right in front of their apartment building. The trombone player passed around a silver dish. Neighbors dropped coins into the bowl.

"Do we have to pay to hear them play?' asked John.

"Of course not, but that's the Salvation Army. They're good deed doers. Today is Decoration Day. They're collecting money for veterans and their widows. Here's a nickel, John. Go down there and put it into the collection plate," said Grandma.

"Stop that racket. You woke me up." Vinnie Romano stood on his fire escape shooting at the Salvation Army. His first shot hit the street, ricocheting into the crowd. His second shot knocked the tray out of the trombone player's hand, scattering the coins into the street. The band and spectators quickly dispersed.

"*Dummkoph.* You're gonna kill somebody someday!" Papa shouted at Mr. Romano. "Let's go inside. It'll be safer."

As Emily and Grandma helped Papa inside, she thought about what Papa had said. Someone could have gotten hurt. Someone like her brother. If Mr. Romano had come out onto the fire escape any later, John might have been standing by the collection plate.

John had a rough time sleeping that night. One hand securely held his teddy bear; the other burrowed into Emily's arm. His nails hurt. She tried to keep her mind on something else. Recalling her day was a good start. She thought about Mr. Romano. Why was he sleeping in the middle of the day? He must have been drunk; why else would he shoot off his gun? Papa was right; somebody could have gotten hurt. She thought about the Salvation Army and their money collection for the poor. Poor people. What makes people poor? Emily looked around her apartment with the light of the full moon. There was no furniture and hardly any food or coal. Did that qualify her as poor? Surely there must be people worse off than her. Grandma tried hard, and she loved her. Emily vowed that she would never partake in the offerings of the Salvation Army. But then again, wasn't that better than stealing milk and begging for bread?

The next morning, Emily woke up to her grandma's ranting, "Get out of bed right now. What is wrong with you? You're still wetting the bed at eight years old?" She shoved John onto the floor.

"Don't worry Grandma. I'll wash the sheets," Emily said as she put her arm around her brother's shoulder. "Don't I always?"

"It's not the washing. That God-awful smell will linger here for a week. It's bad enough I have to take care of my crippled son, but I don't need the extra burden of caring for his two wayward children. Pack up your clothes. I'm taking you out of here."

"Are we going back to Mama?"

"No. I don't know where she is."

"So where are we going?"

"You'll find out soon enough."

As Emily packed her clothes, she wondered what got into her grandmother. Was it really John's bed-wetting or something deeper? Perhaps Mr. Romano's behavior affected Grandma as much as it did John. But where was Grandma taking her?

Bergen Street
1912-1913

The Home for the Friendless stood at the top of the hill. In its heyday, it was a family mansion, but today its huge façade with a surplus of windows was intimidating. A stockade fence shielded the children from the Miller family standing at the front door, but Emily could still hear them playing.

The matron, Mrs. Dixon, answered the door. She was a small woman, not much taller than Emily. Her hair, tied in a tight bun, emphasized her high cheekbones and stern mouth. Her dress, shoes, and tights were all black. A single strand of pearls added the only color to her outfit. She carried a ruler in her right hand, which she tapped nervously into the palm of her left hand.

"You must be Emily and John. Welcome. And you must be Mrs. Miller." She transferred the ruler to her left hand and shook Grandma's hand. "Let me give you the tour and we'll get the children settled in."

The vast foyer boasted a black and white linoleum floor with a bust of Christopher Columbus perched on a marble pedestal. Mrs. Dixon's office and sitting room lay to the right. Emily could see two Queen Anne chairs and an oak coffee table lined with magazines through the open door. The dining room to the left included a long table with 20 chairs and six smaller tables scattered around the main one. Two winding staircases led to the second floor. The group ascended the one to the left. From the landing, Emily could see at least three washing machines on this side. The room to the right was a playroom, where two young girls played jacks while two boys amused themselves in a game of checkers. The group ascended another set of stairs.

"These are the girls' quarters. Emily, this is your bed." Grandma plopped Emily's belongings onto her new bed. Ten beds lined each side of the room. Her bed was the third from the back, on the right-hand side. "I'll leave you to unpack. Mrs. Miller, if you follow me, I will show you the boys' quarters one flight up."

"You mean John won't be sleeping in here?"

"In the girls' quarters? Of course not. Say your goodbyes now."

Emily hugged her brother and her grandma. What was this place? Would she ever see her grandmother again? Would she simply disappear like Mama?

"Emily, you can let go now." She let go, turning her head so Grandma wouldn't see the tears forming in her eyes. She waved goodbye over her shoulder.

As Grandma left, her soon to be roommate called out to her. "Don't worry, everybody cries on the first day. Hello, my name is Betty. I'm your big sister, so to speak."

Emily wiped the tears from her eyes and found a girl a bit older than her on the bed next to hers. Betty sat with her left leg folded underneath her right one, revealing the petticoat underneath her yellow dress. She styled her blonde hair into two pigtails with yellow ribbons.

"What is this place? Is it an orphanage? Is my grandma leaving me here?"

"No, it is supposed to be temporary. Your parents are poor, right?" Emily thought this girl was too personal, but she nodded. "They'll come back to get you when they get back on their feet.

You'll see it's not too bad here. The meals are good, and Sunday is visiting day. Most parents come to visit and bring a picnic lunch."

Would her papa and grandma come next Sunday? She hoped so; it was only a week away. "What about school? Can I start tomorrow? I'm so far behind on my studies."

"We go to the regular public school here. But you won't be going until Tuesday. Monday is laundry day, and Mrs. Dixon wants you to help me. We have to wash all the sheets and towels and remake the beds. It is an all-day project, so we get to skip school. And whatever you do, don't tell the other kids at school that you live at the Home for the Friendless. Just say you live on Bergen Street."

"Why?"

"They don't understand poor people. They'll think we're different, scum of the earth. Trust me, if you want any friends at school, don't tell them."

Emily thought about what Betty had told her as she unpacked her clothes into the bureau attached to the foot of her bed. She put her teddy bear, Henry, on top of the sheets. There were no pillows. All the other girls had dolls or stuffed animals too. She looked at the calluses on her fingers. Would her job as a laundress make them worse?

The next day, Emily dressed quickly and raced to the dining room for breakfast. Her stomach was rumbling, and she wanted to get a seat by John to find out how his first day went. Betty waved to her. She clearly wanted Emily to sit by her. Emily reluctantly joined her and immediately started scanning the room looking for her brother. "What are you looking for?"

"My brother."

"The boys aren't here. They don't let the boys and girls mix. They have a separate dining room in the basement."

"But yesterday, I saw boys and girls in the playroom."

"That's because it was Sunday visiting day. That will be the only time you'll see your brother." Betty was right, there weren't any boys in the room. Emily felt disappointed, but she enjoyed her pancakes, savoring her first breakfast in over four months.

After breakfast, it was time to tackle the laundry. Betty explained the procedure. "Everyone strips their own beds here. They take their bottom sheets off and throw them on the floor together with their dirty clothes. They put their top sheet on the bottom so they can reuse them for another week. Our job is to gather the dirty clothes and sheets and wash them. You go get the girls' things and I will get the boys' laundry, and we'll meet in the laundry room. Do you know where it is?" Emily nodded. She gathered the laundry, but she didn't see any laundry baskets. It took four trips to haul all the wash to the laundry room.

"What took you so long?"

"There were no baskets. I had to make several trips."

"You silly girl. You don't need one. Just lay out a sheet and wrap everything else inside it." Emily would remember that next time. "We'll wash the sheets first. If you see any threadbare sheets like this one, put them in a separate pile. The older girls will rip them into rags."

The electric washing machines made doing the laundry quicker and easier. Together, they washed the sheets and hung them on the line to dry. It was so windy, Betty had to hold the sheets in place while Emily clipped them on the line. Then they washed all the towels and clothes. By the time the girls finished washing them, the sheets were dry. They took down the sheets, hung the towels and clothes, and put all the clean sheets back on the beds. Then they took down the towels and clothes and gave them to another group of girls to iron them. Betty was right. It was an all-day project. Emily retired to bed early so she could be ready for her first day of school tomorrow.

In the morning, she wore her blue dress with a white pinafore and added a blue bow to her hair. Remembering to take her slate, primer, and lunch pail, Emily stepped onto the porch.

"Where do you think you're going?"

Emily stopped to face Betty. "To school."

"You're not allowed to walk alone until you are eleven years old. Wait for me." Emily paused while Betty buckled her patent leather shoes, and the two girls set off to Clinton Street School.

Betty took Emily to the office. "Meet me here after school; you can't walk home alone either."

Because of her age, they assigned her to the fifth-grade class, but the secretary said they would test her, and if she wasn't reading on the fifth grade level, they would reassign her to a lower grade. Emily reviewed all the vowel sounds in her head as the secretary escorted her to her classroom.

"Hello, Emily. I'm Mr. Post, your teacher. Please have a seat in the back. As soon as we finish our lesson, I'll be back to test you on your reading and spelling." She walked to the back with her shoes echoing loudly on the tile floor, slipping into the first available seat.

She had never had a male teacher before. He wore a black suit and white shirt, and she found him intriguing with his handlebar mustache. She patiently listened as he told the class how Arizona became our 48th state in February. Since it was mid-April now, Emily counted the stars on the huge American flag mounted on the wall. It had 47 stars. She wondered when the school would get the new flag with all 48 stars. Mr. Post then gave the class a reading assignment and walked toward Emily.

"Alright, Emily. Take out your slate. We're going to start with some spelling words. Spell goose."

Emily said the word as she spelled it- "g-o-o-s-e."

"Very good. Now try frost."

"F-r-o-s-t."

"Mr. Post, Emily is writing with her left hand," the girl in the next desk said. Emily looked to see who the busybody was. The girl had thick, blonde hair. She wore a buttoned-down pink dress with a high collar, a handkerchief sticking out of her lacy sleeve.

"Thank you, Edna. You can get back to work now."

While Emily looked at Edna, she felt a sharp pain in her

hand. Mr. Post had smacked her with a ruler. "We don't use our left hand in this classroom."

"Why not?" Emily asked as she rubbed her hand.

"It is the sign of the devil; right hand only. Next word, camera."

Emily grasped the chalk with her right hand and spelled out c-a-m-e-r-a and f-u-r-n-i-t-u-r-e. She then read the required text with fluency. Mr. Turner said, "Excellent. Your reading and writing skills are perfect. We'll test your arithmetic skills after lunch." He then addressed the class. "Time for recess."

As Emily walked into the schoolyard, she felt proud of herself. Her reading and writing skills were excellent, but writing with her right hand would be a challenge; she would have to work on it. But that girl Edna, what a squealer. She waited to see where Edna sat for lunch, then headed to the other side of the playground by the swings and sat on a bench by herself, as did Edna on her side. Emily thought the other kids didn't like her either. No one likes a tattletale. As she took a bite of her ham sandwich, Edna approached her. "Can I sit here?"

"Suit yourself."

"Where do you live?"

"At the home- on Bergen Street." Emily almost forgot not to mention the Home for the Friendless. It's a good thing she caught herself.

"Me too. I live that way," Edna said, pointing to the left.

"I live the other way." That was good; they wouldn't have to walk home together.

"Do you want to see something?" Edna removed a news-paper clipping from her pocket and unfolded it. She started reading about a ship called the Titanic that sank in the icy waters of the Atlantic Ocean. When she got to the part about the children dying, Emily took the article from Edna's hand.

"Oh, my God. It actually includes the names of all the children who died." All Emily could think about was her mother and how embarrassed she was when Emily's name appeared in the paper. What if they were on this ship? Would her mother leave her to die? Now that would be embarrassing. She handed the clipping back to Edna as the bell rang. Recess was over; time to test her math skills.

Mr. Post worked through lunch and had an arithmetic test sitting at every student's desk except for Emily's. When the class was fully engaged, Mr. Post sat on a stool and rolled it over to Emily with his feet. "Are you ready? What is 327 multiplied by 6?" She picked up the chalk with her left hand, beginning to write out the problem. She wrote the three and the two before the ruler came smashing down on her hand. "I told you not to use your left hand."

"I forgot." It was going to be hard to remember; her left hand was the dominant one.

"Well, I'll help you remember." Emily watched Mr. Post rifle through his desk and come back with a rope. He tied Emily's left hand behind her back. "Now, let's try that again. What is 327 multiplied by 6?"

She wrote the problem on her slate, but her handwriting was illegible. She read the seven as a one and got the incorrect answer.

"That is incorrect. Let's try a few more."

Emily took her time writing the numbers, and she tried to write them larger. Her insight worked because she got every other problem correct. By the end of the afternoon, Mr. Post said, "Welcome to fifth grade." He untied the rope.

Emily strolled back to the Home for the Friendless with Betty, massaging her aching arm. She looked ahead and behind her for her brother, but she didn't see him. She missed John and needed a friend to talk to. Betty would have to do. "Let me tell you about my day."

On Wednesday morning Betty woke up Emily. "Get up. We have laundry to do."

"Laundry? It's not Monday."

"I forgot to tell you. Every morning we have to check the

bathtubs. If anyone wets the bed during the night, they'll leave their soiled sheets in the tub to soak in soapy water and peroxide. And we have to wash them."

Emily followed Betty to the boys' bathroom, where they found two dirty sheets. In the girls' bathroom, there were no sheets, but bloody rags. Someone must be badly hurt to have that much blood. What happened? She didn't notice any girls with bandages. Emily and Betty ran the sheets and rags through the washing machine twice, using extra bleach to get out all the urine and blood stains.

Betty laughed as they hung the sheets and rags to dry. "What's so funny?" Emily asked.

"Everyone knows today is not laundry day, so when all the residents see the sheets and rags they're probably wondering who is on the rag or who wet the bed." Emily didn't know what "on the rag" meant and she didn't care. All she could think about was her brother. Was he the boy who wet the bed? Poor John.

Friday was Ruth Nelson's birthday, and it was also treat day. All the girls gathered in the dining room around Ruth, who sat at the table wearing a pointed birthday cap. Mrs. Dixon brought in a chocolate layer cake with six flaming candles. All the girls sang to Ruth, and then Mrs. Dixon sliced the cake, giving a generous slice to each girl. While the girls ate, Mrs. Dixon disappeared into the kitchen and reappeared with bags of candy. Emily watched her call out the girls' names one by one, each one taking their bag. Some bags had lollipops, others Tootsie Rolls, and some had Life Savers, the new invention this year. But Emily didn't get one.

"Excuse me, Mrs. Dixon. I didn't get one."

"Oh, I'm sorry, Emily. Parents send in birthday cakes and candy on treat days. Your papa didn't send any sweets with his grocery money. You'll have to ask him about it when you see him on Sunday." She was grateful to Ruth's parents, who sent a cake for the entire group, and Betty shared some Life Savers with her. But she would ask her father about it on Sunday, that is, if he showed up.

Sundays were the days that the boys and girls could mingle in the backyard under the watchful eyes of Mrs. Dixon and two aides. All the children scattered, looking for their visiting parents. But Emily wanted to find John first. She found him sitting under the oak tree in his khaki shorts. "I missed you so much," he said, giving Emily a big hug.

"I missed you more. Hey, did you wet the bed this week?"

"No. I didn't have any accidents."

"Good for you. Do you think Papa and Grandma will come today?"

"I don't know. Let's go wait by the gate."

A pack of parents filtered through the gate, but no Papa or Grandma. Emily took a string from her pocket and played cat's cradle with John. About ten minutes later, John yelled, "Look. There they are."

Grandma, wearing a pleated brown skirt and white blouse, carried two overstuffed baskets. Papa hobbled behind on crutches.

"I'm sorry we're late, Princess. It's hard to walk on these darn crutches."

"I'm glad to see you getting around. Your foot must be getting better."

"Little by little. Wait until you see the feast your grand-mother prepared." Grandma was already spreading a blanket on the ground. The family munched on chicken soup with home-made bread smothered in butter. The adults drank beer while John and Emily shared a quart of milk.

They spent the afternoon playing Chinese checkers and hearts. Before Emily realized it, it was time for Papa to leave. "Will I see you next week?"

"Wouldn't miss it for the world."

"And can we talk in German next time? It'll make me feel more at home."

"*Ja.*"

"Oh, Papa. Do you know about Treat Day?"

"Of course I do. But that is just for special occasions. We can't afford to send treats every week. Besides, all that sugar will rot your teeth."

"I understand." As she hugged Papa goodbye, she realized how selfish she was for even suggesting such a thing.

Throughout the next year, Papa and Grandma visited every Sunday. Emily watched her father's foot slowly heal; he graduated from crutches to a cane, and finally to just a limp. There was no mention of him returning to work. Emily so desperately wanted to go home and be a family again.

September 7, 1913, was Emily's eleventh birthday. It fell on a Sunday, so Emily had to wait patiently until Friday to celebrate Treat Day. This was a special occasion, so she hoped Papa would keep his word and send a cake with his grocery money. But Emily worried for nothing. Mrs. Dixon walked out with a big chocolate cake that said "Happy Birthday Emily" in red letters.

"Where's the candles?" Betty asked.

"Emily doesn't need candles. Your papa sent a birthday present instead." Mrs. Dixon handed Emily a gift wrapped in red wrapping paper. "Why don't you open it so the girls can see what you got?"

Emily savagely ripped the paper to reveal a red and white knitted scarf with a matching hat and mittens. "I bet my grandmother made these."

"Emily, they're very practical. I hear that this year is going to be a cold winter and you'll be prepared. By the way, how old are you Emily?"

"Eleven."

"I thought so. That means Betty won't be your big sister anymore. Now you get to be a big sister for our newest resident, Clara. Clara, meet Emily. Emily, meet Clara," Mrs. Dixon said.

Clara was six years old. She wore a long-sleeved dotted Swiss dress with a hole worn through the right elbow. Her big smile with the missing baby teeth was infectious. She looked severely underweight. Emily hoped Mrs. Dixon would cut her an enormous piece of cake. "Nice to meet you. I'll walk you to school in the morning." Emily knew they would become instant friends.

One day in October, Emily woke up in wet sheets. But why did she wet the bed? She didn't have anything to drink after supper. Looking at the sheets, she saw blood. Quickly, Emily stripped the sheets and threw them in the bathtub. She sat on the toilet for the longest time, but the bleeding wouldn't stop. Finally, Betty came in. "Betty, I have a bleeding that will not stop."

She heard Betty rummaging through the bathroom cabinet. "Here's some rags. Pin them in your underpants."

Emily did as she was told. But she couldn't imagine what was wrong with her. She got hit in the stomach with a basketball yesterday on the playground. But it wasn't hard enough to cause this bleeding, was it? The walk to school with Clara and the morning school lessons were all a blur; she couldn't stop thinking about her problem. She went to the bathroom twice, but the bleeding still hadn't stopped. By recess time, she was really worried.

"Are you alright?" Edna asked Emily on the playground.

Emily still didn't like Edna very much, but she was desperate to talk to someone, anyone, about her problem. "No, I'm dying," Emily said.

"What do you mean?"

"I'm bleeding to death."

Edna laughed.

"What's so funny?"

"No, you're not. You're having your period. You're a woman now. This will happen for about a week every month."

"Every month?"

"Yes, unless you're having a baby. It is perfectly normal. Didn't your mother explain it to you?"

Her mother? Where was she? This was a time when every girl

needed her mother, and Emily's mother was nowhere to be found. And what was wrong with Betty? How come she didn't tell her about it? Emily would let her have it.

Menstruation was such a new concept for Emily. Could people tell she was menstruating? Would they look at her differently? Emily found the whole thing embarrassing. She would have to find the right time to talk to Betty, out of earshot of everyone else. That time didn't come until bedtime.

"Betty, how come you didn't tell me about my period? All day long, I thought I was dying; I was terrified."

"I'm so sorry. I thought you knew," Betty said as she gave Emily a big hug.

"Don't worry. It wasn't your fault." How could Emily accuse Betty, her dear friend, like that? It really wasn't her place to tell her. Darn her mother.

As Emily laid in bed that night, she thought about her period. She was a woman now, no longer a little girl. Women don't sleep with teddy bears. She rolled out of bed with Henry, walking to the trash can. But she couldn't quite bring herself to throw him out. Instead, she buried him deep under her clothes in her dresser. And women don't call their mothers Mama. From now on, she would address her mother as Mom. That is, if she ever saw her again.

One day in mid-December, Emily set off to school with Clara as usual, but she spotted her brother 50 feet ahead. In all the times that she had lived at the Home for the Friendless, their paths had never crossed outside of their Sunday visits. She started running after him. "John, John, wait up."

"Emily, stop. Don't leave me alone." Clara tried to catch up, but her little legs could not reach Emily. She tripped on a tree root and fell down. She stood up wailing, her face a bloody mess. Emily looked back at Clara and paused for a minute. Should she go back? The desire to see her brother was so strong, she ran ahead.

Later that night, Mrs. Dixon asked Emily to come down to

her office. It was the first time she had ever been there. Mrs. Dixon sat behind her roll-top desk dressed in all black. Didn't she ever wear any other color? Emily could also see the back of Clara's little head barely clearing the top of the chair. "What is the meaning of this? Clara, show her your face." Clara turned around. She had a split lip and a black eye.

"I'm afraid you'll have to be punished for this. Stand up." Mrs. Dixon removed her belt and swung it like a lasso in the air. Emily could hear the whirring sound as it circled in the air. Then Mrs. Dixon cracked it like a whip on Emily's backside. The impact dropped Emily to her knees. She tried to ward off three more blows with her hands unsuccessfully. As she lay in bed that night with her hands and buttocks still stinging, she asked herself, was it all worth it just to see her brother? She removed her teddy bear from the cabinet, hugging him tightly until she fell asleep.

Later that month, the residents of the Home for the Friendless received a rare surprise. Mrs. Dixon said, "I want you all to be part of history. We're taking a walk to Military Park for its first Municipal Christmas tree lighting ceremony. Thank you, Thomas Edison for the invention of the electric light bulb. Everyone, meet on the porch."

An excited Emily, bundled up in her new hat, scarf, and mittens, arrived on the porch first. A blustery wind gave her a chill; she tightened up her scarf and pulled her hat firmly over her ears.

Clara barged through the door with her coat wide open. "Here, let me help you." Emily buttoned Clara's coat and tied her scarf. As the rest of the group arrived, Emily maneuvered Clara toward the center of the pack for warmth.

As the group approached the park, the crowd grew thicker. Emily worried they wouldn't be able to get close enough to see the tree, but she was wrong. Once they passed a statue of Major General Philip Kearny, she had a clear view of the towering tree. "Wow, that tree must be 100 feet tall," Clara said.

"Silly girl. It's 48 feet, to be exact. I read it in the newspaper," Mrs. Dixon said.

"How did the men get it here? It looks heavy."

"I'm sure they used a crane and some scaffolding to set it up."

"How come it's not lit up yet?"

"Boy, you're full of questions today. Be patient. I'm sure it will only be a few more minutes."

The crowd counted down, "Five, four, three, two, one--."

And the tree lit up to the oohs and aahs from the crowd. Emily thought it was the neatest thing she had ever seen in her life. The lights were so bright, they reflected on Clara's white coat. "Mrs. Dixon, do you know how many lights are on that tree?"

"800 lights." Emily and Clara stared at the tree until the crowd started thinning out. "Come on, girls. It's time to go."

Emily looked at the spectators on the other side of the street. Was that Mama over there? "Mrs. Dixon, can you watch Clara for a minute? I think that's my mother over there?"

"Yes, but be quick. We need to go. It's getting cold out here."

Emily hadn't seen her mother in a few years, but the closer she got to this woman, the more convinced she became it was her mama. "Mom, Mom," she yelled. When she got no reaction, she tried again. "Mama, Mama."

The woman slowly turned around, and that was when she saw Bill; she couldn't miss that pointed chin and nose. He looked exactly how she remembered him, but Mom's hair was silver in color.

"Emily, is that you?"

"Oh, Mom. I've missed you." She threw her arms around her mother.

"Since when do you call me Mom instead of Mama?" Margaret patted Emily on the arm, peeling Emily's arms off.

"I'm all grown up now. I'm too big to call you Mama."

"Where have you been? I've been looking all over for you," said Margaret.

Emily wondered if she really was looking for her. Somehow, she doubted it. "We were with Papa, then he got hurt, and Grandma put us in the Home for the Friendless."

"The Home for the Friendless? Are they treating you alright?"

"Mama, they beat me." She took off her mittens and showed Mama the black and blue welts that remained on her hands.

"No kid of mine is living in that place. I'm going to come and get you tomorrow."

"Why can't we come home tonight?"

"There are too many people around. We'll be there in the morning."

Too many people. What did she mean by that? Was she embarrassed again? Is she too worried about what other people think? Emily rejoined Mrs. Dixon.

"Was that your mother?"

"No, it was somebody else." Emily amazed herself at how easily the lie rolled off her tongue. Somehow, telling a lie was easier than telling the truth, and she wasn't convinced that her mother would show up tomorrow.

Camden Street
1914

"Emily, you're going home. Pack up your things." said Betty.

"Wait. What? How do you know?"

"Your mother is waiting for you in the office. Mrs. Dixon sent me up to get you."

Emily couldn't believe it; her mother's words were genuine.

"Oh, Betty. I'm going to miss you." She gave her a big hug. "I promise I'll come visit you. Maybe on Sunday."

"Good luck. I hope everything works out for you."

"Me too."

Emily gathered her belongings and headed to Mrs. Dixon's office to meet her mother and John. Mom signed the papers, and they walked to their new home on Camden Street.

"Here we are."

"Mom, I'm confused. I don't see any houses. This is the business section of town," said Emily.

"This is it. We rented the apartment above this Chinese laundromat. And our rent includes free use of the washing machines." Mama used a key to open the door next to the laundromat. After climbing a steep staircase, they were in the front parlor of their railroad apartment. The brick fireplace sat between two ancient bookcases. Mom wasn't much of a reader; the only books on the shelf were *Twenty Years at Hull House*, the Bible, and a dictionary. Instead, she filled the shelves with potted plants and her sewing basket. The polished hardwood floor accented the claw-legged couch and high-back chairs. Mom pulled back the curtain to reveal the green panel walls of the kitchen. The stove, sink, and icebox lined one wall while a cabinet and breakfast nook adorned the other. They walked through the kitchen to the main bedroom, furnished with a canopy bed and washstand. A table runner covered a dresser. A man's pocket watch rested on top of it. Emily thought that Bill, the boarder, still lived here.

"Mom, where's Bill?"

"He's at work, He'll be home for supper."

The next room housed the bathroom consisting of a claw-footed bathtub, a freestanding sink, a white toilet with a black seat, and a pull chain electric light bulb. "The bathroom is in the house, and we don't have to share it with another family."

"Wow! How did you ever afford this apartment?"

"I work in the Chinese laundry downstairs, so the rent was drastically reduced. I saved the last room for you. This is where you and John will be sleeping." Mom pulled a curtain to reveal a spindle bed with carved flowers and a two-drawer dresser. "I will leave you two to unpack and explore. I have to go to work. Tomorrow we will register you for school."

Bill came home with veal for dinner. Mom added onions, pickles, and mustard to make *rouladen*. Emily slid into the breakfast nook against the wall so she wouldn't bump John's arm while eating with her left hand. Although she had to use her right hand in school, in the comfort of her own home, Emily ate with her left hand. Bill slid in opposite Emily. Watching him eat still appalled her. His pointed chin and hooked nose almost touched. As he slurped his beer, Emily noticed he was missing a front tooth. She felt bad for him. She hoped he didn't lose another tooth or that chin and nose would touch for sure.

Having Bill around created a sense of normalcy in the house. They ate decent meals. Emily had fewer chores to do and more time for schoolwork. But her mother never had time for her, not to talk or play hearts, which was becoming her favorite game. It took three people to play hearts, and neither Bill nor Mom ever played. She missed her father. Funny when she was with Mom, she missed Dad, but when she was with Dad, she missed her mother.

One hot day months later, Emily sat on the windowsill, stealing the breeze as it entered their apartment. She glanced into the alley and saw four men playing bocce. One man had a slight humpback and limp. Was that her father? "Papa, Papa is that you?"

He turned around, "Emily, is that you?" She waved, and he shouted, "I'll be right up."

Emily threw her arms around her father. "I've missed you so much. Won't you come back home?"

"That's up to your mother." Margaret and Henry headed to the bedroom while Bill sat quietly smoking his pipe. Bill, Emily, and John couldn't miss the raised voices coming from the bedroom. They were arguing in German, loud enough for the neighbors to hear. Emily wondered if speaking German still embarrassed her mother, but then again, who would care? There certainly was enough Chinese spoken in the laundromat.

"Where have you been? I've been looking for you for months. I can understand you kicking me out, but how could you abandon your kids? I want to come home and be a proper father to those kids."

"It's your drinking that is the problem."

"I'll behave myself, I promise."

"I've heard that before."

"My drinking is no worse than you abandoning our kids."

"Let's get back together and be a family again."

When the conversation waned, Emily stepped away from the door; she didn't want to get caught spying. Crossing her fingers

81

for good luck, she imagined her parents in each other's arms reconciling. She sat in the parlor, pretending to be absorbed in her schoolwork.

Margaret and Henry emerged from the bedroom fused together with his arm around her shoulder and her arm around his waist. "I'm sorry, Bill, you're going to have to leave."

"Margaret, think about this. Are you sure you want me to leave?"

"Yes, it's for the best."

By the end of the day, Bill moved out, and Henry moved in. And Papa was true to his word. He no longer drank in the house, but he still drank at work. Emily could smell the liquor on his breath when he came home. He played a lot of bocce with a beer in his hand. But he still made time for Emily and John. John and Papa were formidable opponents when they played Chinese checkers or poker.

One day, soon after that, Papa said, "We have a surprise for you. Your mother is going to have a baby."

"Oh, Mom, how exciting! I can't wait."

"Hold on, we have some preparing to do before the blissful day. With another mouth to feed, money will be tight. Your mother will have to go right back to work after the baby comes, so Emily, you're going to have to quit school and take care of the baby while she works."

"Why me? Doesn't John have to help?"

"Taking care of children is women's work."

"But what about my schoolwork?"

"You don't need to know how to read to care for children."

"Yes, I do. I know nothing about feeding or changing babies. I'll have to read to learn how."

"Nice try. There is a gracious lady who lives next door, Mrs. Reynolds, and you're going to start taking care of her baby boy tomorrow."

Emily hated being punished for being a girl. No pants to ice skate, a period once a month, and now no education. Why wasn't she born a boy? Looking at her mother's stomach, Emily hoped for the baby's sake that it would be a boy.

The next day, Margaret took her to Mrs. Reynolds's apartment. They had a similar railroad apartment above a tobacco store, but each store and apartment was a separate entity. Emily had to go down the stairs to the street, and then back up another set of stairs to reach the apartment.

Mrs. Reynolds was 20 years old, with a slight case of acne still on her face. Emily figured she didn't know much about babies, either. But she was wrong. "This is baby Thomas."

"Oh, he's so cute."

"Do you want to hold him?"

"No, I might break him."

Mrs. Reynolds laughed. "No, you won't. Sit on the couch. I'll give him to you. Just make sure you support the baby's head in the crook of your elbow." She plopped Thomas in Emily's arms. Thomas, swaddled in a tight blanket, stared at Emily with his toothless grin and big blue eyes.

After a short lesson on heating bottles, changing diapers, and swaddling blankets, Mrs. Reynolds departed for her job selling socks on the street corner, leaving Emily in charge. It took a week to master babysitting skills, and she quickly discovered how much time babies slept during the day. Taking care of babies soon bored her, so she used the time when Thomas was asleep to perfect her reading skills.

One day, Thomas woke up from his nap shaking violently, his eyes rolled back in his head. Emily scooped him up and ran down the stairs and burst into the Chinese laundry.

"Mom, help. I think Thomas is having a convulsion."

Her mother stopped folding the laundry. "Hurry, let's take him up to our apartment." Margaret filled up the sink with water and mustard. Taking baby Thomas from Emily, Margaret plunged him into the water. It seemed to have a calming effect on him. After the bath, she tied a raw onion around baby

Thomas's foot with a string of yarn. Miraculously, the convulsions stopped.

"Thanks, Mom. You were a big help."

"Make sure you take some onion, mustard, and string tomorrow, in case this happens again."

"I'll take the mustard and onion. I don't need any string. Mrs. Reynolds has enough yarn to open up a wool factory."

Emily became complacent, taking care of baby Thomas. She had to admit this was much easier work than gathering coal, doing laundry, or baking bread. Her only complaint was her schoolwork. She could no longer read the vocabulary words in the book, and her parents would be no help. Although they could speak English fluently, they had limited ability to read it.

One Sunday morning, out of the blue, Margaret said, "Emily, John, put on your Sunday clothes. You're going to church," Mom said.

"Church? Why? We haven't been there in years."

"When your little brother or sister comes into the world, we'll be baptizing him or her. We don't want Pastor Rawlings thinking we are a bunch of heathens."

"Mom, you don't look dressed for church. Aren't you coming too?"

"No. Your father and I have work to do around the house."

There would be no arguing with her parents. She put on her green dress in the bedroom while John put his khaki suit on in the bathroom. They gathered in the parlor. "Put out your hands." Emily and John reached out simultaneously. Papa dropped three cents into each of their hands. "For the collection. Now scoot, or you'll be late."

Emily couldn't help but notice the gleam in her brother's eye. "You don't want to go to church, do you?" he asked.

"Of course not."

"Do you?"

"No. So let's not go."

"I don't want to get in trouble with Mom and Dad."

"Well, aren't you a goody goody. Who's going to know?"

"I will."

"Goody goody. Goody goody," John started chanting. "Can't you do something daring for once in your life?"

Emily thought about it for a minute. "What do you want to do?"

"Well, we have six cents; let's see what's playing at the movies."

They walked three blocks to the theater. The marquee read: *Gertie the Dinosaur*, Admission seven cents. John walked up to the woman behind the window with his puppy-dog eyes. "Wouldn't you let a kid in for six cents?"

Emily smiled, remembering how that worked to get day old bread, but they were older now and not as cute. The woman behind the glass paused and said, "Alright."

John dropped six cents into her hand.

"Each. Here's your six cents back. Come back when you have enough money."

"What are we going to do now? It's too early to go home."

"Well, we can play bocce."

"John, Mom and Dad will see us."

"Not if we go to the alley behind my friend George's house."

"Alright. We can come again next week, but let me hold the money. I don't trust you. You'll lose it." Emily put the six cents into her pocket and placed her handkerchief on top of it to hold it in place.

The alley behind George's house was even smaller than the one that Papa played in. Emily didn't like it; she was afraid they might break a window. But as soon as she picked up a ball, the weight of it eased her mind. She would be lucky to have the strength to throw it across the court. A few times, when Emily bent down so low to throw the ball, she thought the money might fall out of her pocket. Each time she checked, it was always there. They played two games, with John winning one and Emily winning one.

"We can go home now." Emily stepped out of the boxed court and caught the hem of her skirt on a nail, putting a two-inch gash in the material. "Oh no. John, why did I let you talk me into this? Now we're going to be skinned alive."

"Not necessarily. I can distract Mama while you go to your room and sew your hem."

"And if she sees it?"

"Just tell her you caught it on a nail on the church pew."

Emily hoped she wouldn't have to lie about her hem. One lie was bad enough, especially about going to church. When they got home, their mother stood in the doorway. "How was church? What was the sermon about?"

When John started babbling about forgiveness, Emily escaped to her room, changed clothes, sewed her dress, and hid the six cents in her cachet bag that had long ago lost its scent.

The following Sunday, Emily put her green dress on again and transferred the six cents from the cachet bag to her pocket. Mama gave another three cents to John and Emily. They set off for church but went to the theater instead. They felt disappointed when they realized that the lady from last week was not here. Instead, a bearded man with thick glasses sat behind the glass window.

Emily handed him the twelve cents. "You're short two cents."

"The lady last week said we only had to pay six cents each."

"She's wrong. We're not running a charity here. Come back when you have seven cents each."

Emily and John left with frowns on their faces. "Don't look so disappointed, John. If we get another six cents next Sunday, we'll have 18 cents and since the movie only costs 14 cents, that leaves four cents extra that we can spend on something else. Any ideas?"

"Let's get some ice cream."

Not wanting to be seen by their parents, Emily and John walked another three blocks until they spotted a small ice cream cart pulled by a lone white horse. The wagon had two vats of ice cream in metal containers being kept cold by the ice beneath it and the red and white striped awning above it. The vendor's shirt matched the awning. "How much for an ice cream, mister?"

"That'll be five cents."

"That's too much. We only have four cents."

"Alright. You look like nice kids." Emily reached into her pocket, trying to only pull out four cents, but grabbed five cents instead. She promptly put a penny back. "What are you trying to pull? You have the money. Are you trying to cheat me? Get lost."

John took his sister's arm and steered her across the street toward a pretzel vendor. "Maybe pretzels will be cheaper."

This vendor stood over six feet tall. He resembled a monster, with his face covered in a full beard and an Irish cap pulled low over his eyes. The fresh pretzels sat in the biggest wicker basket that Emily had ever seen. "How much for a pretzel, mister?"

"Three cents."

This was perfect. They could have a pretzel with a penny to spare. Emily broke the pretzel in half, sharing it with her brother. They played bocce again, but this time Emily remembered to lift her dress when she exited the bocce court.

The following Sunday, Emily found it hard to hide her excitement as she got ready for church. She took out the nine cents she had left from her cachet bag and put it in her pocket. Mama handed her and John the additional three cents each and they were on their way.

The man with the thick glasses was in the booth again. "You two again. Do you have the right amount of money this time?" Emily dropped 14 cents on the counter and watched the man pick up each penny one by one. "Enjoy the show."

This was Emily's first time in a movie theater. It wasn't what she expected. She saw a screen mounted on the wall beneath an arched ceiling. Rows of patrons sat in folding chairs wearing fancy clothes. Emily thought to herself, lots of folks were skipping church today. She and John squeezed into two empty seats in the middle of the last row.

Gertie the Dinosaur rolled across the screen. "Emily, my reading is not so good. Can you read the words for me when they come up?" She nodded. Here John was the one in school and he asked her to read for him. She felt flattered.

Emily began narrating. "We've got a puncture. Let's go in the museum while he fixes it." Later she read, "After six months' work, McCay finishes drawing the cartoons." And later still, "I made ten thousand cartoons, - each one a little bit different from the one preceding it."

"What does preceding mean?"

"I don't know. Just watch the movie."

"Preceding means the one before it," said the lady next to Emily.

"Thank you." Together they watched an animated dinosaur come out of its cave, eat everything in sight, including a rock and a gigantic tree, then raise its paw to bow to the audience.

The whole movie was about eight minutes long. "What did you think?" Emily asked John when they were back on the street.

"I liked it. Movies are pretty amazing. Do you think they will ever have movies where people can talk?"

"I doubt it."

That night in his sleep, John began tossing and turning. "Don't let it eat me. Stop! Stop! I'm not your dinner." His flailing knocked Emily out of bed and Margaret came running.

"John. Wake up. You're having a bad dream."

"I'm sorry, Mama. I thought I was being eaten by a dinosaur."

"Where on earth did that come from?"

"I don't know."

"Well, go back to sleep."

When Margaret left the room, Emily slapped John on the

arm. "You idiot. That was close. No more talk about dinosaurs or Mom might figure it out."

The following Sunday, with a fresh six cents in their pockets and an extra penny for good measure, the children set out on another "church," adventure. "What do you want to do today? It will take three weeks to save for another movie, and from the size of Mama's belly, I don't think we have that long."

"How about we see how much it costs to ride the trolley? It's so hot; it would be nice to get out of the city for a while."

The children approached the trolley parked at the end of the block. It resembled a bus with wheels that ran along a track in the street. A long rod connected the roof to the electrical wires above. The conductor wore black pants with a long sleeve white shirt. A black vest and gold pocket watch chain completed the uniform. "How much to ride the trolley?" John asked.

"Well, it all depends on how far you want to go, lad."

"The end of the line."

"That would be two miles to Maplewood. It's three cents each for children."

John hopped up without even consulting Emily. She had no choice but to follow along. The bus held 25 people, but being a Sunday morning, it was light on passengers. Emily and John chose a window seat, sticking their heads out the window to suck in the cool breeze. Soon the city buildings gave way to country trees.

"End of the line. The last trolley back departs here at 4:00."

When John and Emily got off the bus, a whole new world appeared in front of them. Maplewood was nothing but open fields as far as the eye could see, with a few scattered farms and apple trees mixed in. Emily didn't know which way to go; she felt a little scared as she heard the clang of the trolley car fade away. "Come on Emily. Let's go apple picking."

John ran on ahead, with Emily panting behind him. He paused at the first tree and reached up for an apple. "Stop. That's stealing. Just take one off the ground." John bent over and picked up four apples. "They're all rotten," he said, dropping them.

Emily scooped up a promising one, wiped it on her dress, and took a big bite. It was full of worms. She spit it out while John laughed at her.

"I guess there is a reason they are on the ground." He picked an apple from the tree for Emily and one for himself. They sat under the tree eating them. Together, they watched a red pickup truck approach them on the dirt road. Emily hoped it would just pass them, but it came to a halt with screeching brakes. A man in overalls and no teeth said, "You kids don't belong here. Get off my land." John held his ground, taking another bite from his apple in defiance. The farmer reached for his shotgun on the seat beside him and fired a warning shot in the air. "Skedaddle."

Emily and John ran back toward the trolley stop as fast as they could, constantly looking over their shoulders to make sure the farmer wasn't following them. Emily lost her footing and fell into a manure pile. She rose to her feet, gagging from the stench.

"You stink, sis."

"No kidding. Did you notice any streams or brooks on the way here? Maybe I can clean up a little." John shook his head. As they walked to the trolley stop, John tried to keep a respectful distance from his sister. He turned his head to take a breath, but the oppressive, stale August heat did nothing to lift the smell.

When the trolley came, John tried to board first. "That'll be three cents to ride."

"You mean it's not round trip ticket?"

"It's not, and even if it was, I wouldn't let her board smelling like a sewer rat." The trolley pulled away, leaving John and Emily to begin the two-mile walk home. They followed the trolley tracks back to Irvington. By the time they arrived home, they didn't notice the smell anymore.

But once inside, the smell permeated throughout the house.

"Where have you two been?" Margaret asked with her hands on her hips. "And what is that God awful smell?"

Emily burst into tears, telling her mother everything- about skipping church, the movies, riding out to Maplewood, and falling in a manure pile. "Get yourself cleaned up. We will discuss your punishment when your father gets home."

Emily took a long bath, scrubbing herself until her skin turned red. Then she soaked her dress in the sink. By the time she redressed, Emily could hear her parents talking in the parlor. No matter what punishment her father imposed, it wouldn't be as hard as seeing the disappointment in his eyes. Emily hated disappointing him.

Emily sat beside John on the couch and tried to avoid her father's eyes. "Your mother told me about your little Sunday adventures."

"I'm sorry."

"It's not me you owe an apology to. It's the church. You cheated them out of some money. I'm going to find you both a job until you work off the debt. In the meantime, you are both grounded; no leaving the house except for school and taking care of Thomas. Understood?" Without making eye contact, Emily nodded.

During the night, Papa pounded on Emily's door. "Your mother is in labor. We're on the way to the hospital. Remember to stay put in the house."

"Alright, Dad."

Emily and John couldn't fall back asleep. They wandered into the kitchen to find something to help them sleep. John took a pint of beer from the icebox. "Maybe this will help."

"Are you crazy? We're in enough trouble already. I'm not drinking Papa's beer. I'll make us some tea." But the tea did nothing to help them sleep. They played Chinese checkers and poker until the sun came up.

There was no word from Henry the next day or the day after

that. On the third day, Margaret came home swaddling a baby close to her chest. "Where's Dad?" asked Emily.

"He won't be living here anymore. I thought one of you would have noticed. He moved his things out one day while you were at school and Mrs. Reynolds's apartment."

"But why?"

"I don't know. Maybe your behavior caused him to leave." Emily didn't believe it for a minute. "Meet your new baby sister, Helen." Margaret let Emily hold the baby. She had Mama's big brown eyes, a nose that pointed down, and a chin that pointed up. Oh mother, what have you done?

Catskills, New York
1915-1916

It was obvious to Emily why Papa had left, and it had nothing to do with her ditching church. How could Mom make her feel like her father had left on her account? How could any mother lay that guilt trip on a child? Emily disliked her mother for a while, but it was now morphing into hatred. It did not surprise her when the following winter, Margaret said, "Pack up, we're moving."

"Where to this time, Mama?"

"I don't like your tone, young lady."

"Sorry."

"Bill has a farmhouse that he is renting with "an option to buy," clause in the Catskills. We're going to join him there."

"What about all our furniture?"

"It will be delivered later. Just take your clothes for now. And dress warmly. Upstate New York is much colder than New Jersey."

John, Emily, Margaret, and baby Helen boarded the bus the next day. It was the longest ride of Emily's life. Each passing mile brought her further and further from her father. She wondered if she would ever see him again. The metal seats were hard, cold, and uncomfortable. It didn't help that the bus made frequent stops, turning a two-hour ride into a three-hour one. Emily couldn't wait to get off the bus. Too many eyes drifted in their direction, as her mother had no shame bearing her breast so baby Helen could suckle. Emily felt embarrassed, but apparently Margaret had lost her inhibitions.

At last, they disembarked at the bus stop. The cold winter air brought tears to Emily's eyes. She pulled her pea coat tighter around her neck as she scanned the people milling around on the platform, looking for Bill's familiar face. "Margaret, Margaret, over here."

Bill stood in front of a horse-drawn sleigh. John ran over and started petting the two brown mares on their noses before Emily and Margaret had time to wave back.

"John, wait for permission."

"It's fine, Margaret. The one with the diamond on her face is Trudy. The other one is Bessie. This is one benefit of living in the country, free transportation."

Bill loaded the suitcases on the floor of the back seat of the open sleigh. Emily and John hopped in. There was no room for their feet, so they plopped them on top of the bags with their knees up to their chest. Bill, Margaret, and baby Helen sat in the front seat. When Bill dropped the crop on Bessie's back, Emily's head jerked back, and they were off on a country horse ride. Emily enjoyed the two-mile ride through the forest to their new home.

In the clearing ahead, Emily got her first glance of her new home. The small white farmhouse had a green tin roof with matching green shutters. An attic dormer protruded at the center of the roof. Emily hoped that would be her bedroom. Brown wicker rocking chairs adorned the wraparound porch. The red barn to the right of the house was bigger than the house itself. The tire swing suspended from an oak tree looked inviting until she saw the outhouse behind it. Would she have to use it? Emily stepped forward, taking a whiff until her nose confirmed it. The entire perimeter was surrounded by a white picket fence in dire need of painting.

"Mom, we don't have to use the outhouse, do we?"

"Of course, we're in the country. There is no indoor plumbing or electricity."

Emily didn't want to believe her mother, but she looked up and saw no electricity poles or wires running into the house. She grabbed her valise and ran into the parlor, plopping her bag on the plank floor. She saw a comfortable wrought-iron bed with a patchwork quilt and a rocking cradle for Helen. There was a stone fireplace with three rifles freely mounted above it. The hand pump in the kitchen sink and the kerosene lanterns suspended from the ceiling confirmed it. No indoor bathroom or electricity.

"Take your bags upstairs. You and John will sleep up there," said Bill. The children climbed a staircase so steep that Emily felt like she was on a ladder. Their room was void of furniture. A spider web stood in the corner with the corpses of its prey lying on the floor. The spider was nowhere in sight. At least the attic was toasty warm with the heat rising through the vent in the floor. "Here are some blankets and pillows. You can sleep on the floor tonight; your furniture should arrive tomorrow."

Emily and John woke early to a cacophony of sounds: a rooster crowing, baby Helen wailing, and Bill's booming voice. "Get up."

"Why do we have to get up so early? The sun isn't even up yet." Emily felt like she was back in the bakery again.

"A farmer's day starts early. We have little daylight to work with in the winter, and there are chores to do before you go to school. Emily, you help your mama in the kitchen, and John, you come with me. We have farm work to do."

Emily watched her brother put on his plaid coat and galoshes. When Bill opened the door, a rush of cold air burst in. The boys quickly disappeared through the door. Emily felt glad to be inside with her mother. "What chores do we need to do?"

"We must get the fire going again. Bring in some wood. You'll find the wood stacked on the porch." Margaret's knowledge of where every pot, dish, and utensil was stored seemed impressive to Emily. Had Margaret been here before?

Emily put on her coat and boots. She pulled her collar up, tied a scarf around her neck, and reached for the doorknob. "Aren't you forgetting your gloves?"

She would not let her mother tell her what to do. "I won't be outside that long; I don't need them."

"Suit yourself."

Emily walked around the corner of the porch to the wood-pile that needed replenishing. She sure hoped chopping wood wouldn't become her chore. It was impossible for her to grab an armful of wood because it was frozen solid. She picked up a metal rod and chipped away enough ice to loosen the wood. By the time she had her first armful of wood, her fingertips were numb.

She entered the house and stacked the wood in front of the fireplace to dry. Before returning for another load, she rubbed her hands and put on her gloves. Emily thought she heard her mother snicker, but she ignored it.

"I'm all done with the wood. What's next?"

"I'm going to make potato pancakes, but we'll have to wait until the boys bring in the milk and eggs from the barn. We can have some coffee while we wait."

Emily never had coffee before, but she would try anything hot to warm up her stiff body. She watched her mother pump cold water from the sink into the coffee pot and add the coffee. Mama already had the stove going, so the coffee was ready in no time.

Emily blew on the mug of coffee before taking her first sip. "Yuck. It tastes awful! How can anybody drink this stuff?"

"You have to acquire a taste for it."

"Why bother?"

. . .

John followed Bill into the barn, passing by an empty pen. "What's the pen for?"

"Pigs. We buy them in the early spring, fatten them up, and then slaughter them in the late autumn. Their meat lasts the whole winter." John spotted an icebox in the corner of the barn. He opened it, finding plenty of bacon and pork stuffed inside.

"Have you ever milked a cow before?'

"No, I'm a city boy."

"Come on; I'll show you how, city boy. This will be your job every morning." John watched Bill distribute his round bottom on a short, three-legged stool and place a pail under the cow's udder. Bill grabbed two teats and squeezed until milk began flowing into the pail. "Come closer, son, so you can see what I'm doing." John leaned over as Bill twisted the teat and sent a flow of white milk right into John's face.

It surprised John how warm it was. "Hey!"

"Your turn."

John switched places with Bill, only pausing a moment before he grabbed the teats. He was a quick learner. Farm life was going to be great. "What's next?"

Bill removed a basket hanging on a nail and tossed it to John. "We gather eggs."

Together, they collected the eggs and took them with the milk into the farmhouse.

"It's about time. We're waiting on those eggs and milk to make the pancakes."

With their bellies filled, there were still chores to do. Margaret, Emily, and John boarded the horse-drawn sleigh, while Bill began chopping and stacking wood. Margaret sold their surplus eggs at the market before dropping Emily and John at their new school.

Emily loved her new school. The first thing that impressed her was the class size; there were only 14 children. Classes in the city were much larger. Emily thought that this would be an asset. With her sporadic education, she feared she might be behind her country classmates, and this would give her teacher, Miss Tucker, more time to give her individual attention. But Emily worried for nothing. She quickly discovered she was on par with her classmates.

When Emily got home from school, she couldn't wait to tell her mother about her day and start her homework. She felt delighted that Bill had finished chopping and stacking wood. He was snoozing on the couch. From that day on, Emily looked at school as a sanctuary away from the grueling hours of farm work.

The following weekend, Bill said to John, "How would you like to go hunting?" John's eyes lit up like a Christmas tree. Bill removed a rifle from above the fireplace and took a box of shells from the mantle and put them in his pocket. He placed an empty jar in his other pocket.

"What's the jar for?"

"Use the outhouse before we go. We will bring the jar in case we have to pee in the woods. Animals can smell human urine miles away."

"You can't be serious."

"Dead serious."

John used the outdoor bathroom. When he returned, he asked, "What are we hunting?"

"Rabbit and deer." Bill glanced at his watch. "It's a little late in the day to get started, but maybe we'll get lucky. A few rules before we go. I'll carry the gun. Notice how I carry it pointing down? You never aim it at a person, even when it's unloaded. Are we clear?" John nodded. "And once we get into the woods, no talking. If I need to talk to you for any reason, I'll use hand signals. We don't want to scare the animals away. Are you ready?"

Bill and John trudged through the snow to a remote wooded area on the outer edges of the property. John stepped on a tree limb. Bill grabbed his arm, stopping his forward progress while putting his finger to his lips to signal silence.

They paused for a few minutes when Bill tapped John on the arm, pointing off to the south. There stood a huge buck looking in every direction, like it was expecting danger. John and Bill silently dropped to their knees. John watched Bill load the rifle, take aim, and bring the deer down to the ground. He hit him in the heart, killing him instantly.

"Great shot. Can I have a turn?'

"One buck is enough deer meat to last for a while. Besides, it will take the two of us to carry one back. Maybe next time I'll teach you how to hunt."

Bill took out a knife, cutting a long gash in the deer's torso.

"What are you doing? It's already dead."

"I'm taking out the entrails."

"Here? I really don't want to watch this. Can't you do it back at the house?"

"This buck weighs about 130 pounds. Do you really think you can carry it?"

"I'd like to try." John stuck his hands under the deer but couldn't lift it up.

Bill laughed. "See what I mean? If we take out the entrails, this buck will weigh 20 to 30 pounds lighter. If you really don't want to watch, go find a stick long enough and thick enough to carry this deer and I'll gut it while you're gone."

John felt delighted to hear this. Finding a stick didn't take long, but John waited an extra ten minutes just to make sure Bill was done gutting the deer. When he returned to the slaughter site, Bill was sitting on a rock, patiently waiting for him. John took one look at the pile of entrails and vomited right into the snow.

"You have a long way to go before we make you a hunter." Bill wove the stick under the buck's skin. "Are you ready? I'll take the back and you can take the front."

"What about the guts? You can't just leave them here."

"Why not? They'll make a fine meal for the raccoons."

John grabbed his end of the stick, resting it on his shoulder, and headed home. He felt like an Indian boy bringing dinner home to his family. He didn't have to stop for a rest until they plopped the carcass down on the barn floor. "Mama's going to be delighted to have deer for supper."

"We can't eat this tonight. It'll have to prime for a week." Bill hung it on a meat hook, letting the rest of the blood drain from the deer. "That should do it. Let's go eat lunch. I'm starving."

John wasn't sure his stomach could handle ever eating meat again, so when Mom provided peanut butter and jelly sand-wiches, he ate his full share, washing them down with a glass of milk.

After lunch, the furniture had finally arrived, a month late. Margaret and Bill hauled the mattress into the loft while John and Emily heaved all the other crates of their belongings into the parlor. John handed the pieces of the bed frame up the stairs to Margaret, followed by the dressers. Emily made several trips up the steps with her clothes and began refolding them into the dresser drawers. She watched Mom and Bill put the bed frame together and the mattress on top. They scooted it across the floor, but with the dresser taking up one wall, there was no way it would fit against the low ceiling on the other side of the room. "I'm sorry, Emily. You and John will have to sleep on the mattress without the frame. Just don't stand up too quickly, or you'll bump your head."

Emily couldn't help but laugh as she watched Bill carry the bed frame back down the stairs to the barn. She climbed down the stairs just as John emptied the final crate of his belongings. He removed their Chinese checker set, and from the bottom of the crate, he lifted out their ice skates. "Bill, how did you ever find these? I thought they were gone for good," said John as Bill reentered the house.

"I have my ways."

Emily looked at them closely. She wasn't sure if they were the same pair.

"You can throw them right into the trash; I don't want to skate ever again."

"Come on, Emily. Don't be a poop. Isabel died from the fire, not the skating. There is a nice shallow creek behind the house that will be perfect for skating."

"Leave your sister alone. I'll hang these in the barn with the bed frame. Someday, maybe you'll change your mind." Emily never liked Bill so much in her life.

Margaret made a delicious turkey dinner. She left John and Emily to clean up while she and Bill played poker in front of the fireplace with beer in their hands. With the dishes done, Emily and John played Chinese checkers, and the subject of her ice skates never came up again.

A month later, John found himself bored. Mama was at a quilting show, Bill was fixing his tractor, and Emily was making an apple pie for dinner. He wanted to go hunting and surprise his family with another deer, so he removed a rifle from the mount and took a box of bullets out to the porch. John couldn't recall watching Bill load the weapon, but he was pretty sure he could do it himself. Sitting on a wooden stool on the back porch, John opened the chamber and fed two bullets inside. When he snapped the chamber closed, the gun went off, sending a bullet through the kitchen window.

Glass fell at Emily's feet, just missing her leg. She ran outside to see what had happened. Her brother sat on the stool with his hands on his ears, the discharged weapon on the ground. "Are you alright, John?"

"Yes, but are you?"

"I'm fine, but what were you thinking? You could've killed somebody."

"Oh man, am I ever gonna get a licking." His voice and body shook uncontrollably.

"I'm surprised Bill isn't here yet. I guess with the tractor running, he didn't hear the gunshot. Go upstairs and try to calm down. I'll clean up the mess down here. Maybe you'll get in less trouble."

"Thanks, sis."

Emily gouged the bullet out of the wall and lowered the picture of a fruit basket a few inches to cover the hole. Then she swept the broken glass into the trashcan and stuffed a rag into the window to keep out the cold. She thought about her brother's plight and was glad to not be in his shoes. By the time Bill walked in, Emily was engaged in a book.

"What happened here? Emily, what did you do?"

"It wasn't me. John accidentally broke the window with one of your rifles."

"Where is he? I'm gonna kill him."

"He's upstairs, but go lightly on him. He feels bad enough."

"You mind your own business, little miss."

Bill climbed the steps to the loft. An eavesdropping Emily heard every word from the bottom of the steps.

"Come here, John. I think we both need a hug."

"I'm so sorry. I just wanted to surprise you with another deer."

"No, I'm the one who's sorry. I did everything wrong with you. Our first lesson should have been gun safety."

"Are you gonna punish me?"

"No, from all the shaking you're doing, I think you learned your lesson. But promise me, you'll never touch a gun again without me."

"I swear."

Emily couldn't believe it. No punishment for John. If that had been her, she would have gotten it for sure. She got blamed for everything being the oldest. When she heard Bill's footsteps approaching the stairs, she ran back to her book, pretending to be absorbed.

"Emily, tell your mother to hold dinner for me. I'm going to go into town to buy a locked case to store my guns. It's something I should have done a long time ago."

It took John a week to gain his composure back. Seeing the locked gun cabinet every day added to his confidence. Each day he did his chores, and every night he played Chinese checkers with Emily, while Margaret and Bill drank themselves into a stupor playing cards.

One night while Margaret and Bill were at the neighbors' house playing cards, John helped himself to some beer from the icebox. Emily watched him take three large sips and let out a loud burp before she spoke. "What do you think you're doing?"

"What does it look like I'm doing?"

"Looks like you're asking for trouble to me."

"Just having some fun. You want some?" He turned the growler toward Emily. She shook her head.

"Oh, come on, you're such a baby. Don't you want to be a grownup?"

Emily couldn't resist his pleading eyes. She took a swig. "Yuck. It tastes so bitter."

"You have to acquire a taste for it."

"You sound like Mom. That's what she said about coffee. Why bother? I'll just drink something I like." Emily opened the icebox, pouring herself a glass of apple juice. "Come on, let's play some Chinese checkers."

John chugged his first glass of beer while they played Chinese checkers. "Do you want to play another game?"

"Sure, Sis. But I have to make a trip to the bathroom first. Nature calls."

Returning from the outhouse, he took another glass of beer from the icebox and polished it off while they played another game. "We each won one game. How about a rubber match?" asked Emily.

"Alright, but I have to go to the bathroom first."

John's ability to hold his liquor amazed Emily. The only part of his body that it seemed to affect was his bladder. She patiently waited until he returned to the table with yet another beer. This time, he nursed his beer as they played. He started moving his marbles around the board at a snail's pace, missing easy moves. Then he lost his fine motor coordination, dropping a marble onto the board. The impact sent five other marbles rolling out of their holes, abruptly ending the game.

"Sorry, Sis. I'll put the game away." But as he stood up, he leaned on the board, spilling all twenty marbles onto the floor. He bent down to pick them up, smacking his head on the table, and then he vomited right on top of the marbles just as Mom and Bill walked in the door. There was no hiding this, the evidence laid right in front of Mom and Bill.

"Margaret, I'm gonna teach your boy a lesson. He got away with the gun, but not this time." Bill unbuckled his belt, pulled it through the belt loops, and took a swing at John. John ducked but lost his balance, falling on his stomach with his arms breaking his fall. Bill took another swing that connected with John's backside. John let out a harrowing scream. The second lash ripped a hole in his pants.

Emily could see blood oozing out of it. "Mom, aren't you going to stop him? He's hurting John. Mom?" But Margaret stood there silently, like a deer in the headlights. Emily cried and grabbed Bill's arm, but not before he landed two more blows.

"Stop it, you're hurting him." Bill stopped to look at Emily, a sense of normalcy returning to his eyes. John used the opportunity to scurry up the stairs and collapse into bed. Emily ran after him.

"Where do you think you're going, young lady? You have a mess to clean up here first."

Emily didn't argue, she didn't want to suffer the wrath of the belt. She cleaned up John's vomit, washed the marbles one by one, and put the game away. By the time she got to John, he was fast asleep in bed, but when the numbness of the alcohol wore off, the sting of the belt set in. John moaned.

"Let me get you some ice." Emily tiptoed down the stairs.

She used the icepick to chip off a piece of ice without waking her mother. She stepped over Bill, passed out drunk on the floor, and brought the ice to John.

"Thanks, Sis."

The next morning brought a new set of problems to John. His backside stung, and he had a massive headache. He wasn't sure if this was just a hangover or whether his head hurt thinking about his mother. Why didn't she stop Bill from beating him? Didn't she love him?

John spent the next two days in bed. On the third day, Bill climbed the stairs and yanked him out of bed by his ear. "Come on, you have chores to do."

John walked slowly down the stairs. He discovered that the stiffer he kept his back, the less his backside hurt. With a labored gait, John walked across the floor and put on his coat. "Here, you're gonna need this." He turned around. Margaret threw a pillow from the couch in his direction. John planned on smuggling the pillow to school tomorrow.

"Thanks." Maybe Margaret had a heart after all. John staggered to the barn and placed the pillow on the stool to milk the cow. Bending over to gather eggs created a new problem that John remedied by sitting on the cushion and reaching into the coop to gather the eggs.

In between his daily chores and school, John rifled through his comic books. He barely spoke, and in the evenings with Margaret and Bill playing cards with the neighbors, he refused to play cards or Chinese checkers with Emily.

As the days wore on, John's walking improved. His backside healed, but his heart and brain had not. "John, you need to stop fretting. All of this anger toward Bill doesn't hurt him; it only hurts you."

"It's not Bill I'm mad at, it's Mom. I can't believe she didn't help me."

"I can't believe it either, but I don't think she's going to change either, especially when she's living with Bill. You need to stop being so melancholy. Come on, play Chinese checkers with me."

"No, thank you. I never want to play that game again."

"Come on. It'll help to get your mind on something else."

After a brief pause, John said, "I don't want to play cards or Chinese checkers. I would rather go ice skating."

Emily thought about the suggestion. Skating was not something she wanted any part of, but perhaps this was the solution. She could help her brother with his depression and overcome her fear of skating at the same time. Reluctantly, she agreed. Seeing the smile on John's face told her she had made the correct decision.

Emily and John walked arm in arm and retrieved their skates, hanging from a nail in the barn. She scrutinized the skates. Were these the same skates? They looked the same. She reached her hand inside and pulled out the old stuffed socks. They were the same ones. Since her feet had grown, she wouldn't need the socks anymore.

They walked to the brook and put their skates on. The brook couldn't have been over two feet deep because Emily could see clear to the bottom. But skating would be challenging maneuvering through the obstacle course of rocks and protruding sticks. Emily convinced herself that when she got cold this time, she would warm up by the fire in their farmhouse; no bonfires for her. She closed her eyes while images of Isabel danced in her head. Her brother's scream brought her back to reality. He had fallen on his bottom about twenty feet away. Emily skated as fast as she could, avoiding three rocks on the way. "Are you alright?"

"Yes. The ice actually feels good on my behind."

Laughing, Emily reached out her hand to help him up. "What's that over there?" She saw a golf ball frozen under the water.

John looked over the brook and saw a golf course on the edge of their property. "Wow! Somebody has an amazing stroke to reach this far."

Emily looked in that direction. "Maybe we should be nice and return it to the manager of the golf course."

"Great idea! You wait here. I'll go get the ice pick so we can get it out of the water."

Before Emily could respond, John skated toward home. Without stopping to put his boots on, he continued walking through the snow in his skates with his knees wobbling back and forth. Emily felt proud to see John with a purpose. A man on a mission.

He returned with the ice pick, and they took turns chipping away at the frozen golf ball, rescuing it from its prison. They put on their boots and half jogged and half ran to the golf course office with the ball carefully placed inside John's glove.

In the winter, nobody visited this place. Between patches of water and melting snow, sections of yellow grass were visible. Golf carts covered with a large tarp lined the side of the club. A sign in the window said "Reopening on April 1st. See you then."

"Boy, are we stupid. Of course, they aren't open in the winter," Emily said.

"Let's just leave the ball here at the door so they see it when they open," John said as he removed the ball from his glove.

"No. The wind will blow it away. Let's just come back on April 1st."

"Sounds like a plan. But I want you to hold it until then. I'm afraid I'll lose it."

"Alright." Emily knew the perfect place to keep it in her underwear drawer.

On April 1st, John and Emily met the manager of the golf course. The nameplate on his desk read Otto Schneider, Proprietor. Mr. Schneider wore white pants that ended at his knees and a white shirt that ended at his elbows. He had a red and black plaid vest with matching knee socks. His white shoes had large cleats for playing golf outdoors. It surprised Emily that he was wearing them indoors. He was practicing his swing, putting golf balls into a cup.

"Excuse me, Mr. Schneider," Emily said. Mr. Schneider turned around. He had a deep tan despite the time of year.

"How can I help you?"

"I am Emily Miller, and this is my brother, John. We found this golf ball on our property, and we wanted to return it to you."

"That is so nice of you. I like honesty. Your Mama and Papa brought you up well." Emily and John looked at each other. "Hey, I have an idea. I lost a lot of money on missing golf balls last year. How would you like to make some money? I'll pay you a dollar a week to gather all my missing golf balls. You can work after school and on weekends."

"I don't think we can work on Sundays. Mama would always say that Sunday belongs to the Lord." Emily found it amusing that even though Margaret wasn't a churchgoer, some Christian rules like this were still ingrained in her head.

"That's fine. You can collect twice as many balls on Monday then."

"You got yourself a deal," John said as he shook Mr. Schneider's hand.

"Good, you can start on Saturday. Here's a bucket to gather the balls."

On the walk home, John was so excited. "This is my first job. I can't wait to tell Mom."

"John, you can't tell Mom. She would probably make us give her the money."

"No, she wouldn't."

"Of course, she would. Remember how poor we were when we had to gather all that coal?"

"That was Dad and Grandma, not Mom."

"You're right, but I still think this should be our little secret. Find a good hiding place for the money."

They worked through the spring and summer. The money was piling up, but there was no way to spend it. It was too far to walk into town, and Bill won't let them take the buggy. How Emily longed to live in the city with her father. She could almost taste that ice cream from the corner vendor. She stored her money deep in her ice skates where no one would find it, and John's money remained in Emily's underwear drawer for a rainy day.

Autumn came early with its heavy morning dew and torrential rainstorms. One morning, shortly after Emily's 14th birthday, Bill woke Emily up extra early. "Get the fire started for breakfast. I have to go to work early today."

Emily rolled out of bed, rubbing her eyes. She put on her heavy socks and boots and her lightweight jacket. She opened the door and walked around to the woodpile. The wood was still wet from last night's downpour. She gathered an armful of wood and reentered the house. She placed the wood in the stove and made a little tepee like she always did. Crumbling some newspaper under the wood, she struck it with a long match. A small flame ignited and quickly withered out. Emily blew on it, reigniting the flame. As the fire grew, she quickly added some newspaper and small pieces of wood. The flame died again, sending a light wave of smoke into the kitchen.

Bill staggered in, coughing loudly. Was he hacking from his usual cigarette smoking, or was it from the smoke accumulating in the house?

"Where is my breakfast? I'm going to be late for work. I thought I told you to have it ready. You are going to learn to mind me." With that, he slapped Emily right across the face.

Emily spotted Margaret cowering in the corner. "Mom, Bill hit me for no reason at all." Emily hoped her mother could understand her. Her face stung so much that her words came out with no more than a stutter.

"Why didn't you mind Bill? He told you to have his breakfast ready."

"Can't you see I couldn't get the fire going? The wood is too wet."

"Your children don't listen. If they want to live under my roof, they better learn to do their chores." Bill raised his hand, ready to strike another blow.

"Mom, stop him. You know it's not my fault." But Margaret just stood there like a block of ice, not saying a word. Why isn't she helping me? What kind of mother just watches her child get beaten? But then Emily remembered how she did nothing to defend her brother.

Emily ducked under the impending blow. As Bill teetered and fell to the floor, Emily could smell the whiskey on his breath. Did he wake up drinking or was he still under the lingering effects of a late-night party? "You ungrateful little brat." Bill reached into the crevice between the icebox and the wall and pulled out the broom. Using the handle, he landed a crushing blow on Emily's forehead right above her eye. Blood came spewing out of the wound into her eye.

Emily bolted out the door and kept on running. She didn't stop until she needed to catch her breath. She looked over her shoulder; no one was in pursuit. She picked up some dried leaves from the ground, patting them on her head, trying to stop the bleeding. Where was she going to go? Certainly not back home. She got angry with herself for not taking her saved money from working at the golf course. But there was no time, and she couldn't possibly go back now. She kept on walking past the school and then into neighborhoods she did not recognize. Day turned to dusk, but Emily trudged on. When it got too dark to see, she cursed the country living. In the city, the streetlights would illuminate her way. A chill was in the air. Emily knew she had to find shelter soon.

Fear, coldness, and loneliness overwhelmed Emily, numbing her face. She didn't know if it was tears or her wound dripping blood again. Would anyone ever find her if she died out in the country? Just about when she was ready to give up, she spotted a light in the distance like a beacon, welcoming her. She plodded on and came across a farmhouse. She was about to knock on the door when her mother's words echoed in her head. The Lord helps those who help themselves. Not wanting to bother the occupants of this home, she found a hanging swing on the porch stacked with rugs. Exhausted, Emily crawled onto the swing and rocked herself to sleep, using the rugs for a blanket. With any luck, she could escape from here before anyone discovered her.

Emily didn't know how long she slept, but she missed the sunrise. She awoke to a woman dabbing at her head. "I'm so sorry. I didn't mean to bother you."

"Easy, child. I'm Mrs. Larson. That's a nasty bump you got on your head. Let me help you." Emily sat still as Mrs. Larson dabbed alcohol on her forehead. Mrs. Larson was so close, Emily could look down her paisley dress at her enormous bosom. She felt the warmth of this caring woman and thought about her cold as ice mother. "What on earth happened?"

"My mother's boyfriend beat me up, and my mother did nothing to stop him. I can't ever go back there."

"Well, I think I can answer your prayers, and you can answer mine. You see, I'm a nurse. I work long hours, and I need someone to cook and clean this place while I'm gone. Do you think you could do that for me?" Emily nodded. "But instead of paying you, you can have free room and board."

Did Mrs. Larson really need the help, or was she just giving a poor girl some help?

"Oh, Mrs. Larson, you are wonderful." Emily gave her a big hug.

"First, let's see about that wound. I think I can stitch it up. Come on inside."

The parlor was as warm as Mrs. Larson. A blazing fire emanated from the room. A cozy couch and two rocking chairs surrounded a braided rug with a cocktail table resting on it.

Emily turned her head to the thumping tail of a cute little collie. She thought about Queenie and wondered if she was still alive and in a happy home. "That's Rex. Don't worry. He's friendly." Emily scratched his head, and he licked her hand. "Now, let's see about stitching up your head." Mrs. Larson grabbed her sewing kit from the closet next to the fireplace. Emily watched as she opened it. "Do you have a preference of color?"

"You mean I can have any color?"

"Yes."

"I'll take purple. It's my favorite color."

Emily watched Mrs. Larson sterilize a needle over a lit candle on the coffee table. The hole in the needle was so small Emily didn't think Mrs. Larson could see well enough to thread the needle, but she was successful on the first try. "Sit down, dear. This won't hurt a bit."

The closer Mrs. Larson got to Emily's face with the needle, the more scared she became. Pure panic developed, and Emily ran for the door. "Oh, honey. It'll be alright. It looks worse than it is. There are not that many nerve cells in the forehead. I promise you won't feel much."

She sat down in the lumpy chair and closed her eyes as Mrs. Larson stitched her up. The whole procedure was over lickety-split. "I'm done dear. Here, have a look." Mrs. Larson handed her a mirror.

Emily looked at the stitches on her forehead. "I look like Frankenstein."

Mrs. Larson giggled. "Oh, come now; it's not that bad. Are you hungry? I have some batter left. I can make you some pancakes."

"That would be lovely."

Emily realized how hungry she was. She wolfed down the pancakes and washed them down with some orange juice. She immediately went to the sink and began washing the dishes.

"What a thoughtful girl. I think our little arrangement will work out just fine. The carpet sweeper and cleaning supplies are in the corner closet in the kitchen. After you finish cleaning, you can spend the rest of the day playing with Rex. How are your cooking skills? Can you have dinner ready for us when I come home from work? Fry up some ham and potatoes."

"Don't you worry about a thing. I have it all under control."

Emily watched through the window as Mrs. Larson pedaled off on her bicycle. She wasted no time doing her chores. After finishing the dishes, she took the carpet sweeper from the closet and wiped the carpet. This job was harder than she thought. With Rex's hair clogging up the sweeper, it had to be emptied several times. Then she took the feather duster and dusted all the furniture in the parlor. She moved on to the bedroom. Mrs. Larson's bed was unmade. Emily made the bed, remembering her mother's advice to make the corners taut. She dusted all the furniture and Mrs. Larson's nursing certificate displayed on the wall.

By 2:00, the housework was done. To show her appreciation to Mrs. Larson for taking her in, Emily polished all the silver in the hutch. She picked some dandelions for the centerpiece and had dinner ready by the time Mrs. Larson got home. Emily finished all the dishes without being asked. And Mrs. Larson played Chinese checkers with her when she was done.

A week later, Mrs. Larson told Emily it was time to remove her stitches. It surprised her how little it hurt. "Mrs. Larson, you are the best. Do you think I could stay with you forever? You are nicer to me than my mother."

"I don't see why not. In my good conscience, I don't think I could return you to abusive parents. And I don't think they even want you back. No one has come looking for you."

"You are the best." Emily hugged Mrs. Larson, and Mrs. Larson hugged her back, surprising Emily. It was a warm hug, the type she never experienced from her mother.

The next day, Emily finished her chores so quickly she had most of the afternoon free. She wandered into Mrs. Larson's bedroom and sat on the stool in front of Mrs. Larson's make-up table, spraying a large amount of perfume on her wrists and behind her ears. She knew it was too much when she began coughing, and Rex let out a huge sneeze.

She wound up the key in the back of the jewelry box, opening up the lid. The ballerina began spinning. She raked through the jewelry with her finger, pulled out a strand of pearls, and put them around her neck just to see what she looked like. Opening up the bottom drawer of the jewelry box, she found a rose headband with a pearl trim. Emily put it on her head and adjusted the height to cover her scar. She put on some rouge and lipstick and looked at her reflection in the mirror. A clown was staring back at her. Why didn't my mother ever teach me how to put on make-up? Isn't that what mothers are supposed to do?

She opened up the drawer on the make-up table looking for a tissue or anything to take off this excess. Instead, she found a roll of money tied shut with a rubber band. She couldn't tell how much was there, but it was mostly one-dollar bills with a few fives mixed in. Emily dropped it back in the drawer, slamming it shut. She opened the drawer again and smelled the money. Wasn't she entitled to this money? Mrs. Larson hadn't paid her anything, except room and board. Emily put the money in her pocket and developed a plan. She would use this money to go back to New Jersey and find her father. Surely, he would take her back in. When she retrieved the money that she left home from working at the golf course, she would pay Mrs. Larson back. This wasn't stealing; this was just a loan. But if she took the necklace and headband, that would be stealing. She put them back in the jewelry box.

Emily walked into town and caught the last bus for New Jersey. Trying to look inconspicuous, she took a seat in the back of the bus and slumped down. An old man smelling of liniment sat next to her. The smell was so strong it drowned out the perfume scent emanating from her own body.

She moved to another vacant seat, and a young Negro man sat next to her. "Hi honey. You look like you could use a friend."

"No, I just want to be left alone." She found another empty seat with a discarded newspaper. She pretended to read just to avoid the two men for the rest of the ride.

When she got off the bus, Emily realized there was a flaw in her plan. Where did her father live? How would she ever find him? He did like to drink, so she went back to Brookside Avenue and boldly walked into Sullivan's pub.

"Hello, Mr. Sullivan. Do you remember me? It's me, Emily."

"Of course I do. Boy, you are all grown up."

"Hey little lady, can I buy you a drink?" Emily turned around to see a heavyset man hovering over her, reeking of beer.

"You get out of here, Joe Dixon, and leave the lady alone." Mr. Sullivan had come to her rescue. "Emily, don't say another word. You go right to the back and wash all that make-up off your face before the men in here think you are a prostitute. Then you come back here and tell me what you want."

Suddenly, it all became clear to Emily. She forgot to wash off the make-up before she left Mrs. Larson's. No wonder the men on the bus and Joe Dixon were pursuing her. She went to the powder room, scrubbed every bit of make-up from her face, and rejoined Mr. Sullivan.

"Mr. Sullivan, can you tell me where my father is?"

"He comes in here regularly enough. That last I heard, he was living on 18th Street above the gun shop."

"Thank you, Mr. Sullivan. And if you see my father, tell him I'm looking for him."

"You got it."

Emily walked the mile to 18th Street and found him playing bocce just like old times. She snuck up behind him and gave him a bear hug just as he released the ball, causing his shot to veer off sharply to the right.

"Emily, whatever are you doing here?"

"Oh, Dad. I ran away. I can't live with Mom and Bill. Look what he did to me." She showed him her healing scar.

"Good God. That bastard. You are welcome to live with me."

"Are you gonna tell Mom?"

"Not on your life. Let's go upstairs. You look like you could use some hot chocolate."

Suddenly it was like old times. Emily enjoyed her hot chocolate and fell asleep on the couch.

The next morning, the police were banging on the door. "Open up in there. We have a warrant for the arrest of Emily Miller."

Emily ran for the backdoor. Her father grabbed her arm. "Why are you running? You did nothing wrong, or did you?"

Henry let the police in. "What is this all about? You can't arrest my daughter for running away from an abusive man."

"No, it is not for running away. It is for theft and prostitution. She robbed a woman named Mrs. Larson from upstate New York."

The last thing Emily saw was disappointment in her father's eyes as they slapped on the handcuffs and whisked her away.

Essex County Courthouse
1916

E mily never hated herself so much as she did on that ride to the county jail. Why did she take that money? This was not like her. And after Mrs. Larson treated her so kindly. She was so ashamed. From the back seat of the squad car, she looked at her reflection in the rear-view mirror hoping to see some other girl, but she only saw herself with tears streaming down her cheeks.

At the police station, they removed her handcuffs and shoved her into a processing room void of windows. "How old are you?" a young officer asked her.

"I'm 14."

"I knew it. Another juvenile. The third one tonight. You'll have to appear before the judge tomorrow to learn your fate, but we can release you into the custody of your parents tonight. The phone is right there. Call them."

Who should she call? Her mother? Emily certainly didn't want to go back to Bill, a man who could beat her again with no provocation, and a mother who would stand by and let him do it. Would her mother stand by her side in court? Probably not. Her father? Would he show up drunk and make things worse? She remembered that look of disappointment in his eyes when she got arrested, realizing that he would be a useless proposition. The point was moot, anyway. Neither of them owned a telephone. What about Mr. Sullivan? He helped her train Queenie. Would he help her now? She called him.

"Mr. Sullivan? It's me, Emily."

"It's nice to hear your voice. Did you find your father?"

"Yes, but that's not why I'm calling. I got in trouble."

"What kind of trouble?"

"I got arrested."

"Arrested? For what?"

"Theft and prostitution. I have to appear in court tomorrow. I'm allowed to be released into the custody of my parents. They won't want any part of this. I was wondering- could I stay with you?"

"I'll be right there."

Arriving within the hour, Patrick Sullivan, looking official in his best tie and jacket, walked right to the front desk with a dress draped over his arm. "I'm here to sign out Emily Miller."

"Are you her parent or legal guardian?" asked the clerk.

"No, I'm not. But her parents are unavailable, and I want to help her."

"Well then, I'm sorry. I can't help you."

"Surely you don't expect a young girl to defend herself in court without an adult present, do you?"

"You can ask the judge tomorrow to be appointed as her advocate, but tonight, she stays here."

"Can I at least see her? I need to deliver this dress. She'll need it in court."

"I guess that will be alright. Follow me."

Emily sat alone in the first cell. Patrick waited as the guard fiddled with his ring of keys. The cell opened on his fourth try. Patrick entered and the guard relocked the cell.

"Call me when you're ready to leave."

Emily threw her arms around Patrick Sullivan.

"Thank you so much for coming."

"Easy child. You'll crush the dress." Patrick held up the tan dress with blue lace trimmings for Emily to admire. She loved the high collar, extension sleeves, and blue silk buttons. "What do you think? It's my daughter's dress. You can borrow it. I want you to make a good impression on the judge tomorrow."

Emily looked at her own green house dress hanging loosely on her shoulders. It was missing two buttons and there was a hole in the elbow. She knew he was right. "Thank you so much. Now let's get out of this horrible place."

"Not tonight, I'm afraid. I'm not your legal guardian. You'll have to stay here tonight, but tomorrow I'll ask the judge to appoint me as your advocate and see if we can get you out of this terrible mess. Now try to get some sleep tonight." He patted Emily on the arm, trying to reassure her. "See you tomorrow. Guard!"

Somehow Emily made it through the night despite the parade of prisoners and guards marching past her cell all night. Each time they passed, Emily prayed they would not stop at her cell; she was in no mood for a roommate. And the pillow was so skimpy it gave her a kink in her neck.

In the morning, she put on the dress that Mr. Sullivan lent her. It fit perfectly. Splashing cold water on her face, she was ready for the walk across the street to the courthouse when the guard came to escort her.

Emily had never been in a courtroom before. She had time to check it out while they waited for the judge to arrive. In the courtroom, the chandelier hung low on its chain with six lights, but one didn't work. The lights accentuated three cracks in the white plaster ceiling, but they didn't need to be on. With the window open, sunlight and wind spilled into the room. Four other children sat with their parents waiting for the judge. At least their parents came to lend their support. Emily's parents were nowhere to be found. And neither was Mr. Sullivan. Where was he?

"All rise. The honorable Judge Jude Baxter presiding," said the bailiff.

The judge walked in, his ominous black robe swirling around his ankles. He took his seat below a gigantic clock stuck at 2:07, just like Emily's brain was stuck in time. She would remember this day forever. "You may be seated. Bailiff, call the first case."

"The State vs. Rodney Watson. Young man, have a seat at the defense table with your lawyer." A Negro boy about Emily's age moved to the table. He wore navy blue knickers made from wool serge with a matching cap.

"Young man, remove that cap in the courtroom."

"Yes, sir," he said, removing it.

"He doesn't have a lawyer. We can't afford it. I'm his mother. May I sit with him and be his advocate?" Rodney's mother wore a green percale bungalow house dress with a loose-fitting belt running through two over-sized belt loops. The white braiding completed the outfit.

Emily thought they looked too well-dressed to be poor. Were they trying to scam the judge, or did they have a knight in shining armor like Mr. Sullivan who lent them some nice clothes? Where was Mr. Sullivan? He still wasn't here.

"Proceed with the state's case," said Judge Baxter.

Across the aisle from Rodney and his mother, the prosecutor stood up. He was a large man, although more muscular than fat, wearing a suit a little too small for him. Emily couldn't help but notice how hairy he was with his thick curly hair, unibrow, and day-old stubble. He took off his suit jacket, hanging it on the back of his chair. As he casually rolled his sleeves up, Emily couldn't help but notice the dense hair on his arms. "Matthew Bannon for the state.

"The defendant is charged with arson. How do you plead?" asked the judge.

"Not guilty, sir."

Arson? Emily wondered what kind of person could burn something down on purpose.

"Call your first witness."

"The state calls Kenneth Warner."

After being sworn in by the bailiff, Kenneth Warner took the stand. He had eyes so small that Emily couldn't tell if they were open or shut from her seat in the gallery. She wondered how he could have seen anything at all.

"State your name and occupation for the record."

His lips were so thin, Emily wondered if he could speak. "Kenneth Warner. I'm the principal at the Roosevelt School."

"Mr. Warner, I'm going to show you some pictures. Can you verify what they are for the court?" said the prosecutor.

"They're pictures of fire damage to the science wing of our school."

Matthew Bannon took them from Mr. Warner and showed them to the judge. "And can you tell us how much the damage will cost to repair?"

"Our estimate is $150."

"Does the defense wish to see the pictures?"

"No, we're not disputing the fire. I'm just saying that my son didn't do it."

"Mr. Warner, how do you know that Rodney Watson is the one who started this fire?" asked the prosecutor.

"Apparently, Rodney failed a science test. Many witnesses in his class, including his teacher, Mr. Clark -and I can produce them if you want to waste the court's time repeating the same story over and over- said he tore the test into pieces and threw a few science textbooks across the room. He then spent the rest of the class rocking in his chair with his hands on his head like he was in some type of trance."

"What happened next?"

"Rodney went to the lunchroom with his classmates. According to his friends at the table, Rodney said, 'I hate that Mr. Clark. I'm going to teach him a lesson.' He then left the cafeteria, heading back toward his science classroom. Again, I can produce these witnesses if the court would like."

"That is not necessary at this time," said Matthew Bannon, the prosecutor. "Continue."

"Three band students, Leslie Whalen, William Tate, and Richard Anderson, were heading to the music room when they saw Rodney throw a match onto a heap of papers and books. In his haste to leave the room, he knocked Leslie to the ground. He used some type of accelerant because the fire flared up quickly. These three students were instrumental, if I may use a pun, in reporting the fire and getting everyone out safely."

"The prosecution rests."

"Now it's the defense's turn. What is your defense, young man?" asked the judge.

"I don't remember doing any of this, so I couldn't have done it."

"There's no disputing the facts. Either your son is a colossal liar or-"

"My son is not a liar," said Mrs. Watson, interrupting the judge.

"Well, if he seriously doesn't remember doing it with all this incriminating evidence, then he has deep, deep problems. I feel sorry for him and for you. But I have no choice but to sentence him to incarceration at the Oakland Reform School for Boys until he is of age."

"But, your honor, that's three and a half years."

"I'll reduce the sentence by one year if you make reparations to the school."

"One hundred fifty dollars? I can't afford that."

"Then I'm sorry. Bailiff, take him away."

Emily watched in horror. Three and a half years. Clearly, there was something wrong with Rodney. Why couldn't the judge see that? If the judge could so cavalierly sentence a damaged boy to three and a half years, what would her fate be? Three years is a lifetime.

"Next case," said Judge Baxter.

"The state vs. Emily Miller."

"Emily Miller, take your position at the defense table."

Emily walked at a snail's pace to the table, trying to delay the inevitable.

"Young lady, where are your parents?" asked the judge.

Before she could answer, Patrick Sullivan entered the courtroom, banging the door against the wall. "If it begs the court's pardon, I would like to be appointed advocate for Emily Miller."

"Who are you?"

"My name is Patrick Sullivan."

"Are you a relative?"

"No, a close family friend. As you can see, her parents are not here, and she needs representation. May I fill in?"

The judge nodded, and Patrick took his place beside Emily. "You look so pretty in that dress."

"What took you so long? I was worried you weren't coming."

"I've been here for an hour. Since I wasn't a relative, they wouldn't let me in until your specific case. Don't worry, I'm here now."

"The charge is theft and prostitution. How does the defendant plead?"

"Well, we can hardly deny the theft since she was caught red-handed with the money, but we do plead not guilty to this ludicrous prostitution charge," Mr. Sullivan said.

How could anyone think I am a prostitute? Emily thought. I have never even had time for a boyfriend with all the work I have to do.

"Call your first witness," said the judge.

"The prosecution calls Sarah Larson."

Mrs. Larson took the stand, clad in her nurse's uniform. Emily didn't have the heart to look this kind woman in the eyes.

"State your name and occupation for the record."

"My name is Sarah Larson, and isn't my occupation obvious?"

"Yes, it is, but I need you to say it for the record."

"I am a nurse."

"How did you come to know the defendant?"

"She showed up on my doorstep one night with some sob story about being beaten by her mother's boyfriend. She had a huge gash on her forehead. Looking back on it now, I know she is nothing but a con artist."

"Oh, Mrs. Larson, that part is true. Bill beat me."

"Mr. Sullivan, I need you to control your charge. The defense will have its turn to present its own evidence." Patrick patted Emily's arm to reassure her.

"Continue, Mrs. Larson," said the prosecutor.

"I felt sorry for her. I took her under my wing, stitched her head, and offered her a job to cook and clean for me in return for room and board. For about a week, everything was fine, and then she ran off with my money."

"How much money are we talking about?"

"I had over fifty dollars rolled up and tied with a rubber band."

"Oh Mrs. Larson, I'm so, so sorry. Can you ever forgive me?" Emily burst into uncontrollable tears.

"Again, Mr. Sullivan, I'm going to have to ask you to control your charge."

"Sorry judge." Again, Patrick patted Emily's arm.

"The theft is not in dispute. Please, Mrs. Larson, tell us why you believe the prostitution charges are justified."

"Not only was my money taken, Emily also got into my make-up, and she used a significant amount. Only a prostitute could wear that amount of make-up."

"The prosecution rests."

"And now it is the defense's turn. Call your first witness."

"Emily, I have a surprise for you. The defense calls Henry Miller," said Mr. Sullivan.

Henry took the witness stand, winking at Emily as he walked by.

"What is your relationship to the defendant?"

"She is my daughter."

Emily felt worried. Papa knows she is not a prostitute, but would the judge believe him? How many fathers lie for their children? Emily glanced at the judge. There was no emotion on his face.

"My daughter is not a prostitute."

"Why should we believe you?"

"We come from a hard-working family, and that means my children too. I can assure you, if my daughter wasn't at school, she was home with me doing housework."

"Where is her mother?" Emily glanced around the court-room. Her mother was nowhere to be seen. That figures.

"We have separated."

"How do you know what she did when she was with your wife?"

"She lived on a farm where there is even more work to do. They live far from town. There is little opportunity to meet men."

"That will be all."

"Call your next witness."

"I call myself. And for the record, my name is Patrick Sullivan and I'm a bartender for a living."

Is he supposed to be a character witness? A man who owns a saloon? As soon as he tells them about my make-up, I'm doomed. Emily looked down, avoiding eye contact with Mr. Sullivan.

"I own Sullivan's pub, and I have known Emily since she was a little girl. I helped her train her dog to fetch beer. Some of you might have heard about it. The story made the paper and brought many customers to the bar to see the famous dog."

"But how do you know she is not a prostitute?" asked the prosecutor.

"Because she knows how to handle men. She takes no abuse

from them. She comes to the bar, buys her father's beer, and leaves."

"Have you ever seen her dress like a prostitute or wear make-up like a harlot?"

Mr. Sullivan paused. Emily looked down. This is it. It's off to jail for me.

"No never. Emily is a good girl. If Mrs. Larson thinks Emily stole her make-up, I'm sure it was simply a young girl experimenting for the first time. The defense rests."

Emily couldn't believe it. What a nice man. He lied for her under oath. She hoped it helped.

"Will the defendant please rise?"

Emily stood up slowly. She moved her feet further apart so her shaking knees wouldn't knock together.

"It is obvious to me you are not guilty of prostitution, but you are guilty of theft. Never have I seen a defendant show such remorse, so instead of reform school, I sentence you to the Convent of St. Mary until you become of age. Let the good sisters cleanse your soul, educate you, and teach you a trade. Consider yourself lucky."

"Thank you, judge. I promise I will straighten myself out."

Emily hugged her papa. "Why am I going to a Catholic convent? Don't they know I'm not Catholic?"

"You know I was Catholic before I married your mother, so you qualify to go there." Emily vaguely remembered her father saying "Hail Marys" and his sister, her Aunt Annie, teaching her how to say the rosary. "Just count your blessings. Convent life will be so much better than reform school."

Emily turned to Mr. Sullivan and hugged him. "How can I ever thank you?"

"Just be good, Emily Miller. I see good things in your future."

"When I get settled at the convent, I'll wash this dress and get it back to you somehow."

"Don't worry about it; you keep it. Don't tell my daughter, but it looks better on you."

The court bailiff escorted Emily to the car that would take her to her new home. "Have a seat, young lady. We are waiting for another prisoner."

Emily's mind spun out of control. *Am I sitting in the proverbial paddy wagon waiting for another prisoner? Why was he calling me a prisoner? Surely, I am not a prisoner anymore, or am I? What lies ahead in the convent? Do they know I am not even Catholic? Well, I won't tell them. This has got to be better than reform school,* she tried to convince herself.

The car door opened, and Emily watched a girl about her age take the seat next to her. She was painfully thin, but she had the prettiest green eyes. She never saw a girl with such short hair. If she hadn't been wearing a dress, Emily would have thought she was a boy. "That's it, Ralph. Just these two today. The rest are off to reform school. I'll leave their files on the front seat for Sister Francois. Good luck to you ladies," said the bailiff as he slammed the car door shut.

St. Mary's Convent
1916–1919

The Convent of St. Mary sat high on a hill. It was a huge, intimidating building. At first Emily thought it was a prison, surrounded by a high brick wall, but once the "paddy wagon" drove through the gate, its charm developed. A statue of Jesus greeted them, and the bells were playing "Onward Christian Soldiers." Emily peered up and saw an enormous cross mounted on the roof.

Sister Francois greeted them. "Who do we have here?"

"I'm Cora Radcliff." So that was her name.

"And you, child?"

"I'm Emily Miller."

"Welcome to St. Mary's. Thank you, Ralph. I will take it from here." The driver handed their files to Sister Francois and saluted her as he left. "Now, ladies, if you'll follow me, we can get acquainted." Cora and Emily followed the nun into her office, their feet echoing loudly on the marble floor. "Have a seat."

There were three chairs in front of her desk. Cora sat in the middle one. Why didn't she sit in the left chair so Emily could sit on the right and leave a space between them? Now she would have to sit right next to Cora. It's not that Emily had anything against Cora. She just wanted her own space. Emily sat to Cora's left.

Both girls sat speechless as Sister Francois read their files. "Wow, your birthdays are only one day apart. That means you both arrived together and will be discharged the same day, in just under three years. I hope you become good friends. Care to tell me why you stole a loaf of bread from the bakery?" She looked right at Cora.

"My family was starving."

Emily knew that was the truth. She was thin as a rail. But stealing bread and fifty dollars weren't the same. Why did Cora receive the same punishment as Emily? Was there more to her crime, or did she have an unforgiving judge in her courtroom?

"And you?" Now she was looking at Emily.

"My mother's boyfriend beat me, and I took money to run away."

"I feel sorry for both of you girls, but you sinned and broke God's law. The first thing we're going to do is get you to Confession. Here comes Father Quinn to escort you to the church."

Father Quinn's face was round with a shapely gray beard and mustache. As the three of them walked to the church, Emily couldn't help but notice that Father Quinn had more hair on the back of his neck than the top of his head. Emily found this so amusing that she thought she might forget what she must say in the confessional. But when Father Quinn was out of sight, concealed on his side of the booth, the words came right back to her.

"Bless me father for I have sinned. This is my very first confession." Emily bared her soul about her thieving ways- the money she stole from Mrs. Larson, the church money she took when her sister Helen was born, and the milk she drank when she gathered coal. Her penance- two "Our Fathers" and three "Hail Marys." This ritual may have cleared her soul, but her conscience still made her feel guilty.

Cora was in the confessional booth a lot longer than Emily.

She thought Cora must have been a bigger sinner than her, but if they were going to be friends like Sister Francois said, she would never ask her about them.

"Follow me, ladies. Let me show you your room," said Sister Francois. The room, in the back of the first floor, was more like an army barracks. Ten beds hugged the wall with a chest of drawers for each girl opposite the bed. Engraved on each dresser was a small cross. "I have asked your parents to send none of your personal belongings for now. You will find your school uniforms in the drawers. In time, your parents may send some of your belongings- with permission of course."

Emily hoped they wouldn't have to wear nun's clothing. To Emily's pleasant surprise, she saw a brown pleated skirt, a white Oxford shirt, and a brown cardigan. "One thing you'll learn here is how to sew. When you are released, that will make you marketable. On days when you don't have quotas to fill, you can pick out some fabric and make your own clothes." That didn't sound so bad. Emily hoped they had some pretty lavender material.

"As you can see, the second drawer has all your toiletries."

Emily opened the drawer and found a toothbrush, tooth-paste, deodorant, soap, shampoo, and a hairbrush. In addition, there was a Bible that had seen better days and a set of rosary beads. But there were no sanitary products, and Emily felt her period coming on.

"Sister Francois, I think my period is coming. I don't see any rags."

"I intentionally did that. As soon as your time of the month comes, tell me and I will get the rags for you. I know the courts determined that you two are not prostitutes, but we have to make sure you are not with child. Once we know for sure, you will have no trouble getting what you need."

"Well, I need it now," Emily said. As she waited for Sister Francois to get her the rags, she felt sorry for Cora. How humiliating it would be when her time of the month came and she would have to ask for rags.

Sister Francois returned with a bunch of rags, handing them to Emily. "The bathroom is at the end of the hall. You can join us for dinner when you're ready. Come with me, Cora." Cora looked like a baby duck following its mother as they filed out the door.

The kitchen and dining area was in the basement. The sixteen nuns of the convent sat together at one table, while ten resident girls sat together at their own table. Emily found an empty seat next to Cora. Three girls scooched in their chairs so Emily could squeeze between the sideboard and the table to take the empty seat.

"It was good of you to join us, Emily," said Sister Francois's booming voice. "We were waiting for you to say grace.

"Bless us, O Lord, and these Thy gifts, which we are about to receive from Thy bounty, through Christ our Lord. Amen. In the name of the Father, the Son, and the Holy Spirit." Emily remembered every word. The girls each made the sign of the cross. Emily almost blessed herself with her left hand, but quickly remembered to use her right.

Dinner was surprisingly good- fried chicken, beets, and rice, but the portions were small. In the middle of the table, sat a basket of bread. One girl grabbed the biggest piece of bread for herself and passed the basket around. By the time it got to Emily, there was only one slice left, and Cora didn't have any yet. Emily broke her piece in half and shared it with Cora. "Thank you," she said. Emily hoped this gesture would win her a new friend. All the other girls had dour expressions on their faces; no one said a word during dinner. Was silence a convent rule, or were the girls intentionally excluding her and Cora from the group? Emily glanced over at the nuns' table, they too were eating in silence.

After dinner, the rest of the evening was free time. The girls had the freedom to complete their homework or read at their leisure, but since Emily and Cora hadn't been to school yet and the library was locked, they were compelled to read the Bible. They lounged out on their beds; Emily read the book of Matthew while Cora fiddled with some paper and pens.

"What are you doing?" asked Emily.

"I'm making a chart to count down the days we will have to spend here. We get released on September 7, 1919. That's 1,074 days from now. Each day I cross off the chart puts us one day closer to being released."

Emily didn't agree with Cora. In Emily's mind, the chart would only prolong the agony. She returned to her Bible reading, but Cora's stomach released a big growl, breaking her concentration. She looked at Cora and the two girls shared a laugh. "I'm hungry. Let's go exploring and see if we can find a snack."

"Are you sure that's a good idea?"

"Come on; it'll be fun." When Emily hesitated, Cora continued. "Let me tell you a brief story. When I was born, it took my parents a few days to come up with a name for me. I was a fussy baby. Cried all the time. My mother predicted I was going to be incorrigible, so they named me Cora. Now I have to live up to my reputation."

"Is that a true story?"

"I'm in a convent. I wouldn't lie."

"Alright. I'll go with you. An adventure might be fun."

The girls tiptoed down the stairs, wandering through the dining room to the kitchen. The heavy pantry door squeaked as Cora pulled it open. "Is someone there?" came a voice from inside.

Emily knocked a saltshaker over as they ran out the door. The girls watched a heavyset woman with rollers in her hair appear in the kitchen.

"Who is that?" Emily said.

"I don't know, but my guess is the cook. She probably lives

here in a room off the kitchen. Come on; let's get out of here before she sees us. Follow me."

Emily followed Cora into the attached church. The streetlights gave off just enough light to see the empty pews. "Let's see if we can find some food." Cora took Emily's hand, steering her around the altar and majestic pipe organ into the sacristy. The room was the size of a closet. All the priests' robes and stoles hung neatly on wooden hangers. Extra Bibles and hymnals were stacked on the floor. Cora opened a cabinet door, revealing bottles of wine and boxes of unconsecrated hosts.

"Want some wine?" Cora asked.

Emily thought about her brother John and the beating he received when he was drunk, not to mention cleaning up her father's vomit. "No, thank you."

Cora opened a box of the unconsecrated hosts and shoved a handful in her mouth. Emily gasped. "That is so sacrilegious. We can't eat that."

"Why not? It's only a piece of bread until the priest blesses it."

Emily thought about it and realized her friend was right. She took a host and put it on the tip of her tongue like she was in church. She ate two more, but they tasted like cardboard. Cora kept eating them like a starving child.

"Do you hear that?" Footsteps echoed across the marble floor of the sanctuary, rapidly approaching the girls. This room had no window; there was no place to hide. The girls grabbed a Bible pretending to read, just as a dark figure loomed large in the doorway. He had a limping gait. Could Emily knock him over and run away? No, then she would be in more trouble.

"What are you two doing in here?"

The dark-skinned man wore a janitor's uniform with a tool belt around his waist. Emily could see the silhouette of a hammer and screwdriver hanging from it.

"You scared us half to death. Who are you?" Cora said.

Emily was happy that Cora was doing the talking. She would just play along.

"The name's Lindsey. I am the maintenance man for the church and convent. And I will repeat myself. What are you doing in here?"

"Well, Mr. Lindsey."

"No, not Mr. Lindsey. Just Lindsey."

"We thought we would come in here to read our Bibles in peace."

Emily knew that excuse would not work. She scooted over to sit on the crumbs and block the box of hosts from his line of vision. Lindsey pushed her over, revealing the evidence left behind.

"You have no business here. Put that box away and then we'll have a little visit with Sister Francois."

"Oh please, Lindsey. Don't turn us in. This is our first day here and we don't want to go to reform school. Please?" Emily said with her big pleading brown eyes that always melted Papa's heart away.

"Well, there is something you can do for me," said Lindsey.

"Oh great. I hope he will not ask me what I think he's going to ask. I'm not a prostitute, Emily thought.

"Well, maybe there is. Can you teach me how to read?"

"You don't know how to read?" Cora said.

"Never had the opportunity. But if you can meet me every night after supper behind the church for about an hour and teach me how to read," I'd be obliged."

Emily thought about it. Depending on how much homework she had, they could make it work. Even if she had to sacrifice an hour of sleep each night, it would be better than going to reform school. "Lindsey, you've got yourself a deal."

"We'll meet you tomorrow night," Cora agreed.

. . .

Before retiring to bed for the evening, Cora crossed a day off the chart. "One down and 1,073 more to go." How did Cora know how many days were left? Emily thought she must be some kind of math whizz.

Emily had little sleep that night. Her back hurt from sleeping on the thin mattress, while her head hurt thinking about Lindsey. Could they trust him not to turn them in? Wasn't this blackmail? How long would they have to keep on teaching him how to read? Emily woke up at 11: 57, then 1:03, 2:17, 3:49, 5:23, as the minutes ticked slowly away. And each time Emily woke, she checked on Cora, sleeping soundly in her bed. At least Emily's restlessness didn't wake her friend.

At 6:00, Emily and Cora began the basic training of convent life. Sister Francois walked down the aisle of the barracks, rattling off her alarm clock until each girl sat up in bed. Is this what military personnel had to endure? A quiet breakfast and a long Mass followed. Then, the girls received chores for the rest of the morning. Emily took care of the laundry, and Cora was responsible for the dishes in the kitchen. Then all the girls would regroup for lunch in the dining room.

Sister Francois told Cora and Emily that the afternoon was education time. This implied that Sister Francois taught most girls how to sew and knit so that they would be prepared for good jobs after leaving the convent. The girls with "a good head on their shoulders" could spend half the time in the classroom and half the time sewing. Sister Francois walked the girls to the second floor. Emily could see some girls already knitting and sewing.

They continued up to the third floor. Classrooms ran half the length of the hallway. A green curtain blocked access to the other side. Emily wondered what was behind it. She was afraid to ask, but Cora must have read her mind when she said, "What's behind the curtain?"

"That is the nuns' quarters. It is strictly off limits to students. Do you understand?" Emily nodded. Sister Francois continued,

"Each classroom is for a different grade, grades five through twelve. Since you are both 14, I am putting you in the ninth-grade class. After taking a placement test, the teachers determine if you will move up or down a grade," said Sister Francois. It sounded reasonable to Emily; she hoped she could stay with Cora. "Have a nice day, ladies."

Sister Erma introduced herself to Cora and Emily. Her habit was so tight she had a tough time speaking, and Emily had an even tougher time understanding her. She assigned the rest of the class some math work while she tested Emily and Cora. "This is a quick test with a combination of skills from fifth through twelfth grade. This will give us a good assessment as to your math level. You may begin."

Emily looked at Cora who was already plowing through the math problems. Emily picked up her pencil. "Emily, use your right hand," said Sister Erma.

"Yes, ma'am." Emily switched the pencil to her right hand. She put her name at the top, but she could hardly read her own handwriting. She became so flustered that she forgot her times tables. That made it almost impossible to do fractions and long division. Why didn't Mama let her go to school more often? Was Emily going to be sent down to a younger grade? Would she be able to stay with Cora?

"Alright girls. Now it is time for your reading assessment. Class, begin reading *Silas Marner* while I take Cora out in the hall to read to me." Emily tried to concentrate as she strained to hear Cora read. But the door was soundproof; Emily couldn't hear a word. She focused on *Silas Marner,* but she had difficulty understanding it. When the classroom door opened up again, Sister Erma entered without Cora in tow. Oh no, did Cora get sent down a grade? Would they be able to stay together? "Emily, your turn. Bring your book out in the hall and read to me."

"Yes, ma'am."

Emily struggled through Chapter 1 of *Silas Marner.* When she finished, she looked at Sister Erma, hoping for some praise;

all she got was a blank stare. "Now give me a summary of what you just read. What was it about?"

"I read it, but I didn't understand what it was about."

"I'm afraid this is too hard for you. Your reading level, combined with your math scores, tells me you belong in seventh grade."

"But Sister Erma, I'm 14, those girls are only 12. I don't belong there."

"But that is where you are academically. You can join them when you catch up, but some girls are better equipped to learn life skills. Education is not for all girls; maybe you are one of them. Now what will it be, the sewing room or the seventh-grade classroom?"

Could she join those girls? Would it be too embarrassing? Was this Emily's last chance for an education? At least Cora would be there so they could go through it together. But when they walked to the seventh-grade classroom, Emily saw her friend was not there. She swallowed hard. "I think I'll join the girls in the sewing room." A girl snickered as Emily walked out the door, wiping a tear from her eye.

Another nun, Sister Peggy, greeted Emily at the sewing room door. She was short and chubby with rosy cheeks. Dressed in black and white, she looked like a penguin. Emily tried to stifle a laugh. What was it her mother always said-children should be seen and not heard? Sister Peggy wore a brown leather belt around her thick waist, with rosary beads draped on her right side. In the front, she had stuffed twenty knitting needles fanning out like porcupine quills. She extracted two needles and handed them to Emily. "Here. Do you know how to knit?"

"I'm afraid not, Sister Pen-." Emily caught herself. She almost said Sister Penguin.

"Have a seat on the couch. I'll start a scarf for you, and we'll have you knitting in no time. What colors would you like?"

Emily walked to the wall where bins held just about every color of yarn. "How about lavender and white?"

"That is a splendid choice."

Sister Peggy sat with her back to Emily, preparing the yarn and needles for Emily's lesson. Emily couldn't see what she was doing, but she could see all the other girls deeply engaged with their knitting. One girl with thick eyeglasses held the needles so close to her face Emily thought she might poke herself. Emily thanked God for her good eyesight. She sat patiently on the gold couch that sagged in the middle. Her bottom fit nicely into the indentation. Putting her arm on the armrest, she noticed a hole in the fabric. She wondered if another juvenile delinquent had picked at it with her knitting needles in total frustration. She picked out another thread with her finger until Sister Peggy crept up behind her.

"It is time for your lesson." Sister Peggy wrapped her arms around Emily and put a needle with some completed stitches of yarn in her right hand and an empty needle in her left hand. "I started this with a slip knot and a single cast on. I will show you how to start this when you know what you are doing, but for now, this is where we'll start. Put the single strand of yarn and the needle in your left hand and make a fist with your thumb up in the air." Sister Peggy positioned the yarn and needle where she wanted it and wrapped her hand around Emily's hand to form the fist. "Now wrap the yarn around the stick from back to front- like this." Emily felt like a marionette puppet while Sister Peggy controlled all the strings. "Pull it tight like this, slipping it onto the right needle." Sister Peggy repeated this four times in slow motion. "Now you try."

Emily took one stitch and waited for Sister Peggy's response. "That's too tight. You'll never be able to get the needle under it for the next row." Emily watched Sister Peggy struggle to loosen up the stitch. "Here, try again." Emily's next attempt made the stitch too loose. "That's too loose. Watch what happens." Sister Peggy tilted the needle down and the stitch fell right off the needle."

"Can't I do it the other way?"

"What do you mean?"

"Can't I hold the empty needle with my right and take the stitch with my left hand? I can control it better that way."

"Oh, I'm sorry Emily. You live in a right-handed world. Just keep practicing. You'll get the hang of it."

Emily kept on practicing. Some stitches were too tight, some too loose. She wondered when she would get it right. After a few hours, she was getting the hang of it; she just couldn't work as quickly as the other girls and feared she would never master it if she had to knit with her right hand.

A girl whispered, "Here come the bookworms," and broke her concentration. Emily looked up to see the schoolgirls pile into the room, with Cora in the midst. She ran over to her friend. "What happened to you? When you didn't come back to the classroom, I assumed you got moved down a grade or two. But when I moved down, I didn't see you."

"That's because I got moved up to eleventh grade."

"Emily, don't you have work to do?" said Sister Peggy.

"Yes, ma'am."

As Emily returned to her seat, she heard Sister Peggy ask Cora, "Do you need knitting lessons, or can you get right to work?"

"I know how to knit."

Sister Peggy said, "Pick out two colors and get started." She pointed toward the yarn bins on the wall. Cora chose deep purple and black and got right to work on her scarf.

Is there anything Cora couldn't do? Emily was jealous of all of Cora's accomplishments.

"Sister Peggy?"

"Yes, Cora. What is it?"

"I heard Alice Paul is protesting again outside the White House. She and the other suffragettes plan on staying there every day until President Wilson takes up their cause and gives women the right to vote. And I also heard women were donating coffee, scarves, and mittens to help them protest through the cold winter. Couldn't the convent take up the cause and donate some of our scarves and mittens to her and her companions?"

"Don't get me wrong, Cora. I am in favor of women's rights, but now is not the time. I think the brave soldiers fighting the German tyranny in Europe are in much greater need of our supplies."

Cora couldn't argue with that, so she simply nodded her acceptance.

After a dinner of lamb stew, it was time to give Lindsey his reading lessons. "I'm not going," said Emily.

"What do you mean, you're not going?" Cora said. "You have to. That was our deal with Lindsey, to stay out of trouble."

"I got moved down two grades today and felt too embarrassed to stay. Then I couldn't get the hang of knitting. I'm just a stupid little left-handed twit."

"Everyone can learn to read; it just takes some people longer than others. Did you know Woodrow Wilson didn't learn to read until he was ten years old? And look at him. He graduated from Princeton, and now he's our president."

"Really?"

Cora nodded. "You just have to find something you're good at, and I think I know just the thing. You speak German, don't you?"

"How do you know that?"

"You were talking in your sleep last night in German. I'm jealous. My grandparents immigrated from Germany, and they spoke both German and English, but somehow, me being third generation, I got lost in the shuffle and I never learned it. Do you have any German books? Can you teach me?"

"I have a German primer book that my Aunt Annie gave me for my sixth birthday. She told me she never wanted me to lose my heritage. But are you sure you want to learn German? Frankly, I would be scared speaking it now. Wouldn't Americans look at us as traitors?"

"Don't be silly. Speaking German would make me bond

more with the family I still have living in Germany. I pray every day that they will be safe. War does nothing but tear families apart. So, is the book here at the convent?"

"No, it's at my father's house, but I should be able to get it. Sister Francois said if she approved it, we could get anything from home."

"Good. Why don't you get it? Sister Francois is reasonable. I already got permission to get my clarinet. Then we can make a deal. You teach me German, and I will teach Lindsey to read. Just come tonight and stand guard until we know we can trust Lindsey."

"Alright," Emily said.

The following week, with seven days crossed off the calendar and 1,067 days to go, Emily and the other girls moved across the hall to the sewing room. There were ten sewing machines, but Emily knew as much about sewing as she did about knitting, almost nothing. She hoped Sister Peggy would be a better sewing teacher than she was a knitting coach.

"Today we're going to teach you sewing. Once you learn, you'll have the choice of sewing or knitting every day unless we have a job to complete."

"What kind of job?"

"Well, your sewing has two purposes. First of all, we will train you for a job when you leave here. But more importantly, we can sell the things we make, and that income helps us run this place. Right now, we have no orders, so you are free to make a dress for yourself. Take advantage of the time because when Christmas comes, you'll be very busy."

Sister Peggy grabbed a tape measure and yanked Emily's arm to measure it. Then she told her to spread her legs. She reached her fist into Emily's crotch and measured her leg length. Emily's body felt violated as the nun measured her waist and hips and her still developing bust. Why did Sister Peggy have to put her through all that humiliation? Why couldn't she just let her try on clothes to determine her size? "The next step is to pick a dress style." She plopped an enormous book in Emily's hand. "Here, pick out a dress you like, but don't be all day."

Emily settled on a simple red cotton dress with a white collar. "Great choice for a beginner." Sister Peggy took a bolt of red fabric, cut the length of cloth for the dress, and then cut a smaller length of white material for the collar. She handed Emily the cloth and pattern pieces. "Your first job is to pin the material to this pattern and cut the cloth around the pattern. When you finish that step, let me know, and then we will move to the sewing machines."

Emily noticed the immense table where several girls had already spread out their material to cut. She stayed seated to pin the material to the pattern. By the time she finished pinning, some girls had already moved to the sewing machines. Emily began cutting. So far, this was a simple task, although she stopped several times to wiggle her fingers.

Just as she took the last snip, the "bookworms" arrived. Once again, Cora knew exactly what to do. Without coaxing, Cora rummaged through the patterns and material and began pinning and cutting. Boy, Cora really was a jack-of-all-trades, while Emily felt like the master of none.

Sister Peggy steered Emily toward an empty sewing machine against the wall. All the other girls claimed the machines with a window view. This was Emily's punishment for being so slow. She sat patiently as Sister Peggy showed her how to thread the machine and bobbin.

More than a useful tool, the sewing machine was a genuine work of art. It was hand-painted with intricate roses. The first thing Emily noticed was that it had to be hand-cranked with her right hand, leaving her left hand to guide the material through the machine. She was in left-handed heaven. Each stitch she took was perfect. She smiled to herself when all of her right-handed colleagues mumbled under their breaths when they had to rip out a crooked stitch and begin again. It took the entire day for Emily to complete the neck and arm stitches. She found her forte. From now on, she would spend her work hours in the sewing room.

Sister Peggy assigned a bin to Emily and Cora where they could keep their work until they finished. Emily glanced at Cora's work, but it didn't look right. "Cora, I think you made a mistake with your dress. It looks like you cut the skirt down the middle. Did you do that on purpose?"

"No, I didn't," she replied. "I'm making a pair of pants for myself."

"But girls don't wear pants."

"Says who? Pants are much more practical. They don't get caught on things as easily as dresses do, and they keep your legs warm in the winter. And I bet a progressive woman like Alice Paul wears pants."

"I've seen her picture in the newspaper many times, and I've never seen Alice Paul in pants."

"But that doesn't mean she doesn't own them."

Emily realized Cora was right. She thought about her late friend Isabel. She too, wore pants under her dress on that fateful day when they went ice-skating. But to wear just pants without a skirt in public, could she do that? Probably not. Cora was a rebel and someone Emily needed to take lessons from. She didn't want to be like the cowardly lion in *The Wizard of Oz*. As all the girls filed out for dinner, Lindsey came in with a broom and cleaned up the sea of scrap material strewn across the floor, one of his many jobs at the convent.

Before long, Sister Peggy noticed how fast Emily learned to sew. Being left-handed was an asset, but so was the fact that she took her time. Slow and steady wins the race. Emily said this repeatedly in her head as she sewed away. As a result, she never ripped out her stitches and always made them in a straight line. "I am quite pleased with how you are progressing," Sister Peggy said. "How would you like to try sewing on something other than cotton?"

"Why? Aren't all materials alike?"

"No, the materials that make up a fabric affect how you sew them. For example, silk is very slippery when you thread it through the machine, making it hard to stay in a straight line. And if you have to rip out the seam because it is crooked, the material will have holes. Then there is chiffon. It is important to keep the stitches straight here too, because if you veer too close to the edge, the material will fray. Not everyone can master it, but I think you are ready to work on both materials. Do you want to try?"

Emily looked around at the other seamstresses. Of the 15 girls in the room, only two girls were good enough to work with silk and chiffon; Emily would be the third. "Yes," Emily said, with a beaming smile on her face. Even Cora could not work with silk or chiffon, although Cora could sew pleats better than anyone in the room.

Evenings were the best time of day at the convent. When Emily's German primer book arrived two months later, she couldn't wait to teach Cora German. It made her feel so proud; it was the second topic that Emily actually knew more about than Cora. Cora was a fast learner. She devoured the entire book in no time at all and the girls would converse in German. Sometimes they talked about the day's activities or politics or something as silly as how to fold the laundry, anything for Cora to perfect her German.

Other evenings Emily listened to Cora play her clarinet. She played "The Clarinet Marmalade Blues" and "The Skeleton Jangle" beautifully. Cora also accompanied Sister Francois while she taught formal dances like the Tango and The Hesitation Waltz, but Emily's favorite was the Grizzly Bear. She loved the dips and the hand motions that made her feel like a bear.

"You play the clarinet beautifully. You make it look so easy," Emily said to Cora.

"Do you want me to teach you how to play? Trust me, it's easy."

"But I'm left-handed."

"Is that your excuse for everything? It doesn't matter. You use both hands equally to play. Here, put your right thumb under the bridge and blow."

Emily reluctantly put her thumb under the bridge and blew, but no sound came out. Cora laughed. "You're not puckering right." Cora changed the angle of the clarinet until it was up tight against the back of Emily's teeth. "Now blow."

A pitiful sound bellowed out on Emily's first try. She learned a few notes, but she could never quite perfect it. While Cora's tone sounded like velvet, Emily's sounded more like fingernails on a blackboard. It just seemed simpler to let Cora play while Emily mastered her dancing skills with the other girls. She wondered if she would ever meet a man to dance with. Before she knew it, Cora's chart reflected they had been in the convent for 555 days, more than halfway through their confinement.

As time moved on, the dance nights became less frequent, as Cora spent more time with Lindsey. After their reading lessons were over, sometimes they would gravitate toward the garage and talk. Emily would try to read a book but found watching them more interesting. There would be Cora, boldly wearing the pants that she had made, puffing on a cigarette she shared with Lindsey. Emily watched Lindsey show Cora how to blow smoke rings. Another time he lifted the hood of the convent's Ford, showing Cora the engine. This wasn't right. Didn't Cora know enough already? Did she really have to learn about cars too? Emily was so jealous of their friendship; she just wished Lindsey would go away.

One night, when Cora and Lindsey deserted her, Emily finished the last ten pages of her book, *The Wizard of* Oz. She became so bored she didn't know what to do with herself. She thought about Cora and how bold she was, not afraid to try anything new. What could she do to be daring like Cora? Or adventurous like Dorothy? And then it came to her. Like Dorothy, she would pull back the green curtain and see how the Sisters of St. Mary's lived. This would be suicide if she got caught. But how good would it feel bragging to Cora about it?

Emily crept up to the third floor, pausing at the curtain. Peeking around it, and seeing no one, she stepped inside, keeping the curtain drawn. The doors on this side were a carbon copy of the classrooms on the other side, except each room housed one nun. A sign on the first door read Sister Francois, but the room was dark, so Emily moved on to the next one. The next sign read Sister Peggy, her sewing teacher, and the light was on. Emily crept in front of the door, peering in. With her habit draped over the drying rack, Sister Peggy sat on her bed in her bloomers, reading *The Amazing Interlude* by Mary Roberts Rinehart. This shattered two misconceptions about nuns that Emily had believed for years: that nuns don't spend all day reading the Bible and they actually have hair on their heads. And Sister Peggy's was totally gray. Emily gasped.

"Who's there?" said Sister Peggy.

Emily wanted to hightail it out of there, but the long empty hallway left her vulnerable for detection. She spotted the dumbwaiter next to Sister Peggy's room, squeezing herself into it just before Sister Peggy came out into the hallway. Emily waited to hoist the rope down to the first floor until she heard the door of Sister Peggy's room close. With her heart still pounding, Emily felt lucky to be alive as she returned to her room. She never told a soul about her experience, not even Cora. The dumbwaiter became her secret hiding place when she wanted to read in peace.

One day in January 1918, with 255 days left on Cora's calendar, Sister Francois barreled into the sewing room with a look of panic on her face. "Everyone, stop what you're doing. Rebecca Williams is missing. We need everyone to help find her. I don't think she left the convent; her boots and coat are still here." Rebecca was one of the bookworms. Emily hardly knew her, but she knew what she looked like with her red hair.

All the girls and the nuns spread out and searched every inch of the convent, but to no avail. After about an hour, Sister Francois said, "I guess I better call the police."

"Did anyone think to look in the dumbwaiter?" said Emily.

"The dumbwaiter?" With that, Sister Francois opened the door and found Rebecca sitting in the dumbwaiter, studying her social studies book with a flashlight.

"Didn't you hear us calling you? Why didn't you answer us?" said Sister Francois.

"I'm trying to study for my test. This was the quietest place I could find. I guess I lost track of time. When I heard you calling, I thought it was funny, so I didn't answer you."

"Well, young lady, it wasn't funny at all. You had me scared half to death. Get yourself to confession."

"Yes, ma'am. But how did you know I was in here?"

"That's a good question. Emily, how did you know?"

Emily couldn't say that she hid in there to avoid a confrontation with Sister Peggy, so she said, "I don't know. It just seemed like a good place to hide."

The encounter changed Sister Francois. She got stricter, more worried about her charges. Her words became sharper, and she made negative comments like, "The toilets are backed up. You'll have to use the latrines" or "No free time tonight. We didn't make our quota on making shirts." The girls began calling her the Grim Reaper behind her back. However, Sister Francois pleasantly surprised the girls when she said, "Girls, we have a surplus of chickens, so we're going to have a chicken pickin' party on Saturday." Emily thought that sounded like fun.

So on Saturday, June 22, 1918, with 77 days left on Cora's calendar, Lindsey set up tables outside with red and white checkered tablecloths. Sister Francois hired a band, and the girls feasted on hot dogs, potato salad, baked beans, and watermelon. They ran potato sack and three-legged races. Emily was having fun, but she didn't know what any of this had to do with chickens.

"Alright girls, it's time to start the party. Each of you go into the chicken coop and pick out a chicken. Then come back here and sit on the grass in front of Lindsey," said Sister Francois. Emily was glad they were in the coop. It made them much easier to catch.

With all the girls sitting in front of Lindsey with their chickens, Emily noticed a hatchet stuck in a big wooden block. Sister Francois said, " I have a blue ribbon for the girl who picked the winning chicken. Emily, you go first. Hand your chicken to Lindsey."

"Oh no, you're not going to kill it, are you?"

"Of course. How do you think chicken gets onto your plate?"

Emily knew animals had to be killed to eat them. She remembered seeing the deer hang in the barn on Bill's farm and all the other animals in the icebox that he slaughtered, but she never actually saw one being killed.

She handed her chicken to Lindsey as the band played on. Is this what it was like to be on the Titanic, drowning as the music played? That poor chicken. Emily closed her eyes until she heard the blade hit the wood. When she opened her eyes, the chicken was dancing around the yard without its head. It seemed like an eternity until that chicken dropped dead. "Thirteen seconds. That's the record the rest of you girls need to beat to win the ribbon," said Sister Francois. That was one prize Emily didn't want to win.

Each girl led her chicken to the slaughter. After killing each bird, Lindsey picked them up two at a time and threw them into boiling water. Then the girls plucked off the feathers. This was a tedious job to do by hand. By the time Emily finished, she had a blister on her finger and multiple cuts on her hands. She hoped this was the end of her work because her hands hurt. Fortunately, Lindsey finished the job gutting the chickens and bagging them. He kept three for the convent and drove the rest to the store to sell.

Cora won the blue ribbon. Her chicken lasted 37 seconds. She claimed the blue ribbon but threw it out that night, declaring that she was a vegetarian and would never eat meat again. In the morning, it was all forgotten as Cora ate sausage and eggs for breakfast.

Just a few days after the chicken pickin' party, Lindsey developed a hacking cough. Emily thought he got what he deserved with all of his smoking and killing all those chickens, but then he developed a fever and broke out in a sweat. He collapsed right at her feet in the sewing room as he was sweeping up the scraps. Sister Francois and Sister Peggy picked him up and laid him on the couch in his apartment above the convent garage, while Sister Erma called the doctor. Doctor Cummings diagnosed the Spanish Flu. Emily knew it was rampant in the area, but no one except Lindsey ever left the convent. They lived in a perfect bubble that had kept out the flu, but now that bubble had burst.

Doctor Cummings ordered all the residents of the convent to isolate in their rooms for two weeks, except for Cora. Her exposure was greater than anyone else's, so she volunteered to take care of Lindsey, wearing a face mask. Two days later, Lindsey coughed up some blood and had trouble breathing. Despite Cora's nursing of Lindsey, he died the next day. Emily felt so guilty for being jealous of Lindsey and Cora's friendship. She prayed the rosary every day while in quarantine, asking God for forgiveness and to watch over Cora. She concluded there must be something to the power of prayer because the only other person who caught the Spanish flu was Cora, and her case was no more than the sniffles.

In her last month in the convent, a letter arrived for Emily from her mother. She didn't know what to think. Her father visited her twice and wrote often, but this was the first contact with her mother in the almost three years that Emily lived here.

She tore open the envelope, giving herself a paper cut on her finger. She licked the wound as she read the letter.

July 5, 1919

Dear Emily:

I hope this letter finds you well. We all enjoyed a fireworks display yesterday, except for your baby sister, Helen. And I mean, baby. The loud noise made her scream like a banshee, and she covered her ears throughout the entire show. All the neighbors stared at us. I don't think she'll be ready for school anytime soon.

Your brother continues to sneak the booze. Bill thinks he is turning into an alcoholic. He will be out of here on his 18th birthday. Bill says he needs to be a man.

Bill's butcher business is very successful. He hired a few employees and bought a truck for deliveries. We talked it over, and we decided that under the circumstances, we think it best that you do not come here to live. Besides, you are an adult and need to find your way in the world.

I don't think you'll be able to run to your father for help, either. Besides, I don't know where that no-good bum is. I tried to serve him with divorce papers, and they got returned to me because he moved again.

Good luck to you in your future. Remember, even though you won't be living here, you will always be welcome for a visit.

Your loving mother

Your loving mother? There was nothing loving about this diatribe. Bill this and Bill that. Doesn't she have an opinion about anything? Mama clearly has no use for Papa. A divorce? Where would Emily go? She returned the letter to its envelope and tossed it into the smoldering fire as a tear formed in her eye.

"Is everything alright?" Emily turned around; Cora stood right behind her.

"No. It's not. My mother said I'm not welcome when I get out of here. Where will I go?"

"Believe it or not, I have no place to go, either. I mean, I do, but my parents moved to West Virginia so my father could get a job in a coal mine. I can't live there. It's way too far from the city."

"I know how much you like the city. Isn't there anyone else in the city you could live with?" asked Emily.

"I have a grandmother who lives there whose mobility has declined in recent years. I thought she could help me out financially and I could help her out with the cleaning and shopping, but she wants no part of it. I don't think she is ready yet to admit she needs help. Grandma says I cannot live with her, although I am welcome to visit anytime. What do you say we get jobs and share an apartment?"

"Do you mean it?"

"Of course I do."

"That sounds like a perfect solution." Emily looked forward to spending more time with her good friend.

Pierce Street
1919

Armed with Sister Francois's letters of recommendation and the confidence of experienced seamstresses, Emily and Cora spotted the "Help Wanted" sign in the garment factory window and applied for the job. The girls trudged up the narrow steps, one behind the other to the employment office on the third floor. About halfway up they met a woman coming down. As there was no room to pass her, they marched all the way back down. When the girl passed, the girls proceeded up to the third floor.

Stopping on the landing, the girls paused to stare at rows of men cutting fabric from patterns placed together so tightly on the material that it resembled a jigsaw puzzle. One man placed his finished products on a dumbwaiter and hoisted it up to the fourth floor. Cora nudged Emily to follow her to the employment office door. Cora knocked boldly on the door.

"Come in." The girls entered the small office of one Paul Wainwright, proprietor, or so read the sign on the water-stained desk, littered with mounds of paper. Mr. Wainwright stood up. He was a little man, his head just an inch shorter than Emily's head. He had been chewing on his cigar for so long that the excess moisture was disintegrating the cigar and making his bushy mustache glisten. "Can I help you?"

"We're here about the seamstress positions. We come with references." Cora handed the owner the letters of recommendation from her worn satchel.

As Mr. Wainwright perused the letters, Emily spotted a woman with thick glasses and a tight bun busily typing away. "I see you come with top honors. But let's see how you can work. Edith, get us some material for these girls to practice on."

"Yes sir, Mr. Wainwright." Edith opened the closet and rolled a heavy sewing machine into the room. She then brought out some pre-cut fabric.

"One position will be to pleat and sew the front, and the other is to sew on the sleeves. You decide who goes first and which job," said Mr. Wainwright.

Emily looked at this sewing machine; it differed from the one she used to at the convent. For one thing it had a foot pedal instead of a hand crank. Emily thought that this could be a good thing because guiding the material with two hands might speed up her sewing. But would the foot pedal make the material feed through too fast? She also hoped that Cora would take the pleating job since she was still the best at sewing pleats.

Cora spoke up. "I am an amazing seamstress, and it just so happens that pleats are my speciality."

"Alright, let's see how you do." Cora folded her pleats like an accordion and then masterfully stitched them together while Emily eyed the amount of pressure Cora placed on the foot pedal. She was confident that with little pressure on the pedal, the speed would be the same. "Excellent job, Cora. Now it's your turn, Emily," Mr. Wainwright said.

Despite being nervous, Emily took her time and sewed the sleeve together in a perfectly straight line. She held up the finished product with a smile on her face.

"We are hiring both of you for your great work. You'll work a

12-hour day from 6:00 AM to 6:15 PM with a 15-minute lunch that you provide yourself. You are expected to complete a quota of 60 sleeves or pleats in an hour, or you will be required to stay later until you finish them. Your pay is six dollars a week. I will see you bright and early tomorrow, and I suggest you tie up your hair in a bun so that it doesn't get caught in any machines."

Emily thought that the way Mr. Wainwright rattled off those rules so quickly, he must have said them so many times before. Was everything in the factory based on speed? Emily's secret to sewing successfully was because she took her time. Slow and steady wins the race. Could she sew 60 sleeves in an hour?

Down in the street, the girls hugged each other, proud of landing their first jobs. Next on the agenda- finding a place to live. They found a furnished one-room apartment that looked perfect. The full-size bed hugged one wall, with a sheet hung to separate it from the other half of the room that doubled as a parlor and kitchen. Emily was delighted to find out that the apartment already had electricity and running water. But when they heard the rent was twelve dollars, they knew it was out of their price range. Paying for it would require both their full salaries, leaving no money for food and other living expenses.

The girls ventured further into the poorer side of town until they stumbled upon a rooming house with a vacancy sign in the window. From the outside, the rooming house looked impressive. The brick house stood on a corner lot. It had a turret on the top resembling a medieval castle. They proceeded up the stone path to the front door until they could read the fine print on the vacancy sign. The rent was only four dollars a week, which was more in line with their price range. They noticed a cracked window next to the front door. As Cora rang the doorbell, a cockroach crawled out from under the doormat. Emily turned around to leave when Cora grabbed her.

"Come on, Emily. First impressions can be deceiving. Let's check out the house. We can afford this rent."

Emily knew Cora was right, so she patiently waited until the house matron opened the door. An intimidating woman, who stood well over six feet tall and wore a black cotton dress with a row of gold buttons down the front, greeted them. Emily thought she looked like a prison matron. All that was missing was a badge to complete the image.

"Can I help you?" she said.

"We were wondering if we might have a look at the house. We need a place to rent," Cora said.

"Follow me. At one time I used to live here with my husband and nine children, but the children have moved out and my husband has passed on. I thought the best thing to do was to upgrade my home into a rooming house," the matron explained as the threesome entered what used to be the parlor.

Emily thought "upgrade" was a terrible choice of words; downgrade was more like it. Men and women shared the converted parlors as sleeping quarters together. Two-by-four bed frames held thin mattresses. Some boarders had placed nails above their beds to hang clothes, while others stored the clothes in laundry bags at the foot of the bed, further cementing Emily's image of a penitentiary. There would be no privacy here.

In the kitchen, the girls found a single light bulb hanging by a wire from a peeling plaster ceiling. There was a water source in the sink and a four-burner stove for cooking. The table had six chairs around it, but with all the laundry hanging to dry, only two people could sit there at a time. The room lacked an icebox. Emily thought it was a plus that there was a food market next door since they would have to buy their food daily and store it in their own assigned cabinet with a lock and key. The building still had outdoor latrines and a running shower that each boarder could use once a week.

"What do you think, Em? Should we take it?"

"It's not spacious, but at least it's clean; I don't see any rat droppings. Only that one cockroach."

"Is that a yes?"

"Yes."

The girls signed the lease, and the landlord assigned them their beds. They left their clothes on the bed and went to the food market. They established an account to buy on credit and purchased carrots, beans, potatoes, and cabbage to make a soup for dinner, some bread and cheese for lunch, and oatmeal for breakfast. Cora locked her clarinet into the cabinet with the food.

There was no schedule on kitchen time, so the girls had to wait for a free stove burner. It was eight o'clock by the time they had gathered the water, cut the vegetables, cooked, ate their dinner, and cleaned up.

With no privacy in the room, the girls changed into their pajamas under the blankets and went right to bed. Cora set the alarm for 4:30. Between all the conversations going on and the snoring, it was well after midnight before Emily fell asleep.

The next morning, about ten minutes before the alarm went off, Emily laid in bed. Her brain and legs were still asleep, but her bladder wasn't. She staggered to the bathroom in her bare feet, proud to be the first in line. Returning to the sleeping quarters, Emily saw Cora was still asleep. She didn't have the heart to wake her, so she shook her gently. "Cora, you take an extra ten minutes' sleep. I'll make the lunches today, and then tomorrow we'll switch."

Cora mumbled yes as Emily dressed into her clothes under her blanket. Emily sat up and swung her feet over the bed, blindly trying to find her shoes, but they weren't there. "Where are my shoes?"

Emily didn't realize how loudly she said it until three residents, including Cora, sat up. "Sorry, Emily. I'll make the sandwiches today to give you time to find them."

"Thanks, Cora." Emily watched Cora leave the room, and then she rummaged under the bed looking for her shoes.

"You know you won't find them, don't you?" said the voice in the bed across the room.

"How do you know?"

"You're new here. If you want to keep your shoes, you need to sleep in them."

"Are you trying to tell me that somebody stole them?"

"If the shoe fits."

"Very funny." But Emily didn't think it was funny. She reached to the bottom of her bag for her old pair of shoes with the floppy sole. She removed a string from one of her corsets, using it to hold the sole on tight, and made her way to the kitchen.

Cora hadn't made the sandwiches yet. She had to wait in line behind the other boarders before she could get near the table. The girls waited another ten minutes, and each made her own lunch of a cheese sandwich and an apple to save time. "I think we better get up earlier tomorrow. We'll probably be late for our job on the first day," Emily said. Cora nodded.

Despite walking quickly, the girls arrived five minutes late for work, and Edith greeted them with a stopwatch in her hand. "You girls are off to a less than stellar start. Each of you will have five cents deducted from your pay for being five minutes late. Hang your lunch pails and jackets on a peg and I'll take you upstairs."

Besides the coat hooks, the rest of the first floor had a cafeteria-style table and two bathrooms, one for the ladies and one for the gentlemen. Emily was glad to see that they had flush toilets. The girls hung their coats and followed Edith up the narrow stairs. On the second floor, the drapers, both male and female, were hard at work making patterns. On the third floor, the cutters, all male, were already pinning patterns to the material.

When they reached their destination on the fourth floor, the supervisor assigned each girl a sewing machine around the perimeter of the large room. In the middle of the room sat the clippers, diligently cutting away the loose threads from the finished products. Some of them looked no older than ten years old. These girls, like Emily, would also be denied an education, and she felt sorry for them.

Remembering her quota, Emily got right to work. It was a tedious job. By lunchtime, her back hurt from leaning forward, her ears hurt from the drone of the sewing machines, and her throat and mouth hurt from inhaling the fabric dust in the air.

All the women on the fourth floor ate together. Maneuvering her way through the crowd to join Cora felt like threading a needle. They were the last two to file out past the dour-faced Edith. Didn't she ever smile?

Fifteen minutes would pass quickly, so the girls spent no time talking. Emily noticed one of the ten-year-old girls crying when she was almost done with the first half of her cheese sandwich. She promptly put her arm around her like a mother hen. "What's the matter?" The girl stared down at her uneaten sandwich, still sitting on the brown wrapping paper with rat dung running through it. "Oh honey, didn't you have it in a lunch pail with a lid? You should have figured there would be rodents around here."

"I didn't know," said the girl, with tears welling in her eyes.

Cora came to the rescue. "Here, take half of my sandwich."

"Oh, thank you. You are so kind," the girl said, with a smile returning to her face.

Emily broke half of her remaining sandwich and handed it to Cora. Emily thought about Cora's kindness. She was an amazing friend, always thinking of others. They finished the sandwich and their apples when Cora noticed all the girls waiting in line to use the bathroom. "Come on, we better get in line," Cora said, joining the queue.

But just when it was their turn, lunch was over. Edith was hustling the girls back to work. What would they do? If they stayed to use the bathroom, Edith would dock them another five cents each for being late. Cora decided to wait while Emily went back to work. It was still early in the day. Could she hold it until 6:15? Probably not. Surely, she would allow her a bathroom break later.

Somewhere around 2:30, Emily couldn't wait any longer; she

had to use the restroom. She approached Edith, guarding the exit like it was Fort Knox.

"Where do you think you're going?" Edith said.

"I need to use the restroom. It's an emergency. Is that allowed?"

"Of course. But I am setting a timer. If you are not back in five minutes, that will be another five cents coming off your pay."

Emily darted down the three flights of stairs to the first level. She guessed that took two minutes off the clock. It would be at least another two minutes back up and that only left her one-minute to do her business and wash her hands. This was an impossible task. She tried her best, but when she met Mr. Wainwright coming down between the second and third floor, she had to retreat and let him pass before she could proceed back up.

She returned to Edith, who informed her that she was three minutes late and would be docked another five cents. No wonder all the girls were in the line at lunchtime. She vowed she would be first in line tomorrow.

By the end of the day, almost everyone was done by 6:15, but not Emily. She looked around; only two other girls had not met their quota. It took Emily another 20 minutes to finish. When she left, massaging her aching back, the other two girls were still working. Emily felt delighted that she wouldn't be the last one to finish.

When she got home, Cora had already cooked dinner. Emily did the dishes. That was the rule while they lived together. Whoever cooked, the other one cleaned up. Just as she finished, she heard the sweet sound of Cora's clarinet. But this wasn't the fun-loving dancing group of the convent. No one got up to dance. Emily thought if she started dancing, the others would join in. They did not. One man reading his newspaper said, "Stop that racket!"

Cora, being the sweet girl that she was, honored his request.

She locked the clarinet back in the cabinet. Emily wondered when Cora would ever play again.

It took the next few days to perfect their routine. The girls started making their sandwiches at night; they were never late again. Emily brought a pillow to sit on to help her back. Cora and Emily shoved cotton balls in their ears for earplugs. After all, they didn't want to lose their hearing. They also wore handkerchiefs across their noses and mouths to prevent inhaling tiny fabric fibers, and they ate their lunches sitting outside in the fresh air on the fire escapes. Emily thought about the Triangle factory fire that killed several workers a few years earlier. Because the doors were locked, the young girls couldn't escape. Cora believed this type of accident would be unlikely here because they kept the doors open, and the risk was minimal due to Mr. Wainwright chewing his cigars more than smoking them.

But the one problem that still persisted, was the excessive line at the bathroom at lunchtime. Emily got docked ten more cents before she came up with a solution- she just wouldn't use the bathroom. She created a makeshift diaper out of rags and simply urinated in her underpants. Of course, this created an extra job at night washing out the rags, but this was better than losing any more of her hard-earned money.

About three months later, Emily noticed a new job posting, this time for a draper. The position paid ten dollars a week. "Cora, look at this. If you take that job, we can move into a one-bedroom apartment and out of that horrible rooming house."

"Em, I don't think I qualify. That is skilled labor."

"I beg to differ. I seem to remember you taking those dress patterns at the convent and turning them into pants all by yourself."

"You're right. I'll give it a shot. But I'm not promising I will pass Mr. Wainwright's test."

But pass it, she did. The girls moved into their one-bedroom apartment with a new roommate- the sweet sound of the clar-inet. But with the increase in rent, there was still little money left over to buy meat at 18 cents a pound. Many nights, the girls ate a meatless dinner and poor nutrition ensued.

One day, Emily woke with a toothache. A dentist was out of the question. She nursed it by gargling and filling up on aspirin. The pain didn't subside until the molar fell out. Emily was in tears. She tried to put a big smile on her face and looked at her image in the mirror. She twisted her face at every angle and found she could still smile with no one seeing the missing tooth.

Watching Emily struggle with her tooth loss infuriated Cora. "You know, Em, there is something wrong with a society that doesn't help women enough. Why do men get paid more for their work? There is no skill in cutting patterns at the factory, but those men make more than I do as a draper. It's simply not fair. But I have an idea. My parents still have a membership at the Elks Club. Why don't we go there on dance nights to meet some men? We can find some amiable gentlemen too, and they can pay for our dinners."

Emily liked the idea. But dating? She had no experience with men. In fact, she couldn't recall the last time she talked to a boy her own age. Maybe it was time to try. "Alright as long as we double date. I might be a little awkward with men."

"I'm sure you'll be fine." Cora picked up the newspaper, shuffling through it to the social page. "Look, there is a dance tonight."

This was an occasion for her best dress. Emily wore her blue dress with the lace collar and pleated front. She spent extra time combing her long hair. Should she wear a braid or leave it straight and loose? Should she wear a bow? Gloves? She glanced at Cora, clad in a short sleeve burgundy dress with fringe on the front and long black gloves that reached halfway up between the elbow and shoulder. She had a matching burgundy headband. Emily immediately let her hair down, discarding the bow. "Do you have a headband I can borrow that might match my blue dress?"

"Of course." Cora fished through a small box with miscellaneous necklaces and headbands, pulling out a blue headband that would suffice. Emily wondered where Cora got the money to buy such niceties. In her own practical world, Emily would have spent money on meat, not jewelry and headbands. The girls wore no make-up. At least, that was a luxury that the girls agreed they could go without.

When the girls opened the doors of the Elks Club, live music greeted them. Walking down a long corridor garnished with pictures of past and present members, they soon came upon the action in the grand ballroom. Some couples were already on the dance floor. Many men hovered around the bar in the back of the room. There was a plethora of round tables with wooden chairs. The men sat alone on one side of the room, while the women gathered on the opposite side. The tables in the middle were designated for couples. Emily wondered if the duos came together or hooked up for the evening. Cora grabbed Emily by the elbow, steering her toward an empty table on the women's side.

The girls enjoyed three songs before two men wearing gray suits with black bow ties and top hats approached their table. Both were the same height and had round faces with oversized jutting ears. They had huge smiles, showing off their perfect white teeth. Emily, feeling self-conscious, thrust her tongue into the empty tooth socket.

"Would you ladies like to dance?" one man said.

"We would love to," Cora said, taking one man's hand. Emily took the arm of the other gentleman, and they were off to the dance floor. The girls were skilled dancers, keeping up every step with their partners. Sister Francois's dance lessons paid off.

At the end of several dances, the foursome took a table in the middle of the room. Here is where the courting began. What would Emily say? But she needn't have worried. One boy did most of the talking. "I am Ronald Bennett, and this is my brother, Donald." That much was obvious.

"What do you do for a living?" asked Cora.

"I'm a car salesman, and my brother here is an accountant. How about you ladies?"

"We work at the shirt factory," the girls said simultaneously.

Ronald told amusing stories about his customers. The funniest one was about a lady who wanted to add a second steering wheel for her poodle to drive. Donald, the younger brother, had little to add to the conversation. Emily wasn't sure if he had nothing interesting to say about his job, or more likely, with a loquacious older brother, he couldn't get a word in edge wise.

"Well, what do you think?" asked Cora later in the bathroom.

"Ronald is great. He is marriage material, but Donald is a dud; no personality."

"Let's call him Mr. Personality," Cora said giggling.

By the end of the night, it was clear they would set up a double date for tomorrow night. It was also clear that Emily would be stuck with Mr. Personality.

The next day, Cora told Emily that she had to go into New York City to visit her grandmother, who was in the hospital with a broken hip.

"Oh Cora. What about our double date tonight?"

"Don't worry. I'll be back in plenty of time."

Cora took the bus into New York City and began the grueling walk to Mt. Sinai Hospital. A commotion was brewing at the Metropolitan House. A group of women and one brave man had gathered, blocking the sidewalk. They held banners that read "Wilson is Against Women" and "President Wilson

How Long Do You Advise Us to Wait?" Cora mingled into the crowd. This was a suffragist group that she always wanted to be a part of. Why shouldn't she have the right to vote like men, and why did men get higher salaries than women? Was that Alice Paul holding the biggest sign? She wished she had her clarinet; maybe playing it would attract more people to the cause.

Suddenly the police stormed the crowd, trampling the women and destroying their banners. Cora shoved a police officer after he violently shoved Alice Paul to the ground. As she helped Alice up, the police officer arrested her, along with Alice Paul and three other women. A paddy wagon drove up to take the women away. Cora felt mortified to be arrested again. But this time, she was an adult. Would they send her to an adult women's prison? She started shaking. Maybe Alice Paul would know a way out of this quandary.

"Don't worry, honey. Everything will be fine," Alice Paul said as she put her arm around Cora.

"That's easy for you to say. You're famous. You'll never go to jail. I'm just a little nobody."

"No, you're not a nobody. You're an American hero. Thanks for saving me back there. And the women's rights movement thanks you too. Does this little nobody have a name?"

"I'm Cora." The van hit a bump, and Cora hit her head on the roof. "Ouch! You don't understand. I cannot be arrested; I'm an adult now."

"Well, so am I. What does that have to do with anything?"

"I avoided jail before because I was underage. But this time? I'm not so sure."

"Oh honey. I'm sure nothing will happen to you."

"How can you be so sure?"

"Because I have a history of being arrested."

"You have?"

"Yes. Several times. Trust me. I know how this works. They can't hold us; we did nothing wrong. They'll put us in a cell for a little while until they calm down and then they'll let us go."

Alice was so confident as she spoke. Cora hoped some of it would wear off on her.

The van arrived in front of the precinct. A police officer opened the back door of the van, letting the cool air rush in. "Let's go, ladies," he said.

The women filed out of the wagon in single file, with Cora being the last one out. The officer abruptly slammed the door shut. Cora took a quick sidestep to avoid her skirt getting caught in the door. She looked at the front of the line and saw the first woman fall. But with her arms behind her back locked in hand-cuffs, she had nothing to break her fall. An officer helped her up, and she was bleeding from her nose. When Cora reached the steps leading up to the jail, she was determined not to meet the same fate. She kept her eyes down and walked slowly until she successfully reached the apex.

Another officer, or was it the same one? Cora wasn't sure. They all looked alike in their tight uniforms and handlebar mustaches. He removed the women's handcuffs, shoving them into an overcrowded cell, like cattle being led to the slaughter.

There were two beds with thin mattresses. Four women were already sitting on each of the beds, forcing the rest to stand or sit on the filthy floor. Cora wondered what their offenses were. Some looked like prostitutes, but most looked just like her, young and afraid.

A windowless brick wall lined the back of the cell, while the other three walls held bars. A chamber pot sat in the corner, with the putrid smell of urine permeating the air. There was not an ounce of privacy. Suddenly Cora felt like she had to relieve herself, but she had gone only an hour earlier at the bus termi-nal. She convinced herself that it was only psychological.

With none of the women engaging in conversation, Cora's mind wandered. What would her grandmother or Emily think when she didn't show up? Would they worry? Call the police? She shuddered just thinking about it.

It felt like an eternity in that cell, but in reality, it was probably just over an hour when the clanking of the key in the lock set them free. "You, you, you, you, and you, get out of here," said the officer as he pointed at Cora, Alice, and the other women arrested with them. Cora scooted out of the cell before he could change his mind.

Outside, Alice patted Cora on the back. "See, I told you so. Nothing to worry about. Now, how about dinner? My treat. I need to repay you for your kindness."

Cora knew she should decline. The clock on the courthouse across the street read 5:00. If she hurried, she might just make it home in time to join Emily and the twins for their double date. But this was Alice Paul. A once in a lifetime opportunity. Clearly Emily would understand. "Yes, I would love that," Cora said quickly, before she had time to talk herself out of it.

Dinner was at Delmonico's. The four marbled columns and red awnings at the restaurant's entrance looked expensive. Cora was glad Alice was paying.

"I know what you're thinking. It is high-priced, but it is the only place in town that allows unescorted women to enter its premises. That is one thing the women's suffrage movement is trying to change. Why should we have to have a man with us in order to eat at restaurants?"

The maitre'd led the ladies to a table for two on the third floor and handed them menus. The inside of the restaurant was as elegant as the outside. Golden sconces with lit white candles covered the walls. The ambiance extended to the tables, each covered with a spotless white tablecloth and a candle centerpiece.

"So tell me about yourself. How did you get arrested as a child?"

"I stole some bread and *wiener schnitzel* from the local market. My family was poor."

"*Sprechen Sie Deutsch?*"

"*Ya*. My grandparents were German immigrants, but I never

got the chance to learn it being third generation until my friend taught me recently."

"Did you know I spent time in Germany growing up?" Alice said.

"No, I didn't."

"Let's converse in German tonight. I need to brush up on it. I don't get to use German often enough. Can you order off the menu in German?" Alice said as she handed Cora the menu.

"*Wurste.*"

"Ah, sausage. I'll have the same," Alice told the waiter when he took their orders.

They chatted all night in German. They debated about who had the best Jewish apple cake recipe and discussed women's rights. When Alice told Cora about her love of music, Cora couldn't help but brag about being pretty darn good at playing clarinet. She talked about playing it at the convent while the other girls learned to dance. She felt so comfortable with Alice that she had to say, "Do you mind if I ask you a personal question?"

"Fire away."

"Do you own pants? I've never seen a picture of you in them, and my friend and I were wondering if you had them."

"Of course I do. What modern woman doesn't own them? But I only wear them at home. I think it is best to dress like a lady when I am protesting for women's rights. The rest of the world may not be ready to see me in pants." Cora couldn't wait to tell Emily.

As the evening wound down, Cora had an idea. She knew her path would never entwine with the great Alice Paul again. "Do you think I could have your autograph to remember this evening by? My friend will never believe I met you."

"Of course."

Cora rummaged through her purse, searching for anything that Alice could write on, but found nothing. She thought about the cloth napkin on her lap, but the signature would probably fade when she washed it. Scanning the restaurant looking for something suitable to write on, she settled on a menu left absent-mindedly on the next table. "How about this?"

Alice laughed as she signed it and watched Cora stuff it down her bra to smuggle it out of the restaurant. Out in the street, Cora said, "Thank you for a lovely evening, Alice."

"No, thank you for saving me and helping me brush up on my German. I hope our paths meet again someday."

As Cora walked back to the bus station, she knew they would never meet again. She pulled the menu out of her dress and looked at it again. She would cherish it for the rest of her life. But she realized she might have to part with it as a reconciliation gift to overcome Emily's wrath for standing her up on the double date.

Emily stared at the clock on the living room wall. Where was Cora? The Bennett boys would be here in fifteen minutes. She wanted her friend to help her choose what to wear for her first official date. She settled on her black skirt with the yellow blouse. Its wide low collar hung low over her breasts. Should she cancel the date if Cora doesn't show up? Go out with both men? She wasn't even sure where they were going.

Emily gulped as a loud knock on the door aroused her from her thoughts. "Who is it?" she said.

"It's us. Are you ready?"

Emily opened the door. The brothers wore impeccably dressed in black suits and gray fedoras with black bands. It was hard enough to tell them apart. Did they really have to dress alike? Emily couldn't wait until one of them spoke; then she would know who was who.

"Hey, sunshine. That yellow blouse brings out your brown eyes."

What a smooth talker; that was clearly Ronald. "Hey,

Ronald, Donald." Each man tapped their hat as she called their names.

"Where is Cora?" asked Ronald.

"I don't know. She hasn't come home yet. I think maybe we should cancel."

"You don't have to do that. The three of us can have fun. We'll be outside the entire time if you are worried about our intentions," Ronald said. Didn't Donald ever talk?

"Where are we going, anyway?"

"It's a surprise, but trust me, you'll like it. Bring a sweater. It might be cold outside where we're going."

The men looked respectful, and Emily wanted to go. She took her sweater off the rack, convincing herself that if this evening ended badly, she would kill Cora. She'd better have a good excuse for standing her up.

Emily followed the men to their green 1915 Chevrolet Royal Mail parked in front of her apartment building. "Wow, that looks like a race car," Emily said. Donald opened the long hood, cranking the car into action. She looked up and down the street hoping to show off to one of her neighbors, but no one was near. Emily slid into the leather seat, sandwiched between Donald and Ronald as the car roared up the block.

Buttoning her sweater and rubbing her hands to fend off the cold air atop the Brooklyn Bridge, Emily enjoyed the view. "Can I guess where we are going?"

"Sure," said Ronald.

"Are we going to Steeplechase Amusement Park?"

"I guess I can't surprise you. It's so much fun. Everyone needs to go a few times a year," Donald said.

"Absolutely," Emily said. She would never admit that this was a dream of hers; she had never been there in her entire life. This was a luxury her parents simply couldn't afford. She was determined to have a great time with or without Cora. Where was she, anyway?

Emily didn't mind the long queue to enter the park because

it gave her time to absorb the elegance of the park. Bright lights on the glass ceiling shone down on the patrons as they inched their way up the steps. A view of the ocean made waiting less painful, as did a band dressed in red jackets with green collars and cuffs playing "The Grizzly Bear." Emily couldn't help but move her feet in time to the music.

"Do you want to dance, Emily?" Ronald asked.

"No, but thanks for asking. I don't want to get out of line."

"This is your day, Emily. Where do you want to go first then? Skating? Rides? Eating? Or the arcade?" Ronald said.

Emily wanted no part of skating. She didn't care if it was roller skating; she was never skating again. "Let's eat first, then the rides. And if we have time, we can stop at the arcade on the way out."

"Your wishes are my command," Ronald said.

Feltman's Cafe was the biggest cafeteria-style restaurant that Emily had ever seen. The trio weaved their way to the empty tables in the center of the room. Emily and Donald inspected them to find a clean one while Ronald went to order their hot dogs and sarsaparilla. Emily tried twice to engage Donald in conversation, asking him about his work and hobbies, but his taciturn personality prevailed. Her only entertainment was watching a young boy trying to take gum off his shoe by scraping it on the chair at the empty table next to her. She felt sorry for the next person who would sit on the chair. When Ronald returned with her meal, Emily inhaled her food, excited as a small child to get on the amusement park rides.

Her first choice was the Steeplechase ride, which included four horses with two riders each, with a track completely encircling the Pavilion of Fun. But how could a group of three ride this? Darn that Cora for standing her up.

"Emily, do you want to ride that?" asked Ronald. He must have read her mind.

"Yes, but how can the three of us ride?" she asked.

"You can ride twice. Once with me, and then I will wait at

the end and you can go back and ride with Donald. Is that okay with you, Donald?" He nodded.

After a brief wait, Emily and Ronald mounted the innermost horse. She sat in the front and Ronald wrapped his arms respectably around her waist. Without warning, a cable lifted all four horses about 20 feet in the air and dropped them onto a wooden track that wound across a miniature lake, through a tunnel, and up and down some hurdles before it stopped. Their horse came in first place, but not by more than a second. To exit this attraction, they had to crawl through a doghouse on their hands and knees. As they stood up, they walked slowly across a stage, enjoying the antics of a cowboy, a farmer, and a dwarf clown. Then, without warning, one compressed air jet blew off Ronald's hat, while another jet blew up Emily's skirt. As Ronald ran for his hat, Emily repositioned her skirt. That is when she noticed an audience roaring with laughter at their mishaps.

"I'm gonna wait here and watch everyone else's reaction as they come off this ride. You go back and ride again with Donald. But don't tell him about the ending. I can't wait to see the expression on his face."

Emily met Donald and rode again. His arms wrapped around her waist, a little too close to her breasts for her liking. When they got to the end, Emily clenched her skirt down when she met the air jets. And Donald was a good sport when his hat went flying.

"Let's find more rides that we can all ride together," Emily said, thinking about her companions.

Despite the long lines, they rode the carousel, the Ferris wheel, the Human Pool Table, the Hoopla, and the Human Niagara before the night ended. They walked through the arcade as the park was closing.

"Look at the kiss-o-meter over there. It measures the intensity of a couple's kiss. You want to give it a try?" Ronald asked Emily.

Emily watched how it worked. A man put his hand firmly

around a handle as he kissed his date. A light moved around different results before it landed on "sexy." As much as she wanted to kiss Ronald, she would never admit to him that she had never kissed a man before, and she didn't want her first kiss to be in public. She needed time to practice first with a mirror in the comfort of her bedroom. What excuse could she muster? "I would love to, but those people are crazy. The Spanish flu is still going around," Emily blurted out as she thought about Lindsey.

"Okay. That makes sense. Maybe another time," Ronald said.

Instantly, Emily regretted the excuse she came up with. Would he ever kiss me now? Would Emily have to wait until the Spanish flu ended? When would that be? She hoped she didn't blow her chances with this nice man.

By the time they returned to Emily's apartment, Cora was home reading a book at the kitchen table. "What on earth happened to you?" Emily asked her friend.

Slamming her book closed, Cora said, "You'll never believe it. I got arrested."

"Arrested? For what?"

"I joined Alice Paul, and we were apprehended fighting for women's rights. But they let us go. I'm sorry I missed our date tonight. Can I have a raincheck?"

"How about next Saturday night? The four of us can go out for dinner. I want to hear more about that story," Ronald said. "Alice Paul? Really?"

Cora hustled Ronald and Donald out the door and turned to confront her friend. "Am I forgiven?"

"Well, that all depends."

"On what?"

"On who dates who. I want Ronald. You can have Mr. Personality," Emily said.

"No, I want Ronald. But I have something that might make you agree to take Donald as your date."

Cora whipped out the Delmonico's menu signed by Alice

Paul. "Look what I have! I'm willing to part with my souvenir if you can bear to part with Ronald for one night. After this you should feel confident to date on your own. No more double dates. What do you say?"

"Cora, are you bribing me?"

"Call it what you want."

"Alright. It is a great keepsake." Emily quickly put the menu in her closet before Cora could change her mind.

"Emily, you're a great friend."

Somehow, Emily thought she got the short end of the stick.

The following weekend, the brothers picked up the girls, and they went out to dinner at the Pirate's Den in the city. Emily was happy with this selection because as Cora and Ronald spoke, she could enjoy the corny sword fighting entertainment to fill in the many lulls in conversation with Mr. Personality. By the end of the evening, Emily could sense a chemistry brewing between Cora and Ronald. By the end of the month, Cora and Ronald became exclusive. By the end of the year, they were planning their marriage, and Emily would have to find another roommate.

Spruce Street
1920

In the months leading up to Cora's wedding, Emily's time was consumed with two tasks- helping Cora make her wedding gown and searching for a new roommate. What started out as a long-sleeved, scoop-neck wedding dress became more and more intricate, as the girls spent hours sewing on lace accents by hand.

Emily believed that no guest should outshine the bride at a wedding, but since pictures would be taken, she also believed that the maid of honor should not look like a pauper "Cora, your dress is so exquisite. It will put any dress I own to shame. When we finish your dress, can you help me make an appropriate dress?"

"What are you talking about? You must have made ten dresses at the convent that were all beautiful."

"Actually, it was six."

"Pardon my mistake. Bring me your best dress, and I bet it will work perfectly."

Emily fished through her closet, picking out her favorite, holding it up for Cora to inspect. Made from a mixture of wool and cotton material, the dusty rose dress had a V-neck with loose quarter sleeves and pearl buttons down the back. The oversized white silk collar had little pink rose buds on it. Emily used a pink whipcord to make a belt and trim the edges of the collar.

"Emily, I love this dress. That whipcord on the collar is so unique. You should be a fashion designer."

"Stop teasing me."

"I'm dead serious. We're going to embroider some little pink roses onto the collar of my wedding dress, and anyone who sees a picture of my wedding with my maid of honor will think a professional made these two dresses together."

"Oh, Cora, you know how to make me feel good," said Emily, hugging her friend.

As the girls sewed, they discussed how to find a roommate for Emily. Emily tried posting an advertisement on the bulletin board at work, but Mr. Wainwright ripped it down, stating that she didn't have permission to post it. Cora assured her she would ask around at work. There must be somebody looking for an apartment.

One week before the wedding, Cora found Emily a new roommate. She told Emily about it on the walk home. "Her name is Henrietta Lansing. She is a young girl I work with. She wants to break away from her parents and live on her own. I think you two will get along just fine. And the best part is she can move in on Sunday."

On the day of Cora's wedding, a crown of daisies arrived from the local florist. The girls promptly sewed the chiffon veil to it and placed it on Cora's head. "You look beautiful," Emily said, with tears in her eyes. She wondered if she would ever get married.

They splurged for the train ride downtown. Patrons congratulated Cora and asked where the groom was. She explained they were meeting him at Town Hall and that the mayor was going to marry them.

Ronald and Donald, together with Mayor Charles P. Gillen,

were waiting for the girls in the lobby of the courthouse. The groom wore a crisp new suit with a pink boutonniere. The nuptials took about ten minutes, and Emily and Donald signed the marriage license as witnesses.

They all celebrated at the Robert Treat Hotel. The lobby touted a high ceiling with marble columns. The newlyweds posed for some pictures in front of the immense fireplace and then meandered into the dining room, which had windows from floor to ceiling. Royalty radiated in the room, with its marble wainscoting and potted plants everywhere. Emily felt like a queen. She ate like a queen too, indulging in an expensive roast beef dinner.

When the evening was over, the newlyweds drove off for a honeymoon somewhere on the Jersey shore; Cora wouldn't say where. Donald offered to escort Emily home, but she politely declined. She couldn't fathom the idea of hearing herself talk with no response from Mr. Personality, and she didn't want to give the impression that she was interested in him.

Arriving home, she found a woman sitting on a valise at her doorstep. "You must be Emily," she said, extending her arm to shake Emily's hand.

"And you must be Henrietta," Emily said, accepting her hand. "You're a day early. I thought you were coming tomorrow."

"I was, but I was hoping to get settled in before work on Monday, and I had to get away from my mother. Is that a problem?"

"No, not at all. Come on in." Emily waved her into the apartment, wondering what the problem was with her mother. But then again, considering the relationship she had with her own mother, Emily wasn't one to pry.

If Henrietta was as young as Cora said, she didn't look the part. She wore her blonde hair pulled back into a tight bun. Her frumpy brown dress and thick eyeglasses made her appear about 40 years old.

"If you don't mind me asking, how old are you?" Emily asked.

"I'm 20."

Only two years older than Emily. But outward appearances can be deceiving. It was what is in the heart that's important. Emily would give her new roommate a chance. She opened the wardrobe and pushed her own clothes to the side, making space for Henrietta to unpack.

Emily watched as Henrietta unpacked, not offering to help. Henrietta took each dress out of the valise and ironed it before hanging it up. Then she lined her shoes carefully in a row, each with its mate. Emily looked at her own side of the wardrobe where she had haphazardly thrown her two pairs of shoes, lying on their sides, looking for mates. Henrietta stood each of Emily's shoes upright,.

In the months that followed, Henrietta's quirks became more apparent. She rose extra early each morning to iron her dress before putting it on. Emily couldn't understand how the dress could be wrinkled hanging in the wardrobe, but Henrietta said she didn't like the little bump the hangers left on the shoulder. She was too much of a neat freak for Emily. Henrietta would never sit on the bed, and she forbade Emily to do it either. And since the bedspread was Henrietta's, Emily had no say in the matter, so she made cushions for the wooden kitchen chairs, and read her books at the table instead of in bed. And the apartment floor got washed every other day whether it needed it or not.

Meals should be an enjoyable time of the day, but for Emily they were torture watching her eat. Henrietta made a ritual of dividing her meat, potato, and vegetables into three separate piles with ample space between each, only taking a bite of one food at a time. Emily loved to watch the expression on Henrietta's face when she buried her green beans into her mashed potatoes and ate them with a piece of meat in one bite.

Emily tried to teach Henrietta how to play Chinese checkers, hearts, poker, and gin rummy, her favorite go-to activities, but it never seemed to work out. Emily couldn't decide if Henrietta was just a slow learner, or she couldn't sit still long enough to learn the rules of the games. Henrietta would often storm off to the park in the middle of a game to go for a jog and come home drenched in sweat, her clothes reeking of body odor. She would leave the dirty clothes in the closet to fester until laundry day, making Emily gag from the smell. If Emily opened the windows to cleanse the apartment of the stench, Henrietta would close them, stating she couldn't sleep with the street noises.

The smell nauseated Emily, but it didn't seem to bother Henrietta or her long line of gentlemen callers. Where Henrietta met these men, Emily couldn't figure out, but Emily spent many nights alone playing solitaire while Henrietta went gallivanting with her beaus.

One night, after reading too long, Emily retired to bed early with a smashing headache. Somewhere around 1:00 in the morning, she woke up to a hullabaloo- cars honking, men yelling at Henrietta. What was going on? Emily staggered to the window, not quite awake. What had Henrietta done? Were they drunk? It was Prohibition, but that meant nothing. Emily had seen many drunks in the street on prior occasions. She couldn't tell what they were saying, but she noticed several lights in the neighborhood go on, one by one. Boy, was Henrietta making a scene. She was afraid that a man might strike Henrietta. Should she call the police? But then, just as suddenly as it began, it ended with Henrietta trekking into the building, while the cars disappeared into the night, leaving a loud backfire in their wake. Emily ran to the bathroom, and when she came back to bed, Henrietta was laying on the couch pretending to be asleep. Being non-confrontational, Emily decided to say nothing.

The next morning, the landlord, Mr. Whitaker, slid a note under the door telling Emily and Henrietta that this was a peaceful neighborhood and he didn't like troublemakers. If they were to cause another disturbance like the one that occurred last night, he would evict them.

Evicted. Emily remembered the time when she, her mother, and her brother were evicted from their apartment. Would that happen again? Could Mr. Whitaker padlock their apartment? As much as she disliked Henrietta, Emily wanted her to stay. Needed her to stay. She couldn't afford to live on her own, not on her salary.

The Catskills
1921

About a month later, Henrietta came home from work with a big announcement. "I'm tired of working at the factory; it's bad for my health," she said, coughing for emphasis. "I answered an ad for a nanny-housekeeper job in the Catskills, and they called me to come for an interview."

It came as no surprise to Emily. This arrangement wasn't working out, and maybe Henrietta felt the same way. Yes, it was time to sever the relationship, but was she ready to find another roommate? Boy, did she miss Cora. The music of the clarinet would feel good right about now. But to her surprise, Henrietta said, "And I want you to come with me to the interview for moral support. Can I borrow your pink dress? I want to make an impression, and none of my dresses look as stunning as yours."

Beaming with pride, Emily didn't know what to think. After all, this was her special dress- the one she made in the convent, the one she wore at Cora's wedding. Could she lend it to a friend? Would she get it back in good condition? If anyone would return it without incident, it would be Henrietta. At least it would be wrinkle-free. After all, Henrietta was the ironing queen. "Yes, you can borrow it as long as you return it. When is the interview?"

"The day after tomorrow."

The girls arrived at a yellow house, accentuated with green shutters. The enclosed porch had a sign hanging on it that read, James Stafford, Attorney-at-Law. "This is the place," said Henrietta.

The aroma from the roses in the rock garden was so strong it made Emily sneeze. Mrs. Stafford greeted Emily and Henrietta at the door, wearing a navy blue serge dress with a high lace collar that covered her entire neck. The shoulders of the dress ran halfway down her arm. The silk belt, tied in a bow, accented her slim waist.

"Hello, Mrs. Stafford. I'm Henrietta, and this is my friend Emily. She came along to keep me company on the bus ride."

"If you can just point me toward the kitchen, I'll get out of your way so you and Henrietta can talk," said Emily.

"It's just through the dining room."

Emily whispered "good luck" to Henrietta as she walked past the mahogany coffee tables and baby grand piano to the dining room. She counted twelve chairs at the dining room table and thought about how much house Henrietta would have to clean. She continued through a swinging door into the kitchen.

Planted in the middle of the black-and-white checkered floor stood a four-year-old boy wearing a white sailor outfit trimmed with a blue tie, putting the finishing touches on a chocolate doughnut. With his mouth still full, he wiped his hands on his shirt and extended his arm to shake Emily's hand. "Hi. I'm James Allen Stafford Jr."

"I'm Emily. Pleased to meet you," Emily said, trying not to giggle. "Oh, my goodness, I'm afraid you have made a mess of your face and your outfit. Come to the sink, let's wash off that chocolate before it sets in your clothes."

Emily removed a dishrag hanging on the stove, dipped it into the soapy water in the sink, and washed off James's face, hands, and shirt. "Now that's better. You look much cleaner. I'm sure your mother won't be angry."

"Thanks, Emily. Can I color you a picture to thank you?"

"Yes, that would be lovely."

James picked up the coloring book and held it close to Emily's face. "You pick the picture."

Emily flipped through the book. "How about this one of the firemen? My papa was a fireman once and I haven't seen him in so long."

As James got to work coloring, Emily tackled the mound of dirty dishes overflowing the sink. She thought that Mrs. Stafford needed a housekeeper in the worst way, and she hoped Henrietta would get the job. Finishing the washing, she placed the clean dishes on the drying rack, and dried two plates. James interrupted her cleaning by throwing a yellow crayon across the room, yelling, "I messed up. This is too hard."

"Wow, calm down little man. What's the problem?"

"I can't color the buttons on the fireman's uniform. They're too small. I went way out of the lines."

"That's easy to solve. Pick up that crayon and let me help you."

With a pout on his face, James stomped across the linoleum floor and scooped up the crayon that had rolled partially under the icebox. He plopped into the chair. "Now what?"

Emily slid a chair next to James, placing the crayon in his hand. She placed her hand firmly around his, and together they steadily colored the remaining buttons on the fireman's uniform. "Thank you. But what about the first two? I went way out of the lines?"

"You're in luck because the uniform is dark blue, and you can color over the yellow with the darker color. Try it."

As James began correcting his mistake, Mrs. Stafford whisked into the kitchen with Henrietta at her heels. "What do we have here? The dishes are washed, and I have never seen JJ sitting so still working on a project. You're hired," Mrs. Stafford said, leaving Emily speechless.

"What about Henrietta? She's the one who wants the job."

"But she has no experience. You have the initiative to take on the dishes without being asked. And as for JJ, he's a rambunctious child. You have a calming effect on him."

Henrietta rushed out of the kitchen, stomping her feet. "Henrietta, wait."

But Emily felt restrained when Mrs. Stafford grabbed her arm. "Let her go. She'll get over it. Do you want the job or not? It pays $3.50 a week with room and board included. You start at 6:00 and work until after the dinner dishes are done, with Sundays and Wednesday evenings off. I'll need you to keep JJ out of my hair and out of Mr. Stafford's office while I teach piano lessons. Let me show you where you would sleep while you think about it."

The attic bedroom was bigger than her entire apartment in New Jersey. The temperature was perfect now in the spring, but what about winter and summer? Then she noticed a small fan and heater stored in the corner. This job would surely be an improvement over the heavy labor at the factory. "I'll take it."

"Good. Let's have some tea in the kitchen. If you wait an hour, you can catch the next bus and not run into Henrietta."

"You've got yourself a deal," Emily said, shaking Mrs. Stafford's hand.

Emily's plan was to return to her apartment, pack up her things, and catch the first bus back in the morning. What would she say to Henrietta? She wouldn't blame her if she never talked to her again. Oh no,- the dress. She wondered if she would ever get it back again. Of course Henrietta would be reasonable, wouldn't she?

She spent the evening packing her clothes, shoes, and keepsakes, deciding to leave all the kitchen items in place. Henrietta never came home all evening; Emily had to come to terms with the fact that she would never see Henrietta or her best dress again.

As Emily unpacked her belongings into the pine wardrobe, she had to do it under the scrutiny of Mrs. Stafford's watchful eyes. Why was she watching her? Was she afraid Emily might steal something? Suddenly Emily thought of Mrs. Larson and the money she had stolen. Mrs. Larson didn't live far from here. Did Mrs. Larson and Mrs. Stafford know each other? Emily realized she was being ridiculous; if Mrs. Stafford knew about the theft, she would never have hired her. Watching Mrs. Stafford anchored to the floor just staring made Emily uncomfortable. Fortunately, it didn't take very long to unpack her few earthly possessions. As she closed the wardrobe door, JJ shoved her from behind. "Here. Take the fireman picture. I finished it."

"It's beautiful! I'm going to hang it right here across from my bed so I can think of my papa every morning when I wake up and look at it. Thank you so much."

Emily fell into the morning routine very quickly, rising at six, gathering the wood from the porch, starting the stove, cooking breakfast, cleaning, and taking JJ to the park. In the afternoons, the music of the piano emanated up the stairs while she entertained JJ in his bedroom. Emily was delighted to have music back in her home, even if it wasn't Cora's clarinet. In the evenings, Emily would cook dinner and serve the Stafford family in the dining room while she ate alone in the kitchen. By the time she put JJ to bed and did the dishes, she was ready for bed herself, only to repeat the same routine the next day.

When Emily's evening off arrived, she asked Mrs. Stafford if there were any dance halls around to have some fun and meet some nice people. "You don't have a car, do you?" Mrs. Stafford asked. Emily shook her head. "Well then, I'm afraid not. Don't forget, you're not in the city anymore. The nearest one is about twenty miles away. But if you want to meet nice people, I have a better idea. In two weeks, we're having an all-day church social. Why don't you come with us?"

Emily thought that was a wonderful idea. "Can I borrow your Montgomery Ward catalog? I need to buy a nice new dress. Do you remember that pink dress that Henrietta wore to the job interview?" Mrs. Stafford nodded. "Well, that was mine. She never returned it."

"Ouch." Mrs. Stafford disappeared into her bedroom and reappeared holding the catalog. She handed it to Emily. "Here. I'm sure you can find a lovely dress."

Emily skimmed through the catalog and couldn't believe her luck. She found a pink dress that looked almost exactly like the one she had loaned to Henrietta. It had the same V-shaped neckline and the same color. The only difference was that it had a front closure and the belt was not braided. She promptly ordered it and prayed that it would arrive in time for the church social.

All that praying didn't work; the dress hadn't arrived on time. Emily stood in front of her wardrobe, trying to decide which dress to wear. Bolder prints were becoming popular, so Emily tried on her only floral-printed dress. It showed a little too much ankle for church. She decided on the more conservative navy blue dress with the white collar. A frumpy looking woman stared back at her in the mirror; this would not attract any male callers. Emily added her navy blue headband with the white trim, and suddenly a younger woman appeared. She felt satisfied with the look.

The Lutheran church service exceeded the length of the Catholic Mass that Emily was accustomed to. If anyone were to ask her what the sermon was about that day, she could not recall, but if anyone asked her about her favorite part, it would be watching the cute red-headed young man in the choir. She felt delighted that the Protestants sang every verse of every hymn because it allowed her to make eye contact several times. She made a mental note to herself to meet him at the picnic.

Following the congregants to the basement after the service, Emily stretched up on her toes, trying to find that red-headed fellow in the crowd. He was easy to spot, and she began weaving her way toward him, until Mr. Stafford stepped in front of her, impeding her view. It was bad enough that Mr. Stafford was over six feet tall, but his brown derby added another few inches, making it impossible to see over him. Emily maneuvered around him and lost sight of the red head. Where did he go? It was like he disappeared into thin air. Emily thought it was just as well. After all, she wasn't a forward enough girl to start a conversation with a boy. At that moment, she thought about Cora and wished she had just a little of her spunk. Cora would say, of course, you can talk to a man. This is 1921.

The day was young, and Emily hoped she would get the nerve to approach the red-haired choir man when he reappeared. She helped Mrs. Stafford and the other church women set up the buffet to take her mind off things. One table held mounds of fried chicken, home-made potato salad, baked beans, corn-on-the-cob, coleslaw, and ham and turkey sandwiches on rye bread. A dessert table teemed with brownies, cupcakes, watermelon, and all the ice cream you could eat. Emily didn't think she had ever seen so much food at one sitting. Was this Thanksgiving?

The families began serving themselves. The Stafford family and Emily took plates and joined the queue. As they waited for their food, Emily scanned the room, looking for that mysterious redhead. Suddenly, he was walking right toward her- or was he? Emily looked over her shoulder and didn't see anyone else he could be approaching.

"Hi, you must be Emily. Allow me to introduce myself. My name is Timothy O'Keefe. I wanted to be the first one to welcome you to Christ the King Lutheran Church." He had shed his choir robe and was now wearing a single-breasted black serge suit with a white shirt and a black batwing bow tie.

"How did you know my name?" Emily felt delighted that he had made the first move.

"Didn't you read your bulletin? You can thank Mrs. Stafford. Turn to the back."

Emily flipped to the back and saw a small ad that Mrs. Stafford had placed. "Please welcome Emily Miller, my new employee, to our congregation." Emily profusely thanked Mrs. Stafford, especially since she called her an employee, and not a maid and governess.

"May I join you to eat?" Timothy asked.

"Of course." Emily was beaming inside. They had reached the front of the line and Emily filled her plate with a turkey sandwich and some potato salad, avoiding the fried chicken and corn-on-the-cob. Greasy fingers and corn stuck between her teeth would be no way to make a first impression.

They found a table far away from Mrs. Stafford's listening ears and the howling of little James as he ran laps around his mother's table. Emily was glad Sunday was one of her days off.

Timothy shared his biography with Emily, telling her he was an immigrant from Ireland, and that he was studying to become a welder so he could work on the big ships in New York City. Emily shared her story, leaving out the part about the convent. She relished every moment of their conversation and enjoyed playing badminton and croquet with Timothy.

With their time together waning, Timothy said, "When will I see you again? Do you want to join the choir? We practice every Monday evening."

"As much as I would love to, I can't. I work on Monday evenings. But I am off on Wednesday nights. Why don't you stop by and visit me?" Emily jotted down the Staffords' address and shoved it into Timothy's jacket pocket. "If you stop by, come around the back and knock on the kitchen door. No need to bother the Staffords."

"I might just do that." With that, he tipped his hat and said his goodbyes.

On Monday, Emily's dress arrived. On Tuesday, she baked oatmeal cookies, hoping beyond hope Timothy would come calling on Wednesday. She felt guilty hiding them in her room, but if JJ discovered them, there would be none left for Timothy. Emily felt delighted that Wednesday's dinner was a one-pot meal of beef stew. Fewer dishes to wash. She left the dishes to dry on the rack and the pot to soak in the sink and hurried upstairs to change into her new dress. Glancing at herself in the mirror, she pinched her cheeks to add some color to her drawn face. When she felt satisfied with her appearance, she grabbed the cookies and playing cards before heading back downstairs. The dishes on the rack were dry, so Emily put them away and washed the pot, leaving it on the drying rack. Then she sat at the table and practiced the in-hand riffle shuffle that Papa had taught her as a child, remembering to keep her thumbs over the bridge. Perfection. She hadn't lost her touch. She practiced it again just to make sure. This would be a way to impress Timothy if he ever showed up.

Timothy's knock on the kitchen door was so timid, it sounded more like a pebble hitting the glass than a knock. Emily smiled as she let him in. "I'm so glad you came."

"I wouldn't miss it for the world." Timothy took one look at Emily, clad in a silky robe. Would this be his lucky night?

Emily poured Timothy a glass of lemonade and offered him some of her oatmeal cookies. "Do you want to play cards? How about a game of gin rummy?"

"Absolutely. I love that game."

She brandished the in-hand riffle shuffle to Timothy, who watched in amazement. Emily did it three more times for effect. Thank you, Papa, wherever you are.

"What is going on in here?" said Mrs. Stafford, scooping her cigarettes off the kitchen counter.

"It's my night off. Timothy came over to play cards with me."

"I don't recall giving you permission to entertain gentlemen callers in my home. What if JJ walks in here? That's not an image I want him to see. Out young man. Out."

Timothy skedaddled out the door. Emily wondered if she would ever see Timothy again. Why couldn't she entertain men here? Maybe the country was better on her physical health- her hearing, her posture, her lungs, but what about her mental health? At least in the city, she was free to come and go as she pleased and see whoever she wanted to see. This was like living in prison.

"And why are you dressed like that? Are you a prostitute now? Were you planning on sneaking him up to your room to sleep with you?"

This was the second time in her life Emily was called a prostitute, and she didn't like it. After all, she had never slept with a man before. "What are you talking about? This is my new dress."

"You mean the one you ordered from the Montgomery-Ward catalog? That's no dress; that's a bathrobe."

"A bathrobe?"

"Let me get the catalog, and you show me what you ordered."

With a forlorn face, Emily waited as Mrs. Stafford rummaged through the credenza, looking for the catalog in the dining room. How could she be so stupid? Mrs. Stafford was right to send Timothy away. Did Timothy know it was a robe? She shuddered just thinking about the predicament she could have gotten herself into.

Mrs. Stafford was back in a flash. "Here. Show me what you ordered."

Emily wet her index finger with her tongue, rifled through the catalog to page 43, and pointed out the dress to Mrs. Stafford.

"Emily, that's not a dress."

"I didn't know."

"How could you not know? It says right here that it's a kimono made of rayon."

Emily didn't know what "rayon" or "kimono" meant, but she would never admit that to Mrs. Stafford. She simply said, "I

189

guess I missed that. I just saw the color, and the style was so much like my other dress, I got excited."

"Well, no harm done," Mrs. Stafford said, with her tone softening.

Maybe Mrs. Stafford didn't think any harm was done, but Emily did. She had never been so embarrassed in her life. Timothy seemed like a reasonable young man. Surely he would understand her mistake. She just had to explain it to him, but when would she see him again if Mrs. Stafford wouldn't let Timothy come calling at the house? There must be a way around it.

Emily racked her brain, trying to find a way to see Timothy again. She tossed and turned most of the night, unable to sleep, but then she had an epiphany. Mrs. Stafford said Timothy couldn't come to the house, but she never said Emily couldn't see him outside of her home. She would go to church again on Sunday and speak to him after the service. If Emily played her cards right, they could go out on Wednesday evening on her other day off.

The following Sunday, Emily wore the same conservative dress to church that she wore the week before. Sitting with the Stafford family towards the front of the church, Emily had a clear view of the choir. She kept her eyes peeled on Timothy, but he never made eye contact, keeping his eyes buried in his hymnal. This was not a good sign. She would have to confront him after church.

Emily waited patiently for the service to end. As the congregation filed out the back of the church to shake hands with the minister, Emily followed the choir to the basement. Timothy had already hung up his robe, but just as Emily was ready to approach him, she saw Timothy holding hands with another girl. As they headed to the exit, he planted a kiss on her cheek.

Emily thought her eyes were deceiving her. How could Timothy have moved onto another girl so quickly? How could the interest he showed in her be gone already? Was Mrs. Stafford right after all? Was Timothy only after one thing? Well, Emily was sure of one thing. Timothy was no "choirboy." No one would make a fool of her again. She swore off men until she could educate herself better.

The next day, Emily took JJ on two outings. First, they strolled to the drugstore where Emily purchased a notebook and a penny sucker for JJ. Then they trekked further to the library, where Emily received a library card. She asked the librarian for a book suggestion that could help her hone her reading vocabulary. The librarian recommended *Main Street* by Sinclair Lewis. She told Emily that she would love the bestseller because it was about a young girl trying to find her way in the world, like Emily.

The self-teaching began that night in the privacy of her bedroom. After borrowing Mrs. Stafford's dictionary, she wrote vocabulary words in bold letters across the cover of her notebook. The first entry was rayon, a new synthetic material similar to silk, followed by kimono, a Japanese bathrobe. Two months later, after finishing *Main Street,* she had added another 100 words to her vocabulary. She was proud of herself for making it all the way through the book, but she didn't like the story very much. How that book was a best-seller she would never know. For her second choice, she decided not to ask the librarian. She chose *Ladd: A Dog* by Albert Payson Terhune. It was easier to read, and Emily could share the stories with JJ.

In the beginning of the summer, Mrs. Stafford had an announcement. "Emily, we need to talk. Mr. Stafford and I are taking JJ to Europe for an extended vacation."

"How long?"

"Let me finish. About six weeks, so we will not be needing your services."

"You mean permanently." Emily thought this might be a blessing in disguise.

"No. Just for the six weeks. You're doing a fine job. But you can't stay here alone. Is there any place you can stay while we're gone?"

Emily wondered why she couldn't stay here, but Mrs. Stafford probably didn't trust her alone in the house. Emily thought about her family. She hadn't seen them in years. It would be great to see Mama and her siblings again, but Bill? She had no desire to see him. He couldn't hold his liquor; he was a nasty drunk. Everything bad that ever happened in the family seemed to revolve around alcohol. But then she realized it was Prohibition. "Sure. I can stay with my family. I'll call my mother tonight."

A week later, Emily stood on the porch of the Staffords' house with her valise in hand, waiting for her brother John to pick her up. The family was all packed, just waiting for Emily to leave so they could depart for New York City and cruise the Atlantic to England. When John's red Hatfield coupe came to a sputtering stop, the Staffords left without waving goodbye.

John raced out of the car and gave Emily a long overdue bear hug. "Oh John, it's so good to see you again. Look how tall you are. My baby brother is taller than me. When did that happen?"

"It's been a long time. Things change."

"I'll say. That's a fancy car. Bill must be doing well. And he let you drive it?"

"He sure did. And wait until you see the place. You won't recognize it."

John took Emily's valise, threw it in the back seat, and held the door open for Emily. He held her hand as she stepped into the coupe and closed the door after she sat down. That wasn't the John she remembered. Where did he learn how to treat a lady? Some things do change.

During the ride, Emily started firing questions at John. "How's Helen?"

"She's not a baby anymore. She's seven."

"And Mama?"

"Good as gold."

"And Bill? I almost didn't come. The last time I saw him, he smacked me right in the face. Look here. I still have a scar." Emily turned her head so John could get a good look at it. "But he should be good now that he's not drinking."

"Who told you he's not drinking?"

"Nobody. But it is against the law, so I just assumed he stopped drinking. He stopped, didn't he?"

John suddenly got silent. "I'm going to say no more and let you see for yourself. Here we are, home sweet home." The car lurched forward and stopped with a loud backfire.

"The truck is gone. Where is Mom?"

"She is with Bill and Helen. They are on one of their runs to Canada."

"What business do they have in Canada?"

"Like I said, you'll have to see for yourself to believe it."

Emily forgot about her brother and focused on the house. trying to decipher all the changes. The first thing she noticed was the freshly painted house and fence. She felt delighted to see both telephone and electric wires running into the house. Rows and rows of wheat and corn replaced most of the cow pasture. "What happened to all the cows and horses?"

"Bill got rid of most of them. We still have a few. He decided that corn and wheat farming was a much more lucrative business."

"Better than cattle? But Bill is such a good butcher."

John picked up Emily's valise and steered her toward the house. The house was exactly as she remembered it- the same couch and table, the same bedspread on Mama's bed, although more weather worn.

"Here's the best part. Indoor plumbing." John ran the faucet in the kitchen for show.

Emily rushed to the bathroom and slammed the door. As she did her business, she noticed the faded wallpaper curled back at the seams, the crack in the vanity mirror rusting around the edges, and the claw-legged bathtub covered in a layer of dirt. That didn't seem like Mama. The one thing Emily remembered about her mother was her meticulous housekeeping skills.

When she came out of the bathroom, both John and her valise were missing. Her brother yelled, "I'm up here." Emily climbed the steep stairs. "I'm going to sleep on the couch, and you can sleep up here with Helen. Why don't you rearrange Helen's things into two drawers so that you can put your clothes into the bottom drawer? She won't mind, and even if she does, who cares? She is only seven, and you're an adult."

Emily chuckled as she took Helen's elaborate headband and hair ribbon collection out of the drawer and placed it on top of the dresser next to Helen's hairbrush and comb. Then she transplanted the remaining collection of junk- three coloring books, broken crayons, a picture of Cinderella, an old maid card game, and a jump rope- into the second drawer. Now, all that remained was a large sack of coins. Emily looked inside. "John, there must be twenty dollars here. Where did Helen get that kind of money? Surely the golf course isn't paying that much, is it?"

"Oh, those were fun times for us. But no. She made the money waiting on tables."

"Waiting tables? What do you mean?"

Before John could answer, Emily heard tires crushing over gravel and a car backfire announcing the rest of her family's arrival. She hurried down the stairs and out the front door to greet them.

Margaret's hair was grayer than Emily remembered, and she was rounder in the middle. But she would recognize those big brown eyes anywhere. "Mom, it's so good to see you again." Emily gave her a hug and Margaret gave her a peck on the cheek. "And you must be Helen. You probably don't remember me, but I'm your big sister, Emily." Helen hid behind Margaret, avoiding Emily like she was a stranger.

"There's no time for pleasantries now. Let's unload the truck before prying eyes see us," Bill said.

"Oh hi, Bill. Glad to see you again. Thanks for letting me visit." Emily waved. She couldn't bear to hug him.

Everyone ran to the back of the truck. Emily couldn't understand why someone had loaded lumber onto the truck. Why did her mother and Bill drive to Canada to get wood when there were plenty of wood and paper mills right here in the Catskill Mountains? But then she watched Bill remove a section from the back of the truck, finding that it was hollow inside. Bill hoisted Helen into the small opening, and she began handing out containers of whiskey and beer. Suddenly everything made sense- Helen's pile of money, Mama's dirty bathtub, and John's evasive demeanor. He couldn't bear to tell her he was part of the family bootlegging ring.

"Get that shocked look off your face and get busy helping us unload," Bill said as he handed Emily a barrel of beer and pointed at the barn. Bill, Mama, John, and Emily formed an assembly line that Henry Ford would be proud of, hauling all the booze into the barn.

With Helen safely out of the truck, Bill replaced the fake door on the back. Emily looked at it carefully and couldn't see any seams. It was quite an elaborate design. Even if the police stopped them, they wouldn't see anything.

"Pretty good, huh? I have become the safest driver in all of New York State. I obey all the traffic signs and don't drive one mile over the speed limit. I don't give them a reason to stop me. I'm just a man out on a drive with his family."

Emily didn't know what to say. Nothing seemed appropriate.

"Come into the barn and I'll show you the rest of the operation."

Emily followed Bill into the barn as he turned on the electric light and closed the barn door. Not only did the barn have an electric light bulb swinging on a wire, but it also had a telephone mounted on the wall. Make-shift plywood tables had several folding chairs scattered around them. They had installed shelves around the perimeter of the barn and stacked them with rows of mason jars, cans of black paint, and a victrola lodged in the middle. A curtain hid the few cows, horses, and pigs that remained in the back of the barn. It was quite a nice nightclub if the smell of manure didn't overcome the patrons. Bill deposited the liquor into the root cellar and scattered hay across the trap-door. John snuck up behind Emily and said, "I told you Sis, you would have to see it to believe it. Wait until you see the entire operation tonight."

At 7:00, the Miller speakeasy was in full operating mode. Emily was glad that nobody expected her to work tonight. Bill told her she could just observe, but tomorrow she had to help "earn her keep" as he put it. Emily carried a chair into the corner and planted herself, trying to look inconspicuous. Some guests brought their own mason jars, while others took some from the shelves. Each guest received black paint to write their names on their jars. One man sped up the drying process by blowing on the paint, spraying Emily with saliva. She decided standing would be a better option to avoid further germs.

Once painted, the guests used the jars as place cards to claim their seats at the tables. They took some playing cards or board games and returned to their seats, waiting for Helen to serve them. Helen took two orders from each patron for each of their two glasses. One order was for iced tea, lemonade, or apple cider, the other for whiskey or beer. Emily was impressed by how little Helen kept the orders straight. and how generous the tips were in return. Who could resist the charm of a cute little girl?

Emily, staying sober, enjoyed watching the spectacle. The more the alcohol flowed, the louder the talking got. One man started the victrola, and the dancing began.

"What do you think, Sis?"

"Totally amazing. But it is getting loud in here. Isn't Bill worried that someone may call the sheriff?"

"No. Look." John pointed at Sheriff Jenkins, taking a slug of his whiskey.

"Oh, my gosh."

The telephone buzzed with a ring so loud everyone could hear it over the music. They all watched Bill take a big swig of beer and run to answer it without spilling a drop. "Sheriff Jenkins, it's for you."

The sheriff staggered over to the phone. Mama shut off the victrola. Everyone watched in silence. "Okay. Thanks, Bill. Quick, everyone, the feds are in the area. You know the drill."

After his third attempt, Sheriff Jenkins placed the receiver back on its cradle. Bill gathered all the liquor bottles and passed them down to Mama, who was already in the root cellar. All the guests firmly sealed their glasses of beer and whiskey and ran with them behind the barn, with Emily shadowing behind. John and Helen were hiding the alcohol in the creek. Each guest calmly returned to their tables drinking cider and lemonade, playing cards or dancing when the authorities arrived.

Sheriff Jenkins tipped his hat at the officers as they walked from table to table looking for liquor. He smirked when they found nothing. About fifteen minutes later, Helen and John retrieved the beer and whiskey from the creek and the drinking resumed.

"So Emily, what do you think?" asked John. He was still huffing and puffing from his multiple trips to the creek.

"Ingenious. Does this happen every night?"

"Well, the drinking does while supplies last. But the feds rarely come. It helps having the sheriff on our side."

"Listen, John. I'm glad you're here to look out for Helen. This can be dangerous."

"I won't be for long."

"What do you mean?" said Emily.

"When I turn 18, I'm joining the army."

"What? And who is going to look out for Helen?"

"She'll be alright. Don't forget, Bill is her father. I've never seen him raise a finger to her. We are not his children."

Emily thought about it. She sure hoped John was right.

The summer flew by. Emily helped Mama pick the corn and wheat. Together, they would make the alcohol in the bathtub, but it would never taste as good as the liquor they imported from Canada. Emily thought about the loving cup she won making bread. She would never win one making whiskey, but then again, she didn't want to end up in jail either.

One day in late August, about a week before the Staffords were expected to return from Europe, the telephone rang. It was one of those calls that Emily would remember exactly what she was doing for the rest of her life. She was coloring at the kitchen table with Helen when Aunt Annie called to tell Margaret and the family that Papa had died.

And Margaret had the gall to say, "That son of a bitch. If I knew he was going to die, I could have saved all that money I spent on the divorce."

"Mama." Emily thought her mother was cold as ice.

Grove Street
1922

The Miller brood was piling into the truck to head back to New Jersey for Papa's funeral when the clouds launched their attack. Didn't it always seem to rain or snow when someone died? Mom called it "God's tears." Emily would have preferred to lie down under the fake lumber in the back of the truck to stay dry, but John vetoed the idea. "That would be like laying in a coffin," he said. Instead, they sat unprotected from the elements with the raindrops pelting them like bullets as Bill sped around the curves.

By the time they arrived at Aunt Annie's apartment, Emily was soaked to the bone, shivering uncontrollably. She deposited her wet shoes in the vestibule and stepped into the parlor.

"Welcome to our humble abode," said Aunt Annie's macaw. Emily walked over to the cage. It was a colorful bird with its red head, yellow body, and blue wings. And it talked. It made her smile and forget about Papa for a minute until she saw her aunt slumped over in a velvet chair positioned in front of Papa's coffin. The room was empty of any other furniture. Some type of white powder was falling out of papa's coffin. As Annie hugged her sister-in-law, Emily could see her aunt's eyes swollen and red, all the tears drained from her eyes. "It's not fair, you know. I'm older, my baby brother shouldn't have gone first."

"Who are we to question God's plan?" Margaret said.

"I suppose you're right, Margaret." Aunt Annie said as she spotted Emily and John staring at the macaw. "Leave Freddy alone. Come children. Give me a hug and kiss your father goodbye."

This was the first funeral Emily had ever attended, but kiss a dead body? How creepy. How could she get out of this? "In a minute, Auntie. I'm soaking wet. I need to get out of these wet clothes first."

"Okay, child. Your papa is not going anywhere," she said as she burst into another round of crying. Emily darted to the bathroom, trying not to cry as her aunt removed a lace handkerchief from her sleeve, dabbing her eyes.

As Emily looked around the bathroom, she realized Mama's claim that Aunt Annie was the richest member of the family had merit. Built in 1921, this apartment had all the plumbing pipes and electrical wires nicely concealed behind the walls. She smiled as she turned on the faucet. As she waited for the water to warm up, Emily lit the lavender scented candle on the shelf above the bathtub and dropped her saturated clothes into a heap on the floor. She submerged herself in the water until the shivering stopped. She had so many questions-Why was Papa's body in Aunt Annie's house? Why do you have to kiss a dead body goodbye? What happened to Aunt Annie's couch? Was she poor, or rich like Mama said? And what was that white powder? Trying to avoid kissing Papa, she stayed in the water until it got cold and the shivering returned.

After dressing herself in dry clothes, Emily entered Aunt Annie's bedroom. Draped across the wrought iron bed was a heavy green Chenille coverlet that matched the curtains. Emily sat on the edge of the bed in front of the mirror brushing her hair when she heard a scream. She ran to the parlor still holding the brush in her trembling hand. Her mother was pulling Helen toward the casket. "Come on, Helen. Kiss your papa goodbye."

"No, no, don't make me. He's not my papa," Helen screamed, her arms flailing wildly.

"Stop it this instant; you're making a scene," Margaret said.

Emily didn't want to go near the coffin herself. She couldn't imagine what was going through Helen's seven-year-old mind. After this experience, poor Helen might have nightmares for years. Emily retreated to the kitchen, sitting at the table covering her ears to block out the barrage. She jumped when Aunt Annie's arm wrapped around her.

"Are you alright?"

"I think there is something seriously wrong with my mother. How can she be so cruel?"

"I agree with you. At first I used to think it was her stoic personality."

"Stoic? What does that mean?"

"A person who endures pain without showing their feelings or complaining. In your mother's case, I think she doesn't show her emotions because she is worried about what other people might think."

"That sounds like my mother." Emily made a mental note to add the word stoic to her vocabulary journal.

"But now I think it's more than that. I think Margaret has a flaw in her personality. Something that makes her cruel."

"Well, she had a tough life. Living with Papa wasn't always easy. We were poor, and Mama always had to worry about feeding us and keeping a roof over our heads."

"Poverty is only part of it. True, there was never enough money to go around for all the material things, but there are other things you can give."

"Like what?"

"Time. What does it cost to spend time with your children and give a hug once in a while? Think about it, Emily. I can't think of a time that I ever saw your mother give you a hug. That's selfishness and cruelty, not poverty."

Emily thought about what her aunt was telling her. Margaret was definitely not the lovey-dovey type. In fact, Emily could count all the times that her mother had hugged or kissed her on one hand, and those kisses were more like pecks than kisses. Suddenly the old adage "Two peas in a pod" came to mind. "Oh, my God. Do you think it runs in families? Am I going to be like my mother someday?"

"For your sake Emily, I hope not. I want you to promise me something. If you ever have children, don't treat them the way your mother treats you. It might be a hard habit to break, but there is no reason to be selfish and distant. Be mother material."

"I'll try to remember that."

"Good girl, now let's go back and pay our respects to your father."

By the time Aunt Annie and Emily returned to the parlor, Bill had taken Helen outside. Emily didn't like Bill very much, but at this moment she was grateful for his help in pacifying Helen. Emily trekked up to the coffin like she was facing her own death. But the closer she got, the more at ease she became. Aunt Annie did a good job laying out Papa for the viewing. He was wearing his best double-breasted suit and a blue bowtie. The mortician had folded his bands across his chest, with a rosary draped through his fingers. With his eyes closed, he looked like he was asleep. Aunt Annie had placed a hat rack next to the coffin, holding Papa's hat. Emily thought this added a delicate touch. After all, Emily couldn't think of a time in her life that he wasn't wearing it. Laying in the coffin next to Papa's emaciated body, Aunt Annie had placed some of his favorite things in life-a bocce ball, a pack of cigarettes, a growler of beer, and a deck of playing cards. Maybe he would take them to Heaven if he were buried with them.

Emily touched Papa's arm, hoping that this was all a mistake. Without blood flowing through his body, it was cold to the touch. She squeezed it hard, praying he would wake up, but he just laid there. Emily leaned in and kissed him on the cheek, dropping a few tears on his face. "Goodbye, Papa. I'm going to miss you." Backing away from the casket, Emily sneezed as she shook the white powder from her hands and clothes. "What is this stuff?" she asked.

"It's lime," Aunt Annie said, explaining that it is used to pack dead bodies in order to absorb bodily fluids and prevent them from smelling until the burial.

"Sorry I asked. And what happened to your couch?"

"That old thing? I donated it to the church thrift shop. Your papa deserves only the best. Besides, it had to go to make room for our guests. I'll buy a new one after the funeral."

Aunt Annie must really be rich. Emily couldn't imagine giving away furniture so easily. Interrupting her thoughts, a tall thin man burst through the door carrying two folding chairs in each arm.

"Welcome to our humble abode," squawked Freddy.

"Emily, John, have you ever met Peter Dufort?"

"I don't think so," said John.

Although Emily didn't recognize the man, his name was somewhere in her brain. "Don't you own a restaurant on Brookside Avenue?"

"You have a wonderful memory, mademoiselle," Peter said with his thick French accent.

"John, why don't you help Mr. Dufort unload the rest of the chairs from his truck?" said Aunt Annie.

"Alright," John said flexing his muscles.

Emily opened the chairs and placed them in a row behind Aunt Annie, taking the seat closest to the macaw. She enjoyed looking at the bird instead of the casket, which only made her cry. Cousin Blanche arrived next. "Welcome to our humble abode."

Aunt Annie got out of her chair. "That's enough out of you," she remarked as she threw a cover over Freddy's cage. Blanche hugged her mother and immediately walked over to the coffin to kiss her uncle goodbye. Emily couldn't believe how effortless this was for Blanche until she remembered this wasn't Blanche's first funeral. It had been three years since her own father had died. That would have been Emily's first funeral too, if she hadn't been confined to the convent.

A parade of mourners came and went all day long, including Papa's bocce ball friends, his coworkers from the firehouse, two scraggly looking pals from the bar, and some neighbors. When Mr. Sullivan came in, Emily rushed over to greet him personally. As sad as Emily was, it made her happy to know her father was so well liked by so many people.

It was a stressful day, and Emily fell asleep in her chair until a loud buzzer woke her up. "What was that?"

"It's just the telephone," said Blanche.

Of course it was, but how could Emily have known that? Other than Mrs. Stafford, Mr. Sullivan was the only other person she knew who had a telephone in his home.

After a brief phone call, Aunt Annie said, "That was Mr. Dufort. He'll be back in the morning to pick up the chairs. Why don't we all turn in? The church service is tomorrow, and it will be another long day."

Aunt Annie's apartment only had two bedrooms- one for Aunt Annie and the guest room for Margaret, Bill, and Helen. John, Blanche, and Emily slept in the parlor in sleeping bags. It reminded Emily of all the fun sleepovers she had with Blanche when they were children. But this wasn't fun. In fact, it was eerie sleeping in the same room with a corpse.

In the morning, a hearse arrived with six men dressed in black suits. They waited patiently for the family to say their final goodbyes. Emily knew this was the last time she would ever see her father again. She held John's hand and tried not to cry when the men closed the lid and carried the coffin to the hearse.

The next stop was St. Mary's Church. The six men wheeled the casket down the center aisle, and Emily took a seat in the first pew with her family. Mama and Aunt Annie each wore a black velvet hat with black crinoline pulled down over their faces to hide their tears, although she was certain Mama would shed no tears. Emily's hat had no such option. The entire world could see her tears for Papa for all she cared. Emily couldn't help but notice the opulence of the church, with its huge stained-glass windows and crucifix lined with gold. Emily wondered why the church had such luxuries. Wouldn't the money have been better spent helping poor families like her own? Would God strike her dead for having such thoughts? Was she thinking like a socialist now? For all the money that Aunt Annie gave to this church over the years, Emily was expecting a better funeral. The priest spoke of Papa as if his time on earth was inconsequential.

The next stop was Holy Cross Cemetery. This was also Emily's first time in a graveyard. She always thought it would be scary, but as she looked around at the manicured lawn, she found it peaceful. Many graves had flowers on them, placed there by loving family members, she supposed. Emily paused at the first headstone to read the inscription- Sarah Elizabeth Thomas Born 1899 died 1905. Only six years old, a child. Emily wondered how she died. Each headstone was a tribute to the life of the deceased. What a nice way to honor the deceased for all eternity. They passed by a family having a picnic by a gravesite. Emily stopped to gawk at a little boy of about ten, talking to his dead grandfather. "Grandpa, I got an "A+" on my spelling test. My teacher says I might be good enough to enter the spelling bee. And I got chosen to be the captain of the basketball team. I wish you could see me play."

"Emily, stop dawdling," said Margaret as she grabbed Emily's hand, pulling her along.

"That is so creepy. Talking to the dead like that. Will we be doing that with Papa?"

"No. But every family mourns in their own way."

Upon reaching Papa's grave, they noticed that his coffin was suspended above a deep hole. The priest said the final prayer and the six pallbearers lowered him into his ultimate resting place. Each family member said their last prayer and dropped a flower onto his coffin, and the men covered it with dirt. Emily shuddered thinking about Papa in that cold ground, but then she remembered his soul was already in heaven.

"Are you alright, Emily?" Aunt Annie asked.

Emily was still staring at Papa's grave when the rest of the family left, "I'm as good as I can be. But I have a question. How come Papa doesn't have a headstone like everyone else?"

"Oh, he will. It takes time to do all that carving. Look over here. That is my husband, your Uncle Paul's grave. That stone took almost a year before it was done. You remember him, don't you?"

Emily nodded. "It's too bad you couldn't attend his funeral. He was a fine man like your papa. This is our family cemetery. Someday me, your mama, your brother, you, your future husband, and your children will all be buried here."

It was a nice thought, but if Emily didn't meet somebody to marry soon, she might just die an old maid.

The last stop of the day was the repast at Peter Dufort's Restaurant and Dance Hall. Mr. Dufort hadn't let go of his French roots. Two flags, one French and one American, stood on each side of the vast fireplace. Emily thought the roaring blaze was too hot for a late summer day. Small round tables huddled close together made room for the dance floor. So many ferns suspended from the array of wooden ceiling beams made Emily feel like she was outside in a jungle.

Peter Dufort ushered the grieving family to a table close to the fireplace. "I'm sorry for your loss," he said. "Have you ever tried French food before?"

Emily shook her head. "I'm sorry to say that we have not," Margaret said.

"Then you are in for a treat. Dinner will be on the house tonight."

"Thank you; you are so kind," Bill said.

Peter Dufort drew his belt to the smallest hole and his trousers still hung loosely on his thin frame. Emily laughed to herself, wondering if French cuisine would be very satisfying. But still, this was such a kind gesture.

"The first course has arrived. *Escargots and baguette fromage,*" said Peter, bearing two trays which he placed in the center of the table.

"Ooh! What is that? Bugs?" shrieked Helen as she jumped up from the table, knocking her chair over.

"*Escargots.* Snails. This is a staple in France. Served with mushrooms and garlic."

"I'm not eating them," said Helen.

"Sit down and be polite," said Mama.

"Thank you, Mr. Dufort," said Helen, holding her nose.

"You're welcome, little lady," said Mr. Dufort as he headed back to the kitchen.

"Don't embarrass me like that ever again," said Margaret. Emily's mother hadn't changed in all these years. Even Bill couldn't mellow her out.

"That's all right. That's more for me," said John.

"What are you, a tough guy? When in your life have you ever eaten snails?" said Emily.

"Watch me."

John fished out the first snail with a little fork and paused before putting it in his mouth. He washed it down with a sip of water.

Emily laughed as she reached for the *baguette fromage.* It had cheese baked inside of the bread. The girls polished it off while Bill and John finished the snails. The main course was *coq au vin*- chicken, bacon, mushrooms, and carrots cooked in a rich red sauce that tasted a lot like wine. Where on earth did he find the wine to cook with? Emily concluded he must have either imported it from France or bootlegged it himself. The meal ended with chocolate eclairs. They just finished as the band was setting up for the evening and the dinner crowd began shuffling in.

Back home at Aunt Annie's house, the family talked. "I'm so glad this day is over. It was so stressful. I can't wait to get back to normal tomorrow," said Emily.

"Whoever told you things would be back to normal tomorrow? Tomorrow is when the grieving starts. You will go about your life, and you'll think about your papa a lot, and you will be sad. But after a while, and it could take years, you will think of all the nice memories he left you with, and you will smile. What are your plans, Emily? Are you going back to the Staffords?" asked Aunt Annie.

"I don't really want to."

"Why not?"

"It was something you said today at the cemetery that got me wondering. About being buried with my husband. First, I have to find one. Mrs. Stafford wouldn't let me have guests at the house. How will I ever meet men?"

"Why don't you move back to New Jersey and work here?"

"But I gave up my job at the factory. Where will I find another job? Where will I live?" said Emily.

"I can help you with both. You can live here. I have been so lonely since your Uncle Paul died. And I have an extra bedroom. How would you like a job as a telephone operator?"

"I would love it, but are there openings? Are they hiring?"

"Yes, and yes. Don't forget, Uncle Paul used to work there. I know the manager, Mr. Brown. If you want the job, it's yours."

As Emily stood on the stoop with Aunt Annie waving goodbye to her mother, Bill, John, Helen, and Cousin Blanche, she hoped she made the right decision to stay behind.

Grove Street
1923

The next morning, Emily headed off to Bamberger's department store, buying two white blouses and two skirts- one navy blue and one black. Aunt Annie told her this would be the required dress code at the telephone company. Not only did Aunt Annie come with her to the store, but she also paid for the clothes. Aunt Annie was quickly becoming her favorite aunt (her only living aunt anyway).

The interview with Mr. Brown turned out to be just a formality because the job was hers, just like Aunt Annie had said. Emily found Mr. Brown to be a man with a kind smile and caring eyes, and she felt delighted not to see a cigar dangling from his lips, nor any sign of an ashtray on his desk. The only opening he had was the night shift, working from 11:00 in the evening to 8:00 in the morning, at a salary of 20 dollars a month. The bad news was that she had to work for free for the first two weeks while she trained. He handed her a headset and told her to report back to the telephone company promptly at 11.

Emily thanked Mr. Brown profusely. This salary was incredible compared to her $3.50 a week working in the factory. She checked her watch. It was already 2 in the afternoon. Should she stay awake until then and risk falling asleep on the first day of her new job, or go home and try to get some sleep? She decided on the latter.

But falling asleep in the daylight hours was difficult with the local train roaring by every ten minutes. And Aunt Annie proved to be quite the social butterfly. The telephone rang three separate times, each time jolting Emily from an already unsatisfying sleep. This was a luxury she never had before. Was owning a telephone really necessary? And she never noticed how loud Aunt Annie's voice was before. Or does everything seem louder when you are trying to sleep? All she knew was Aunt Annie's friends were calling to ask about the time tomorrow that the ladies would be playing cards. One o'clock Aunt Annie said each time, followed by Freddy's echoing chorus, "Cards at one." Darn that bird. But perhaps the most annoying problem was the strong rays of the sun shining right through the thin curtains. It was like her body knew it was daytime and wouldn't let her sleep. She vowed to make room darkening curtains and earplugs her first priority with the proceeds of her first paycheck.

One thing Emily's mother successfully drummed into her head was to always be on time. It was a good thing she allowed herself a half hour to walk the six blocks to work because after walking only two blocks she realized she forgot her headset and had to double back to get it. Despite the mishap, she arrived with five minutes to spare.

A girl wearing a black dress without a splash of color, greeted her at the door. She wondered if the girl was in mourning or had simply chosen to wear this drab frock. Emily hoped that her white blouse and black skirt were acceptable attire. "Hello, you must be Emily. My name is Marion. I am one of the chief operators, but for the next two weeks, I will be your trainer. You get to shadow me for two weeks until you learn the ropes. Rule Number one: Always take the steps. I don't know why, but only the morning girls get to take the elevator. The night shift must walk six flights of steps. Do you have your walking shoes on?"

"I do." Emily was glad she had chosen her comfortable shoes.

"Then follow me."

The girls proceeded up the wide stairway, so wide, in fact, that Emily felt like a princess in a palace. She thought about the claustrophobic stairs of the dress factory and realized she would never have to turn around to let someone else pass through. The first two flights were marble. When they approached the third floor, Marion said, "Watch your step. The stairs are turning to a rubber covering, and I have seen many girls fall here."

"How come the marble doesn't go all the way up?" asked Emily.

"Because marble is elegant and impresses our visitors who do not go beyond the second floor. Rubber is cheaper and absorbs sound, so as not to disturb our guests."

Emily liked the springy bounce in her steps; it massaged her feet.

When they reached their destination, it was not what Emily had envisioned. Enormous windows encircled the room. Although they were too high to see out above the switchboard, they let in an abundance of fresh air. Emily took in a deep breath, enjoying the clean air, free of the microfibers she inhaled at the dress factory. The clicking of the circuits was nowhere near the deafening sound of the sewing machines either. Perhaps Emily wouldn't lose her hearing after all.

"You'll be at Station 33. I will sit, and you can stand behind me and observe for now. In a few days we'll let you take on the duties one at a time." Marion plopped herself into a swivel chair with a hardback. "Rule Number Two: You never use your real name when you are talking to customers. From now on, your name will be Mable."

"Is Marion your real name?"

"I'll never tell."

"But why can't we use our given names?"

"Because sometimes you may take a phone call from

someone you know, and they are supposed to know you as the operator, not as your relative or friend." Marion put on her headset and attached a heavy microphone to it. The contraption left both of her hands free to work the switchboard. "Now watch. This is your board. You're responsible for these 100 phone numbers. Start learning where your customers are located."

Memorizing the location of 100 numbers on the board was a daunting task, but Emily had two weeks of training ahead of her. She broke down this task into smaller chunks. Isn't this what teachers do? They couldn't possibly learn all their students' names in one day. By the end of the day, she would learn ten numbers. She would add another ten tomorrow, and by the end of her two-week training she would know them all.

"The first thing that happens is a disk will fall down with a number displayed on it. Your job is to take this wire and plug it into the matching number on your panel. Then you ask your customer, 'what number please?' If you are lucky, your customer might be calling another of your customers, and you simply plug the other end of the cord into that number and say, 'go ahead, please.' More than likely, it won't be. If it is not, you press this calling circuit button. You will get the trunk line switchboard and tell the operator the number. She will make many connections before getting back to you. Do you see this row of numbers labeled one to twenty?" Emily nodded.

Marion continued, "She will come back to you and tell you to plug into one of those numbers. You plug it in and finish the connection."

"That seems easy enough," Emily said.

"Just be glad you're working the night shift. During the day, it can get pretty hectic. The stress has caused many girls to faint. You'll have the opposite problem. It'll be so slow in the middle of the night that you will have trouble staying awake."

"I have a question," said Emily. "What happens when my board is all filled up with connections?"

"It won't be because you're only half done. Then, disconnect the wires at the end of the call to be ready for the next call. Once the customer finishes, they are expected to ring off, and then you disconnect the cords. But sometimes they forget. You may have to listen in to a call to determine the call has ended and then unplug the connection."

Emily wasn't sure she was going to like that. After all, weren't some telephone calls supposed to be private? What if it was someone she knew? She didn't want to be privy to anything like that. What if they recognized her voice? But then she realized that even if they did, she would say she was "Mable."

They assigned Mable a half hour for lunch break. But why would she eat in the middle of the night? But then she realized, if she was going to be working nights, she would sleep through breakfast and lunch during the day. Suddenly she felt hungry. Marion told her that the telephone company supplied the meal in the cafeteria buffet style. Today's menu was a generous amount of beans, tea, and bread with butter. Marion told her this was the regular fare and suggested it might be a good idea to supplement the meal with some fruit and vegetables.

In addition to lunch, Marion granted Emily a ten-minute recess in the break room. Marion left her alone to acclimate herself. The current issues of just about every magazine stacked the long table. Emily leaned back in a plush pink chair to skim through her favorite- *Vogue*. There was no long line at the bathroom, and even if there was, she learned she could leave her station at the switchboard by asking the chief operator for a "necessary"- an emergency bathroom break. She shuddered thinking about her days in the factory wearing rags to avoid getting docked in pay.

Returning to work, Emily noticed a bulletin board mounted just by the exit where all the employees were bound to see. It had the pictures of four girls fired this week. Two for fainting on the job, one for being habitually late, and the last for removing her headset. Emily promised herself that her picture would never grace this board.

As she walked home at the end of her shift, Emily thought about her first day. She would call it a successful day, but she cared little for Marion. Does Marion even realize how she appears to her employees? So formal, almost like a robot. Emily thought she would make a better chief operator. At least she would smile once in a while. Emily made a promise to herself that in a year's time not only would she be chief operator, but she would also work the day shift.

When Emily received her first paycheck a month later, she learned a new lesson about finances. The check was only for $18.80. $1.20 in federal income taxes had been expected, but Aunt Annie's unexpected comments threw her for a loop. "The rent for this apartment is $30 a month. Your share will be $10.00 a month, but I want to be fair and give you a chance to get back on your feet, so you can start paying next month."

Emily thought that was more than fair. "Oh thank you, you are so kind."

"And I also want you to learn about budgeting. Tomorrow we'll go to the bank to open up a savings account in your name. $3.00 should do it."

"And why would I want to do that?"

"Because this is the twenties, and you can buy big items on time. Why should you have to wait to enjoy the luxuries in life? You just keep adding $3.00 a month, and when you have enough for a down payment, you can buy whatever you want, like a bicycle, a piano, furniture, even appliances or a car. Then, you make monthly payments until you fully repay the loan. It usually takes 12 to 18 months to pay off, sometimes longer."

This all seemed a little greedy to Emily. Was Aunt Annie really as rich as Mama had claimed? Aunt Annie still hadn't replaced her couch. She looked around the apartment at the rest of Aunt Annie's belongings. Did Aunt Annie want to make people think she was rich? Was this just all a show? Then she thought about her mother and Papa. They never taught her about saving or putting money in a bank either, but then again, they probably didn't have any money left over after paying the bills. About as close as they came to saving was putting the rent money in a tin can above the stove, until that fateful day when the dog catcher took the money along with Queenie, her beloved dog.

"Emily?"

"Sorry, I drifted off for a minute."

"So, what would you like to save for?"

"Certainly not a car. That would cost way too much. Besides, I don't even know how to drive."

"You don't have to decide right now. You'll know what to buy when the time comes."

Emily did the math in her head. With $3.00 in the bank, that would leave her $15.80 for the rest of the month. Could she make it last? But Aunt Annie had other ideas for that money too.

"Now it's time to get you out to the club to meet men."

"Aunt Annie, I would love to. But how is that even possible when I work nights?"

"You just have to get creative. You usually sleep from 8 until about 4 in the afternoon. So, you wake up, eat dinner and go to the club. You would just have to leave around ten to get to work on time."

Suddenly, Emily felt like Cinderella going to the ball to meet her Prince Charming and having to leave early before she turned back into a working girl in drab clothing. "Oh, Aunt Annie, you're the best."

"The first thing we need to do is get you a proper dress. I would lend you one of mine, but I haven't been as slim as you in years. Look through the Sears catalog and pick out a nice dress."

Emily quickly turned to the dress section of the catalog, being careful to avoid the robe section. She would not make that mistake again! Emily settled on a purple wool crepe dress with

3/4 length sleeves. Plaited lace adorned the collar, sleeves, and waist. The dress had an overhanging skirt and a silk bow in the front. She divvied out another $5.90 for the dress- only $9.90 left for the month.

"I think I know what I want to buy on time- a sewing machine. I can make my dresses much cheaper than Sears, and I'm actually quite good at it thanks to the convent and the dress factory."

"Great choice. And while we're waiting for the dress to come, we need to work on your hair and make-up. Didn't your mama ever teach you how to style your hair and apply make-up? Nobody applies it better than her."

Emily couldn't think of a single time her mother helped her with anything. Mrs. Baker taught her how to bake, the nuns to sew. Mama had no time to teach her to skate, or play Chinese checkers, or help her with her homework. She wasn't around when she had her first period, so why would Emily expect her to be here now to teach her about make-up? "No, she never did. I'm so glad to have you, Aunt Annie. You're my favorite aunt." She wished Aunt Annie had been her mother instead.

"Thank you for saying that. You flatter me. Now, let down your hair for me."

Emily pulled the pins out of her bun, shook her head, and let the hair cascade down her back. It fell past her bottom.

"We're off to the barber to get that mop cut."

"Cut it?"

"Of course. You're a young woman of the twenties. And wait until you see how much easier it will be to take care of."

Ray's Barber Shop stood just a few blocks from Dufort's Restaurant. It was hard to miss with the spinning red, white, and blue pole luring patrons to its door. The sign in the window read "Men's haircut and shave still 25 cents."

"We can't go in there; it's for men only," Emily said.

"Trust me, you can," Aunt Annie said.

Emily peered through the window like a small child looking

into a candy shop, just in time to see a man draped in a white gown get out of his chair to use the spittoon. Disgusting. Another customer was reading a magazine while a barber applied some kind of gel to his hair, and yet another customer had shaving cream on his face as the barber used a straight razor on him. No women in sight. Six other barbers, waiting for customers, stood at attention like soldiers ready to go into battle. Emily was about to be the next war casualty.

Emily entered and asked, "Do you cut women's hair?"

"Of course. My name is Al, and I would be happy to accommodate you." Al's thin mustache and gel-saturated hair made him look like Errol Flynn. Confident that he could give her a good haircut, Emily took a seat in the chair closest to the door. "What style would you like?" he asked.

"I don't know. Aunt Annie, you're the expert. How do I want my hair cut?"

"Give her a bob. Cut it about even with her chin. Good luck. I'm going to take a walk around the block. When I come back, you'll be a new woman."

Emily was so nervous, but her aunt's confident demeanor was reassuring. Emily watched her aunt leave the barbershop. Then, she looked in the mirror and watched Al chop off her long, straight hair. The whole haircut took only 15 minutes. "That'll be $5.00."

"Five dollars? Why so much? Men's haircuts only cost twenty-five cents."

"Women have more hair than men," Al shrugged. "Your next haircut will only be $2.00."

Emily divvied out the $5.00 from her paycheck- only $4.90 left. She met her aunt outside and immediately began speaking her mind. "I can't believe they charge women $5.00 for a haircut, and men only pay twenty-five cents. That's not fair. Women got the vote, but things still aren't fair."

"I agree. Give it time. I bet someday they will have hair salons just for women with more reasonable prices."

Hair salons for women? Emily thought that would never happen.

"Would you like to get a manicure?" asked Aunt Annie.

"How much?"

"That will only cost you twenty-five cents."

"Maybe next month." Although a manicure sounded nice, she could think of better ways to spend her money.

"Alright. Let's get home, finish styling your hair, and practice applying your make-up."

Styling hair was much easier than Emily thought it would be. Aunt Annie assured her she would have no trouble styling her hair. First, she wet her hair under the faucet and then rubbed bandoline through it. It smelled like rose oil. Aunt Annie showed her how to make finger waves by simply rolling her hair around her finger and then holding it for a few seconds. Emily loved the instant curls it created.

"Lovely. Now let's work on the make-up. First, we have to do something with those eyebrows. Have you ever shaped them before?" asked Aunt Annie.

"No."

"Hold still while I tweeze them for you."

Emily couldn't believe how much this hurt. It seemed to take forever, and her eyes wouldn't stop tearing. When Aunt Annie was done, there was nothing left but a thin line above each eye. Aunt Annie then used a pencil to apply kohl to one eyebrow, coloring and shaping it. She let Emily imitate her on the other brow. Emily couldn't understand why you take off the eyebrows only to paint them back on again, but she had to admit the finished product produced an evenly shaped brow.

"Oh my, your eyes are so red. Let's do your face and lips next and give your eyes a chance to calm down," said Aunt Annie. "First, you apply powder from the compact, evenly but lightly, over your face. Just enough so the rouge will have something to stick to." The powder dust in the air, together with Emily's watery eyes, made this step hard to follow. Too little powder and the rouge wouldn't adhere, too much and she would look like a circus clown. Emily knew she would have to practice this step again and again to get it right.

"Achoo!"

"*Gesundheit*," said Aunt Annie as she opened up another compact containing rouge. "Look at me." Emily stared right into Aunt Annie's eyes.

"This step is important. You have a wide face, so you want to apply the rouge high on the cheekbones, close to the nose. It will draw people's attention to the color, away from a broad face. Watch. Apply it in a small circle and rub it in." Aunt Annie had a delicate touch; her fingers felt like silk as she maneuvered them across her face, blending in the rouge. "Now, you try it on the other cheek."

Emily tried to mimic her aunt, but she rubbed a little too hard. The result- Aunt Annie's application left a beautifully bright cheekbone, while Emily's was a faded mess. She felt lopsided.

"Not bad for your first attempt. Again, it takes practice. Now for the lipstick, and I guarantee you won't mess this up." Aunt Annie reached into her bag of tricks, pulling out a lip stencil and a lipstick tube, handing both to Emily. "Line the stencil around your lips and apply the lipstick. It comes out perfect every time. In fact, I am so sure you can do it yourself without my help."

Emily looked into the mirror, holding the stencil with one hand while applying the lipstick with the other. When she removed the stencil, her lips exploded in vibrant red.

Aunt Annie handed her a Kleenex. "Now dab the excess off so you don't smear it all over your face," she said. Emily did as she was told. "Good girl. Now let's get back to your eyes. Eye shadow comes in gray, blue, green, brown, or plum. Brown-eyed girls should only use brown or plum. Fortunately, your eyes are brown like mine, and I have both brown and plum. Which color do you want to try?"

"Brown please."

Aunt Annie removed another compact with brown eye shadow, handing it to Emily. "You don't need me to do it for you. You can do it yourself. Just apply it on the eyelids with your fingers." Emily followed directions.

"Nice. Now the last step is the eyelashes." Aunt Annie removed yet another compact from the makeup bag. "This you will also have to practice applying. Mascara comes in cake form. You'll have to wet it first and then apply it with a brush. Do it yourself. I don't want to poke you in the eye. Go ahead, I'll watch."

Emily scooted up close to the mirror and applied the mascara to both of her eyelashes. No matter how hard she tried, she couldn't get the clumps out. She blinked hard, her eyes feeling as heavy as bricks. A line of mascara appeared under each eye. Oh great, I look like a raccoon, she thought.

"Way too thick," said Aunt Annie as she handed Emily a Kleenex. "Wet it and wipe the excess off."

Thank God for the invention of Kleenex. Emily wiped her face. "How's that?"

"Better. But it's still clumpy. And I have the perfect solution for that too."

Emily watched her aunt pick up some type of contraption that looked like forceps.

"What's that?"

"This is the Kurlash eyelash curler. Pinch your eyelashes between it, and not only will it remove the clumps, but it will curl your lashes as well. No man will take his eyes off you." Emily's lashes glided through the device with ease.

"Stunning. Now keep practicing. By the time your dress arrives, you'll be a makeup professional."

"Aunt Annie?" said Emily, frowning.

"What is it, child?"

"I've spent most of my paycheck already. I don't have money

left over to buy makeup this month. Would it be all right if I borrow yours until then?"

"Of course."

"Oh, Aunt Annie, you're the best."

Three days later, wearing makeup, her new hairstyle, and dress, Emily walked with Aunt Annie to Peter Dufort's club and restaurant. She wondered if Dufort's would operate the same way as the club she went to with Cora and the Bennett brothers- tables for men on one side, women on the other, and mixed couples in the middle.

As they entered, it took Emily a minute to adjust to the dim lighting; the multitude of hanging plants cast an eerie shadow on the patrons. Young people gathered in the front, close to the band, while older patrons sat in the back.

"Ann, Ann, over here. We saved some seats."

Emily saw a short gray-haired woman of about 60 in a blue satin pleated dress waving frantically at them. Emily didn't want to be tethered to that table all night. After all, how was she going to meet anyone while sitting next to two old ladies who looked like her chaperones? Her eyes must have reflected it. "It's alright. I'll sit with my lady friends. You go enjoy yourself," said Aunt Annie.

"Are you sure you don't mind?"

"No, have fun. Just don't forget you have to leave by ten."

Aunt Annie must have thought Emily was still ten years old with a remark like that. She ignored it; anything she could have said would have appeared disrespectful. Instead, she wove her way through the tables and took a seat on the girls' side at the only empty table nearest the band. Men had already paired up with girls, either on the dance floor or engaged in conversation at the center tables. One girl was even smoking a cigar. Emily looked at the men's side of the room. A man wearing a dark blue pencil striped suit sat alone. As he looked at Emily, the light reflected off his face, creating a halo over his head. Was this a sign from God?

Emily approached him. Creeping closer, she soon discovered the source of the light. The man sat directly under a chandelier, its light reflecting off his glass eye, that looked right at Emily. Now she understood why he was sitting alone. She made a quick pivot to return to her table.

"Don't go away, pretty lady. There is a seat right here," he said as he gestured toward the empty chair beside him. Not wanting to appear rude, Emily reluctantly sat in the chair. He was older than her. With his dark brown hair and sideburns beginning to gray, she guessed him to be in his mid to late thirties.

"My name is Frank. To whom do I have the privilege of speaking?"

"Emily. Nice to meet you." She wanted to make an excuse to leave, but the glass eye had a hypnotic effect on her.

"I don't think I've ever seen you around here before," he said.

"That's because it's my first time here. What about you? Do you come here often?"

"I've only been here a few times. I'm new to the area."

"Where are you from?"

"Pennsylvania."

"Where in Pennsylvania? It's a big state," said Emily.

"I have a Gettysburg Address."

Emily couldn't help but smile; she loved men with a sense of humor. "So, what made you come to New Jersey?"

"I had a career as a bartender, but I lost it when Prohibition hit. So I moved to the city to get a job in a factory. The electric company hired me to work the assembly line, making fans."

"Is that how you lost your eye? If you don't mind me asking."

"Yes," said Frank, looking down at the floor.

"I'm so sorry. So where do you work now?"

"Boy, you sure are full of questions. I got a job as a florist, but I had to leave when they ran out of irises."

"That didn't actually happen, did it?" Emily asked, trying to conceal her laugh.

"No, I got a job as a teacher, but I got fired when they ran out of pupils."

"Now I know you're teasing me. Really, where do you work?"

"Newark Electric is a great company to work for. When I lost my eye, they kept me on as a janitor. It pays the bills. Enough about me. Tell me about yourself."

Emily told Frank about her life, leaving out the part about being in the convent. When the band began playing "Rhapsody in Blue," she hummed along. "Would you like to dance?" asked Frank.

"I would love to." It surprised Emily how good of a dancer Frank was. She thought his balance might be off with one eye, but he was steady on his feet. They danced several more dances and shared an apple cider. Ten o'clock arrived too quickly.

"Will you be here again tomorrow night?" asked Frank.

"Well, that all depends. Will you?" Frank nodded. "I'll see you then."

The next day, as Emily prepared for Dufort's Club, her aunt confronted her. "I hope you will not spend another evening with that one-eyed man."

"He was such a nice man; I certainly hope to see him again."

"That is not a good idea."

"Why not?" said Emily.

I promised your mother I would look out for you, and I know she wouldn't approve. He's too old for you, and he's a damaged man. He won't be a good provider- clearly not marriage material."

"Not marriage material," squawked Freddy.

"Shut up, Freddy."

Emily felt devastated. Just when she thought she was connecting with Frank, Aunt Annie was trying to put a stop to it. "We made plans tonight. Frank is expecting me. It wouldn't be right if I didn't show up."

"Alright. You can go, but make sure you put an end to it tonight."

Emily met Frank, and this time she didn't even see his glass eye. She looked beyond it into his warm heart, hoping she wouldn't break it when she told him she couldn't see him again.

For the next few months, Emily moped around the house, sinking into a deep depression. Her eyes and hair lost their sparkle, and she lost some weight. She couldn't bear not seeing Frank again, so she stayed away from Dufort's restaurant. Some days, it was hard to get out of bed.

One afternoon when Aunt Annie was off playing cards, the doorbell rang, waking Emily from a sound sleep. She put on her robe and slippers, shuffling to the door. "Who's there?"

"It's your little brother."

She opened the door and gave him a big hug. "John, you look great. What brings you by?"

"Sis, you look like crap. What happened to you?"

"Nothing that your visit can't fix. How long are you in town?" asked Emily.

"I hope for a while. I was hoping Aunt Annie would let me stay here until I find a job."

"I thought you were going to join the army."

"I can't. I couldn't pass the physical. The doctors told me I have a bad ticker."

Emily thought about their younger years sifting through the coal dust and remembered John's coughing fits. Could that have caused his heart condition? "Aunt Annie isn't here right now. We'll ask her if you can stay as soon as she gets back. But I'm sure it will be alright. She never says no to family."

Aunt Annie was receptive to the idea, but with Emily in one bedroom and Aunt Annie in the other, there was no place for John to sleep. "I have a great idea," said Emily. "Tomorrow I'm going to take my money out of the bank and buy a couch on time, so John will have a place to sleep."

"What happened to saving for a sewing machine?" asked Aunt Annie.

"That can wait. My brother needs a place to sleep."

"You are my two favorite ladies. Thank you," said John, as he extended his long arms around his sister and aunt for a family hug.

Emily cleared a drawer in her bureau so John could store his clothes. He only had to sleep two nights on the floor before the brown leather couch arrived. In no time at all, he landed a job as a butcher. Living with Bill all those years had its advantages. Emily and John reestablished their routine of playing Chinese checkers in the evenings. Soon Emily was back to her old self.

But the good times did not last long. Only a few months after John's arrival, Aunt Annie passed away in her sleep. Emily felt devastated. How could Emily make it through another funeral? How could she live without Aunt Annie? Where would she live now? Emily cried herself to sleep.

Grove Street
1923-1925

As sad as Emily was about her aunt's passing, she felt confident enough this time around to help her cousin Blanche with the planning of the funeral. The viewing took place in the parlor again, but John slept on the couch, and since Emily handled the payments, she wouldn't allow it to be thrown out to make room for the casket. Instead John, Emily, and Blanche half-carried, half-dragged the couch into Aunt Annie's room. They decided that John would sleep in Emily's room in the meantime, and Blanche and Emily would crowd together in Aunt Annie's room.

Emily remembered to cover Freddy's cage to keep him quiet, while a steady flow of mourners strolled through the apartment. They were mostly Aunt Annie's neighbors, church members, and her card playing friends. She couldn't help but notice that there were fewer people than at her father's funeral. Visibly absent were Margaret, Bill, and Helen, who couldn't attend because Helen was performing in her school chorus concert. Emily thought this was a flimsy excuse, but who was she to judge?

Did her father have more friends than Aunt Annie? That was impossible. Aunt Annie was the nicest person in the world. She asked Blanche about it. "My mother is quite older than your father. She has outlived most of her family and friends. The younger you are when you die, the more people you know are still alive to attend. And no offense to your father, but I don't know any of his friends that would turn down a free meal at a funeral." Emily supposed that was true. Sad, but true.

Emily wore the same black dress for her aunt's Mass that she wore for her father's funeral. She hoped she wouldn't have to wear it again soon. But this time Emily was an active participant in the Mass, reading Romans 8:35, 37-39. Blanche sang her rendition of "Amazing Grace" that brought tears to Emily's eyes. She thought about Helen's chorus concert. With any luck, Helen might inherit Blanche's singing voice that somehow had passed Emily by.

A new section of Holy Cross Cemetery had opened up in the few years since her father's death. If not for the open plot, Emily would have never found the gravesite. After burying her aunt next to her uncle, she wandered a few rows over to her father's grave and placed flowers on it. She noticed a bowling alley under construction, just beyond the perimeter of the cemetery. This would be a significant landmark to find her family's graves. She also noticed a new grave one row over from her father. Emily noticed the date on the tombstone- Edna Wilson, mother and wife 1904-1925. Edna was just 21 years old when she died- almost the same age as Emily. What a shame to die so young, before she had time to live. For the first time ever, Emily faced her own mortality and vowed to make something of her life.

Deja vu. That was a new word Emily learned from Peter Dufort when they entered his restaurant for the repast. Only this time, it was just the three of them- John, Emily, and Blanche. Peter did not offer to pay this time, so they each ordered a simple sandwich, similar to grilled cheese, called *croque monsieur.* It finally gave Emily some time to express her feelings to Blanche.

"What are your plans for your mother's apartment? Are you

going to let the lease go? John and I would love to stay there, but without Aunt Annie, we can't afford to live there."

"I can't either, and it's too bad because it's so close to the Charms Candy Factory. I could walk to work instead of taking the bus," said Blanche. "But hey, maybe all three of us together could swing it, and then you wouldn't have to move. Do you want to try it?"

The three of them discussed their finances. Combining their salaries and considering money for the telephone bill, food, and Emily's monthly payments for the couch, they all agreed it could work. So John moved back to the couch, and Blanche settled into Aunt Annie's bedroom.

One day Blanche came home with a radio. "How on earth are we going to afford that?" Emily asked.

"Don't worry. I bought it on time."

Emily worried, but after several months of keeping up with the monthly expenses, she began to relax. She gave up on reading. Her budget wouldn't allow her to buy books, and the library was too far away. No longer did she play Chinese checkers or pinochle with John. He had grown so distant lately, sleeping more and more each day. She was worried about his health. Was his heart worse than he was telling her?

Emily's new pastime became listening to the radio programs, especially "The Everyday Hour." Wendell Hall's ukulele music was heavenly, and his hit song "It Ain't Gonna Rain No Mo" was so catchy that Emily couldn't get it out of her head. She sang it everywhere- even in the bathtub.

On June 24, 1924, Wendell Hall married his sweetheart, Marion Martin, on the air. John slept through the entire event, while every girl with the luxury of a radio tuned in, wishing she could be Marion Martin. Blanche listened with her eyes closed, strumming an imaginary ukulele while Emily thought about Cora's wedding, wondering if her wedding day would ever come.

The next day, Blanche came home with a ukulele. Emily quickly learned that Blanche had extravagant tastes. "I'm never going to get married, so my new love is going to be the ukulele," she said, while hugging it next to her face.

"We can't afford that," said Emily.

"Yes, we can. I bought it on time."

"But we have to pay the rent first. In fact, it's due next week. Do you have your share of the money?"

"Not exactly."

"Then take it back."

"Who are you, my mother?"

"No, I'm just being practical. My name is the one on the lease, and I don't want the landlord to hunt me down when we don't pay him."

Blanche returned the ukulele and had her share of the rent, but when Emily asked John for his share, he told her he didn't have it.

"I lost my job last week."

"What happened?" asked Emily.

"I can't be a butcher anymore. I get sick around raw meat."

That didn't sound right to Emily. He sure has no problem eating it. "So get another job."

"I'm working on it."

"What am I going to tell the landlord?"

"Just ask him for a week's extension. I'll have a job and the money by then. I'm sure when you flash him your big brown eyes, he won't be able to resist your charm."

"You sound like Papa. He always talked about my big brown eyes too."

To Emily's surprise, the landlord was very understanding. John got a job as a roofer and had the rent money one week later as promised.

With the long hot summer days, John's workday began at 6:00 and finished most days by 2:30.

One day, the sound of coins jingling on the table and Freddy squawking awakened Emily. "Deuces are wild." She glanced at the clock next to her bed. It was only 3:00. Burying her head under her pillow, she tried to go back to sleep and reclaim her last hour of sleep. When Freddy squawked, "Jacks are wild," she knew it was a hopeless cause. Emily put on her robe and stomped into the kitchen.

"Sorry, sis. Did we wake you?" John and several of his work buddies sat around the kitchen table, playing poker and smoking cigars.

Emily coughed, fanning the heavy smoke in the air. "Well, I guess I'm up now." She turned on the radio and flipped through a Life magazine that she had "borrowed" from work. When 5:00 rolled around, Emily had to cook dinner, and the poker game was still in full swing. Since she had no intention of feeding John's friends, she shooed them out the door.

"Are you mad at me?" asked John.

"Not really, as long as you don't make it a regular habit. And I'm not inviting them to dinner. We aren't running a diner here."

"You got it, Sis."

But soon the card game became a regular occurrence. And the next month, just before the rent was due, John lost his job again. Now Emily had to face the landlord for the second month in a row, telling him they would be late again with the rent money. This time he wasn't as understanding. Although he accepted the rent a week later, he told Emily there would be a penalty this time. She would have to scrub the back stairs on the four-story building. Emily wanted John to wash them, but when he came home and put the rent money in her hand after landing a job as a shoe repairman, she let him slide and washed the steps with Blanche.

One morning, Emily dragged herself home from work, exhausted. As she turned the key in the lock, she heard Freddy squawk, "Hide the booze." Opening the door, she caught John scrambling to hide empty liquor bottles under the couch. One bottle rolled across the floor, only stopping when it hit Emily's foot.

Suddenly, it all made sense. Sleeping long hours, getting sick at work, and losing his jobs. Emily's tirade began. "After watching Papa drink himself to death, how could you do this? It's Prohibition for God's sake. You could get arrested or worse. You don't know what's in that. What if it's Jamaican ginger? You could end up blind, paralyzed, or dead. Have you lost your mind?"

John's eyes were bloodshot. He remained speechless, teetering on his feet.

"Get out." Emily pushed him toward the door.

"What about my tings?"

"Don't you mean your things? You're so drunk you can't even talk straight. I'll leave them on the porch. Come back tomorrow and pick them up." Emily hoped she was doing the right thing. She thought about the day Mama kicked out Papa and the downward spiral that ensued.

Emily explained the situation to Blanche. She was shocked but supportive of Emily's decision to throw John out. The girls reassessed their finances, cutting back on their food bill. They stopped making payments on the radio and on the couch, but they still couldn't survive without John's income.

"We need to find a new roommate. Let's put up signs at our workplaces and in lots of store windows, if their owners will allow it," said Blanche.

"Great idea."

The girls spent Saturday hanging signs. It didn't take long to get a response. On Monday, Blanche came home from work with a prospective tenant. "This is Frank. He might be interested in renting with us and wants to check out the apartment."

"Aw, we meet again," said Frank, his right eye looking right at Emily while its glass mate stared off into space.

"Do you two know each other?" asked Blanche.

"Yes, we met at the club. We wanted to date, but Aunt Annie said my mother wouldn't approve, and since I was living in her home, I had to respect her wishes," said Emily.

"That sounds more like my mother talking than yours. I

brought three beaus home over the years, but Mama would never approve- not marriage material, she would say," said Blanche.

"Not marriage material," squeaked Freddy.

"See, even Freddy backs me up. Why do you think I never married all these years?"

"I never knew." Emily saw an opportunity open here, and she planned to take full advantage of it.

"Anyway, Frank, this is our apartment. It's not much, and you would have to sleep on the couch. Are you interested?" said Blanche.

"Please say yes," Emily said hopefully.

"How can I say no when it reunites us again?"

Emily tried to contain her smile. She didn't want to appear eager to Frank.

Blanche and Emily offered to help Frank move in, but he declined. It took him only three trips to move in his few possessions. When Friday rolled around, Frank said to Emily, "Since we are both off from work tomorrow, how would you like to spend the day with me?"

"Are you asking me on a date, Mr. Rittenhofer?"

"Of course. This is way overdue."

"Well, it all depends."

"On what?"

"You never said where you wanted to go," Emily said, with a big smile on her face.

"I didn't, did I? Have you ever been to the Statue of Liberty?" Emily shook her head. "Well, neither have I. I heard someone at work yesterday talking about how many tourists a year visit it, and it got me thinking. Do the locals go there? We have two right here in this room that have never been. What do you say? Do you want to go?"

"I'd love to." Emily felt excited to try this new experience, especially with a man who appeared to like her as much as she liked him.

Since Frank didn't own a car, they took the bus to Liberty State Park. Their timing was perfect to catch the ferry to Liberty Island without waiting in line.

"I think we'll see better if we sit on the top," said Frank.

Emily took the first two steps but lost her balance when the boat pitched against the dock in the rough waters. Frank caught her as she fell backwards. "Steady now. You better hold on to the handrails," he said.

Emily grabbed the railing, and Frank left his hand on the small of her back for reassurance as they proceeded to the top deck. They sat on the front bench so they could see in two directions. The ferry continued to rock, making Emily's stomach queasy. "Do you mind if we go back down? I think it will be better on my stomach."

"Absolutely. We can't have you getting sick now, can we?"

They walked back down against the flow of other passengers going up. Choosing to stand, they held on to a pole as the boat lurched forward, leaving the dock. The ferry glided past Ellis Island, where a vast ship displaying the black, red, and yellow flag of Germany was unloading passengers onto the dock. Emily wondered how those people could have survived so long at sea when her stomach couldn't handle the brief trip to Liberty Island.

Standing up was an excellent choice, as Frank and Emily were the first passengers to disembark. Emily stopped to admire the sheer size of the statue and all of its intricate details.

"Did you know that there is a type of frog in the United States that can jump higher than the Statue of Liberty?" said Frank.

"Wow, that's amazing! No wait, you're fooling me. The Statue of Liberty can't jump! I'm glad to see that you didn't lose your sense of humor."

"I almost got you. What kind of shape are you in? There are 354 steps to the top of the statue, but if you think you can't make it, we can take the elevator up to the pedestal and save 176 steps."

"I want the total experience, so we are walking all the way. If we get tired, we can take a break on the pedestal until we catch our breath and admire the view a little longer."

Pacing their way, Emily and Frank arrived on the pedestal, only mildly out of breath. Despite the relentless wind at this height, Emily and Frank were rewarded with a breathtaking view of the harbor and the Brooklyn Bridge. There was little room to maneuver, and they soon found themselves plastered against the concrete wall, leaving a narrow pathway for other tourists to pass by. The man next to Emily held firmly onto his hat while he explained the history of the statue to his companion. Emily thought he must have been a teacher because he was so knowledgeable. She eavesdropped on the middle of the conversation. "He must have been obsessed with the number seven. The crown has seven spikes. It has 25 windows- five plus two equals seven, and it stands 151 feet tall- one plus five plus one also equals seven."

Emily found it hard to tear herself away from the conversation when Frank said, "I've caught my breath and rested my legs. Let's climb up the statue."

The narrow, winding staircase made it difficult to stand upright. Emily's back ached. The heat was unbearable, and it was only spring. She couldn't imagine making this climb in the summer. Reaching the apex, they only had about 30 seconds to look out through the crown before the momentum of the ascending crowd pushed them back down. When they reached the pedestal, they took the elevator down.

When Emily's feet reconnected with the green lawn, she collapsed, her legs feeling like rubber. Her overworked muscles shook ever so slightly. Being sure to leave his hands on top of her skirt, Frank gently massaged her thighs as Emily recapped her day. She concluded she would never climb the statue again. It was a thing she would only do once in her life, but it was an amazing first date.

The next day, Emily couldn't wait to call her mother and tell her all about the Statue of Liberty and the not so new man in her life. The problem was it was a long-distance call. Could she afford it? Emily sat in the chair, her eyes glued on the clock, determined to make the call last no longer than ten minutes. She was just about to ring the operator when she realized it was a Sunday morning. Would Mom be in church? She gave it a try and felt delighted to catch her mother at home.

Her mother told her she didn't attend church anymore. Emily laughed to herself, remembering the year Mama forced her and John to go to church when baby Helen was born. What a hypocrite.

Before Emily started talking about Frank, Aunt Annie's words reverberated in her head. "Your mother won't approve of a damaged man with a glass eye. He's not marriage material." But then, didn't Blanche say it sounded more like her mother than Emily's mom? Emily left that part out when she told Margaret about her date with Frank.

Margaret told Emily that she was happy for her and couldn't wait to meet Frank. Emily didn't think her mother sounded very convincing until she said, "I have a great idea. How about I call you every Sunday morning, say around 11:00? And you can share more of the juicy details of your relationship. I just adore love stories."

Margaret never struck Emily as the romantic type, but she agreed, especially when her mother was the one willing to pay for the cost of the long-distance phone charges. If it's free, it's for Emily. As she hung up the phone, Blanche was standing in the doorway. Was she listening to her conversation?

Overhearing Emily's conversation, Blanche said, "I'm happy that things are working out for you and Frank. I really am, but I feel like a third wheel. Maybe I should move out."

"Don't be ridiculous."

"Come on Emily. How would you feel if I were living here with my boyfriend?"

Emily hated to admit it, but she knew Blanche was right. "But how can Frank and I pay the rent without your share? I'm sorry. I didn't mean that. You must think I'm a callous person."

"No, I don't. I understand. I'll tell you what. Since the lease is signed until the end of the year, I will remain until then, and then we can all go our separate ways."

"That's a good idea. It will give us plenty of time to look for new apartments."

The following Saturday afternoon, Emily awoke to the aroma of a fresh-baked apple pie wafting from the kitchen. With her stomach growling, she staggered to the kitchen just as Frank, wearing khaki pants, a white shirt, and Emily's apron, pulled an apple pie from the oven.

"Oh good. It's about time you got up. Are you ready for your date today? I have prepared a feast - a picnic in the park."

Emily watched Frank pack the basket with cold broiled chicken left over from dinner, potato salad, pickles, bread and butter sandwiches, cheese slices, the apple pie, and a thermos of hot coffee. Did she die and go to heaven? This was the perfect man, and one who could cook too.

Frank carried the heavy basket to the park while Emily carried the light blanket. He didn't complain once about his load, but Emily noticed him flex his fingers when he plopped the basket on the ground.

Together, they enjoyed their dinner with an entertaining show. A squirrel tried to jump from a small bush into a garbage can and missed. He tried again and missed. On the third attempt, he fell right in. "Oh dear, how is he going to get out?" said Emily.

"Don't worry. Squirrels are pretty ingenious."

Sure enough, he hopped out with a half-eaten apple in his mouth and scurried up a tree. Emily's eyes followed him up to the highest branch until she was looking at the sky.

"Frank, look at that cloud up there. What do you see?"

"I see a horse."

"Me too. How about the one next to it?"

"A dragon."

"Dragon? It looks more like an igloo to me."

They laid on their backs, finding additional shapes in the clouds, but it quickly got boring. "What do you say we take a ride in one of those rowboats?" said Frank.

"I'd love to."

Stepping into the boat, Emily leaned on Frank until she anchored her feet. She waited until the boat steadied itself and took a seat in the back of the boat, facing Frank. He gave her a big smile, showing off his perfect teeth as he sat down and immediately began rowing. Emily couldn't help but notice his big biceps as he pulled on the oars. His strokes were hard and fast as they hugged the shoreline. The water was so shallow here that sometimes the oar struck bottom, stirring up mud and severing lily pads from their roots. Frank ducked as he steered under a low-hanging branch. Emily tried to follow his lead, but she wasn't fast enough. The branch clipped her head, littering its leaves in her hair.

Frank stopped rowing. "Oh, I'm sorry; that must have been unpleasant." Emily said nothing as she brushed the leaves out of her hair with her fingers. She wanted to look perfect for Frank. "My mama always used to sing to me whenever something bad happened. Why don't we try that? Row, row, row your boat gently down the stream. Merrily, merrily, merrily, merrily, life is but a dream," he sang. Emily joined in and soon they were singing in rounds. Boy, how those words rang true- life is a dream with Frank.

Frank stopped rowing to give his arms a break. From all his hard work, the boat continued drifting. Emily looked over her shoulder; they were in a secluded part of the lake. She wanted to massage his arms like he massaged her legs at the Statue of

Liberty. Should she do it? No- she didn't want him to think she was a floozy.

Their forward progress ended in front of a small cemetery. "People are dying to get in there," he said, pointing at the graveyard.

"Hahaha," Emily said, laughing at the corny joke.

"I have another one for you. Why can't you play cards in a boat?"

"I don't know. Why?"

"Because you're sitting on the deck." Although this joke was corny too, Emily politely laughed. "Emily Miller, I think I'm falling in love with you. Can I kiss you?"

She nodded. Frank leaned forward and kissed her. First, he gave her a peck on the cheek, followed by one on the lips. He looked into her eyes. She returned the stare, and suddenly the glass eye didn't matter. Emily saw two loving eyes and felt like she was looking into his soul. Frank reached in and gave her a passionate kiss. He was a perfect gentleman, never using his tongue or putting his hands where they didn't belong. They hugged and kissed until the mosquitoes started biting. Emily slapped her arm, drawing blood.

"It's getting dark. I better get you home," said Frank. He stood up, quickly reaching for the oars, and the boat began listing to the right. Emily held on tightly, feeling nauseous, while Frank steadied the boat. Try as she might, Emily couldn't control her stomach. She leaned over the side, vomiting the remains of her dinner into the lake.

Emily was never so embarrassed in her life. She thought about all the times she had to clean up Papa's vomit, how disgusting it was. What is Frank thinking about me now? He probably thinks his kisses made me barf. Would he ever want to see me again? She felt like jumping out of the boat and swimming to China, but she pushed her hand deep into the lake, scooping up some water to rinse her mouth and lips.

She turned around to face Frank with tears in her eyes. "I'm so sorry. I've ruined everything. It's not you. Your kisses were good, wonderful, in fact. It's me. I get seasick sometimes. You probably never want to see me again."

Frank wiped the tears from Emily's face. "Don't worry about it. It happens to the best of us. You got a little nauseous on our last date too. Let's forget all about this; put it behind us. Will you give me the honor of taking you out again next Saturday?"

"You mean you still want to go out on a date?"

"Of course, if you'll still have me."

Emily hugged Frank. "Yes, I'll go out with you anytime. There's one condition though."

"Name it."

"Let's go somewhere where I can keep my feet on solid ground."

"You got it."

A loud pounding on the door woke Emily the following Tuesday morning. She glanced at the clock. It was ten o'clock, way too early to get up. She rubbed her eyes and put on her robe. "I'm coming. I'm coming."

"I'm coming," squawked Freddy.

"Oh, shut up." Emily really had to get rid of that stupid bird. She threw the cover over the cage.

"Who is it?"

"It's Acme Repossession Company. Are you Emily Miller?"

"Why yes, I am."

"Let us in. You are delinquent on your couch payments, and we're here to repossess it. "

Emily didn't know what to do. She wished Frank and Blanche were here, but they had already left for work.

"Go away."

"Miss, open the door. You have no recourse here."

Emily knew they were right, she hadn't made her monthly payments. She reluctantly opened the door, her hand shaking.

Two men in overalls with biceps bigger than Frank's burst in. They threw Frank's pillow and blanket onto the floor and picked up the heavy couch like it was a small child. "Is there any way I can get it back?"

"That's between you and the store."

She watched her couch waltz out the door with the two men and locked the door behind them. She called Sears and asked to be connected with the billing department, where she spoke to a woman with a slight lisp. "This is Emily Miller. Two men just repossessed my couch. I was hoping we could come to some type of agreement so I can get it back."

"The time for the agreement would have been when you first started falling behind. You never contacted us; you just stopped making payments."

"I'm sorry. We temporarily lost our roommate and got behind on the rent."

"Everyone has a sob story. I think many people don't understand how credit works."

"Is there any way I can get it back? Please, I'm begging you."

"You will have to make the three months back payments and then the next three months to start the loan again."

"Thank you. I'll see what I can do." Six months' payments would be impossible.

Emily hung up the phone with tears in her eyes. She was getting more emotional every day. Frank might have been understanding about the vomiting, but would he be sympathetic about losing his bed? And just when things were working out between them. She tried to fall back to sleep, but she was still awake when Frank came home from work.

"What happened to the couch?"

"It got repossessed," said Emily.

"You mean you bought it on time?"

Emily nodded. "It was before you moved in. I was making payments regularly, but when my brother moved out, I stopped making payments so we could afford the rent. That's why we advertised for a roommate." Frank shook his head. "Say something."

"What do you want me to say? I don't believe in credit. If you can't afford to buy something outright, you don't buy it, because if something unforeseen happens, like losing your room-mate's income, you're flat out of luck. You could also lose your job or get sick and be unable to work." Frank took his valise from the closet and began stuffing his clothes into it.

"What are you doing?"

"What does it look like I'm doing? I'm leaving. I can't stay here, not without a bed."

Emily didn't like how angry Frank appeared. "Where will you go? Will I ever see you again?"

"I will probably get a room at the YMCA. As to if I will see you again, most likely, but not as often. The rent will be higher, and the 'Y' is on the other side of town."

"All I have to do is come up with six months' payments to get the couch back."

"I hope you're not asking for me to pay for it."

She was, but she said, "No. It was my mistake. All I'm saying is that it may take me some time to get enough money to get it back."

"When that happens, call me." Frank said as he deposited a kiss on Emily's forehead. When he opened the door, he was taken aback to find Blanche standing there.

Blanche saw the suitcase in Frank's hand. "What's going on here? Did you two lovebirds have a little spat?" she said.

"Yeah, over a missing couch. Did you know Emily bought the couch on time? No one should buy things they can't afford."

Blanche didn't have the heart to tell Frank that she also bought a radio on time. She wondered if that would also get repossessed one day. That would be sure to happen if the girls let Frank walk out the door. Coming up with a quick idea, Blanche said, "I have a solution."

"Let's hear it," said Frank.

"Why don't you share the bed?"

"That's pretty presumptuous of you," said Emily.

"I don't mean in that way. Frank, you sleep in the bed at night, and Emily, you sleep in it during the day. Your time never overlaps."

Emily loved this suggestion, but she didn't want to appear too anxious. She paused a few seconds before saying, "What do you say? I think it just might work. What do you think, Frank? Do you want to try it?" Emily said. "Please?"

"I guess I'm outnumbered by two lovely ladies."

Emily grabbed Frank's valise and hung his clothes back in the closet before he could change his mind.

When Frank emerged from the bathroom the following Saturday night wearing his khaki pants, cardigan sweater, and baseball cap, it became clear to Emily where he was going- the Polo Grounds, to watch the New York Giants play. What happened to their date night? Did Frank forget? Surely he didn't expect Emily to go to a baseball game.

"Have you ever been to a baseball game, Luv?" Emily shook her head. "Then you're in for a treat. Go get ready."

What was she supposed to wear to a baseball game? Scanning her wardrobe, Emily settled on her go to outfit- a white button-down waist shirt and gray tailored pleated skirt. She chose her black stockings and low-top shoes that showed off just enough of her ankles.

They boarded the train out to the Polo Grounds and took a seat in the second car. Frank made a fist and repeatedly drove it into his mitt. "Why did you bring that thing anyway? Aren't you afraid of losing it?" asked Emily.

"You don't know anything about baseball, do you? How do you think I'm gonna catch a ball?"

"Aren't there thousands of fans there? It seems pretty unlikely to me."

"You never know. Let's see how much you know about baseball. Can you name all the positions?"

Emily didn't think the positions mattered, but she rattled them off, counting with her fingers. "There's a pitcher, a catcher, first baseman, second baseman, third baseman, left fielder, right fielder, and a center fielder."

"There's one more."

"Wait, don't tell me. It'll come to me. The shortstop who stands between first and second base."

"Almost. The shortstop stands between second and third base."

"Why is it important to know the positions?"

"Because we are only a short stop away from the stadium."

"There you go again. Don't you ever run out of jokes?"

"For you, luv? Never."

The entrance was at the top of a hill. She could look down into the horseshoe shaped stadium. The clubhouse sat in deep center field. Early arriving fans had already dotted the bleachers in left and right field. Some fans also gathered at the top of the hill to watch the game. Emily thought they must be too cheap to pay for the admission. She hoped Frank wouldn't make her stand here. He could never catch a baseball from this height, but she worried for nothing, because they walked right by the milling fans, down the ramp, and into the stadium.

Frank bought tickets in left field, explaining that if we want to catch a ball, that is the place to sit because more players were right-handed than left-handed, and right-handed players hit more home runs into left field. It made sense to Emily. They took their seats on the bleachers. Frank sat down and stood up again so quickly that Emily thought he must have sat on a nail. "Here, hold my glove. I'm going to buy us some snacks."

"Can I have a hot dog?"

"No. I am getting fresh 'batter' pretzels and a 'pitcher' of beer."

Emily laughed. She read the program while Frank was gone.

He returned just as the National Anthem began playing. "Which players do you like? Who is most likely to hit a home run?" Emily asked.

"My money is on the second baseman, Frankie Frisch. He was a big star in the 1921 World Series, and he has a batting average of .335."

Emily found the game to be boring, but she paid attention when Frankie took the plate. "Wait a minute, he's left-handed. Shouldn't we be sitting in right field?"

"He's a switch hitter. I just hope he doesn't bat leftie all night."

When the count was two strikes and two balls, Frankie Frisch bunted a perfect pitch and got a base hit. His next time at bat, he stepped into the batter's box, ready to bat right-handed. Emily and Frank perked up. Frisch wasted no time. He swung on the first pitch, connecting with the ball. He hit it so hard the bat cracked in two. The ball headed right for them.

Frank stood up, his one good eye glued to the sky. As he took two steps to the right, another fan with his eyes also looking up took a step to the left and they collided. The impact knocked both of them to the ground. The ball hit a pole and ricocheted right into Frank's glove. "I got it," Frank said, rubbing his elbow.

"You really did," Emily said, hugging Frank.

"And you thought it couldn't be done."

"I guess I was wrong."

Just before the end of the game, Frank said, "Let's go."

"Don't you want to stay to the end? Get your money's worth, as my mama would say."

"Normally I would, but I want to hang out by the players' exit for a while. If we catch Frankie Frisch coming out, maybe he'll autograph my ball."

They wove their way through the crowd already established at the players' exit, trying to get up close.

"Hey Mack, where do you think you're going? We were here

first," said a man about twice the size of Frank. Emily hoped Frank wouldn't start a fight with this man.

"I'm looking for Frankie Frisch to autograph my ball. I caught his home run," Frank said, proudly holding up his treasure.

"Are you the knucklehead who collided with another guy up in the stands?"

"That's me."

"And you caught it with one eye? Impressive. Well, I guess that gives you first dibs then. You're welcome to move to the front."

They waited for a half hour before the players began filing out. With the players dressed in their street clothes, Frank wasn't sure if he would recognize Frankie Frisch without his cap. The first two players out of the clubhouse were clearly not Frankie Frisch. He stepped aside to let them pass. The third one could have been him. "Frankie?" Frank said. "No. He's not out yet."

After another half hour, the crowd had dissipated, leaving only Emily and Frank and the burly man they had first encountered. Emily looked at her watch. "We need to leave soon, or we'll miss the last train." Frank pulled out his pocket watch to verify the time.

"What's the matter, Frank? Don't you believe me?"

"I don't trust those new watches to keep the correct time. My pocket watch works just fine."

"They work just as well as pocket watches. Men have been wearing wristwatches for years now. You're about the only man I know who doesn't own a watch. When are you going to get with the program?"

Frank ignored her last remark. "Let's just give it another ten minutes." Emily nodded.

Finally, Frankie strolled out the door. Frank recognized him instantly with his bushy eyebrows and baby face. "Hey, Frankie, I caught your homer. Could you please autograph the ball for me?" Frank asked.

"Sure thing, kid."

Kid? Frank hadn't been called a kid in years. He was older than Frankie. Frisch pulled a pen out of his pocket, as if he expected to be asked for his autograph. As he signed the ball, Frank couldn't help but notice his wristwatch. "Thank you." And just like that, Frankie Frisch disappeared into the night.

"Here, luv. I want you to have this," Frank said, handing the ball to Emily.

"You keep it. It means so much to you."

"The only treasure I need is you. You keep it."

"Alright, as long as you're sure."

"I am."

Emily didn't care if anyone was watching as she gave Frank a sloppy kiss right on the lips. When she got home, she put the ball on the top shelf of her closet, along with her other treasured keepsakes.

As the year rolled on, Emily and Frank continued their Saturday date night. Emily enjoyed the circus and several trips to the movies. If she got the choice, Emily chose horror flicks like *The Phantom of the Opera* and *The Lost World*, where she could pretend to be scared and snuggle up next to Frank. Soon they discovered they didn't have to spend a lot of money to have fun. Simple things like taking a walk in the park, playing cards, and listening to shows on the radio made them happy, as long as they could be together.

Soon Emily thought about Frank constantly. It was like floating on a cloud- the time of year or day of the week no longer mattered. It took Blanche to bring her back to reality. "I'm going to give you and Frank the best Christmas present ever. Since Christmas is on a Friday this year, I'm going to go skiing with some friends for the weekend and leave you two lovebirds alone."

"Oh Blanche, you're the best. Thanks for being so understanding."

Christmas. And this year, Emily would have the blessing of

celebrating Christmas for a three-day weekend. She wondered what Frank would give her. A new couch? Unlikely. He would never buy it on credit, and so far, sharing the bed was working out fine. An engagement ring? That would be perfect.

On Christmas morning, Emily made pancakes and sausage while Frank put Christmas music on the radio. He sang along, putting the finishing touches on the Christmas tree. She wolfed down her food so they could open their gifts, feeling like a little girl again.

Frank opened his gift first. "I love it."

"Are you going to wear it?"

"Of course I am." And just to prove his point, he threw the pocket watch into the trash.

"What are you doing?" Emily said, fishing her hands deep into the garbage to retrieve the old watch. "That could be worth something. I'm going to take it to the pawnshop. We could use the extra money."

"Sorry. You are so right. Here's your gift."

Emily could tell by the size of the box that it was not a ring. She tried not to show her disappointment as she opened it. But it was a lovely gift- a sapphire necklace- her birthstone. "Oh Frank, I love it." And she meant it.

Before they knew it, the long weekend was over, and Frank returned to work on Monday morning. The first order of business was to take down all the Christmas decorations. Why couldn't management wait until after New Year's Day? But who was he to say? He was just a little peon and did what he was told. It took most of the morning to complete the task. After several trips up and down the ladder, removing the ornaments and dragging the bare tree to the incinerator, his knees and back hurt. He finally had time to rest at lunch, munching on Emily's leftover turkey and cranberry sandwich.

After lunch, he began his daily job of cleaning the bathrooms and washing the floor when he heard, "Frank Rittenhofer, report to the machinists' deck immediately." By instinct, he touched his glass eye, remembering the horrible day he lost his eye courtesy of a broken chain on the machinists' deck. He hoped and prayed another disaster was not unfolding, especially around Christmas time.

Frank heard an agonizing scream as he entered the deck. A man stood in the middle of the room, oozing blood from a gaping hole in what used to be his arm. Mercifully, the man had passed out onto the floor. A man tied a tourniquet just below the shoulder, while two others deposited him on a stretcher and whisked him away. Frank cleaned up the blood, skin, bone, and sinew, while all the other machinists looked on in shock. "Alright, the show's over. Get back to work," said the foreman. The company showed little compassion for the mangled man who would never be able to be employed again due to his severe injuries. How those men were supposed to forget about what they saw and go back to work, he would never know. And some of them didn't. Frank would be called back two more times that afternoon to clean up vomit.

He had little appetite for dinner that night. Without sharing the gory details of his day, it was hard to convince Emily it wasn't her cooking. "I hope you're not getting sick." She felt his forehead. "No fever. That's a good sign."

Frank drank three cups of coffee, trying to stay awake and to convince Emily and himself that everything was fine. When Emily left for work that night, Frank crawled into bed, emotionally and physically drained.

Walking to work that night, Emily thought about how boring her job at the phone company had become. Few people made calls in the middle of the night as it was, and she feared the week between Christmas and New Year's Day would be even slower. Most of her customers told her they would still be out of town until New Year's Day. For those who weren't, after visiting for a three-day weekend with family, there wouldn't be much to talk about a day later. The year was winding down, and she still hadn't heard about a day job yet. Tonight, she packed a thermos of coffee and her book to occupy her time through the endless boredom of the night shift.

Arriving at work, Emily completed her regular routine, hanging up her coat and reading the daily notices on the bulletin board. The company fired an employee for reading a book at work. So much for that idea. She took her seat at her station, wondering how she would get through the boring night.

Her first call came immediately, a drunken man trying to call his wife for a ride home. Then nothing for the rest of the night. Emily took a slug of her coffee and then another and another until she polished it off. She sang every Christmas song she could think of- "Away in a Manger," "It Came Upon a Midnight Clear," "Hark the Herald Angels Sing," "Joy to the World," "Oh Come All Ye Faithful," and "Good King Wenceslas Looked Out." Then she challenged herself by reciting "Joy to the World" backwards. "Sing-nature-and-heaven-and-heaven-and-sing-nature-and-heaven-and-sing-nature-and-heaven-and-room-him-prepare-heart-every-let-king-her-receive-earth-let-come-has-lord-the-world-the-to-joy." She glanced at her watch. Only an hour of her shift had passed. Emily asked the chief operator for a necessary. She didn't need to go. The coffee hadn't worked its way to her bladder yet, but she got to kill some time, stretching her legs and reapplying her make-up. Walking back on the floor, she watched her co-worker release a huge yawn, which promptly made her yawn too. Didn't she hear somewhere that yawns are contagious? For the rest of the evening, she let her feet practice the dance moves she had learned in the convent while she counted the yawns of her co-workers. She counted 37 by the lunch break.

On the second half of the shift, Emily stood trying out some yoga moves she read about in a magazine somewhere, although she couldn't recall where. Balancing was harder than it looked. She watched the janitor wash the floor, pointing out a spot of dirt that he missed. When he shot her an angry look, she refrained from that activity and asked for another necessary, this time blaming it on the chocolate cream pie she ate over the weekend that was too rich for her stomach. She counted another 51 yawns before it was time to go home for the day. She dragged herself home, ready to collapse into bed, only to find Frank asleep in the bed.

"Come on, Frank. Get up. You're going to be late for work," said Emily, nudging him in the back.

"Too tired. Called in sick."

"Come on, it's my turn for the bed." Could Emily sleep in Blanche's bed? No, Blanche was pretty particular about her private things. Frank wasn't budging. Feeling that she had no other choice, Emily changed into her nightgown and hopped into bed. She laid on her side, facing away from Frank while trying to fall asleep. His hand cupped her breast through the thin material. Her eyes shot open. Should she stop this before it progressed any further? This would be the time to say something. Instead, she closed her eyes, trying to fall asleep.

Frank expected Emily to raise an objection or grab his hand, but receiving none, he reached his hand under the nightgown, gently stroking his fingers across Emily's thigh. He lingered briefly between her legs and then continued working his way over her abdomen and belly button to caress her breast. He drew circles around her areola and flicked her nipple. Emily could feel her nipples harden. Frank's magic fingers traveled into her underpants. As his fingers gently stroked her between her legs, Emily's underpants became soaked.

Emily rolled onto her back and looked Frank right in his good eye. So many thoughts were going through her head. If she continued, she would no longer be a virgin. What would Mama think? Was her mother a virgin when she got married? Would she somehow look different? Could people tell she lost her virginity just by looking at her? Could she still wear white when she got married? Would Frank still marry her? Or would any other man, for that matter, if she wasn't a virgin? Emily didn't want the warm, pulsating sensation in her loins to end. She nodded.

Frank propped his hands under her bottom. Grabbing the panties on either side, he quickly shimmied them down her legs, throwing them onto the floor. He dropped his clothing onto the floor like a snake shedding its skin. Gently nudging her legs apart, Frank knelt between them. For the first time, Emily stared at a grown man's naked body, a sight she had never witnessed before, except in her imagination. He was so big down there and seemed to grow bigger as he moved closer. Emily couldn't imagine his manhood fitting inside her. "Don't worry, I'll be gentle."

With a soft but persistent push, he was inside of her. Frank collapsed onto her torso with his crushing body weight, their bodies thrusting in unison. Frank kissed her, pushing his tongue deep into her mouth. Experiencing a mixture of pain and pure pleasure, Emily held on to the wrought iron slats of the headboard. She could hardly breathe. After several minutes, Frank rolled off of her, spent, breathing like a steam engine.

"Are you alright, Frank?" Emily thought he was having a heart attack.

"Am I alright? Better than alright. Amazing, in fact." Frank looked at the droplets of blood collecting on the sheets between Emily's legs. "Emily, you are a beautiful woman. Let me make an honest woman out of you. Would you do me the honor of being my wife?"

"Oh, yes." Emily's Cinderella dream was coming true. With their bodies entwined, they giddily discussed wedding plans. They made love again. This time, there was no pain, just pure pleasure.

Netherwood Place
1925-1926

E mily had news to share with her mother, and she wasn't waiting until Sunday to reveal it. "Mom, I'm getting married."

"Oh, that's wonderful. You've been bragging about Frank for a long time, and we still haven't met him. Why don't you get married on New Year's Eve? What a great time for a party. And it just so happens we're having a big one here in the barn. Since it's already planned, it won't cost you anything. You know most of the neighbors, and I'm sure that they'll want to wish you well."

"That offer is too good to turn down. Just let us iron out some things around here, and we'll be there."

The first order of business was her job. Emily liked how Frank called in sick, so she followed his example. It wasn't like they were busy anyway. She called out for the rest of the week, complaining about a sore throat. She feared it might be a mild case of the mumps, and she was only thinking about her coworkers. Wanted to keep them safe. Management bought it.

Next on the agenda was finding a new place to live. There were only a few days left in the month. Emily and Frank had put off finding a new place to live for too long. Frank ran to the corner, returning with the Newark Evening News. Arriving home, he flipped to the classifieds, looking for an appropriate apartment.

Because of the time constraints, they looked for a furnished apartment. One with a bed and couch. They visited three apartments, discovering that they were way out of their price range. Frank crossed each off the list, their prospects dwindling quickly.

"Frank, look at this one. It's the second floor of a two-family house. And it's only $35 a month. Why don't we check it out?"

"I bet that's a misprint. It sounds way too good to be true."

"Only one way to find out."

Just three blocks long, Netherwood Place was a group of newly constructed homes. Frank and Emily knocked on the door of the only house with a vacancy sign in the window. An old woman answered the door. Emily couldn't help but notice the tremor in her hand.

"Can I help you?" she said, with a voice as trembling as her hand.

"We're here about the apartment for rent. Is this the correct price?" Frank said, waving the newspaper in her face.

"Why yes, it is. But there's a reason for it. My name is Barbara Goslowski. You see, I have Parkinson's disease. My husband recently died- a heart attack- and I can't take care of myself, let alone manage this place. I need a tenant to help me out. Buy groceries. Take me to the doctor. Do minor repairs when needed. In exchange, I substantially reduced the rent. Is that something you might be interested in?"

Emily thought she had died and gone to heaven. Between Frank's experience as a janitor and hers as a caregiver to children over the years, they were the perfect fit, and Emily told Barbara so. "Can we see the apartment?"

"Of course." Barbara reached into the pocket of her calico dress, pulling out the keys that rattled in her hand, and passed them to Frank. "I have trouble with the stairs. Just bring them back after you look."

Emily and Frank walked up the steep steps, counting 16 in

all to the top. They opened the door to a large living room and immediately noticed a radio by the large window. A telephone sat on an end table between a dark green easy chair and a green-flowered couch. Frank picked up the receiver, putting it to his ear. "Can I help you?" asked the operator.

"No, sorry. I'm just checking to see if it works." Frank returned the receiver to the cradle.

They moved into the kitchen. Emily opened every cabinet and found the place well stocked with dishes, flatware, cups, pots, and modern kitchen gadgets. This was a big plus. She thought about all the times she had moved in her life, remembering how many trips it took to load and unload all the kitchen items. The kitchen and the bathroom both had running water and electricity, with all the pipes and wires hidden behind the walls.

Each bedroom had a double bed and dresser. Emily ran her finger through a thick layer of dust on the dresser as a sneeze escaped Frank's nose. "*Gesundheit.* Frank, no one has dusted this room in weeks, maybe months, That's a good sign. Nobody else is interested. I bet it's ours for the taking. What do you say?"

"If you want it, baby, it's all yours."

They returned the keys to Mrs. Goslowski and signed the lease. Returning home, Emily left a note for Blanche, who would be home that evening. She filled her in about her wedding on New Year's Eve at Mama's farm, begging Blanche to come.

The first bus out to the Catskills was at 7:00 in the morning. Frank and Emily were on it. This gave Emily the chance to fill Frank in about her family. "Mama is pretty selfish, and Bill is a mean son of a gun."

"You don't mean that, do you?"

"What would you call a mother who neglects her duties, saddling them off on her children? I can't tell you how many times I had to fetch Papa's beer and clean up after him when he got drunk. And what do you think of a mother who leaves her children alone in an apartment for weeks with little food?"

"Wow. Maybe she's trying to make it up to you now by throwing us this wedding."

"I hope you're right. She was never there for me at the key times in my life, like when I needed a mother to teach me about things like fashion and make-up. That's why I'm letting my sister Helen be my maid of honor. It will be a hoot for her, dressing up and learning how to do her hair and make-up. I'm sure my mother never showed her either. Oh, by the way, who is standing up for you?"

"I have a cousin, Joseph. He lives nearby. He agreed to be my best man."

"Oh, and there is one more thing I think you should know about my family, and I'm not sure you are gonna like it. They are a bunch of bootleggers."

Frank laughed. "I'm alright with that. I used to be a bartender, remember?" Emily nodded. "It was a good job. If the government hadn't interfered, I would never have lost my job or my eye."

"But then you would have never moved to New Jersey, and we would never have met. Fate plays a part in our lives."

"You are so right."

Bill met Frank and Emily at the bus station with his horse-drawn sled. Bill had changed little, maybe a little heavier around the middle. He pulled off his glove, saying, "You must be the famous Frank. Let me be the first to shake your hand."

"Nice to meet you," Frank said, looking right into Bill's face.

Emily watched Bill's smile slowly fade into a concerning grin. She was sure Bill couldn't or wouldn't see beyond the glass eye. He was quiet and withdrawn as Emily and Frank babbled on and on about how they met and all their fun dates.

When they arrived at the house, Margaret stepped out of the barn. Bill hopped down from the wagon and whispered something in her ear. Mama put her hand over her mouth and approached Emily and Frank.

Could she make it any more obvious? She was like a child who couldn't keep a secret. Frank met Margaret halfway with his hand extended. "Nice to meet you. Do I call you Margaret or Mom?" he said warmly.

Margaret stared directly into Frank's face. "You can call me anything you want. Emily, may I have a word with you in the barn?" Emily followed her mother while Frank helped Bill unhitch the team. Red and green candles garnished each table, and strands of holly decorated the walls. Bill had a pig already cooking over a fire pit for tomorrow's festivities. Emily appreciated her mother and Bill. They had worked hard getting things ready for her wedding.

"Is this some sort of joke? You can't be serious about marrying that freak of nature."

"He's not a freak. He had an accident, is all. And yes, Mother, I'm gonna marry him. I love him."

"What do you know about love? You don't marry a man for love, you marry him because he will be a good provider. He's a damaged man. Does he even have a job?"

"He's a janitor."

"Janitor? How can he provide for you on that kind of salary? You'll never own a house or a car."

"I don't care. I still want to marry him."

"Not here. If you want to marry him, I can't stop you. You're an adult, but don't expect me to accept it or pay for it, for that matter."

Emily loved Frank and had every intention of marrying him. What was wrong with her mother? Maybe she needed to go back to church because she wasn't being very Christian-like right now, not following Jesus's way. But neither was Emily. "Maybe we'll never own a house or a car like you say, but at least he has a steady job."

"What is that supposed to mean?"

"You're such a hypocrite. Papa had good jobs, but with all that drinking, he couldn't keep them. He was no provider to us. And Bill is a bootlegger who could end up in jail. What kind of provider will he be if he ends up behind bars?"

"You insolent little brat." Mama slapped Emily right across the face.

"Goodbye, Mama. Frank! Frank! Come on, we're leaving."

They lugged their suitcases back toward the bus station through the snow until Bill caught up to them with the sleigh. "Come on, Emily. Come back and apologize to your mama before you regret it."

"Sorry Bill. Right now I can't."

"At least let me drive you to the bus station."

On the bus, Emily removed her boots to massage her frozen feet. Aunt Annie's words resonated in her head, "Your Mama won't like Frank. He's not marriage material." She sure had Mama pegged right.

Emily woke Thursday morning, New Year's Eve, more determined than ever to marry Frank that night. But with no preparations or money, how could she make it happen? She called her old friend, Cora, who she hadn't spoken to in years. Cora was exceptionally skilled at improvising and making quick decisions. If anyone could help her, it would be her.

Cora and Emily reminisced about old times, and then Emily brought Cora up to speed about her current situation. "So you see, I don't know what to do."

"Leave it to me. Emily, I am going to throw you the best wedding you can ever imagine, and I will stand up for you. We'll be there in a few hours."

"Thanks Cora, you're the best."

Emily had just hung up the phone when it promptly rang again. "Cora, what did you forget?"

"This isn't Cora. This is the telephone company. I'm looking for Emily Miller."

"This is she."

"First, how are you feeling? I heard you were a little under the weather."

"Better, thank you. I should be back to work on Monday the fourth." Emily hated lying.

"That's why I'm calling. We would like to offer you the position of chief operator on the day shift. Are you interested?"

"Boy, am I. Thank you so much. I'll be there bright and early Monday morning." As she hung up the phone, she could see her life falling perfectly into place.

Several hours later, Cora arrived with many surprises. The first being Cora's swollen belly. Emily hugged her. "You'll make a fine mother."

"Just like you'll make a fine bride. Here, try this on." Cora unzipped a bag, revealing her bridal gown.

"Cora, I can't. That's your dress."

"I don't need it anymore, and the way I look at it, you spent just as much time making it as I did."

"Oh Cora, you're the best." Emily disappeared into the bedroom to try on the dress. She admired herself in the mirror, feeling like Cinderella about to attend the ball. Returning to the parlor, she asked, "What do you think?"

"Beautiful. I just love weddings. And before I forget, here is our wedding present to you," Cora said, handing Emily and Frank an envelope.

"Cora, you didn't have to do that. Just giving me the dress and standing up for us is more than enough."

"Well, we did. Now open it. I hope you like it. Consider it a honeymoon present."

Frank tore the envelope open, revealing two tickets for *No No Nannette* at the Palace Theatre on January 9, 1926. Neither of them had been to a Broadway play before. "Oh Cora, of course I love it," Emily said, hugging her best friend. Frank put the tickets back in the envelope and put it in the top drawer of his bureau for safekeeping.

"Now off to the ceremony," said Cora.

"Where did you find anyone to preside at this late date?" asked Frank.

"It was easy. Ronald knows Mayor Raymond. They both attended NY University. He is a ham and loves publicity, anything to help his career. It turns out he is celebrating New Year's Eve at Dufort's tonight. He agreed to marry you as long as you wait until after midnight. The four of us will join him and his wife at his table because the place was fully booked tonight."

The two couples walked to Dufort's restaurant. Emily loved being the center of attention in her wedding gown, as the passers-by stopped to congratulate her. A bouncer told them to wait at the door until he could verify that they had permission to sit with the mayor. Mayor Raymond returned himself to escort them to the table.

Being a celebrity granted Mayor Raymond a great table- not too crowded, not near the kitchen or the bathroom, and just close enough to the dance floor to dance without being over-whelmed by the band. He introduced us to his wife, who was wearing a light blue silk dress with oriental lace sleeves and rosebud trim.

They dined on roast beef, mashed potatoes, and peas. Emily felt delighted that the menu now offered American fare, as well as the traditional French dishes. Cora and Mayor Raymond were the main focus of the conversation- she talked about meeting Alice Paul, and he boasted about his efforts to start the construc-tion of Port Newark. Not being able to get a word in, Emily and Frank enjoyed dancing most of the night. Just before midnight, the band stopped playing to countdown the last seconds of 1925. All the couples paused to kiss their dates.

Mayor Raymond shouted, "Can I have your attention, please?" Several tables looked in his direction, but he continued louder. "Can I have your attention please?" as he banged his fork against his glass. The room fell silent. "I am here tonight to join a couple in wedded bliss, and you all get to witness it. "Frank, Emily, come join me in the center of the floor." Emily loved being the center of attention, but her knees were shaking. She looked Frank in the eye as she recited her vows. When the mayor pronounced them man and wife, all the tables clapped and cheered. Emily noticed a group of girls from the telephone company stand to cheer, each toasting her with a glass of grape juice in their hands. Suddenly a photographer appeared to take their picture, or was it to take a picture of the mayor? "Wait, no flowers?" asked the photographer. Mayor Raymond plucked a rose out of the centerpiece, placing the stem into Frank's jacket pocket. He then handed Emily the whole centerpiece to hold while the three of them posed for pictures. The mayor promised to send them a copy of the wedding picture when it was developed.

Mr. and Mrs. Rittenhofer danced until two in the morning before excusing themselves to go home to spend their last night in the apartment, where they consummated their marriage.

When Emily woke up the following morning, Frank was already up and out of bed. She glanced at the alarm clock. Twelve noon. She couldn't think of a time she ever slept that late on days when she wasn't working. Strolling into the kitchen, she found Frank putting the finishing touches on a fried egg and bacon breakfast. "Glad you're up, Mrs. Rittenhofer. I made you breakfast."

"Oh, you're so sweet, Mr. Rittenhofer." Emily kissed Frank, grabbed her plate from the counter, and joined her husband at the table. Blanche sat opposite Frank, puffing on a cigarette. But Blanche only smoked when she was upset. "You two look deep in conversation. Is everything alright?"

"I was just explaining to Blanche that it would be alright for her to move with us into the new apartment. But she wants no part of it."

"It's fine. We have a second bedroom."

"Nobody wants a third wheel, especially newlyweds."

"Where will you go?"

"I don't know yet, but Mr. Dufort says I can store all the furniture in his extra storage room until I know for sure."

Peter Dufort was such a nice man. Every time there was a family crisis, he was there to help, as was Mr. Sullivan. They were assets to the community.

Peter showed up with his truck, and the four of them spent most of the afternoon moving Blanche's belongings into the storage room. "Blanche, make sure to call me with your new address when you are settled."

"You know me; I will." With that, Blanche gave Emily a big hug.

"It's getting late. What do you say we go home, have a quick dinner, and then move our stuff into the new apartment?" said Frank.

Emily pouted. "But I want our first dinner together to be in our new apartment."

"I can't say no to those big brown eyes."

"You sound like Papa."

Without a car, Emily and Frank would have to make many trips, carrying all their belongings by hand. They took all the ingredients they would need for dinner on the first run, and Emily would stay in the new apartment to cook while Frank made several more trips. If by some chance Frank couldn't finish, Emily would either help him later that night, or on Sunday, if they needed more time.

Arriving on the porch of their new home, Frank said, "Put those groceries down; I want to carry my new bride across the threshold." Giggling, Emily dropped the bags. Two apples rolled onto the street. Frank swooped her up and began his trek up the stairs. Emily's legs hit the wall in the narrow stairway, causing them to ricochet. She thought Frank might drop her, so she tightened her grip around Frank's neck.

When they finally reached the top, Mrs. Goslowski opened her door. "What is all the noise out here?"

"Frank is carrying me across the threshold."

"How romantic, but you're doing it the hard way. Carrying her across the threshold just means the doorway. The apartment door would have sufficed. You didn't have to carry her all the way up the steps."

"I didn't mind. My husband is showing off his strength."

Looking at the bags of food, Mrs. Goslowski asked," What are you making for your first dinner together?"

Emily thought her new landlord and neighbor might be a little nosey. Or was it just loneliness? At any rate, she didn't want to get off on the wrong foot, so she answered the question. "Chicken and dumplings and apple pie."

"Sounds yummy."

"We will bring you a slice of pie," Frank said.

Because of acclimating herself to her new kitchen, dinner took a little longer than usual to fix, but it gave Frank enough time to transfer their remaining belongings. They enjoyed their first dinner together and had time to relax on Sunday before Emily's big work day.

On Monday morning, Emily set her alarm clock ten minutes earlier than she needed. She wanted everything to be perfect for her first day as chief operator. Even spending extra time on her hair and makeup, she made it to work with time to spare. She entered the personnel office. The new manager, Mr. Billings, who Emily hadn't met yet, sat behind his desk glaring at her. One girl who was at Emily's wedding, whose name she couldn't recall, was also in the room. What was she doing here? Was she also starting a new position?

"Come in, Emily, and sit down. Roberta here was just telling me an interesting story." Emily looked at Roberta, a smug look on her face. "Is it true that you were married over the weekend?" he asked.

"Yes."

"I think congratulations are in order."

"Thank you."

"There is a problem though. You weren't sick, were you?"

Emily didn't know what to say about being caught in a big lie. She merely shook her head.

"I can't have people working here who are dishonest. I also don't like married women working for me."

"Why not?"

"Because training workers takes a lot of time. In return, I expect my workers to give me a lot of years of service. Married women only stay until they get pregnant."

"I'm not pregnant."

"I'm sure you will be soon."

Emily thought about all the women who worked at the phone company. She couldn't think of one woman who was married. Suddenly, it became clear to Emily. Roberta had ratted her out. How rude. Or conniving. Was Roberta going to steal the job right out from under her? Women have had the right to vote for years now, but they still had a long way to go. How is this fair?

"I suppose Roberta here is getting my job?"

"That is not your concern. I suggest you go home and begin your wifely duties."

Fighting back tears, Emily left with her head held high. As she walked home, she reflected on her life. Every time she moved, her life began another chapter. But what would the married chapter be like? What would she do with herself all day long without a job? Would she find herself bored out of her mind for the rest of her life? Had she made the wrong choice? No, she loved Frank.

She remedied the situation on her own, with no input from Frank. If she discussed it with her husband, he would be perfectly content to let her stay home and play housewife, and that was not acceptable to her. Emily feared her brain and hands would rot away if she didn't use them. She sold her tickets to *No, No Nannette* and bought a sewing machine. She would begin a business from home, making clothes and knitting scarves, mittens, and socks. Thank you, Sister Francois.

After two months of marriage, she was running a lucrative business. Emily also developed a bond with Mrs. Goslowski. Besides running errands, cleaning her house, and gardening, Emily found time to entertain her. She tried to teach Mrs. Goslowski her favorite game, Chinese checkers, but it was torture for her. Her shaking fingers couldn't hold on to the marbles without dropping them and upsetting the board. They played pinochle and gin rummy instead. And if Frank was available in the evenings, the three of them played hearts. Emily was never bored, and by the end of the month, she discovered she was with child.

This news came with mixed emotions. She was happy to be having a baby, but Emily and Frank had their first argument. "Frank, I want to have my baby in a hospital."

"No, I want you to have the baby here. Women have been having children at home with midwives for years."

"Yeah, and women have been dying in childbirth for years too. You don't want me to be one of those, do you?"

"Of course not. But I'm not convinced that having a baby at a hospital is better."

"If something goes wrong, the doctor will be there."

"True, but hospitals aren't the cleanest places, with all those germs. You could pick up an infection. You're an outstanding housekeeper." Frank inhaled deeply. "I can smell the bleach and lemon. Germs can't live here. No way will you or the baby get an infection in this house. Besides, I want to be here to hold your hand when our son or daughter comes into the world. In the hospital, fathers have to wait in another room."

Everything Frank said made sense, but deep down in her heart, she knew the real reason he didn't want to go to the hospital- they simply couldn't afford it. And no matter how many socks, scarves, or dresses she could sell, it wouldn't be enough. "I'm scared. What if something goes wrong?"

"Midwives are very professional. They are practically nurses.

Why don't I hire one now? She can examine you and put your mind at ease."

Emily knew she was on the losing end of this argument, so she reluctantly agreed.

The following week, Iris, the midwife, came to the apartment to examine Emily. Iris wore a long-sleeved white blouse, white skirt, and white pinafore. She had her hair pulled back into a tight bun, with bobby pins anchoring the white cap on her head. She looked like a snowman. Emily laughed to herself.

"Frank tells me you are very nervous about having a baby. Let me tell you, I've delivered hundreds of babies in my career, and I never lost a mother or baby. That's because I visit the mothers-to-be early on, and if I see anything that might look like a problem, I won't accept the job. Now, let me examine you and see what we've got."

Iris rummaged through her black bag, lifted a pair of forceps, and promptly dropped them back in. Emily closed her eyes, trying to get the image of them wrapped around her baby's head out of her mind. Iris pulled out a stethoscope. "Let me listen to your heart. Take a deep breath." Emily took several deep breaths as Iris moved the stethoscope between her breasts and onto her back. "Nice strong heartbeat. Lie back on the bed." Iris lifted Emily's dress and put the stethoscope on her stomach. It felt cold against Emily's bare skin. "Do you want to hear your baby's heartbeat?" asked Iris.

Emily nodded. While gripping one end on Emily's stomach, Iris put the earpieces in Emily's ears. "So fast. Is that normal?"

"Of course. The smaller the baby, the faster the heartbeat. Your baby is tiny right now, but has a healthy heartbeat." Emily stayed on the bed as Iris moved her hands around the curve of her waist, stopping to poke at her hip. "God blessed you with wide hip bones. Perfect for delivering babies. You should have no problem delivering this baby."

Time seemed to stand still for Emily as the months wore on. The morning sickness disappeared, only to be replaced with strange cravings- pineapples and ice cream, and she could no longer tolerate red meat, much to Frank's chagrin. Her breasts and belly became full, making everyday tasks difficult. Her back hurt as she leaned over the sewing machine, and climbing the stairs made her winded. And cleaning? The thing that Frank praised her for was now neglected. She was afraid if she got down on her hands and knees to clean the toilet, she would never get back up, so she stopped cleaning it. Mopping the floor made her back hurt, so she stopped doing that too. Soon she slept more and more.

One day in early October, Emily got a second wind. She woke up early and cooked bacon and eggs for breakfast. "I don't know what got into you, but I'm glad to see you eating meat again."

"I don't feel so tired today. The baby will come any day now, so I want to clean up this place, make it sterile."

"Sounds like a plan. But promise me you'll take it easy."

"I will," Emily said as she kissed Frank and shooed him out the door to work.

Her first order of business was washing the mountain of neglected dishes in the kitchen sink. About halfway through, Emily had a strong and sudden urge to go to the bathroom. She was lucky to make it to the toilet when a bout of diarrhea came upon her. Since this was the first time in months that she had eaten fatty meat, she convinced herself her system wasn't used to it.

She finished the dishes and tackled the kitchen floor. Emily washed a small section of the floor and dipped the mop into the bucket to rinse it off when she felt a small dull pain in her lower back. Frank's words to take it easy resonated in her mind., so she sat down until the pain subsided. She stood up slowly, and a gush of water flooded her dress and the floor. It was a good thing that the mop was already out. Emily cleaned up the mess and finished the floor. Lifting the bucket with the dirty water to the sink to empty it, a stronger, sharper pain ripped through her back. It felt like a lightning bolt had struck her back and traveled through her spine to her stomach.

Dribbling a fresh deposit of water onto the clean floor, Emily dragged herself to the telephone and called Iris. "I think I'm in labor. Get over here. Should I call Frank?"

"Oh baby, don't bother him yet. You have a long way to go. Labor takes hours. I want you to lie down and try to rest. Count how much time there is between contractions. When they are five minutes apart, call me and I'll be right over."

Emily got the message loud and clear, but if she laid down, would she be able to get back up to reach the phone in the kitchen? She called Mrs. Goslowski and asked her to please come up and sit with her. This was no time to be alone.

Mrs. Goslowski must have had some nursing training in her background because she knew how to keep Emily calm, wiping the sweat from her forehead and giving her ice chips to munch on.

Within an hour, the labor pains were five minutes apart. "It's time to call Iris and Frank. I'll be right back," Mrs. Goslowski said.

"Don't leave me alone," Emily said, gritting her teeth through another contraction.

"You'll be fine."

Emily waited patiently for Mrs. Goslowski to return. "Are they coming?"

"Iris is on the way. She told me to boil water and start a fire in the fireplace."

"What about Frank?"

"The company operator told me he was out in the yard unloading a truck and he would be hard to reach, but someone was running out to give him the message."

Would Frank get here in time? Emily thought about his argument for home delivery- a sterile house and the father could be here. Now neither would come to pass.

Iris appeared in the doorway. "How is our patient?"

"She's doing fine," Mrs. Goslowski said.

"It's about time you got here. I'm in a lot of pain and I'm feeling a lot of pressure down there."

"Let's have a look. You're crowning. I can see the baby's head. You can start pushing with the next contraction. How's that water coming?"

"I'm on it," said Mrs. Goslowski, on her way to the kitchen.

Iris pulled clean rags out of her bag, packing them around the patient. Emily felt like a big baby lying in a diaper. The next pain hurt so badly, she thought she might pass out.

"Push. Push as hard as you can." Iris sat her up with her legs spread far apart.

Emily looked in the mirror across from the bed. The baby's head was out. "Please, cover the mirror. I don't want to watch this."

While Mrs. Goslowski covered the mirror with a quilt, Iris said, "I think one more push will do it. As soon as the shoulders are out, the rest will be easy."

Emily thought it better be because she had no strength left in her. With the next contraction, she pushed so hard her legs shook like a worn-out rubber band. The baby shot out into Iris's hands.

"It's a girl."

"Can I hold her?"

"In a minute. We need to clean her up." Iris reached into her black bag, pulling out a pair of scissors and handing them to Mrs. Goslowski. "Boil these for two minutes and bring them back to me."

Mrs. Goslowski stood as far away from the pot as she could to sterilize the scissors. She didn't want any boiling water to fall on her shaking hands. She returned the scissors to Iris, who cut the cord and tied it off with twine.

"Can I hold her now?"

"Not yet. The afterbirth is coming."

Iris handed the baby to Mrs. Goslowski, while she wrapped the afterbirth in the bloody rags and threw it into the fire. Emily hoped Mrs. Goslowski wouldn't drop her baby with those trembling hands.

Iris took the baby from Mrs. Goslowski, handing her to the new mama. "What's this little angel's name?"

"Meet Laura Regina."

"Are you going to breastfeed?"

"Yes."

With that, Iris pulled a metal comb out of her bag and raked Emily's breasts in a downward pattern.

"Ouch. What are you doing? That hurts."

"Sorry. This stimulates your milk production. Now let her suckle."

Emily pulled the baby to her breast. The baby latched on.

"Emily, I have to tell you. This was the easiest birth I ever took part in. Like I said, your body is perfectly designed for bearing children. I hope you have many more babies. And don't tell anyone your labor was only three hours. Most women are ten hours at least, some 24 hours. They will all be so jealous if you tell them you only had three hours of labor."

Emily laughed. "Alright, I won't. Thank you so much for all your help, Iris."

"Just doing my job."

"And thank you Mrs. Goslowski for filling in for Frank." Emily looked at Mrs. Goslowski, counting on her fingers. "What are you doing?"

"We've been through a lot together. Please call me Barbara. And I'm just counting to make sure your daughter was born in wedlock. Do you realize that today is exactly nine months from your wedding day?"

"So it is."

Iris and Barbara cleaned up the remaining mess, stayed with Emily until Frank came home, and then politely excused themselves.

"Emily, I'm so sorry I wasn't here for you. Darn job. Did everything go okay?"

"It's fine, Frank. I just find it so funny that you wanted me to have a home birth so you could be here, and then you missed it anyway. Here, hold our daughter."

The proud papa cradled Laura in his arms until she started fussing.

"Here Mama, you'll know what to do." Frank handed her back to Emily.

"What makes you think I know what to do?"

"All women know what to do. Mothering comes naturally."

"I don't know about that. Frank, do you remember how my mother said you weren't marriage material?"

"Yes, I'll never forget that," Frank said. Emily couldn't miss the frown on his face.

"Well, my mother is not mother material. I just hope I can be a better mother to Laura than my mother was to me."

Laura continued crying while Emily rocked her. Freddy began cooing ever so slightly, like he was serenading the baby. It lulled Laura back to sleep. Emily was sure glad she kept Aunt Annie's bird.

"See that? You have the mother's touch," said Frank..

"Mother's touch," squawked Freddy. As Emily placed Laura in the bottom drawer of the bureau that doubled as Laura's crib, she thought even Freddy was better mother material than her mother.

The Laura Years
1927-1947

When Laura was born, Emily looked at it as a new opportunity to renew her relationships with her family. She hadn't spoken to Mama, Blanche, or her brother in almost a year. And John was working so hard to overcome his alcohol addiction. Emily rectified the situation as she planned Laura's christening. John and Blanche felt honored to be named godparents, and Mama expressed her delight in coming to meet her first grandchild.

John and Blanche met Emily and Frank at the church on the day of the christening. There was no time to socialize until they returned to Frank and Emily's apartment for a small party. Blanche couldn't wait to show Emily her present. John and Blanche had pitched in together to buy a crib for Laura.

"Thank you so much, but how did you ever afford it?" Emily asked.

"I am back working again, and before you ask, we didn't buy it on credit."

Emily couldn't help but laugh as she watched Frank return the drawer, doubling as Laura's crib to its home in the bureau.

"Where's Mama? Why isn't she here?"

The smile on Emily's face quickly disappeared as she said,

"She's not coming. She gave me some flimsy excuse about Bill getting a new puppy, and she couldn't leave it alone because the dog wasn't housebroken."

"That's not Mama's fault. You know she doesn't know how to drive."

"But she could have taken the bus if she really wanted to be here. She doesn't approve of my husband and since Laura is an extension of Frank, I guess Mama doesn't approve of Laura either. I've tried to make things right with her, but now I'm done. I never want to see her again."

"You don't mean that, Sis."

"Oh, yes, I do."

"I hope someday you change your mind."

"I doubt it. It will be up to Mama to come here. I'm not going to see her."

Although her pre-school years remained elusive in her mind, Emily felt determined to make Laura's years more memorable. Frank brought home a decent salary, and with Emily's little sewing and knitting business, it was enough to keep the new family clothed and fed.

From the day that Laura was born, Freddy and Laura became best friends. Emily moved Freddy's cage into Laura's room. He had a soothing effect on Laura. If she ever stirred in her sleep, Freddy would coo her back to sleep. Emily taught many songs to Laura. When they sang, "She'll Be Coming 'Round the Mountain," Freddy would repeat, "When She Comes." Emily loved the way Laura would roar with laughter every time she heard it. As Laura got older, she learned to sit still long enough so Freddy could rest on her arm.

Emily spent countless hours with her daughter. They were frequent visitors in the park, where Emily could push Laura on the swing for hours. Often, neighbors would compliment Emily about how well-dressed Laura was. No one could say she was a negligent mother. Emily was on top of the world.

When the Great Depression came roaring in, Frank managed to retain his job, but his hours were reduced. This didn't deter Emily one bit. She took extra jobs sewing and knitting to supplement their income, even keeping a rainy-day jar to save money for a bicycle for Laura. Emily often worked well into the evening hours, sacrificing her own sleep before she would give up any time with her daughter. While others in the neighborhood lost their jobs and moved away, Emily and Frank kept their little family together.

When Laura turned eight, Frank and Emily gave her a shiny red bicycle for her birthday. "Do you like it?" Emily asked.

"Like it, I love it! Oh Mama, can you teach me to ride?"

Emily thought about her own mother never teaching her to ice skate. That would not happen with Laura. "Yes. I'm sure you can learn in no time. It's just a matter of balance." Emily sat on the bicycle with Laura in front of her. They rode around the block several times so Laura could get the flow of riding. "Now you try it."

Laura pedaled slowly, with Emily holding on and running alongside. "Mama, don't let go."

"I won't."

Laura pedaled faster, and Emily couldn't keep up. Soon Laura took off, leaving Emily in the dust. Emily watched Laura look over her shoulder. When Laura realized that her mother had let go, she panicked, lost her balance, hit the curb, and fell. Emily ran to her daughter.

"Let me see. Are you hurt?"

Laura was crying. "I skinned my knee. It hurts."

"It's just a scrape. Do you want to try again?"

"No. I never want to ride again. It's too hard."

"You will not learn if you don't keep trying. But tomorrow is another day. Let's go home and clean up that knee."

Laura let out one last sob as Emily walked the bicycle home.

As Emily and Laura approached their home, they saw an ambulance parked right in front of their house. Emily's first thought was Frank, but then she saw him mingling in the crowd with the other gawkers. She snuck up behind him. "What happened?"

"It's Mrs. Goslowski. I went to check on her and found her dead in bed. I called her daughter, Madelyn, and the ambulance."

"That's awful." Suddenly, Emily got a sick feeling in her stomach. Through the years, Mrs. Goslowski became like a grandmother to her. She would miss her dearly. Could Emily attend another funeral? Would they have to move out? That was another promise Emily made to herself and her daughter. She would not keep moving every year like her mother did. Emily wanted Laura to have a steady home so she could have a forever friend and an uninterrupted education. Should she ask Mrs. Goslowski's daughter if they could stay? Would Madelyn be selling the house? But now was not the time to ask. The rent wouldn't be due until after the funeral. Emily would wait until next month's rent was due to approach the subject, when Madelyn would be in a better state of mind.

On the first of the month, Madelyn knocked on Emily's door, looking for the rent money. "I'm afraid to ask. Are you selling the house? Do we have to move?" Emily asked as she forked over the rent money. She handed over the regular rent money, hoping with all her heart that Madelyn wouldn't be raising the rent since she would no longer be watching over Mrs. Goslowski.

"No, we are not selling, and no, you don't have to move. You are great tenants, and you always looked out for my mother. You're welcome to stay as long as you want. I will rent out the downstairs apartment to other tenants." Madelyn said nothing about raising the rent, and Emily wasn't about to mention it either.

Over the next four years, five different tenants rented the

Goslowski home. They never stayed long, coming and going like gypsies. Emily wondered what made them so transient. The reason was always the same- no money, no jobs. Emily thought about how many times she moved as a child. Was it because they were poor too? Suddenly, she saw her mother in a new light. Poverty and homelessness go hand in hand. All these years, she blamed her mother for something that was out of her control. But that would make Aunt Annie wrong when she said Mama's stoic personality made her cold as ice. Which was it? Poverty or personality? Or both? Emily was confused.

Just before Christmas, a new family moved into the first-floor apartment, and Laura found her forever friend in Lisa Martelli. The girls hit it off right from the start. They spent hours riding their bicycles in the park. Lisa told Laura about the Girl Scouts, and she promptly joined the troop. Laura delved right into the community service projects, board game night, and working on badges, especially cooking.

Lisa's family was warm and fuzzy, always greeting Laura with a hug. When Laura thought about it, she probably had more hugs from Mrs. Martelli than she did from her own mother. While Laura knew Emily loved her, she had to admit her mother seldom showed any signs of affection. Maybe it was her German upbringing. Mrs. Martelli taught the girls how to make meat-balls, rolling the chopped meat in their hands until they were just the right size. They also fed the dough that Mrs. Martelli had prepared that morning through a pasta maker. Laura said, "This is something I've never done before. It's so much fun."

"We do this all the time. It's an Italian tradition. Italians love to cook. Does your family have any German traditions?"

"We eat a lot of German dishes."

"I have a great idea. Laura, bring your parents over for New Year's Eve. Let's share our traditions in a real ethnic mix feast."

"That's a great idea."

Laura felt delighted that her parents were on board. The Rittenhofers would provide a German appetizer, while the Martellis would make the Italian dessert. Each family would cook a main dish to share with all. Emily offered to bring the ingredients to make whiskey sours, telling Mrs. Martelli that red wine gives her a headache.

About a week before the event, Emily said, "Laura, bring me your blue and white checkered dress. We need to fix it up for the New Year's Eve party."

"Why Mama? There is nothing wrong with it."

"We're going to dress up in lederhosen. I'm going to make you a white apron and some blue lacing down the front."

"No, Mama. That will ruin the dress. I can't wear lederhosen to school. I will be the laughingstock of my class."

Emily suddenly remembered what it was like to be twelve years old. Such a tender age. Embarrassed about everything. It was bad enough that Laura had a case of mild acne. She didn't want to make it worse for her daughter. "Don't worry. I'll only pin on the lacing and you can take it off after the evening."

"Thank you for understanding, Mama."

The day of the party, Frank and Emily wore their own lederhosen costumes that Emily had made for the Oktoberfest party the previous year. Laura carefully analyzed the temporary outfit that her mother had whipped together, making sure the pinholes couldn't be seen. Laura carried the appetizer, Frank the main course, and Emily the whiskey sour ingredients. Together, they knocked on the Martellis' door.

Mr. Martelli greeted all the Rittenhofers, including Frank, with a big hug and kiss. For Laura, this was the regular fare, and she watched her parents' reaction. Emily rubbed her cheek, and Frank froze like an iceberg, with his mouth agape. Obviously, this was a tradition that didn't exist anywhere in his house.

God bless Mrs. Martelli. She broke the ice by saying, "I love the outfits. I didn't think we had to dress up."

"Speak for yourself," Mr. Martelli said to his wife, as he

pulled down his pants, showing off his bright red underwear. "This is our tradition. Red underpants mean fertility in the new year."

Laura never heard her father laugh so hard. What a way to start off the evening.

Emily had one glass of wine with the appetizers. She had made a cheese fondue that the group dipped pieces of pretzels in. "What a marvelous idea. I've had nothing like this before," said Mrs. Martelli.

"Mama, can I have a glass of wine?" asked Lisa.

"Well, alright. It is the holidays."

"Can I have one too?" asked Laura. "I heard Mr. Martelli made it himself using the wine press his grandfather left him."

"When you put it like that. As long as your father says okay."

"I don't see why not."

"Thank you, Papa." Laura rushed to the sideboard to fill a glass before her parents could change their minds.

"Can I get you another glass, Emily?" asked Mr. Martelli.

"Oh, no thank you. I'm afraid that wine gives me headaches. Would you be so kind as to make me a whiskey sour? I've brought all the ingredients."

"I'd be honored."

While Mr. Martelli made Emily her drink, the two girls sat at the table, waiting for their mothers to unveil their holiday masterpieces. Mrs. Martelli revealed hers first. She had made lentils with sausage. "Well, what do you think?"

Frank liked what he saw. A sausage dish was near and dear to his heart. "Wow. I'm impressed. I guess our nationalities overlap somewhat here. But in Germany, we serve something that is supposed to bring prosperity for the new year, and God knows we need it through this never-ending depression. What might you say is prosperous about this dish?" asked Frank.

"Look at the lentils. Don't they resemble coins?" suggested Mrs. Martelli.

"Well, I guess they do, if I use my imagination. Come on, Emily. Show us your dish. Wait until you see this. My wife is a superb cook." With that, Emily took off the lid of her casserole pot, revealing baked carp and sauerkraut.

Mr. Martelli took one look at the dish and said, "I knew it had to be something with sauerkraut. I love it. But I have to ask you the same question: what does this have to do with prosperity?"

"In Germany. we take the skin off the fish and carry it in our wallets for good luck for the year."

"Well, I'm willing to try anything," Mr. Martelli laughed.

Mrs. Martelli brought out a tray of Italian pastries for dessert, explaining what each was- torre- a mixture of almonds and nougat, tordilli- fritters with wine and cinnamon, struffoli- deep fried donuts with honey and sprinkles, and mustaccioli- chocolate bars with spices. Emily politely took a torre, while asking for another whiskey sour. She hiccupped as she watched Laura take one of each kind of the pastries. "Laura, that is more than enough. Save some for everyone else."

"Alright, Mama," Laura said, giving Emily the typical eye roll a 12-year-old girl gives her mother.

After dinner, Lisa and Laura did the dishes without being told. Then they entertained themselves by playing Sorry and Chinese checkers while the adults played poker. Emily smiled at her daughter. Emily was so happy that Laura had found such a good friend. Suddenly, Emily felt robbed of her friendship with Isabel. What if she had lived? Would she be married today with children? Would they still be friends? And then there was Cora. How long had it been since she saw her? Three years? Four years? Emily didn't want life to get in the way. She made a New Year's resolution to call Cora.

At ten minutes to twelve, Mrs. Martelli put on the radio. After the ringing in of 1938 and a rendition of "Auld Lang Syne," the Rittenhofer family said their goodbyes, thanking Mr. and Mrs. Martelli for a lovely evening. Emily felt a little woozy on her way up the steps. Was she tired, or did she have too many whiskey sours?

A few weeks later, Laura came home from school to find her mother rummaging through Frank's dresser drawers. "Mama, what are you looking for?"

"Red underwear. I was wondering if Mr. Martelli gave your papa a pair."

"Red underwear? Didn't Mr. Martelli say wearing them was for fertility? Mama, are you pregnant?"

"I am. Unfortunately, you're going to be a big sister."

"Mama, that's great news."

"During these hard times? This won't be easy. Money is tight and now we'll have one more mouth to feed. I wish I didn't drink so much on New Year's Eve. Now I'm going to have a whiskey sour baby."

This was more information than Laura needed to hear. She retired to her bedroom to do her homework, feeling sorry for that baby being referred to as a whiskey sour baby.

A few months later, Frank came home with devastating news. His hours were being cut again at work. Emily was worried. This time, no matter how many more dresses, socks, scarves, or hats she made, she wouldn't be able to keep up with the expense of having a baby. Frank tried to find another job, but no company would hire a man with one eye. Was Mama right after all? Was he a damaged man? Frank started his own handyman business to supplement their income. Emily altered their food budget as much as she could, only having meat twice a week. She encouraged Laura to eat with the Martellis as often as she could. She wanted to ensure her daughter was well nourished.

About a month before the baby was due, Emily realized she didn't have enough money to buy a crib for the baby. Why did she get rid of the crib after Laura was born? She looked around the apartment to see what she could sell. But this was a furnished apartment; nothing belonged to them. Emily couldn't sell the radio or the couch. She couldn't sell her sewing machine either. Not when it was a source of income. She thought about all the farmers who had to sell their tractors to survive during the Depression. Emily didn't want to be like them. But she could sell Laura's bike.

"Laura, we need to talk. I'm sure you realize how tight money is for us. We need a crib for the baby, and we can't afford to buy one. We have to sell something to buy a crib. And I'm sorry to say this, but we have to sell your bicycle."

"I understand."

But the look in Laura's eyes said otherwise. How could a twelve-year-old child ever understand losing a prized possession without being resentful of her mother? Or worse yet, of her sibling? Emily felt awful. Damn this depression. Was Emily turning into her mother? She hoped not. Aunt Annie had assured Emily that there was some flaw in Margaret's personality, making her so cold. What was the word she used? Stoic. Aunt Annie also said not to be selfish. Spend time with your children. So, despite Emily's gnawing poverty, she would spend time with Laura and never abandon her.

Selling Laura's bicycle weighed heavily on Emily's mind. Emily tried to remedy the situation by spending even more time with Laura. But the harder she tried, the more Laura pulled away, becoming more and more distant. Emily felt the need to get away once in a while, to unwind, or she would lose her mind for sure. Emily's vice became card playing. She joined a card club that played every Tuesday night to save her sanity. While the other members drank beer, Emily chose a more inexpensive option- water.

Laura barely spoke to her mother throughout the rest of Emily's pregnancy. Every time she looked at the crib in her bedroom, it made her miss her bicycle even more. She avoided coming home, spending more time at the library or working on Girl Scout projects with Lisa.

Emily couldn't bear the silent treatment forced upon her by

her daughter. She convinced herself that things would change when the baby arrived. After all, who could resist the charms of a newborn baby?

One day, the following fall, Laura came home from school to meet her baby sister, Ann Adele. Emily could see the warmth in Laura's smile, the twinkle in her eye. Laura became a mother hen, doting on baby Ann. Whenever Ann woke in the middle of the night, Laura would change her diaper and carry her into her parents' bedroom so Emily could breastfeed the baby.

Within a week, it became apparent to Emily that baby Ann would not be the good baby that Laura was. Ann ate well enough, often falling asleep at her breast. But Emily needed her own sleep too, so whenever the baby started fussing, Emily would lay her back in the crib so Freddy could work his magic and lull her back to sleep. Freddy was a good sport, doing his job well. But Ann rebelled, only wailing louder each time Freddy cooed. Ann's screams were so loud they woke up the entire house. The more Ann cried, the more Freddy tried to calm her. Trying to help, he would shout, "Time to change the baby!" Laura did her best to sleep, burying her head deep under her pillow.

"That does it. That bird has to go," Emily said, barreling into Laura's room. Laura watched her mother put the cover over Freddy's cage and move him to the kitchen. Laura was too tired to argue. She hoped a good night's sleep would change her mother's mind. But the following morning when Laura came into the kitchen, Freddy was already gone. Laura never brought up the subject of Freddy again. She could only hope he went to a suitable home.

Losing Freddy weighed heavily on her mind for days. Laura was glad when Tuesday rolled around so that she could busy herself with the Girl Scout meeting. Tonight, the troop was learning how to roll pie crusts for a cooking badge. As she put on her sash, Emily entered her bedroom without knocking.

"Oh Laura, I hate to disappoint you, but I need you to stay

home and babysit your sister. Your father and I are going to the club."

"But it's Girl Scout night."

"I know, but you know how difficult your sister is. We need a little sanity, and Tuesday night is the perfect night to unwind playing cards."

"Why can't Uncle John or Blanche babysit?"

"I'm sure they wouldn't mind once in a while, but I can't ask them to do it every week."

"Can't you find a different group on another night? You know how much I love Girl Scouts."

"We can't afford a babysitter, and Tuesdays are when our friends play. Can't you join another troop?"

"No, I want to be with Lisa."

"I'm sorry, but it's just the way it has to be."

Laura cried herself to sleep after her parents left for the evening. She hated her mother for using money- or the lack of it- as an excuse for every mean thing she did. As much as Laura didn't like it, she had to admit that selling her bicycle could be seen as poverty-related, but getting rid of Freddy and making her quit Girl Scouts? That didn't save any money. It was just an excuse to hide Emily's selfishness. What a mean thing to do.

As Emily played canasta with her friends, she felt guilty about making Laura quit Girl Scouts. But Laura had to learn about family responsibility. To be a team player. Did this make Emily a terrible mother? She hoped Laura wouldn't see it this way, but if Emily didn't get this time to herself, she would go mad. If that happened, there would be no telling what she might do or say, and then Laura would really hate her.

"Emily, watch what you're doing. You just discarded a king. We have them on the board."

"I'm sorry, Frank. My mind was wandering."

"I can see that."

"Do you think Laura would enjoy this game? Maybe I can teach her to play."

"I don't see why not."

Somehow Emily would make it up to her daughter, making a few extra dresses and scarves to sell so she could afford to buy Laura some board games- Scrabble and Parcheesi. And she would teach her to play canasta. Good quality mother-daughter time. With any luck, it shouldn't take more than a week to earn the extra money.

On the first night, Emily had no trouble staying awake, with the adrenaline rush carrying her through. But after the second night, her body demanded more sleep. She slept late into the morning, not even hearing Ann cry.

Laura buried her head under her pillow, trying to drown out her sister's wailing. Why wasn't her mother coming to get the baby? Ann must be wet and hungry. When Laura couldn't stand it any longer, she rolled out of bed, stubbing her toe on the crib. It only made Ann scream louder. Laura changed Ann's diaper and carried her into her mother's bedroom. Laura couldn't believe that her mother didn't wake up. Ann was making enough racket for the neighbors to hear down the block. Laura shook her mother's arm. Emily turned over onto her side but didn't wake up. Damn her mother. It was bad enough to give up Girl Scouts for her sister. Now she had to take over the morning feeding as well. Laura staggered into the kitchen, heating a bottle with one hand while she rocked Ann with the other. As she fed the baby, she hoped that this would not be a regular occurrence.

After a week, Laura realized that the morning ritual was becoming the new norm. It made her late for school. She started spending more time with Lisa, as far away as she could get from her mother.

One day, Lisa and Laura cranked up the volume on the radio in the parlor so they could hear it in the bedroom. They stretched out on Lisa's bed to listen to "Guiding Light." Laura's mind wandered, dreaming about the life of this happy minister's family. What twelve-year-old girl wouldn't? Why couldn't her family be as happy? Laura thought if given the opportunity, she could write and perform just as well as these characters. She was going to run away to New York or Hollywood if that's what it would take to get away from her mother. Should she tell Lisa? Could she rely on her not to tell her parents the secret? Laura decided against it.

Laura returned home, going straight to her bedroom. She packed her suitcase and would wait until everyone was in bed tonight before leaving. She hid it under the bed just before her mother came barging in. Boy, that was close.

"Laura, I have a present for you."

"Why? It's not my birthday or anything." Laura could see her mother holding something behind her back.

Emily whipped out Parchesi and Scrabble. "I wanted to thank you for all the help you are giving me with Ann Adele."

"Thank you, Mom. That is so nice."

But Emily expected more of a reaction. Staring at her daughter's face, Emily saw no emotion, not as much as a smile. What was that word Aunt Annie had used to describe Emily's mother? Stoic. Emily didn't consider herself to be stoic, but could her daughter be stoic too? Was it possible for a personality disorder to skip a generation in her family? For her daughter's sake, Emily hoped not. "This will keep you busy. I'll play with you anytime you want, and I'm sure Lisa would love it."

As Laura laid in bed that night, she realized how impulsive running away would be. So out of character for her. She immediately thought about Lisa. Lisa, who admires Laura's ability to think things through. Like the times she talked Lisa out of shoplifting a scarf from Bamberger's or smoking cigarettes behind the school. What would Lisa think now? Laura didn't want to get knocked off the pedestal she sat on in Lisa's mind, so she concocted a new plan: stay home until she was sixteen, quit school, move out, and get a job. Laura quelled her anger with the board games, sometimes playing with her mother but more often with Lisa, while still completing her schoolwork and taking care of Ann.

. . .

Although the hours, the days, the weeks, the months, and the years passed as quickly as a turtle crossing a pond, Laura turned sixteen. Now she had to come up with a plan to quit school. This wouldn't be easy, since her mother valued an education so highly. Laura couldn't simply come home and say I want to quit school. She needed a reason her mother could swallow.

Sprawled out on her bed, Laura racked her brain trying to conjure up a solution while attempting to read chapter one of *Silas Marner* for her English class. She quickly learned that multi-tasking was not one of her fortes.

The next day in English class, Laura felt totally unprepared. Why did she let her mind wander so much last night? She hoped the class wouldn't have one of those "pop quizzes" that her teacher, Miss Tobias, had been threatening them with for months now, nor did she want to be asked any questions about *Silas Marner.* Trying to blend into the woodwork, she took a seat in the back of the room behind Stanley Krauss. Stanley was on the basketball team. He was so tall that Miss Tobias could never see her.

"Good morning class. Everyone, take out your *Silas Marner* book so we can begin our discussion." Miss Tobias, dressed in a red and black plaid dress, walked up and down each aisle, ensuring that all the students were prepared with their novels and notebooks. "Let's start out easy. Who can tell me what Silas Marner's vocation was?" Only a few hands shot up. "Why do I see the same hands up all the time? I want to hear from some new students."

Miss Tobias started up Laura's aisle. Laura sank lower into her seat, staring at the acne on the back of Stanley's neck. Miss Tobias stopped right next to Stanley. "Laura, what was Silas Marner's occupation?"

"I don't know."

"What physical handicap did Silas suffer from?"

"I don't know."

"Laura, these are easy questions. Anyone who completed the reading assignment would know the answer to them. If you will not do the work, you can get out of my class," Miss Tobias said, pointing toward the door.

Was Miss Tobias serious? Could Laura leave the classroom? This could be the opportunity that she needed. Since English is a required course, Laura wouldn't be able to graduate without it. All she had to do was muster up the courage to walk out the door. Her legs felt like lead, but Laura trudged out of the classroom, not making eye contact with Miss Tobias or any of her classmates.

Laura headed to the office, pausing at the basketball team's trophy case while she waited for the secretary to deal with a student who was signing in late for school. Stanley's name was on three of them. A high school legend.

"Can I help you?" asked the secretary when she was done.

"I'm here to tell you I'm quitting school."

"Are you eighteen?"

"Not yet."

"Are you at least sixteen?"

"Yes."

"Wait here." Laura watched the secretary open a file cabinet and pull out a form. "Your parents must sign this form. Bring it back and then you can clean out your locker."

Laura took the form, charging for the door.

"You're welcome."

She paused briefly to turn around. "Thank you." What would her mother say, forgetting her manners like that? More importantly, what would she say about quitting school? There must be a way to soften the blow.

Laura went to the bathroom to freshen up her face when an idea came to her. It was still first period. That would give her most of the day to find a job. If she came home with a job in her pocket, her mother would have a hard time saying no.

Laura remembered how Emily talked about her phone company years with mixed emotions- a company that would take a chance on an uneducated girl but then drop her like a hot potato when she got married. Well, Laura was uneducated and single. That would be her first stop.

The brick building that housed the phone company was easy to distinguish from all the other brick buildings in town, with the big copper bell sitting on the front lawn. Laura walked through the revolving door into the lobby. She approached the receptionist, who was sitting behind a mahogany desk, blowing her fingernails dry from recently applied nail polish.

"Can I help you?"

"Yes, ma'am. I would like to apply for a job. Do you have any openings?"

"They're always hiring operators. The employment office is the second door on the left."

"Thank you."

"Good luck."

Another receptionist wearing a navy blue dress with polka dots so big they were blinding, greeted Laura when she opened the door. The name plate on her desk read Mrs. Greason. Laura was glad to see that married women could work here now.

"Can I help you?"

"Yes, Mrs. Greason. I'm here to apply for an operator job."

"Do you have any experience?"

"No, but both my mother and uncle worked here a long time ago."

"Not everyone is suitable for this type of job. You must be quick."

"I can be as quick as you need me to be."

"Excuse me if I don't take your word for it. You must pass an aptitude test first."

Mrs. Greason led Laura behind the desk. Mounted on the wall were 50 huge manila envelopes labeled with letters of the alphabet. Some envelopes had individual letters like "A," while others grouped letters like "Q," "R," "X," 'Y," and "Z," together in one envelope. However, most of the letters were divided among multiple envelopes, such as "Ba-Bed" or "Beda-Bot." It reminded Laura of a dictionary.

Mrs. Greason handed Laura 100 index cards with names on them. "I'm going to set the timer. If you can correctly file these cards in ten minutes, the job is yours. Are you ready?" Laura nodded. "On your mark, get set, go."

Laura hated working under pressure, but she really wanted this job. She worked as quickly as she could, finishing before the timer went off. "I'm done."

Mrs. Greason stopped the timer. "Wow, that only took you six and a half minutes. Let's check your accuracy."

Laura waited patiently for Mrs. Greason to check her work, with her fingers crossed behind her back like a small child. "You got them all correct. A new company record. The job pays sixteen dollars a week. When can you start?"

"How about tomorrow?"

Imagine that. Sixteen dollars a week. More money than she had ever seen in her lifetime. And she would get it week after week. As Laura walked home, she passed an apartment building with a 'For Rent' sign hanging in a window. The building was four stories tall, with at least two units on each floor. Should she go in and inquire? Wouldn't it be nice to go home and tell her mother she got a job and an apartment?

Opening the green door with a cracked window, Laura entered the long hallway. There were three apartments on each side on the first floor. The landlord's apartment was the first door on the right. Laura boldly knocked on the door.

A man answered the door with a cigarette dangling from his lips and a glass of whiskey in his hands. His black pants and white shirt had matching tomato sauce stains on them. "Are you the landlord?"

"Isn't that what the sign says?"

"I might be interested in the apartment. How much is the rent?"

"Aren't you a little young to be renting an apartment?"

"I'm old enough to work, so I'm old enough to rent an apartment. How much is the rent?"

"Twenty-seven dollars a month."

"That's right in my budget, but I won't have the money for two more weeks. Can you hold it for me?"

"Even though I would love a pretty little lady like you moving in, I don't hold the apartment for no one. You can take your chances. Come back in two weeks. Maybe it will be free, but then again, maybe not," the landlord said, slamming the door in her face.

Since the apartment wasn't confirmed, Laura chose not to inform her mother about her upcoming move. Emily would have enough on her plate learning her daughter quit school and found a job.

Laura waited until after dinner that night to discuss the matter with her mother. "Mom, I have something to tell you. I got in trouble in school today."

"What kind of trouble?'

"I got kicked out of my English class. Since I can't graduate without passing English, I want to drop out of school. Can you sign the papers letting me do it?"

"Wait. Back up. What happened in English class?"

"Miss Tobias is kind of strict. We were reading *Silas Marner* in class. I couldn't answer her questions about the book, so she told me to get out. Have you ever read it? It's a hard book to understand."

Emily knew where Laura was coming from. Were they still reading that God awful book in high school? Emily thought about trying to read it at the convent and what a disaster that was. It was the day she put her education in the rear-view mirror and learned to work with her hands. Now it was happening to her daughter.

"Mom, say something."

"You can't quit school until you get a job first."

"I thought you might say that. That's why I got a job today at the telephone company. I start tomorrow as an operator."

Emily frowned. "Are you absolutely sure that there is no chance that your English teacher would take you back? Maybe I should speak to her. I hate to see you throw away a chance at an education."

"Mom, it's for the best."

"Well then, I'm happy for you." Emily thought Laura's extra income could help the family.

A week later, Laura came home with her first paycheck. "Mom, I got paid today. My first paycheck. But I don't understand. I was supposed to make $16.00, but the check was only for $14.40. Why is the government taking my money?"

"Welcome to adulthood. The government needs money to pay for our troops and other things. Speaking of other things, you have household responsibilities too."

"What do you mean?"

"Why do you think people work?"

"To make money."

"They use the money to put a roof over their heads and food in their stomachs. Nobody lives anywhere for free, and neither do you. Your share of the rent is ten dollars a week."

"But that only leaves me $4.40 a week."

"I'm sorry, but that's the way it has to be."

Laura couldn't believe it. She was more than willing to pay her fair share of household expenses. But more than half of her salary? That seemed excessive. She would never have enough money for her own place. Was she going to be stuck home living with her parents forever? She might never get out until she meets a man and gets married. How many years would that be? Laura started looking at her life in phases- the junior years when she had her mother, the phase when Ann Adele was born and her mother changed forever, the school years, and now the working years. When would the dating and marriage phase start so she could get out of this house?

In May 1945, with the war over in Europe, the soldiers started coming home in droves. One day, while Laura was rocking Ann Adele in the backyard hammock, Laura heard a loud party in the yard next door. Because this house was a revolving door of tenants coming and going, Laura had never met these neighbors. Being curious, Laura tiptoed to the stockade fence separating the yards and peered over. A welcome home party was in the works with lots of beer flowing. The returning soldier looked amazing with his crew cut, staff sergeant uniform, and lean body. Laura couldn't help but gawk. When he looked in her direction with his bright blue eyes, Laura ducked down below the fence.

"Hi there." Suddenly, the soldier was right at the fence.

"I'm so sorry. I didn't mean to stare."

"It's perfectly fine. I just came home from Europe. I'm celebrating with my friends and family. Would you care to join us?"

"Oh no. I don't want to impose. Enjoy yourself. And thank you for your service." A thoroughly embarrassed Laura yanked Ann off the hammock and retreated to the house.

The party carried on well into the night. The more the liquor flowed, the louder the music and talking grew. "Laura, I can't sleep with all that noise," said Ann.

"I can't either. Try putting a pillow over your head. Maybe that will help." Laura didn't fall asleep until 3:00 in the morning. It was a good thing that she didn't have work in the morning.

Laura didn't wake up until 11:30 the next morning. She never slept that late before, and she could have slept longer except for the pounding knock on the front door waking her up. She heard her mother answer it.

"Laura, Laura, wake up. It's the boy from next door coming to see you."

"He can't see me like this, Mother. Stall him."

Laura jumped out of bed and threw on some clothes. She plucked the curlers out of her hair one by one and gave her head a good shake before entering the parlor.

Was this the same man from yesterday? Wearing khaki pants and a long-sleeved white shirt, he was staring down at the bouquet of flowers in his hands. He raised his head and their eyes met. Laura would recognize those blue eyes anywhere. "These are for you."

"Daisies. My favorite. What's the occasion?"

"I think we got off on the wrong foot yesterday. I never told you my name. Very rude of me. I'm Sam Rausch. Also, I want to apologize for all the noise last night. I hope we didn't keep you up last night."

"No, you didn't."

"But Laura-"

Laura put her hand over Ann Adele's mouth before she could say more. "Why don't you go play in the bedroom and let us talk?"

"Alright. Can you play Parcheesi with me?"

"I'll be there soon," Laura said. "Sorry about that, Sam. And you weren't rude. I never told you my name either. I'm Laura Rittenhofer."

"A nice German name. My mother would have been so proud. Would you give me the honor of taking you out to dinner tonight and some dancing afterwards?"

"I would love to."

"Great. I will stop by at 7:00."

Emily was so pleased for her daughter. "Laura, this is so exciting. Let me help you pick out the right outfit to wear and teach you how to apply make-up." Emily didn't want her daughter wearing a robe. And this was the perfect opportunity to teach Laura how to use make-up. She would always remember how Aunt Annie taught her how to use lipstick, eye shadow, rouge, and mascara, unlike her own mother.

"Oh mother, I've got this. I certainly know what to wear. I will wear my brown pleated skirt and a white pullover sweater. As for makeup, I'm not wearing any. After all the dirt and blood that Sam saw in the battlefields of Europe, I think Sam will like the natural look."

Emily hoped her daughter was right. She pivoted toward the kitchen so her daughter wouldn't see the disappointment on her face. Oh well, at least I offered, Emily thought.

Laura's intuition about the natural look was spot on. Sam turned out to be an outdoor guy. Dinner that night was a barbecue at a friend's house, followed by a barn square dance. Over the next few months, Laura and Sam spent their dates at the zoo, horseback riding, whale watching, deep sea fishing, and volunteering at the animal shelter. All the dates were outdoors around animals.

One day Laura asked Emily, "Mom, how did you know Dad was the right one for you to marry?"

"Oh, I just knew. We could talk about anything and always seemed to like the same things."

"Did your mother approve of the relationship?"

"It is funny that you ask me that. The answer is no. Your grandmother never liked your father."

"Why not?"

"She said he was a damaged man, not marriage material because he had a glass eye."

Laura paused a moment to process this information. Not marriage material? Was this true? Were Mom and Dad poor because of his disability? Maybe, but they sure seemed to love each other. Laura couldn't think of a single time they had a fight, except over stupid things like who threw out the newspaper or who moved the toaster. At any rate, the fights were never about important things like money. "Mom, do you think Sam is marriage material?"

"Yes, I do. He is a keeper."

"Good, because we are getting married." When Emily didn't say anything, Laura said, "Mom, say something. Do you approve?"

"Yes. Oh, yes. I approve. It is just a little quick. Are you sure? You have only been dating for six months. What are your plans after you are married? Where are you going to live?"

"We are going to live on a pig farm in the Catskills that Sam agreed to manage."

A pig farm. For most women, this would be a horrible situation. But for Laura? Somehow, this seemed perfect for her animal-loving daughter. When Laura and Sam began planning their wedding, Emily felt thrilled to help plan the festivities. She thought about her rotten mother trying to sabotage her wedding to Frank. "Not marriage material" still ringing in her ears to this day. A young couple needs support, and Emily planned to give it.

Emily presented Laura with her wedding dress, which would now be worn for the third time. It could be Laura's lucky dress. Wherever Cora was, she would be so proud. Emily had lost touch with her years ago. Emily wanted to help with the reception as well. No couple should begin a marriage with an enormous debt over their head.

"Frank, I want to throw Laura the best wedding party ever. Let's save her ten-dollar board money each week until the wedding to pay for it."

"But we need it for the household funds."

"But we're going to lose it when she moves out anyway. We might as well get used to it sooner than later."

"Good point. And I know just the place where we can keep the money." Frank pulled an empty jar from the cupboard, and Emily watched him twist his body like a contortionist to nail the lid to the top of the cabinet behind the sink. Emily couldn't help but laugh when she saw his butt crack. "What's so funny?"

"Nothing."

"You can keep the money in here and just unscrew the jar when you want to add money or take it out. Nobody will know it's here except me and you."

Since Laura wanted Lisa to be her maid of honor, it took a little maneuvering to arrive at a wedding date. At first, Laura picked a date in June, but when she realized Lisa had scheduled her college graduation party on the same date, she had to reconsider. Laura decided on Good Friday, April 4, 1947, when Lisa would be home on Easter break. Emily and Frank spent days preparing the food, Frank preparing a pig roast and Emily baking and decorating a cake and preparing all the sides. By the time they finished prepping the meal, Emily had blisters on her hands and Frank's back was hurting, but they considered it a small price to pay for their oldest daughter.

A church wedding was out of the question. Fearing that a priest would find Laura's frequent absences in church appalling, she was too embarrassed to even ask. Instead, she convinced herself that Father Moore would be too busy anyway with Good Friday Mass. Emily offered the remaining money in the jar to Laura to hire a Justice of the Peace who would perform the wedding nuptials in the backyard.

Laura looked radiant in Cora's wedding gown. The flower crown and bouquet of roses and daisies added the finishing touches. The ceremony was over quickly, and Emily had a new son-in-law. "Welcome to the family, Sam."

"Thank you, Mrs. Rittenhofer."

"Don't be so formal. You can call me Mom."

"With all due respect, I have my own mother. I wish she could have been here to see how happy I am."

"I'm sorry, Sam. I didn't mean to tarnish your mother's memory. How about calling me Emily then? Does that work for you?"

Sam nodded.

Later that evening, with the dishes out of the way and Laura and Sam set off on their honeymoon to Niagara Falls, Emily collapsed into bed. She reflected on her childhood and her abysmal relationship with her mother. Emily had lived in so many homes, she couldn't remember them all. Did she do a better job raising Laura? Money was tight, but Laura always had food on the table and only one roof over her head her entire life. Maybe this didn't qualify Emily as mother of the year, but she felt relieved that Laura had grown into a fine young woman who was beginning a new journey into married life.

Lake George, New York
1975

S usan paused on her front porch, popping a red Lifesaver into her mouth to relieve her scratchy throat. She was grateful to have the lead solo in her high school chorus, but these after school practices were brutal on her vocal cords. Opening the door, a tantalizing aroma coming from her mother's kitchen greeted her.

"Oh wow, you're making Grandma's award-winning apple crumb cake." Susan broke off a piece, and Laura slapped her hand.

"Not before dinner. You'll ruin your appetite. And for your information, Grandma didn't win for her apple crumb cake. It was for her bread making skills."

Triggered by the smell of the apple crumb cake, Susan thought about her grandmother and how she had come to live with them when Susan was ten years old. After Grandpa died, Grandma tried her best to make it on her own. But twice Grandma got mugged coming home from the bank after cashing her social security check, once getting a nasty gash on her head. When she fell in the bathtub and sat there for three days because she couldn't get up, Mom put her foot down. Grandma was going to live with them.

Grandma taught Susan how to play Chinese checkers, gin rummy, hearts, and canasta. Whether Grandma had a lot of skill or luck, Susan didn't know, but she was hard to beat. Susan could probably count the times she won a game on one hand. So much for letting a child win. And Grandma was an exceptional cook. Susan loved to watch her make the apple crumb cake. She never used a measuring cup to add the ingredients. It never tasted exactly the same- sometimes it was butterier, sometimes it had more sugar or cinnamon, but it was always good. This was the happiest time in Susan's life; she thought Grandma would live with them forever.

But then the fighting started. Laura had no patience with Grandma when she left the water running in the bathroom sink one night. Mom screamed at her, really screamed at her about the water bill. Didn't Mom understand that sometimes older people were forgetful? Mom continued to cook traditional acidic German dishes like sauerkraut although Grandma developed a stomach ulcer. On her good days, when Grandma could handle the food, Mom would scream at her for taking a second piece of meat. On her bad days, when she ran to the bathroom to throw up, Mama would yell about Grandma wasting food. Poor Grandma could never win. And Dad? He would never say a word. It was clear who wore the pants in this family.

One problem with an ulcer is that it creates gas, and Grandma had a large supply of it. One day, Susan went grocery shopping with Mom and Grandma. In the parking spot next to them, a man sat behind the wheel reading a newspaper with the window open. Grandma stepped out of the car and let one rip right next to the man's head. He rolled up the window. Susan laughed, but Laura? Mortified, she snatched Grandma's hand, steering her toward the store. Susan thought that instead of being embarrassed, it might be more helpful if her mother could help Grandma out by cooking some foods that she could digest.

On her last day with the family, Grandma hung two paper

towels out on the clothesline to dry. "What are you doing? They are disposable. Throw them out. What will the neighbors think?"

"Oh dearie, they're barely wet. Why waste them when you can use them again?"

Susan understood. All of Grandma's actions came from growing up poor and living through the Depression, not wasting anything. But Mom? Her own mother embarrassed her. She and Dad shipped Grandma up to Lake George to live in a small apartment. They convinced themselves that everything would be all right because Grandma's sister, Helen, only lived a mile away, and she would be there to help out if needed.

"Susan. Earth to Susan. What are you thinking about?" Laura said.

"I'm sorry. I was just thinking about Grandma. Do you think we can go visit her soon?"

"Someday."

Someday? Mom has been saying that for six years now, and still they have never visited her, not even on holidays. Susan worried about her all alone in her apartment, especially since she had developed diabetes. Didn't Laura worry too? "I have a chemistry test tomorrow. I'm going up to my room to study. Please call me when dinner is ready." Right now, Susan just wanted to be alone.

She barely took a step when the green rotary telephone nestled in the corner of the galley kitchen rang.

"Hello," Mom said, answering the phone.

"Is this Laura Rausch?"

"Yes."

"Laura Regina Rausch?"

"Yes, speaking."

"This is Phil Newcomb from the Lake George Police Department. Are you related to Emily Rittenhofer?"

"Yes, she is my mother."

"I regret to inform you she has passed away."

Laura gasped, bringing her hand to her mouth. Susan could tell that something was wrong.

"What happened?" said Susan.

Mom shushed her away.

"Natural causes. The coroner said it was complications from diabetes."

"Well, thank you for letting us know."

"I'm sorry for your loss."

Laura hung up the phone, facing her daughter.

"Well."

"Your grandmother passed away. Apparently from her diabetes," Mom said.

Susan's eyes welled with tears. She looked at her mother's emotionless face. No frown, no tears, no nothing. Was she in shock?

As timing would have it, the call came on the Wednesday before spring break. Dad said there was no way he could get off from work. It was late March, and as an accountant, he had too many income tax returns to file. Susan volunteered to accompany her mother to "take care of affairs," whatever that meant. She just had to get through Thursday and her chemistry exam before they could leave. Chemistry was her weakest subject. On a normal day, Susan had to study twice as hard as most of her classmates just to get a "C." But this time, it would be even harder. How was she supposed to study when she couldn't get her mind off of her grandmother? But somehow she muddled through the studying and the exam itself, her fate to be determined after spring break. She put it out of her mind and focused on Grandma.

Mom told Susan to pack lightly. She wanted to leave room in their cream-colored Chevy Caprice station wagon to bring home whatever possessions they could rescue from Grandma's apartment.

After a four-hour drive, Laura and Susan knocked on the

door of Grandma's landlord, Miles Russell, to get the key to her apartment. Miles stood over six feet tall with an enormous belly. His girth obstructed most of the view of his living room, but Susan still noticed a huge gun cabinet behind him. A shotgun was laid across the coffee table with a rag stuck up its barrel. When he spoke, Susan noticed some missing teeth. Miles spent his money on beer and sweets. He didn't spend it on the dentist, she concluded.

"Here's the key. Today is the 29th. Her rent is paid until the end of the month. If you're not cleared out by the 31st, I'm afraid I'll have to charge you another month's rent. It shouldn't be hard being that it's a furnished apartment. Just clear out her personal belongings."

"What about the sheets and towels, and kitchen dishes and pots and pans?" asked Laura.

"Those are hers, but if you don't want them, leave them. It will make it easier to rent to the next tenant."

Grandma's apartment was a detached two-car garage converted into a cottage. It would be too small for more than one person, but for Grandma, living alone on her husband's social security, it was perfect. It rested high on a hill with a breath-taking view of Lake George.

Opening the door, mother and daughter stepped into a world of chaos. Books, magazines, and newspapers covered almost every inch of the living room floor. "Oh, my God! I had no idea that your grandmother was a hoarder."

But it made perfect sense to Susan. With no one to play cards or Chinese checkers with, Grandma had turned to another cheap form of entertaining- reading.

"Come on Susan, let's start in the kitchen and get rid of her food before we get invaded by ants." They tiptoed through the living room into the kitchen in the back corner of the cottage, throwing on the light switch.

Susan realized it was more than ants that they had to worry about, as a cockroach scurried across the floor. "Gross."

She felt like she had walked into Willy Wonka's Chocolate Factory. She grabbed a trash bag from under the kitchen sink, disposing of all the donuts, cookies, cake, and candy on the counter. No wonder Grandma died from diabetes, eating all this junk.

Laura tackled the refrigerator, pouring the milk down the drain. She added expired yogurt, ketchup, mayonnaise, and a leftover pasta dish with mold sauce to the trash bag. Maybe Mom died from food poisoning, Laura thought.

But when she started adding the insulin vials to the garbage, Susan spoke up. "Mom, that's medicine. I don't think you are supposed to throw that out."

"What else are we going to do with it?"

Susan shrugged, holding the bag open while Laura scooped the insulin into it. Then Susan tied the bag shut and threw it in the garbage can next to the house. Using another trash bag, Laura emptied the pantry of all the unopened cereal, pasta, soup, rice, noodles, and spaghetti sauce. "There is no sense throwing out good food. Put this in the car."

Susan threw the bag over her shoulder, carrying it to the car. When she returned to the kitchen, Laura was taking inventory of the dishes, cups, pots, and pans. Laura said, "They are all mismatched sets. We're going to leave these behind. Nothing worth keeping."

With the kitchen done, they moved to the living room. The contents of the bookcase spilled onto the floor because it was completely stuffed with books. Susan sorted them by author: a five-year supply of Alfred Hitchcock Presents, 207 Harlequin romances, and 50 Agatha Christie novels. Susan was not a fan of romance or short stories, but she wanted to read Agatha Christie to find out what all the hoopla was about. She kept Agatha Christie's first book, *The Mysterious Affair at Styles,* as well as *Ten Little Indians* and *Murder on the Orient* Express. Susan had seen those two movies and wanted to decide which was better, the movies or the books. They bagged up all the rest of the books and deposited them next to the already filled up donation bin at the local library.

On the way back to Grandma's house, they stopped at the funeral home to pick up Grandma's ashes and death certificate. Susan's eyes filled with tears when the funeral director handed Laura a cigar box with Grandma's ashes inside. Susan took a Kleenex from one of the tissue boxes scattered throughout the funeral home. She was still crying when they returned to the car.

"Susan, pull yourself together."

Susan couldn't believe it. She stared at her mother. There wasn't a tear in her eyes. "How come you're not crying, Mom? Don't you love Grandma? Don't you miss your mother?"

"It's not a matter of love. Of course, I love her. She's my mother, but I didn't like her very much."

"You didn't like her? Why not?"

"You don't understand. You didn't have to live with her. She took away everything I loved. Girl Scouts, Freddy, my bike, and most of my paycheck when I started working. Your grandmother wasn't warm and fuzzy. She was cold as ice. Clearly not mother material."

Susan didn't have a response to that comment. What was there to say? Her mother still held a grudge all these years later. She remained silent on the ride back to the house, clinging to her grandmother's ashes.

When they arrived back at the cottage, Susan carefully carried Grandma's ashes into the house, zigzagging her way through the myriad of tree roots waiting to trip her. Laura ran ahead, opening the door. "Put the ashes on the table by the window."

Somehow, the table looked different with all the books cleared off it. "Mom, I don't think this is a table. It's Grandma's sewing machine."

"I can't believe she still has that old thing. We're not leaving it behind. It's an antique. Let's put it in the car. It has to be worth something." Laura and Susan half-dragged and half-carried their treasure to the car. Laura was out of breath when they returned to the house to continue cleaning.

The bathroom was easy to purge, throwing out all the open toiletries and leaving behind the skimpy bath towels. The last room to conquer was the bedroom. They started with all the clothes. "We can donate these to the Presbyterian Church. Fold them and bag them, but check all the pockets to make sure there is no money in them," Laura said. They found none.

Susan returned from the kitchen with another trash bag to throw out Grandma's socks and underwear while Laura emptied the closet of its remaining items onto the bed. The first thing Susan picked up was a baseball signed by Frankie Frisch. "Who is Frankie Frisch?" she asked.

"I don't know. Throw it out."

Susan placed the ball inside the bag. It fell to the bottom of the bag with a thud. She picked up what looked like a whistle. "What's this?" She blew into it but heard nothing but a dog howling off in the distance.

"It's a dog whistle," Mom said.

"Can I keep it?"

"Do we have a dog?"

Susan looked at the expression on her mother's face and added it to the trash bag. Next, she picked up a menu from Delmonico's, signed by Alice Paul. "Who is Alice Paul?" she asked.

"I have no idea." Laura took it from Susan, ripping it in two, and added it to the garbage.

Susan picked up the loving cup that read "1910 Bread Making Winner." As she added it to the overflowing garbage bag, Susan realized she was throwing out Emily's prized possessions. It was like she was throwing her grandmother's life away. Susan thought about her own possessions. What was something special to her she would never part with that her future children might throw out someday? Her tap shoes, color guard flag, and

Wayne Newton autographed postcard came to mind. How sad when someone discards a life as if it were trash.

The only thing left to contend with was Grandma's strong box. "This is what I have been looking for. Maybe she had a life insurance policy," Laura said as she turned the key, opening the box.

Several pictures greeted them. Laura and Susan looked through them. Each marked with a date on the back- Emily and Queenie 1908, Emily and John 1910, Emily and Frank's wedding 1926. When they came to the one that said Laura and Freddy 1929, Laura said, "Give me that picture. That's the bird I was telling you about earlier. I want to keep that one. You can throw out the rest of the pictures."

"I'm keeping them." Susan dropped the photographs into her purse before Laura would throw them out.

Deeper in the strong box, Susan found five $100 dollar savings bonds made out to her. "Wow." Grandma never owned a house or a car. She worked hard for the money she had, and here she was giving it to Susan. This money wouldn't even make a dent in her college tuition fund, but it was a lot of money for Grandma. It made Susan think of the Bible story where a poor widow put more money into the collection plate than other richer parishioners. Wasn't it the Book of Mark? There must be a spot for Grandma in heaven.

There was no will or life insurance policy in the strongbox. The only paper remaining in the strong box was a deed to a double plot in Holy Cross Cemetery. According to the deed, Frank Rittenhofer was buried on one side while the other side remained vacant.

"Mom, why did you cremate Grandma? Didn't she want to be buried with Grandpa?"

"She told me she wanted to be cremated and have her ashes scattered in Lake George."

So why did Grandma have a plot then? Didn't she want to

be buried with her husband? It didn't sound right to Susan, but then who was she to argue with her mother.

"I'm going to respect her wishes right now." Laura picked up Grandma's ashes and walked out onto the wobbly dock behind the house. Susan's eyes welled with tears as she watched her mother from the window. With no other family members present to say goodbye, and without so much a prayer, Laura dumped Emily's ashes into Lake George. Cold as ice.

Author's Notes

The idea for this novel came from my grandmother's journal. She was born in 1902 and died in 1992. I find it amazing that in her life span, she lived through World War I, the Spanish Flu, the Great Depression, World War II, and the Vietnam War. She used inventions like radio, television, microwave ovens, flush toilets, and electricity for the first time. Some of this appeared in her journal. It was 12 pages long, written by hand, and reflected her life memories shortly before she died. The first page was a list of some places she could remember living in, and she admitted there were probably more. The remaining pages were a collection of heart-breaking stories that I can't even fathom, but her story needed to be told.

This book took me three years to write, which is probably an average amount of time for a first novel. It is historical in nature, which slowed me down further. Clothes, places, phrases, and prices were hard to describe, so I had to use an invention in my lifetime- the internet- to help me. I tried to use language as it was used at the time to make it more authentic. This is why I chose words like negro and fireman. My spellcheck wanted me to change them to African American and firefighter; I avoided the temptation.

I regret finding this journal after my grandmother died. If she were still alive, I could pick her brain for more details. As a result of her scant recollections, I had to weave some fiction into the story to make it flow. It is up to you, dear reader, to determine how much of this is true.

Acknowledgments

Let me begin by saying that writing a novel is not a simple task. I preyed upon the services of many individuals along my journey and I wish to thank them all. Some of them may be surprised to see their name here and not remember helping me, but I assure you that I required their expertise to make my characters believable. Thank you to Jenn Quinton for her knowledge of training dogs. I confess I have been a dog owner most of my life, but not one of them was as well-trained as Jenn's dog.

I know nothing about guns or their history. That is where Bill Showalter comes in. He was gracious enough to give me an hour of his time to tell me about guns of the early 20th century and how they worked. To thank him, I changed the name of a character in my book from Ed to Bill.

By the same token, I know nothing about embalming procedures. Thank you to Kelly Petrozelli for filling in the gaps here. Growing up with a father who was a mortician didn't hurt.

Courtroom trials have definitely changed over the years, especially when it comes to juvenile defendants. There were no social services available for children yet. Thank you to Mike Raith for pointing that out. He also gave me the word advocate. What a noble word!

The revision process is long and tedious and I am grateful to my beta readers Linda Condrillo, Steve Brown, and Barb McInerney for the positive feedback. I would also like to thank author, Kathleen Grissom, for reading my first three chapters and giving me the encouragement to contact agents. As for editing, I appreciate the long hours that my daughter, Dawn Warnock, and husband Brian Warnock spent reading sentence by sentence. Thank you.

Anyone who knows me knows I am computer illiterate. Thank you to Robert Harrison for formatting my book and designing my book cover, and thank you to Randy Gerard who deserves more than a dinner for my endless phone calls with technology questions.

Lastly, I would like to thank the readers that bought my book and, of course, my grandmother whose horrendous life inspired this novel.

About the Author

Doretta Warnock is a retired elementary school teacher happily living in southern Delaware. She enjoys reading on the beach, playing pickleball, and traveling both domestically and abroad. *Mother Material* is her first novel.

Follow her on Facebook at DorettaWrites.

www.ingramcontent.com/pod-product-compliance
Lightning Source LLC
Chambersburg PA
CBHW032150190626
46814CB00005BA/1927